THREE
MINUTES
TO MIDNIGHT

THREE MINUTES TO MIDNIGHT

A.J. TATA

KENSINGTON BOOKS
www.kensingtonbooks.com

KENSINGTON BOOKS are published by

Kensington Publishing Corp.
119 West 40th Street
New York, NY 10018

All Kensington titles, imprints, and distributed lines are available at special quantity discounts for bulk purchases for sales promotion, premiums, fund-raising, educational, or institutional use. Special book excerpts or customized printings can also be created to fit specific needs. For details, write or phone the office of the Kensington Special Sales Manager: Attn. Special Sales Department. Kensington Publishing Corp, 119 West 40th Street, New York, NY 10018. Phone: 1-800-221-2647.

Library of Congress Card Catalogue Number: 2015958939

Kensington and the K logo Reg. U.S. Pat. & TM Off.

ISBN-13: 978-1-4967-0625-6
ISBN-10: 1-4967-0625-0
First Kensington Hardcover Edition: May 2016

eISBN-13: 978-1-4967-0634-8
eISBN-10: 1-4967-0634-X
First Kensington Electronic Edition: May 2016

10 9 8 7 6 5 4 3 2 1

Printed in the United States of America

For my brother, Bob, and his wonderful wife,
Anne Ferrell, who have always believed in me . . .

CHAPTER 1

U.S. ARMY RESERVE CAPTAIN MAEVE CASSIDY RAN FROM THE interrogation room into the parking lot of the secret compound on Fort Bragg, North Carolina. She could hear boots slapping on the finely waxed and buffed floors of the military facility until the door slammed shut behind her, sounding like a gunshot. Less than twenty-four hours returned from Afghanistan, she had already retrieved her car from the deployment lot. The men who were chasing her had asked her questions with a threatening undertone.

"Did you bring any classified information back with you?"

"Did you help the U.S. government steal natural gas from Pakistan?"

"In country, did your relationship with your CIA handler, 'Jim,' ever turn sexual?"

"Are you concerned about the safety of your husband, Pete, and daughter, Piper?"

"Are you aware of six natural gas container ships that have departed Karachi, Pakistan, bound for the United States?"

Yes, yes, yes, yes, and yes, she had thought but had never answered. That was when she'd run. Unaware of who these men were or why she was required to meet with them as part of her redeployment processing, Maeve had stood and run, catching them all by surprise.

A track star in high school and at North Carolina State University, Maeve created distance between herself and her pursuers and slid over the hood of her SUV as she heard gunfire in the distance. Could be a training range or it could be people shooting at her, she figured.

Inside the SUV, she pressed the ignition button and slapped the gear selector into drive. She sped toward the gate with the single cantilevered arm blocking her egress. She knew there were probably tire shredders that the gate guard could activate, but she was banking on her head start.

No such luck. As she approached the guardhouse, she watched the shredder bare its teeth facing in her direction, meaning her tires would be ripped apart if she drove over them. She pulled to a stop at the guardhouse, knowing that the security personnel were simply glorified rent-a-cops. She lowered her window and gave the overweight man in white shirt and gray slacks her most charming smile.

"In kind of a rush, sir. Mind opening the gate?"

In her periphery she watched two men dash across the parking lot toward her.

"Was ordered to close the gate."

"How about this order, sir?" She brandished her officer's 9 mm Beretta from beneath her seat. She had chambered a round before going into the building, unsure of what might occur. Her instincts had proven good.

"Seriously, lady . . ."

Maeve fired a shot at the man's communication and television console, shattering the device.

"I *am* serious. Two seconds. Open the gate. Next bullet is in your head."

The man pressed a button, and the teeth lowered on the shredder while the metal arm rose. Maeve sped through the gap, then made a series of turns that took her beyond the Fort Bragg drop zones and into the town of Southern Pines. She followed U.S. Route 1 all the way to her home in Cary, near Raleigh.

The stress of the questioning, the hour-long drive, and the fact that she had just returned from twelve months of combat in

Afghanistan came together to create an adrenaline dump. She was exhausted and, most of all, worried about her family.

Parking in her driveway, she noticed a strange car on the street in front of her house. Still wearing her uniform, she slung her rucksack over her shoulder, checked behind her to make sure no one had caught up with her yet, and kept her pistol in her right hand.

The front door of their brick-facade colonial home in suburban Cary was unlocked. She opened the door to the sound of a television and muted conversation in the den. She looked up the steps to her left and saw no activity. After walking through the foyer, she leaned against the wall that separated the den from the kitchen.

Piper. She heard her four-year-old daughter's voice and nearly cried. Then she heard the voice of a young female, most likely that of a babysitter.

She holstered the pistol and turned into the room.

Both Piper and the young woman were startled and screamed. At first, neither recognized her, but then the babysitter, Dawn Jackson, a high school student who lived five blocks away in the neighborhood, said, "Oh my God. Mrs. Cassidy. You're home a week early!"

Maeve kept her eyes trained on Piper, who didn't seem to recognize her. She had deployed when Piper was barely three.

"Piper? Come to Mommy?"

Piper looked at Dawn, who nodded. "This is your mother, Piper."

"You, my mother," Piper said, pointing at Dawn.

Dawn blushed. "No. I just take care of you. This is your real mommy."

Maeve's combat mind kicked into gear. She had no time for this. Her family was in danger, which could arrive with a menacing knock on the door at any moment.

Maeve knelt in front of Piper, staring into her child's hazel eyes. After a brief moment, Piper's face lit up and she started slapping her hands on her mother's shoulders in glee.

"Mommy's home! Daddy's been talking about Mommy coming home."

"That's right. Mommy's home, honey." She hugged her child, wiping tears from her eyes. After a few minutes, she turned to Dawn and said, "I need you to take Piper to your house, if that's okay. I will pay you double."

Dawn shrugged. "Sure, Mrs. Cassidy, but that's not necessary."

Maeve handed one hundred dollars to Dawn and asked, "Where's my husband?"

"He went to a party on Ridge Road in Raleigh. Some client party. Something to do with a natural gas pipeline," Dawn said.

Alarm bells rang in Maeve's head. Was she too late? Had they also gotten to her husband?

"Please just do this, and either Pete or I will come get Piper. Go. Now."

Dawn scurried to pick up the playthings, and Maeve said, "No time. Just please go."

"You're scaring me, Mrs. Cassidy."

"It's okay. Just go to your house."

Quickly, Dawn was out of the door with Piper, who was now shouting, "Mommy! I want my mommy!"

Maeve took her equipment upstairs and removed a half-used bottle of henna extract from her rucksack and placed it on Piper's bureau. She slid a picture out of her combat helmet and drew a pyramid on the white photo paper backing, then inscribed a code beneath the drawing. She then picked up a picture frame from Piper's bureau. In it was a different photo of her and Piper— one directly before her deployment—where she was dressed in the digitized army battle uniform and Piper was wearing a red, white, and blue jeans and T-shirt outfit. She slid the picture from her helmet into a small frame, making sure it was visible between the outward facing picture of her and Piper and the glass cover of the frame. Maeve replaced the frame stand, and stood the picture up on the bureau next to the henna. It was the only clue she could leave.

She dumped her rucksack in her room and then sped out the door toward Ridge Road.

Maeve drove quickly through a couple of neighborhoods until she saw her husband's car: a practical and safe light blue Chevrolet Malibu with a Graco child seat in the back. She recognized the Cary Running Club decal on the window and parked in the street, behind his car. After walking past a dozen or so other cars, all more upscale than their Malibu, she approached the home, rang the doorbell, then knocked. A young, dark-haired female clad in a light blue UNC T-shirt answered by simply pulling open the door and leaving it that way. To Maeve, it didn't appear the woman was wearing anything from the waist down.

"Is Pete Cassidy here?" she asked.

The young lady shrugged her shoulders, said in an accented voice, "Perhaps that way," and nodded her head toward the hallway. In addition to the Eastern European lilt, something about the appearance of the woman made her seem foreign. She had a broad face and an angular nose and was strikingly beautiful. *Something Balkan*, Maeve guessed. The T-shirt and the woman's appearance didn't match. She was young, but not a student, she thought.

The presence of the female only heightened her sense of alarm.

Maeve stepped into the massive two-story home with a hardwood foyer and looked in the grand sunken family room. There were several young women there, either naked or partially clothed. They all had that same European look, Maeve thought. She kept walking until she found herself in the upstairs master bedroom, watching her naked husband have sex with another woman.

Quickly, the woman pulled off of Maeve's husband, reached into the top drawer of the nightstand, rolled off the bed to the far end of the bedroom, and aimed a pistol at Maeve. Pete, her husband, joined the woman on the far side of the bedroom. Their positions had awkwardly reversed. Maeve's momentum and eagerness had carried her into the bedroom, past the bed, and toward the far wall, level with the large master bathroom mirror to her right. The woman's combat roll had positioned her closer to the door. Pete just seemed confused.

So now, on her first full night back in America after twelve months of combat in Afghanistan, Captain Maeve Cassidy found herself in an unfamiliar bedroom, with her troubled marriage bared and as naked as her surprised cheating husband, who looked back at her.

She stood with her back to the wall, keeping the door to the bedroom in her direct line of sight. The room smelled of sex. Oils. Creams. Lotions. Body fluids. A candle flame made shadows dance slowly around the room, as if otherworldly apparitions were having their own strobe-lit orgy.

To her right was the master bathroom. In its large mirror, running at least six feet across both washbasins, she could see the profile of her husband and his companion standing in front of her. Her own reflection was watching her, too. Her loose-fitting Army combat uniform hid her muscular, lithe frame. Her chestnut hair was too long by Army standards and fell around her shoulders, making the uniform appear less official. As if she were an impostor. After her experience in Afghanistan, that was exactly how she felt. Maeve was a faint reflection of the person who had stepped onto the Afghan desert floor twelve months ago.

Her uniform also hid her holstered pistol. She could still smell the smoky residue of the shot she had fired into the guard shack two hours earlier. Her mind registered that she had a round chambered and a nearly full magazine of hollow points in the well.

In her reflection she caught the blackness under her eyes, chiseled there by a year of sleepless nights and impossible missions. Her anxiety was deepened by the burden of the secrets she carried and had to protect at all costs. A year of eating combat rations had hollowed her face, making the planes of her cheekbones more prominent and, oddly, her entire countenance more beautiful. But the stress of her mission and the threats she still endured weighed on her like a heavy rucksack full of equipment she didn't need.

To Maeve's left was a nice poster bed, and beyond that a read-ing alcove with a bay window. Decorative pillows were piled high on the floor, like rubble. Maeve guessed that at some point before she saw an unfamiliar woman riding her husband on the bed be-side her, those pillows had been neatly aligned on the bed. A streetlamp outside cast an eerie glow into the bedroom, compet-ing with the candle's mystic visual effect.

Music wafted down the hall through the open door to the mas-ter bedroom. To her, the tune sounded like the Eagles, maybe "Hotel California," but that song was well before her era.

"How did you find me?" her husband asked. He was standing next to an armoire with family photos in small frames scattered across the top.

Not their family, Maeve thought. The photos did include, how-ever, the naked woman, whose steady aim somewhat impressed Maeve. Maeve knew the pistol was a small Taurus that chambered five .357 hollow-point rounds. She could tell it was the 605 model by the dull blue finish and compact size.

"All I had to do was look beneath her." Maeve shrugged, point-ing at the woman next to her husband. She paused, figuring she was the one who lacked a full understanding of the situation, not her husband and his friend. So she answered the question as she knew it was intended. "Babysitter told me," Maeve said.

"It's not what you think," Pete Cassidy whispered, his voice a tight hiss, like steam escaping.

"Of course not. It never is. But what I think is irrelevant. Your lady friend here wants to shoot me, and that would not be good for either of us, especially Piper. I need to tell you some things that happened . . . overseas." Maeve was attempting to be cryptic. She wasn't sure if any of these people knew anything about the threat she had brought home like a nefarious virus that could in-fect her and her family.

"What are you talking about?" Pete, in what Maeve registered as a submissive move, turned his head toward the woman and said, "And she will not shoot you. Put down the gun. Please."

"Shut up, Pete. She is right. I *am* going to shoot her. And I will kill *you* if you say another word," said the woman with the pistol.

Maeve had endured roadside bombs in Afghanistan. She had been in firefights with insurgents high on khat or opium. Oddly enough, she had killed her fair share of enemy combatants. The war had had no front lines. Or, put another way, Maeve thought, the entire place had been the front line. As a geologist, she had been there only to study shale drilling as part of a top secret United States energy program. She had arrived when most of the troops were either gone or were leaving. But it hadn't taken long to see that America had found significant new interests beneath the earth's dusty shell along the Pakistan border—and those interests had put her face-to-face with Taliban and Al Qaeda zealots.

Now Maeve recognized the crazy, murderous look in the woman's eyes in front of her. She was gazing at something in the distance, obeying some distant god, convinced of the sanctity of her truth. Clearly, the woman was amped up on meth or cocaine or a more upscale and trendy amphetamine. Maeve had been gone for twelve months, so she didn't know. Perhaps they had a new drug. She noticed the subtle contours of her adversary's body: her slim hips, full breasts, and pouting lips, all surgically im-proved no doubt, and her legs slightly spread in a balanced shooter's stance.

"Don't do this. Please," Pete sputtered. Maeve had never seen her husband more meek. "You can't."

"Actually, you can," a new voice said as a fourth person entered the bedroom.

Four people, three of whom were naked, and two actual weapons, both aimed at Maeve Cassidy, filled the room. Usually, people hid guns in their waistband or pockets, Maeve considered. Exactly what kind of swingers' party had she crashed? She could see the invita-tion: *Let's get naked and shoot each other!* Or for the men: *You go soft, you get shot.*

Her well-developed combat defense mechanisms were kicking in, complete with gallows humor. In combat, she had seen enough body parts scattered around like in a modern artist's rendition of van Gogh.

It was true that she had already established a fatalistic approach to life. Her world had been rocked by the horrors of combat, which in her case she believed had been atypical. Perhaps the experience had loosened a screw; she wasn't sure. She had just been a reservist doing her duty as the wars were winding down. She guessed that maybe she was just having a hard time adjusting back to civilian life.

Wasn't it normal to find her husband at a swingers' party just down the road from their home?

"What are *you* doing here?" Maeve said to the new person who'd entered the room.

"Good question, dear, Maeve. We're just celebrating the completion of Daddy's pipeline to Morehead City. Though I didn't see your name on the invite list," the new voice said.

Then a weapon fired. Pete Cassidy screamed. Blood sprayed from Maeve's body.

And, for all practical purposes, that ended the party.

The same morning that Maeve Cassidy was processing out of Fort Bragg, Maxim Petrov received a text message from his boss. The message contained two words.

Star cluster.

The communication was early, and he was unprepared. Where he thought he had a week, he now had a day, if that. Nervous about being the only one clued into this portion of the plan, Petrov thought back to his Russian Spetsnaz days in Chechnya. A former Special Forces soldier, he knew how to do this. Still, he was on unfamiliar ground in central North Carolina.

He drove slowly past the Wallaby gas station in Chapel Hill and saw a line of Hispanic men waiting for work in the hopeful daily endeavor of day laborers. Petrov had seen these men line up every day here and at other gas stations when he had scouted the area for the mission. The men were desperate for work, and Petrov knew they would take any job. It was usually landscapers, construction foremen, and farmers who cruised through early, picking the most able.

He drove his black pickup truck to the line of waiting journeymen. He jumped out, sized up the lot, selected two strong-looking men, opened the tailgate, and motioned for them to hop in the truck. His boss had told him that he would need more men later to complete the outer security fence, but he needed the cell built immediately.

From downtown Chapel Hill, he drove to the isolated construction site about fifteen miles away. With the two day laborers bouncing in the back of the truck, he entered the site off U.S. Route 1. He made a series of right and left turns through an increasingly wooded area and arrived upon a mile-long tangle of trucks, water tanks, pipes, valves, and drills. It looked better than a junkyard, but not by much.

Petrov turned right again, being careful to stay out of the line of sight of the nineteen other men, like himself, who had been brought to the United States as fracking roughnecks. He followed a minor two-track trail around the eastern side of the hill, where he stopped after a mile of bouncing through the ruts. He shut off the engine and waited, checking again to make sure he had avoided detection by the roughnecks, especially the two Chinese guys. They couldn't know about this part of the mission, at least not yet, if ever. Certain he was undetected, Petrov issued instructions to the Hispanic men in broken English.

The two workers dismounted and moved to the preconstruction area Petrov had already completed. They helped him lift and place the floor, walls, and roof. They were good workers, steady men who knew how to build. Petrov didn't ask their names, because he didn't care. They wouldn't be alive long enough for it to matter. Once they had the plywood sawed and nailed to the walls, ceiling, and floor, save the eight-by-six-by-three-foot opening in the floor, they took a break.

He offered both men a bottle of water, which they gladly accepted. They sat on the hill, looking to the southeast, toward Shearon Harris Lake, less than five miles away, and to the single cooling tower of the nuclear plant, its steam rising lazily into the early morning sky like drifting cigar smoke. He heard them speaking in Spanish, wondering why he was using plywood and what the hole might be. They guessed it was for a latrine.

Close, he thought. He was going to use it to dispose of something he no longer needed.

Their part was done. He approached from behind and shot each of them in the head using a Glock 17, the gunshots signaling nothing more than a deer hunter on this bucolic hillside. He dragged their bodies into the cell and dumped them into the remaining hole in the floor. He poured two bags of limestone on top of them, filled the hole with dirt, laid the perfectly cut sheet of plywood on the studs, and hammered the floor shut.

It took him the rest of the day to finish the holding cell. Using a shovel, he spread two feet of dirt on the roof, which was even with the crest of the hill. He sprinkled fescue grass seed and straw on top of the dirt. In less than a week, the only part of the cell that would show would be the door, which faced toward the woods, which were about one hundred yards away. He camouflaged the door with brown and green paint.

He walked to the woods and down to a rill running into Shearon Harris Lake. Petrov studied the swampy area and determined that no one in their right mind would cross anywhere within a quarter mile in either direction. But if they did, he wanted to know what they would see. Petrov walked directly toward the holding cell and didn't notice it until he was out of the woods and within fifty meters of it.

And he was looking for it.

Soon there would be others looking for it also, but by then it would be too late.

At least that was the plan.

Tomorrow he would visit another gas station and find a different work crew, who would need to last a few more days so they could build the rest of the security fence.

As darkness enveloped him, he drove the mile to the graded lot between two hilltops. He saw the crew of roughnecks wrapping up their work, a few of them staring at him as they smoked cigarettes, the orange tips glowing hot.

Sitting in his truck, looking at the lights on the crew trailers up the hill, where they would all sleep tonight, he received a text message.

Package wrapped. Delivery tonight.

CHAPTER 2

THE FOLLOWING MORNING, JAKE MAHEGAN STOOD IN THE LINE LIKE any other unemployed, perhaps homeless, man down on his luck. He had not shaved in a week, and the black stubble of a beard contrasted with his dark blond hair. He wore old, greasy Army battle dress uniform pants, scuffed Doc Marten boots, and a loose-fitting, ripped NC State sweatshirt atop a tan Army T-shirt. But what set him apart from the other day laborers was that he was a good foot taller than most.

He shoved his hands into his pockets, keeping his eyes cast downward at the abused sidewalk next to the Wallaby gas station near Apex, North Carolina. He was fifth in a line of about twenty people looking for work, part of a human assembly line. A truck arrived; a few got on. Another appeared, and some more left. Every day was the same.

He had been here enough days without getting picked that he knew the system. Arrival time equaled line queue number, unless your name was Papa Diablo, who always got the first job regardless of when he arrived.

Mahegan guessed it took about five trips to the Wallaby gas station to earn any bona fides with the perennial group of Hispanic men who lined up here for the assorted odd jobs that came their way. Most frequently, the routine included a pickup truck, a farmer or a construction foreman leaning through the passenger window, and the barking of a number, usually in bad Spanish, such as "*Tres!*" Three men would then clamber into the back of the pickup, and off they would go to do landscaping or ditch digging, something manual and menial.

But the pay was apparently okay, as Mahegan noticed the same faces in the short time he had been lining up. Every morning there was a new topic of discussion among those in the line, mostly normal locker room scuttlebutt, like the talk Mahegan would hear from his soldiers when he was active duty Army. The chow sucked. Not enough combat action or, in this case, work. Someone's girlfriend or wife left him, and so on. This morning, though, the chatter up and down the line tested Mahegan's limited Spanish skills. He heard words like *camion negro, idos, no estan en casa, ricos,* and *borrachos.* Apparently, the rumor was that two men from a different gas station's line had been selected by a black truck, were now missing, and most likely had been so well paid that they had gotten drunk and had never come home.

This line of conversation piqued Mahegan's interest because he was looking for a black, late-model Ford F-150 being driven by a dark-haired man with a long scar running along one cheek. What Mahegan had learned through his network was that the man driving the black pickup truck was looking for men who could do fracking jobs. Hydraulic fracturing, or fracking, of shale gas deposits would soon be big business in North Carolina, and the men lined up with Mahegan prayed for steady jobs that would provide for their families.

The Ford would have the name of a construction company on the side. Mahegan knew the name of the construction company. Other than losing his best friend in combat, it had been all he had thought about for the past fifteen years. One name. One man.

Since Mahegan's cycle of deployments to combat had ceased when he was dismissed from active duty Army, he was now able to focus his attention on this entirely personal matter. He was catching up on old, unfinished business, the way a normal person might use a Saturday to run errands. Before his dismissal from the Army less than two years ago, his life had been full of workweeks, 24-7. He had been either engaged in combat or prepping for combat. Now it was nothing but weekends, with no real kind of job and a lot of time to think.

Mahegan watched trucks come and go, and the line shorten accordingly, until he saw a Ford pull into the parking lot and then turn to the gas pump island. He saw white letters arcing across the door, with mud splattered across most of them, making the words illegible. A buzz like that from a lit fuse sizzled through the line of men as a stocky man of average height, with black hair, climbed out of the truck and began to pump low-test gasoline. Out of his periphery, Mahegan saw the man look at the nozzle and then across the truck bed at the two dozen hopeful men, including him. He felt the man's gaze settle on him, calculating perhaps how much Mahegan could bench-press. Or it may have been a reckoning that he didn't belong in the group.

Mahegan appeared bored, eyes cast downward. He knew that he wouldn't be able to detect the man's scar from over thirty yards away, so he didn't look. So far, everything matched up. Mahegan was in position number five, unless Papa Diablo suddenly appeared. Then he would be sixth. He hoped the man needed at least six for the job.

Mahegan took a sip of water from a water bottle. He had started bringing a case of it every day and putting it at the head of the line so the workers could grab a bottle as they went with their rides. This act had earned both the praise of the common line dweller and the suspicion of Papa Diablo, who now came walking around the back side of the gas station to jump the line. No doubt he had been waiting for the fracking job, also. It was a different kind of work, and the line had been burning with rumors for weeks that hydraulic fracturing was going to provide not just daily chances for work but also steady jobs. This morning's news of the happy drunks had only fueled that yearning.

The black-haired man jumped in his truck and pulled to a stop directly in front of Mahegan, who noticed red clay had etched red stains around the edges of the tires like dark lipstick. The mud was caked on thick, but the red clay was a good sign. The fracking job would be off-road. The fracking fault lines were in the rolling hills of western Wake, Chatham, Lee, and Moore Counties, where red clay was dominant.

The driver walked with an intent focus that Mahegan had seen before. The man was task driven to find the biggest, hardest-working men possible. He had quick black eyes, which rapidly scanned the crowd again. He paced along the row of downtrodden men, who were too proud to act desperate, but too desperate not to act interested.

To Mahegan, the driver's strut looked like that of the goose-stepping Schutzstaffel, whom he'd first seen in a middle school social studies class on Nazi propaganda. The man took long, lazy strides just outside the range of the work-worn boots of his potential charges. His black combat boots resonated like a dropping guillotine blade with each footfall, the red clay rimming his boots looking like dried blood splatter. Mahegan took in his mud-stained dungarees, his sweatshirt, and his black leather coat, which was listing to the right, an indication of something heavy in his pocket, perhaps a pistol.

The driver stopped in front of Papa Diablo, nodded to him, as if to acknowledge Diablo's authority in the group, and said, "*Uno.*" Then he said, "*Dos,*" as he pointed at the biggest man in the group other than Mahegan. The driver's hands were large extensions of thick, powerful arms. When he pointed, the driver aimed his finger like a gun.

Mahegan watched "Dos" and Papa Diablo jump to their feet, open the tailgate, and scramble onto the truck bed.

Turning away, the driver looked over his shoulder at Mahegan, pointed at him, and said, "And you."

That was when Mahegan saw the scar. He paused, purely an act intended to demonstrate submission and hesitation. Then he walked to the truck, stepped on the tailgate, which shifted the weight of the truck considerably, and slid in next to Papa Diablo. The driver climbed back into the truck, slammed his door, and sped out of the parking lot, as if time was critical.

Mahegan didn't know the protocol about talking on the way to a job, so he stayed quiet, which was natural for him, anyway. He watched homes and stores pass by from the unobstructed vantage point of the truck bed. Shortly, they were on U.S. Route 1, heading south toward Pinehurst, with populated Wake County falling away behind them. But they didn't go far. By Mahegan's estimation, the driver turned the truck off an exit ramp less than fifteen miles from where they had entered the limited-access highway. He pulled onto an asphalt road called old U.S. Route 1 and raced the vehicle to about seventy miles per hour.

As Mahegan rode in the back of the pickup truck, he thought about the many elements at play. He was one of three people selected to go to an undisclosed location to do an unknown type and amount of work for an undetermined wage. Times were tough, and they were tougher, obviously, for the two men sitting in the truck bed with him.

The truck bed had a standard plastic liner that wore the scars of hard labor: heavy metal things tossed in the back; tools, like rakes and shovels, bouncing and gouging the floor and the low walls. The back window was a slider but was tinted dark. He couldn't see inside the cab.

"Dos" was probably six feet tall in Mahegan's estimation. His face was square, and he had the flattened nose of a boxer. He wore a buzz cut like a cage fighter. His shoulders were round and appeared powerful. He wore a long-sleeve Under Armour T-shirt, which poked out from beneath a brown and gray Carhartt coat.

Pablo Diablo was thin and wiry. He had a beak-like nose and a cool, confident demeanor. Mahegan could see he was comfortable in his role as the informal leader of the Apex Wallaby work crew. He didn't know, but Mahegan figured there was a rite of passage here that was similar to the way village elders gained status in Afghanistan.

All in all, Mahegan saw he could have been paired with worse teammates, if that was what he could call them. He had once been a member of the military's most elite team, Delta Force, but Mahegan had killed a handcuffed enemy prisoner of war, which was against military law. His rage had been unleashed only after a bomb maker's improvised explosive device had killed his best friend. In the mayhem caused by the blast, the prisoner had tried to escape, and Mahegan's attempt to disable the fleeing enemy had resulted in the man's death. The buttstock of an M4 carbine to the temple would do that to a person, especially when propelled by Mahegan's powerful forearm.

As Mahegan stared past the bed of the truck at the woods, which moved past them like a movie reel, he thought about freedom. He had fought for freedom but had actually never felt truly liberated. As a kid, he had had school. His parents. Rules. Authorities. Responsibility. When he was a soldier, the same trappings had applied, just in different formats. He had had commanders and soldiers. Authority and responsibility. He had thrived in that environment.

Yet now he was devoid of authority and had little responsibility beyond taking care of himself. And, still, he wasn't free. A memory chained him to his past like prison shackles, binding him to his anger and guilt. His mind pulled against the mental trusses, as if attempting to yank anchors from a brick wall. The memories were of his mother, the only person who had ever shown him what true freedom looked like. Her words and actions had provided Mahegan guideposts by which to live his life. As Mahegan left the Army and decompressed, he had wrestled with the loss of his best friend, Sergeant Wesley Colgate. But he was haunted by the recurring memory of his mother from fifteen years before.

He was a Croatan Indian, born on the Outer Banks of North Carolina. He had spent his youth there and in Maxton, in Robeson County, with his parents—at least until he'd walked home from school one day and found four men smelling of booze and sweat manhandling his mother, calling her an Indian lover bitch. He was fourteen, and by then he was over six feet tall. Young Mahegan had been lifting weights in the gym with one of the assistant wrestling coaches, who was a paratrooper at Fort Bragg.

His mother, Samantha Austin Mahegan, had been a beach-variety blonde. Her skin had been tan and smooth. She had had freckles that dotted her face like a distant constellation and that filled in during the summer, so mostly she'd looked almost as dark as his

Croatan father. Mahegan had loved her as much as any child loved his or her mother, in an adoring, protective way. With his father drifting so much, looking for work and chasing his roots, she had often been all he had.

She had been an elementary school teacher and had had the clear countenance and upbeat attitude that all teachers seemed to share. She had taught him to read, ride a bike, and say the blessing at the dinner table. Her parents had called her Sam, placing her initials together to make a cute nickname, which had stuck. His favorite memories revolved around her teaching him to be a waterman, which included swimming, free diving, and surfing near Frisco, in the Outer Banks. Other memories included sitting on the back porch of their modest home in Maxton as the sun set over the sandy hills to the west. She had shared her life philosophy with him, which essentially centered on *making a difference.*

Sam Mahegan had been no fool, Jake knew, and she had been a tough woman with a gentle heart. She had loved nature and had harbored countless stray animals, from dogs to cats to injured wild pigs and even wounded deer. She had led the Save the Turtle efforts in the Outer Banks and the litter cleanup campaign in Maxton. She'd been a mother with a cause, he liked to say. She had shown him how to be generous while standing up for himself against the bullies who invariably picked on him until he began growing at age thirteen.

"Always give them an out," she had said. "You are strong, Chayton, and you will hurt them." Chayton, which meant "falcon" in Iroquois, was his given name, but he had had trouble saying it as a child. His version had sounded like "Jake," which had stuck, much like "Sam" had for his mother. Mahegan had evolved "a long time ago," according to his father, from Mohegan, which meant "wolf."

Mahegan had tried to let some things go as a teenager, and his mother's advice had mostly worked.

Until that day.

He had walked home from school along the freshly graded dirt road that a construction company was building between his school and their neighborhood. There'd been a pickup truck parked in front of his house. The truck had had a construction company name stenciled on the side. He had found four men in his house.

Flashing before his eyes now was his larger-than-life mother, who had helped him understand his American Indian heritage and fit into society. Sitting in the truck, watching the trees pass, Mahegan recalled what had happened next.

He was fourteen years old and bigger than most full-grown men. Awkward but powerful, he had an athleticism that had not yet been fully honed by coaches and opponents.

Two of the men turned toward Mahegan as he opened the wooden screen door to their trailer. He saw two other men with their pants down, hovering over his mother. A whimper escaped from her.

"Please stop."

Her words were a siren to him. He felt something let go in his mind, like a cable snapping. A flywheel coming loose. A herd of wild mustangs charging through an inadequate corral gate.

The grunts and squeals of the men sounded like those of pigs. The man between his mother's legs was saying, "Indian lover bitch. Bet that Indian ain't got one of these." The man pushed against his mother while another man held her.

Mahegan was no longer in control. Instinct governed his actions. He became Chayton Mahegan, literally "the falcon wolf" in Iroquois. He evolved at that moment into the apex predator that he would forever be against all things evil.

Two men charged him. His forearm snapped the nose of the shirtless guy on his left, because he saw that the one on his right was pulling up his jeans as he ran, which gave him an extra second. After stunning the broken-nose man, he kicked the blue jeans attacker in his gut, making him double over. He slammed his knee into the man's face as he pulled down on the back of his head. By then the first one was coming after young Mahegan hard, like a charging bull. He sidestepped him with a smooth athletic move and wrapped his arm around his neck. Without pausing, he used his free hand to snap the neck clean. He heard the pop and knew he had just killed his first human being. He had no emotion but the fear he continued to feel for his mother.

Barreling toward her, Mahegan saw that she had been cast sideways onto the sofa. He pulled a man off of her and threw him through the sliding porch door. The glass shattered into icicle-like chunks, at least one of which speared the man in the back. Mahegan turned to the last man, whose pants were around his ankles and whose lecherous, stony-eyed gaze was fixed on his mother.

Mahegan rammed into him like a pro wrestler jumping from the ropes, pulled him away from his mother, and smashed his face into the kitchen counter, where it met the sink. The man had a beard and long hair. Mahegan grabbed an oily fistful and slammed and slammed and slammed until there wasn't much left of the man's face.

He was still slamming when a police officer pulled him away.

Mahegan had gone to juvenile prison for two years, while the two assailants who lived had walked because of some connection to a government official somewhere. Despite the fact that four men had raped and murdered his mother, the two men were never convicted, based on insufficient evidence. Mahegan had heard rumors that one of the survivors had blackmailed a judge. When he was fourteen years old, though, that kind of thing had been hard to understand.

At twenty-eight, he had full clarity.

He remembered that his father had visited him once in the detention center, saying to him, *I'll find them, Chayton. And I'll kill them. They took the best thing either of us ever had.* And he had always assumed that his father was on the hunt, like he was, for the remaining two.

And then he had found a picture of his father just two weeks ago in the renovated attic—now a study or library of sorts—of a Raleigh socialite. He had entered the enormous private residence without invitation and had left with the photograph, which he now stored safely in his above-barn apartment in Apex. The picture confirmed to him that he was on the right course.

The picture also made him remember the names the way people remembered where they were when 9/11 happened: James and Raymond Gunther, Tommy Boyd, and Franklin Overton. He had killed Raymond Gunther and Franklin Overton on the scene that day. And he had seen a newspaper article about the death of

Tommy Boyd. It was a story about a meth lab that had exploded in Brunswick County, killing Boyd, but police had a witness who had led them to suspect foul play. Soon the authorities had posted on-line and in the newspapers a rough artist's sketch of a man who resembled his father. He remembered feeling proud at even the thought of his father exacting revenge, but Mahegan had had no clue regarding his dad's whereabouts until his first night in Raleigh a few weeks ago.

While he didn't know the status of James Gunther for a long time, either, he had recently heard some news about the man, as well. Turned out his construction business had thrived and had grown to the point where he had to hire on his son, James Jr., to help him manage the company. Mahegan seethed at the thought. His mother had died a vicious death, while Gunther not only had lived, but also had prospered. Other than the punishment Mahegan had meted out that day, justice had not been served.

At seventeen, Mahegan had enlisted as a private in the Army, and he had quickly become an Airborne Ranger, graduated from Officer Candidate School, and then become a Delta Force operator. But the mustangs inside broke loose again the day he saw his best friend blown to bits. Killing a prisoner of war, though, was probably the best thing that had ever happened to him. That misdeed had led him to his current status as the only domestic contract operative for the Joint Special Operations Command. Major General Bob Savage kept him off the books and called on him only when absolutely required. He was a cleaner. A fixer. A problem solver. A consultant.

But this matter today was personal, and Savage had little idea of what Mahegan was doing at this moment.

The truck slowed, causing Mahegan's massive frame to lean into the firm shoulder of the man the driver had called "Dos." He watched as the truck spun around a cloverleaf exit and turned onto New Elam Church Road. From there, the driver wound along several unnamed roads and turned onto a muddy red-clay path. They dipped through a small wet area, and Mahegan noticed the low ground on both sides of a densely vegetated forest. As the truck's engine roared, they climbed a hill, turning west before reaching the top. Mahegan was staring due east as he looked along the rear axis of the truck. He saw swampy, low ground surrounded by oak, maple, and pine trees. The underbrush was thick, as were the mid-level trees, such as dogwoods. He thought he saw a small herd of deer grazing along a stream.

Looking to the south now, Mahegan noticed the lazy drift of steam from the Shearon Harris Nuclear Power Plant cooling tower about four miles away. Turning to his left, he saw a chain-link fence standing ten feet tall, with menacing curls of razor wire preventing anyone from climbing over it. In either direction. He also saw one-inch ribbons of sensors running through the fence links. Mahegan knew that these were motion detectors and that they were probably connected to cameras that provided surveillance twenty-four hours a day and seven days a week. If the fence moved, a camera zoomed in on the location.

Mahegan felt the vehicle turn back toward the north, and he noticed they were entering a terrain feature called a saddle. It was the low ground between two hilltops. It was a small-scale version of a valley. Mahegan's mind visualized the contracting contour lines indicating the hilltops and the expanding lines between the hilltops, indicating flatter and lower ground.

The saddle probably ran a mile from south to north, Mahegan estimated. He craned his neck, as if checking for snipers and potential ambush locations. The hilltops on both sides were vegetated but not heavily wooded. Sparse trees dotted the high ground. Looking above the cab, a luxury provided by his long torso, he saw the ridge that connected the two hilltops in the far distance. They were isolated. In the center of the small valley were the pieces and parts of a huge industrial operation.

As the truck bounced through a gravel parking lot, they passed into another fenced-in area, an inner cordon, this one with a small sign that read JAMES GUNTHER AND SONS CONSTRUCTION, INC.

CHAPTER 3

MAEVE CASSIDY WAS INJURED.

Well, at least she was not dead, she thought. The general rule in combat had been that wounded was better than dead. Usually. It all depended on what came next, and right now she was in this barren cube of a room. No. It wasn't a room. It was a shelter. It was too rustic to be a cabin and too new to be a previous residence. She searched for the term. *Bungalow?* No, that didn't seem right. A bungalow was a home, and this certainly wasn't a home. *Compartment?* No, not that, either. It didn't seem to be a part of something else.

Then it came to her. *Detention.* She remembered seeing a few detention cells in Afghanistan. They were about this size and equally barren. Five steps across in each direction. Solid plywood screwed into studs, most likely two-by-fours. A plywood box, like a large coffin. *Coffin.* That was about right. And she was here against her will. She was *confined* at a detention site, as the infantry called them in Afghanistan.

Maeve leaned back against the wall and assessed her injury. She was dressed in her Army combat uniform pants, tan combat boots, and a tan, bloodstained Nomex T-shirt. Her ACU jacket lay crumpled on the floor, as if it had been tossed into the cell. Her left arm was in a blue sling that was, she guessed, made out of a table napkin. She had a laceration on her left bicep that had skimmed her triceps. Not exactly a graze, but neither was it a life-threatening wound, barring infection, she surmised. Someone had done a respectable job cleaning, flushing, and bandaging the wound.

Regardless, she thought, *too close for comfort.*

She looked up at the wooden structure that surrounded her. Being held captive, she figured, suggested the intentionally wounded theory. Someone wanted her in this small room, dungeon, cave, coffin, prison, detention cell, or whatever they wanted to call it. For what reason, though, she wasn't sure.

A long-distance runner, Maeve had stamina, though twelve months in combat had lessened that some. The cumulative effects of battle, she knew, had weakened her physical condition, even if that same time period had strengthened her mettle. She caught herself growing emotional and shunted the surge, like a tourniquet on a wound. *No time for feeling sorry for yourself, Cassidy.* "Assess and act"—that was her credo.

She couldn't stop the reflection, though, of her time at war and the decision twelve months ago to step away from her position as a professor of geology at North Carolina State University. The chancellor there had reservedly blessed her departure, not wanting to lose a good professor but admiring her dedication to country. Her husband, Pete, worked as a banker, and they enjoyed a quiet, almost idyllic life in the town of Cary. She had given birth to their daughter, Piper, four years ago, and when she deployed a year ago, she'd been considering having another child with Pete. Now that seemed out of the question, for many reasons.

What confused her was that she should be either dead or at home, not bleeding in some purgatory. They were neither rich nor famous, and ransom was out of the question. Her parents were state workers from Virginia, and his parents were both gone. Their total net worth, including their $250,000 house, was somewhere south of $300,000, hardly ransom bait.

So why, she wondered, had her husband been sleeping with another woman on the night of her return from war? And why had she been kidnapped? She had always considered Pete a loving, caring man, if not a tad too bothered by finances. He wanted the same things she did: a house, children, good neighbors, tailgates at NC State football games, and a happy life. She would never be Martha Stewart, and Pete would never be Warren Buffett. Money would come one day, she had always figured. In her long-range vision—she was a planner—their ship would come in and they would have the house on Figure Eight Island, the beachfront property with the large boat. Before her tour in Afghanistan, she had always believed that day would come through diligence and hard work and perhaps a bit of luck. And she had been just fine with being Maeve Brennan Cassidy.

Then a year in combat had begun to wear on her, like water on a stone. One day at a time, her resolve had weakened, until she'd begun to believe the elaborate stories of her handler, Jim. Together they could make millions, he had promised. She had listened and remained skeptical. But Maeve had redeployed from Afghanistan a changed person, for sure. She harbored secrets and plans that had seemed abstract in the distant confines of her Afghan redoubt.

Until last night. The sight of another woman having sex with her husband had brought her back to reality quickly. The secrets were real. The plans were taking shape, even if she wanted no part in them. Her wound was real; it would heal, but the sting in her arm reminded her that she was not living in an illusion. Ultimately, too, her marriage most likely would not survive, but in truth, the damage had been done in Afghanistan.

Using her right hand, she tucked her auburn hair behind her ears and wiped a few tears away from her eyes. Her world now was this detention cell. New wood. She could smell it. Built just for her? she wondered. Or was she just the first of many occupants to come? There was the slightest whiff of a foul odor that she couldn't quite place. Like a dead animal, but not as bad, yet.

With her left arm in the sling, Maeve stood and paced her cell, pushing at the walls in various places. *Assess and act.* Having been blindfolded and unconscious before being deposited here, she had no feeling for whether she was aboveground, underground, or somewhere in between. There was no give when she pushed on the plywood walls. She used her knuckles to knock lightly in random locations. The duller thuds indicated the studs, and the more hollow sounds signified the gaps between them. One wall, though, sounded altogether different than the other three. To confirm this, she rapped her knuckles on all four walls again, walking in a counterclockwise direction around the small cell.

Whatever was behind the other three walls was not behind the wall with the door. The cell was most likely surrounded by earth on three sides. Reaching up with her right hand, Maeve knocked against the ceiling and heard the same solid thud she'd heard from the three walls. There was only one way out, she figured, which was through the door.

She heard metal against metal outside the door, the unlocking of hasps. The door swung open, revealing sunlight.

And a rifle.

Maeve stepped back into a corner of the cell and waited.

"Food for you," a voice said. "Tonight we get to work." It was a Russian accent, she thought. Perhaps Ukrainian, but more likely Russian. The man tossed two combat rations, called meals ready to eat, or MREs, onto the floor, then added, "Don't do anything stupid."

As he went to close the door, Maeve shouted, "Wait! Work on what?"

The door had stopped about a foot from the doorjamb when the man said, "Later. We tell you everything later. Now eat and rest. You working until we are done."

The man closed the door. She heard him lock at least two hasps. The momentary brightness from the sun made it difficult to adjust to the darkness again. When her night vision returned after a few minutes, she found the MREs, opened one, and began to eat.

What could they possibly need me to do? she wondered. *I am a teacher and a geologist. A mother and a wife. A friend and a neighbor.* And she had just returned from war, for God's sake. This was certainly no hero's welcome, she thought as she munched on the dry crackers.

Sitting in the darkness, her mind volleyed back and forth like two sides in a tennis match: *How do I break out of this cell? What kind of work do they want me to do? Can I bust the hasps? Is the work dangerous?* She cycled through the possibilities, attempting to find comfort in conclusions.

Two hasps, maybe three, with an inward-opening door. Should she wait for him to come again and kick the door into his face? He seemed to be alone. That was an option, but not a good one given her wounded arm. Ask him for a blanket and hope he made a mistake with the rifle? Get him talking? Get him to see her as sympathetic? Possible, but still not likely. The man seemed professional. He wasn't prone to answering any questions, yet at the same time he gave her food and limited information.

What kind of work was he talking about? She was a geologist and a combat veteran. She had participated in the Army's secret program to test a classified series of depleted-uranium drill bits and controversial drilling techniques in Afghanistan. The earth beneath much of Afghanistan and Pakistan was filled with minerals, natural gas, and oil, which were valuable to jewelers, weapons makers, and energy companies. Her specialty had been to study the geology and then maneuver the drill bits thousands of feet into the earth, ultimately searching for gas or oil.

Maeve ran the past twenty-four hours through her mind. She'd arrived back at Fort Bragg after an arduous trip from Bagram to Kandahar, to Kuwait, to Germany, to Pope Field and Fort Bragg. People representing themselves as from the Joint Special Operations Command had debriefed her, and she had told them everything they wanted to know about hydraulic fracturing, or fracking, in Afghanistan, mostly. In Afghanistan she had developed and honed the art and science of using depleted-uranium and titanium drill bits to bore a mile or two into the earth and then to go another mile or two laterally. Next, they pumped massive volumes of top-secret pressurized chemicals to fracture the shale layers and capture the released natural gas. Then the men, whom she didn't know, had asked her questions about the fracking process, money, sex, and the six liquefied natural gas container ships leaving Karachi, Pakistan. That was when she'd run.

Of course, she'd known all along she would never be able to escape the long tentacles of the CIA and her clandestine handler.

And now she prayed that someone would find the clue she'd left revealing the location of vulnerable American targets.

CHAPTER 4

T HE MAN WITH THE SCAR HAD OFFERED HIM A MOTORIZED AUGER to drill the holes, but Mahegan had opted for the posthole digger. Scarface had scowled and shrugged, saying, "Have it your way, dumbass." Mahegan was accustomed to hard work and was enjoying using the digger to complete an outer fence around what he guessed was some kind of energy operation, most likely fracking. Mahegan also wanted a workout since he was skipping his daily regimen of swimming and running.

He needed to be in peak physical condition when he found James Gunther. That was his only focus. His boss, Major General Bob Savage at Fort Bragg, had not texted him a new mission yet. Instead, he'd instructed Mahegan to relax and "stay out of trouble." The problem was, Mahegan drifted toward "trouble" the way a corporate CEO smelled a deal or a top broker made a risky but rewarding stock purchase. Seeing problems before or as they became trouble was Mahegan's sixth sense. Ever since he killed his first man, his lizard brain had dominated, transforming him into a one-man justice system, defending and protecting.

While he would never forgive himself for being too late to rescue his mother, he could still seek justice on her behalf. This operation was the third Gunther and Sons, Inc., construction site at which he had labored, but he had yet to see Gunther or anyone who looked like Junior. Most likely, they sat in their air-conditioned offices while others did their bidding. Problem was, Mahegan would be too noticeable if he walked into an office building in an ill-fitting suit. People would remember him because of his size and his looks: dark blond hair, blue eyes, tan skin, and a six-and-a-half-foot muscular frame. He could do more prying out here, where he was just another American Indian day laborer earning a buck.

Gunther and Sons' headquarters was located in Fayetteville, which was a bit too close to home for Mahegan. Wanting to get Mahegan off the grid, three months ago Savage had ordered him to Apex, North Carolina, where the Army was currently renting an above-barn apartment on a three-acre plot of land. So while he waited for his next mission, Mahegan had stayed local, working as a framer on one Gunther and Sons, Inc., office building project in Holly Springs and as an asphalt spreader on a road-paving project in Cary.

Gunther was the one Mahegan had thrown through the sliding glass door of his home on that horrifying day when he was too late to save his mother. The chunk of glass had cut his back and, Mahegan had heard, nicked a lung. Had the paramedics and the police not arrived when they did, either Gunther would have bled out or Mahegan would have finished him.

He lifted the posthole digger, opened its jaws, and stabbed it into the ground, creating a hole deep enough for Papa Diablo to emplace a metal pole while Dos poured in ready-mix concrete. It was menial labor, which Mahegan almost liked. His mind worked best when he was doing simple tasks, such as swimming or running.

As Dos situated the metal pole in the ground, Mahegan scouted his surroundings. He walked to the top of the ridge. He noticed they had made good progress, having reached the northern end of the western ridge. They had been working west and north around the hill that served as the western ridge of the saddle, where Mahegan had seen what he believed to be energy exploration equipment. Giant water tanks lay side by side next to thick, snaking hoses and assorted vehicles. A construction crew had graded a football field of earth. Today he noticed, at the north end of the leveled area, metal parts, like those of an erector set, which would possibly become a rig for drilling a wellhead. In the middle of the field was a hole about five feet across, with a conical, prefab concrete inlay. He was unsure, but it appeared that the wellhead had already been drilled. From his vantage, the hole looked like a giant inverted cone or funnel, narrowing just slightly from about five to four feet. Surrounding the hole was plastic, orange engineer warning tape, staked in the ground with U-shaped pickets.

A few men milled around in the distance, but mostly the operation was idle today. Two men were smoking cigarettes, until a foreman shooed them away, presumably to a safer area to smoke than a natural gas vent. Coiled like a snake were what appeared to be miles of flexible drill lengths, which would be used to bore into the ground to find the porous veins of natural gas. Next to the stacks of drill lengths was something that looked like a cage full of basketballs, but with grooves like those on a screw, and protruding edges, sharp, with glinting metal. *Drill bits?* Mahegan wondered. They looked like medieval weapons, maces, with their triangular teeth jutting from one end.

Mahegan turned around and looked west. The sun's position indicated the time was about 3:00 p.m. He could see through the forest to Jordan Lake, about a mile or two away. He guessed the fencing was necessary to keep equipment poachers out, as well as the bears and deer that might wander into the construction site.

Mahegan studied the valley, which, he considered, appeared to be a bowl with an opening to the south, scouting for any sign of a Gunther, father or son. He was expecting a big, shiny truck or SUV, but all he saw was the black Ford F-150 that Scarface had driven and the myriad drilling equipment concentrated around the prefab cone. There were trailers—living quarters, he presumed—a quarter mile to the north. In his periphery he saw Scarface walking from the eastern ridge back toward the graded saddle. When he was at the bottom, Scarface walked briskly past the idle crew, bucket loaders, and bulldozers sitting parked like resting animals, and shouted, "What the hell is this? Break time?"

Mahegan lifted his posthole digger with one hand and pointed it at the far side of the ridge, which Scarface couldn't see, and said, "Cement is drying."

"Well, dig another goddamned hole, idiot!"

Mahegan nodded, wishing briefly that Scarface was related to Gunther, then turned and walked back to continue the fencing work.

After another two hours they found themselves at the northwest end of the ridge. They had started due south, where they had entered the area in the truck, then had worked west and north. The sun was still hanging high enough for another couple of hours of work, and Mahegan thought they could probably finish the job. But he was glad when Scarface reappeared and said, "Quitting time."

Mahegan and the two Mexicans walked down the hill to where Scarface was waiting for them. Mahegan surveyed the prefab cone and thought he had it about right. He imagined that the frackers used the opening to extract natural gas the way a surgeon operated through one location on the body.

"We're not done," Mahegan said, putting up a mock protest as he stopped in front of Scarface.

"And you're not going to be done today. I'll pick you three back up tomorrow morning. Right now I need to get you out of here."

"Why so soon? We could finish tonight."

Mahegan could see Scarface's mind calculating why he might be pushing the issue. "Don't worry. You'll get paid today and tomorrow. That's how Gunther does it. Pays out every day."

Mahegan nodded. "Does Gunther do the paying?"

"I do. Why?"

Mahegan shrugged. "We get paid before we get in the truck?"

Papa Diablo and Dos had planted themselves on either side of him, as if to reinforce his message. Mahegan noticed again Scarface's leather coat listing to his right side. He was certain there was a pistol hidden in his coat. Mahegan looked around. The rig workers had disappeared somewhere. The four of them were alone.

Mahegan took a step closer to Scarface. He calculated that the posthole digger was five feet long and, coupled with his arm length, put him within striking distance of Scarface. He gripped the posthole digger and flipped it onto his shoulder like a baseball bat, causing Scarface to flinch and subconsciously send his hand toward his right-side coat pocket.

"Sorry," Mahegan said. "This thing's heavy. So let's see the money, and we'll get out of here."

"Money's in the truck, and you're not in charge, asshole."

Mahegan saw something register in the man's eyes. There was the slightest tic of the crow's-feet on either side of his face. And he detected that the irises of Scarface's black eyes focused inward instead of outward, like a zooming lens. He had seen it a million times in combat, when he was talking to an average Joe Iraqi or Afghan citizen who was really not an average Joe. Rather, he was an enemy combatant, one who understood that Mahegan had figured him out.

Scarface made that calculation and went for the pistol. Mahegan watched. It was a clumsy move, completely predictable. By the time the pistol was out of Scarface's pocket, Mahegan stepped forward with his left foot, as he had been trained in bayonet drill, thrusting the tool like a weapon.

Scarface attempted an ungainly move to his right, but the digger caught him square on the left pectoral. Mahegan's powerful arms closed the jaws of the digger, and he actually felt the pincer bite into the leather coat and some muscle. Mahegan swung Scarface to the ground, and the pistol skittered away through the dirt. In his periphery, he saw Dos pick up the weapon. Mahegan pressed the wooden handles of the digger across Scarface's throat.

"We get paid now. Asshole."

Scarface, writhing on the ground, with a bit of blood oozing from his chest, mumbled, "In the truck."

Mahegan calculated his next move. There was no coming back to this construction site for him or the other two. Not wanting to kill the man, but needing to investigate some before the other workers began milling around, he kept the digger across Scarface's neck and landed a concussive blow on the man's temple. It wasn't enough to kill him, but it did knock him unconscious for the moment.

Digging through the man's pockets, he found the truck keys and a wallet, which he opened, and paid Dos and Papa Diablo handsomely for their hard day's work. They said, "*No gracias*," multiple times, but he made them take the money. He then looked in the identification fold of the wallet and found a driver's license and a green card. The man's name was Maxim Petrov. His country of origin was Russia. On the back of the green card was a stamp that read EB-5 PROGRAM. Mahegan didn't know what that meant, but he kept the wallet. He also took Scarface's smartphone.

Dos handed Mahegan the weapon, indicating he wanted nothing to do with it. They walked to the truck, which Mahegan inspected, and he found a removable Garmin GPS along with a BlackBerry with a tactile keyboard. He thumbed through it and found a calendar. The calendar showed a visit by James Gunther tomorrow morning at 9:00 a.m.

Perfect. Mahegan digested the information. Perhaps he could slay the beast that had been haunting him for over fifteen years. Tomorrow morning he would be one step closer.

The three men climbed into the truck's cab, Mahegan behind the wheel. Mahegan put the truck in gear, reversed the route they had driven that morning, memorizing every detail, and dropped off Diablo and Dos at the Wallaby gas station. He pocketed the smartphone, BlackBerry, Garmin, and the 9 mm hollow points he found in the glove box and drove in front of an adjoining department store in a strip mall to leave the truck in an anonymous spot.

After wiping down the truck to erase his fingerprints, he walked across the mall's giant parking lot, slid a single key from a Velcro pocket in his boot, and fired up a beater-gray Jeep Cherokee. Before driving, he removed the batteries and the SIM cards from the GPS device and the phones to protect against tracking devices, such as Find My iPhone. While driving the few miles to his remote apartment, he thought of Gunther; Papa Diablo; Dos, whose real name, he had learned, was Hector Manuela; and the man with the scar on his face, Maxim Petrov. He had made some friends, and he had made some enemies. Not unusual for a day's work. Tomorrow would be an even better day.

As dusk enveloped the long wooded driveway to the home of his landlords, Maggie and Andy Robertson, Mahegan veered off the drive onto a dirt road that looped around to a barn about a quarter mile from their house. He parked his government-leased Cherokee in the barn and climbed the stairs to his single-room apartment with a kitchen alcove and a small bathroom and shower. He instantly heard his phone chirping from beneath the floor.

He rolled back the throw rug, pried up two eight-inch boards in the middle of the hardwood flooring, and retrieved his backpack. Slipping his hand into the mesh netting where he kept his phone, he retrieved it and answered.

"Check Zebra, damn it," Major General Bob Savage barked.

"Roger."

Both men hung up. General Savage was his boss of sorts. That was the extent of the check-in. Mahegan's foray into chasing his personal ghosts did not include bringing his encrypted smartphone with him. That stayed secured in his backpack here in his Apex flat.

Mahegan lived in that gray area between his desire to disconnect completely from the trappings of society and his sense of duty to his country, drilled into him by his mother and his Army comrades. He tolerated his strained relationship with Savage only because the man had converted his dishonorable discharge from the Army into a rightful honorable one after Mahegan's reflexive killing of that enemy prisoner of war during a combat raid.

Savage was the commander of the Joint Special Operations Command at Fort Bragg, about an hour's drive from Mahegan's rented above-barn apartment in Apex. While the general believed that he owned Mahegan like a master owned a slave, Mahegan knew it wasn't that simple. He could walk away from their handshake deal and the secret bank account at any time and had considered it on many occasions in the past eighteen months.

It was rare that Savage called him. Usually, the general texted him on the secure smartphone issued to Mahegan when he agreed to serve as Savage's off-the-books domestic fixer. The gray area. Many would actually see it as a black area that Mahegan and Savage never should have approached, but after Mahegan had thwarted the American Taliban's terror attacks on the country last year, the two of them had become convinced of the right-eousness of their path.

He palmed the phone, which fit snugly in his oversize hands, clicked on his top secret Zebra app, and saw he had three text messages from Savage, who was the only person in the world with his phone number. The first message was three sentences long and gave him a name, an address, and a mission to find a body. The second message asked him to confirm receipt of the first message. The third message was a threat to do bodily harm to him if he did not comply with the second message.

Mahegan smiled, thinking, *Fat chance.*

He memorized the address and the name as he replied with one word. **Roger.**

The Zebra app automatically erased messages after they had been opened or within twelve hours of being sent, whichever came first. Mahegan had checked the phone in the morning, before heading out to the Wallaby eleven hours ago. He understood Savage's phone call. The man didn't want the message erased before he read it.

And he needed the body of Captain Maeve Cassidy back before anyone learned what she had actually been doing in Afghanistan.

CHAPTER 5

MAHEGAN SHOWERED AND CHANGED INTO RESPECTABLE ATTIRE, which included khaki cargo pants, a long-sleeve dress shirt, and a blazer. In the blazer was an official Army Criminal Investigation Command (CID) badge. He had never been a CID agent, but Savage had had the foresight to outfit him with false identities and false credentials, knowing he would need access on occasion to crime scenes. He knew the chances of his being able to remove a body from a crime scene were limited, but Savage had always challenged Mahegan to reach certain stretch goals, such as capturing the American Taliban.

As he approached the address Savage had provided him, police were everywhere. Lights were flashing, as if this were some suburban rave party. Neighbors were gawking from their yards, and he wondered how many had attended the party and how many were purely gawkers. He also saw a group of teenagers pressing against the yellow tape near the backyard. Mahegan's hearing was in the top range on every hearing test he had ever taken, and he listened intently to the kids as he stepped from his vehicle.

"Totally cool, man . . ."

"What's cool about this? Means the parties will probably stop. Sucks for us . . ."

"But all the cops. A murder. Naked people. Not everybody gets to see this kind of stuff. . . ."

Mahegan walked up to the crime-scene tape and showed the

uniformed officer his badge. He was uncomfortable flipping creds, figuring a Department of Defense special agent badge would not carry much weight in Raleigh, North Carolina. He had never actually used the badge before, so it looked brand new. He wasn't practiced at the technique, and he didn't watch cop shows on TV. But he gave it a shot and held the badge up at eye level.

"Army special agent," Mahegan said.

The police officer was dressed in Raleigh Police Department blue and looked fit and professional. His name tag said HERNAN-DEZ. The man had a broad nose, liquid brown eyes, and square shoulders.

"Sorry. Can't let you in," the sergeant said.

Mahegan spoke in a calm voice, looking the police officer in the eyes. "I understand Captain Cassidy was killed on her first night back from Afghanistan. I'm Special Agent Hawthorne, and we have the Army Criminal Investigation Command en route. After the team arrives, probably not your crime scene anymore." CID was not en route to this particular crime scene, but Mahegan figured they were going somewhere in the country at this moment.

After a short pause, Hernandez said, "Gotta talk to the police chief." He turned his chin toward an older man in khakis and a Windbreaker, looking like he had just been called off the golf course. He was standing on the porch, with his hands on his hips, looking at Mahegan.

Without asking, Mahegan stepped under the yellow tape and walked across the perfectly mown fescue grass. The Ridge Road mansion rose up before him like a monument to architecture. Initially hidden behind Leyland cypress trees and tall oaks, the brick colonial mansion now spread before Mahegan. White columns supported picketed balconies that jutted from upstairs rooms like firing ports in a castle. Large windows stared at him, curtains drawn like the half-closed eyelids of a lurking beast.

"Chief," Mahegan said as he ascended the brick staircase that fanned twenty yards across the facade like a jutting jaw.

"What's your deal?"

"Special Agent. U.S. military. Captain Cassidy just returned from Afghanistan. Need to see the body."

"Don't we all, son."

Mahegan processed the response.

"Body's gone missing. If there ever was one. Got a bloodstain, but given all the crazy stuff going on in there, it could be anything. Some woman might have gotten her monthly, for all we know now. Celebrating the completion of a natural gas pipeline from Raleigh to Morehead City port, or something like that."

Mahegan nodded as he processed the information. "I need to see the crime scene to prep the Army Criminal Investigation Command."

"Let me see your creds."

He replayed the scene with the sergeant, and apparently, Savage had done a decent job, because the Raleigh police chief said, "Be my guest. Damn freak show in there."

Mahegan stepped into the foyer of the home through a wide double oak door with a giant brass knocker on each panel, one a cursive *B* and the other a cursive *T*. Immediately, he was stopped by a dutiful lab tech handing him a pair of surgical booties to put over his shoes.

"Big feet," she said, looking down and then locking eyes with him. She was of Asian descent and petite. She had almond eyes, high cheekbones, and razor-cut black hair that kissed the base of her neck with a slight inward curl.

"Born that way," Mahegan said, slipping the booties on his shoes. "Murder scene?"

"Technically, it's a crime scene. We don't know for sure if it's a murder."

"I'm Hawthorne, by the way," he said to her, logging in his mind that she might be useful in the follow-up investigation. Plus, he couldn't help but imagine her in a black, strapless dress instead of the lab tech smock.

Savage enjoyed literature and had chosen a variety of aliases for Mahegan from his favorite literary works, and Hawthorne worked as both a last and first name. Now that he was in official mission mode, he used Hawthorne. Only his landlords, the Robertsons, knew him as Mahegan.

Standing in the foyer, Mahegan noticed a *Gone with the Wind* staircase to his left. Beyond the staircase's tongue-and-groove oak millwork, he glimpsed a sunken family room with a fireplace, which centered the entire house. On the sofas he saw pillows and sheets randomly strewn about, an obvious sign of a sleepover or what he now suspected had been something more. He recalled the chief's term, "freak show."

"Grace," the lab tech said. "Grace Kagami."

"Beautiful mirror," Mahegan said.

Grace Kagami took a deep breath and said, "Wow. Impressive." Her smile belied the fact they were at a crime scene and momentarily took them beyond the new acquaintance stage.

"Lived in Okinawa for a year with Special Forces. Learned some Japanese and knew some Kagamis over there. They explained the meaning of their name, so not so impressive. Just lucky."

She stared at him for a moment. He could feel her measuring him in a way that was beyond the scope of her duties. He was glad he had showered, but he was self-conscious of his weeklong beard.

"What exactly are we looking at?" Mahegan said to break the awkward moment.

Grace smiled, as if answering another question. What was she looking at? "We are looking at the remnants of a swingers' party turned into a possible murder turned into a missing-person-slash-missing-body case."

"Swingers' party?"

"Yeah, you know. The women throw their keys into a bowl and the men pick, or vice versa. Then everyone has sex. All to celebrate the opening of a pipeline."

Mahegan looked past her into the yawning family room with the pillows and sheets. "Like an orgy," he said.

"That too."

The leftover ambiance of the party infested his senses, as dusty incense lingered in the air like a fog. He spotted a bottle of lotion on one of the end tables and caught the faint whiff of a flowery scent comingling with the incense.

"That way," she said, pointing up the carpeted stairs to a brightly lit hallway.

"Thanks, Grace."

"You're welcome, Hawthorne." She used her fingers to make quotation marks when she said, "Hawthorne."

Mahegan nodded at her and then climbed the stairs, wondering what, exactly, her deal might be. As he passed the various bedrooms flanking the large carpeted hallway, he took a minute to scan inside each one. Oddly, they all resembled one another both in appearance—unmade beds, lotions, and towels—and arrangement: one bed, two nightstands, a bureau, and a connecting bathroom. Two bathrooms connected to a pair of guest bedrooms, like Jack-and-Jill rooms. He spotted the master bedroom at the end of the hallway, its double doors open and revealing a team of forensic experts on their hands and knees, studying a precise spot on the floor.

He scanned the walls of the hallway as he approached the investigation area, work lights shining on the crew, making them look like giants in a miniature sports stadium. His and hers college degrees dotted the walls in full "I love myself" regalia. Bachelor's, master's, and PhDs in business and accounting for him. The same accomplishment levels in education for her.

Dr. Robert Brand Throckmorton and Dr. Sharon Hunter Throckmorton were the recipients, though Sharon's bachelor's degree listed her as Sharon René Hunter. Mahegan had the random curiosity as to why some women chose to use their family name as their middle name after marriage, while others used their given middle name. He quickly lost the thought and removed his smartphone from his pocket as it buzzed.

He looked at Savage's text message, blanked the screen, and pocketed the phone. Complications were going to accumulate quickly, so he needed to move fast. Savage had just informed him that Throckmorton owned several businesses, including a private security company, and hundreds of acres of land in Wake and

Chatham Counties, just southwest of here, and they were prime drill locations for natural gas exploration. In his prep to find Gunther, Mahegan had learned that North Carolina had its own rich basin of fossil fuels that just needed a well and the equivalent of a B_{12} shot in the ass to pump the gas out of the earth.

He stood in the doorway, observing the techs as they studied the approximately twelve-inch circular bloodstain as if it were some new fossil discovery on an Egyptian dig. One of them stood and looked at Mahegan.

"Who are you?" The questioner was a tall man with a few wisps of hair at the top of his head. He wore glasses and a Raleigh Police Windbreaker. His face was ruddy and sunken, as if he had had some type of surgery on his cheeks. Maybe a face-lift, maybe shrapnel from Vietnam. He would be about that era.

"My name's Hawthorne. I work with the Defense Department, and I need to see the body."

"Don't we all."

That line must have been on the standard press talking points memo for this particular crime scene, Mahegan thought.

"What was the time between the original nine-one-one call and the arrival of the police?" Mahegan asked.

The man stepped around the group to Mahegan's left, which gave him an opportunity to move to the right, deeper into the bedroom. He moved all the way to the far wall, opposite the spot where Cassidy had allegedly been shot. He peeled back the curtain and saw a deck off the master bedroom and an outdoor stairway from the deck to the backyard. Multiple points of access and egress. But he already knew that.

"I don't think you should be here," the tall man said.

"Name?"

"Raleigh detective first class Rowland Griffyn. Griffyn with a *y*. Raleigh native all my life."

His second comment was intended as some sort of challenge, Mahegan figured. He had been dealing with that type of condescension all his life, with his frequent moves as a child and his Native American lineage. Mahegan was taller than Griffyn, darker as well, and he detected a hint of bias in the detective's voice. The man probably figured himself to be a direct descendant of Sir Walter Raleigh and had spent a lifetime proclaiming his indigenous status. Mahegan knew that as far as Griffyn was concerned a Croatan Indian such as himself had no right to be in this swank Raleigh palace.

"I'm just an interloper here, but an important one. Army criminal investigation is on its way," Mahegan said, again. Griffyn gave him a blank stare. "You know, like NCIS."

"I know who they are, but nobody told me they were coming."

"I just did. I moved over here so that I could have a private conversation with you, instead of telling you that this all could soon be an Army crime scene."

Making a cop give up a crime scene, Mahegan figured, was tantamount to asking a child to release her teddy bear. Griffyn seemed territorial about all things, and threatening to remove his dominion over the Throckmortons' home was probably a good play.

"So I'm giving you the courtesy," Mahegan said. "Get me some info fast, and maybe I can keep it in your hands. I need blood trails, fingerprints, shoe prints, lists of all participants in the . . . the party, and an opportunity to interview them."

"In exchange for all that, we get to keep the scene?" Griffyn, the Raleigh native, asked.

"I will recommend that to CID. Keep me in the loop, and maybe you can keep control."

Mahegan knew this was the tack Savage would want him to take. The case was far too sensitive for CID. Instead of staying completely out of the investigation or commandeering the entire thing, which he couldn't do, anyway, he wanted to be able to slip in and out, with the appearance of local control. Savage's text message had also indicated that he had informed the Fort Bragg CID commander that this was a Joint Special Operations Command case and would remain classified as such until further notice.

"If I ever get the sense, Griffyn, that you are keeping me out of the loop, CID will be on top of this like a hawk on a rabbit. Understand?"

Griffyn eyed Mahegan warily. Not only was Mahegan taller than him, but he also had probably fifty pounds more muscle. He watched the detective process the information, as if his forehead were an iPad displaying his thoughts: *Federal government, big guy, ethnic of some variety. Got to protect my turf. Raleigh native all my life.*

"Okay. How do I get in touch with you?"

"You don't. I will check in with you. Just need your info."

Mahegan never provided anyone the number to his smartphone. The device itself had protections, such as the ability to track multiple satellites at once or over time while remaining anonymous. If someone with hacking skills were somehow to identify his phone number, they would be able to find him. But there was very little likelihood of that occurring.

Griffyn gave him his card with a handwritten cell phone number, which Mahegan would dial only from a pay phone, if he could find one.

"Thanks. Where do you think the body is?"

"We're taking samples right now. This is where you could help us. We don't have Cassidy's info in our database, but I'm sure you guys do."

"Roger. Give me a vial, and I'll get it analyzed and get back with you."

Griffyn disappeared for a minute and came back with a Baggie with a small test tube.

"Small sample, but should be good enough," Griffyn said.

"We'll see if it works."

"Thanks. I look forward to the partnership."

"Me too." Mahegan nodded and pocketed the Baggie in his blazer.

They shook hands.

Mahegan said, "I'm heading out this way." He hooked a thumb over his shoulder, pointing at the balcony. "You guys may want to process that as a possible egress or ingress route."

"Already planned on it," Griffyn said.

Mahegan turned and slid the balcony door open with his bare hand.

"Hey, you need some latex gloves!"

He put his other hand on the sliding glass door, as if he had stumbled. "Sorry. You're right."

But the truth was, Mahegan knew his prints had been on that door for a couple of weeks. That was when he had found the picture of his father, who apparently had also been hunting James Gunther.

CHAPTER 6

MAHEGAN STOOD IN THE THROCKMORTONS' BACKYARD, WATCHing the adjoining home's lights peek through the wooded acreage like searching beacons. The air was calm and unusually cool. The September sun had set, and the cloudless night allowed the day's heat to diminish upward.

A movement to his right caught his attention, and he saw the tousled hair of a young boy attempting to hide behind a tree trunk. He was sneaking quick looks at Mahegan, as if unaware that Mahegan could see him. Mahegan casually walked to the fence separating the backyard from the side yard as the boy discreetly slid behind the tree, rotating around its trunk to remain hidden. Mahegan drifted slightly toward the tree when he knew it was impossible for the boy to see him. Quickly, Mahegan had a hand on his shoulder, and the young boy yelped, unaware that Mahegan had closed the gap.

"You live here?" Mahegan asked. As he went to drag the boy from his hiding place, Mahegan noticed he was squatting there. The boy was actually nearly six feet tall, gangly, and had a constellation of acne on his face that was so severe, it deserved a nomenclature from Greek mythology.

"No . . . no, sir." He had the scared look of a teenager who was used to being perceived as trustworthy and loyal but who had been caught doing something terribly bad. His eyes darted back and forth, as if he was calculating the fence's scalability.

"Name?"

He did not reply. Mahegan tightened his grip on his shoulder. "Nathan."

Mahegan waited for him to say more, but he didn't. "So, it's like Cher or Bono? Just one word?"

"Nathan Daniels," he said with an edge of defiance, as if the name should mean something to Mahegan. As Mahegan processed Nathan Daniels's name with those of Griffyn and Throckmorton, he began to wonder if he was dealing with Pilgrims just off the *Mayflower*. Fancy names. "Big money names," his mother used to call them.

"What brings you up this way, Nathan Daniels? Out for a stroll?"

"I don't have to answer any of your questions," he said.

Mahegan pulled out his badge for effect. "Actually you do. You've entered a crime scene . . . or perhaps you were here all along?"

"No tape in the backyard. I came across the fence." He pointed with his chin at the slatted wooden fence, which stood eight feet high. Mahegan noticed three horizontal support beams that made for perfect steps. He scanned the backyard, a forested football field of land.

"Just trespassing, then?"

"Just . . . curious. Not trespassing." Then he added, "My dad's a lawyer. I know how this works."

"Okay. I'll let you call him when we get to the station, then. I'm sure he'll be happy to get out of bed and come pick you up when we're done with you around midnight."

"You can't just take me in!"

Mahegan flipped him against the tree and pulled his arm behind his back, as if he was going to cuff him. He pressed the boy's face up against the bark of the pine, which was oozing a bit of sap. "You are violating a crime scene and could be a witness or a suspect in a murder investigation."

"Murder?"

"Yes, Nathan, murder." Mahegan let up on him a bit and said, "Now would you like to talk, or do we need to go to the station?"

Nathan was silent for a moment, then said, "I'll talk, but damn, bro, you need to chill."

Mahegan noticed when Daniels turned around that he was wearing an Aerosmith T-shirt and blue denim pants. He also saw the light from a smartphone pulsing in his pocket. He had placed it on silent and now was receiving a call.

"Need to get that?" Mahegan asked.

"Just my mom probably. Let's do this."

"It's easy. Tell me what you know."

He fidgeted for a second, kicked at a few rocks, and looked up at Mahegan. "I don't think I've committed any crime, but if I have, you gotta promise me immunity of some type."

Mahegan stared at him for a second and then saw it. There was a fiber-optic cable running up the tree. He followed its course onto a branch that extended to the house. The cable terminated at a small blinking camera that was aimed directly at the open windows of the master bedroom.

Nathan stood there, sweating, probably wondering if Mahegan was going to tell his parents he had been secretly taping the swingers' parties at the Throckmorton home. "You're not going to tell anyone, are you?"

Mahegan considered his leverage and perhaps the fact that Daniels had terabytes of Throckmorton quasi porn. "I'm not sure I have any other option, Nathan."

"C'mon, man. You gotta be cool here. What can I do?"

"I don't know. What do you have for me?"

Nathan, an obviously smart kid, processed what Mahegan had just asked him. A slow grin grew on his face. "I have every party they've had for the past two months. Fair trade?"

"Depends on the quality," Mahegan said.

"This will blow you away. The tree is our panoramic vision. We're also inside the house."

Admiring the kid's pluck, Mahegan restrained his interest. "Why'd you do this?"

"You kidding me? One day we're . . . uh, I'm . . . looking in the backyard, and there's, like, ten gorgeous babes lying out by the pool, topless. That's why, uh, I did this."

Mahegan looked at the camera and could see it easily panning to the pool on the far side of the yard. "Okay, here's the deal. In exchange for my silence, I get the recordings, and no one else does. Clear?" Mahegan knew that he was most likely on those recordings, and while he would be impossible to identify, it was a loose end he didn't need.

Nathan gauged Mahegan's intentions for a moment with discerning eyes, then said, "Clear." He then handed him a flash drive. "This is the past two days."

It was almost 10:00 p.m., and Mahegan had been at the scene for over an hour. Before the real cops decided to inspect the backyard, Mahegan told Nathan to remove the camera and the fiber-optic cable and then meet him out front with the previous two months of video. As Nathan scaled the tree, Mahegan began walking toward the house and noticed Grace, the Asian lab tech, step out onto the deck off the master bedroom. Ascending the short stairway, he called out, "Hey."

"What are you still doing here?"

His immediate goal was to avert her eyes from Nathan's activities, so he decided to turn her attention to the inside of the house. "I was just thinking about the bloodstain," he said, motioning beyond the sliding glass door, which she had opened carefully with a latex-covered hand. Mahegan noticed she had slender fingers to match her petite frame.

"Out here?" she asked, placing a hand on her hip, skeptical.

"I thought I might find a blood trail here, but no joy."

She stared at Mahegan a second, and he felt that thrum of connection again. At a different time and under different circumstances, he could visualize them grilling out and knocking back a couple of beers on this nice deck overlooking Nathan's media empire and the pool. Not wanting to make too much of his fantasy, he said, "Either the victim walked out under her own power or someone carefully wrapped her up and carried her away."

She paused, as if to consider whether to reveal something to him, then said, "We didn't find any brain matter mixed in with the blood. Actually, it was just blood so far."

"So it's quite possible she was rushed somewhere to be taken care of."

This time she rolled her large almond eyes at Mahegan and said, "You enjoy the occasional pun, I can see."

"Either to a hospital or a lake, I'm thinking."

"We've called all the emergency care facilities in the area. No joy, as you say."

"That leaves the lakes: Shearon Harris and Jordan."

"Or perhaps she wasn't wounded badly enough," she admitted.

"Any other kinds of 'matter' mixed in with the blood?" Mahegan was looking for clarity regarding the type of wound and whether there might be an entry or exit point on the body, given the report of a gunshot.

"We're running all the tests."

An awkward silent moment passed before Mahegan said, "Any chance I can give you a call . . . to get the results?"

She grinned, and her teeth were perfect, framed by full, pouty lips. "What happened to your big, bad team of Army CID agents? Where are Leroy Gibbs and DiNozzo?"

"That's television and Navy. Wrong on both counts. I'm the lead guy. When they heard there was no body, they decided to let the situation develop some."

She removed her latex gloves, pulled out a pen, grabbed his hand with delicate fingers, and wrote a number on his palm. "Hope you don't sweat," she said.

Mahegan noticed a small tattoo on her wrist: *Esse quam videri.* "To be rather than to seem," he said, translating the Latin.

She turned her eyes upward from his palm and smiled. "State motto. It's henna. I change it every few months, when it wears out." Then she nodded over Mahegan's shoulder and laughed. "Your boy is about to fall out of the tree."

As Mahegan turned around, Nathan landed with a thud on his back, fiber-optic cable and the camera wrapped around his body like packing tape. He appeared okay, and when Mahegan turned back to address Grace Kagami, the beautiful mirror, like a specter, she was gone. Mahegan returned to the backyard, helped Nathan out of his fiber-optic web and removed the GoPro camera with the external battery pack.

"What are you doing?" Nathan asked.

"I'm guessing this stuff cost you some decent change, so while you go and get me an external drive's worth of home movies, I'm hanging on to this. If you're not back in fifteen minutes, I'm ringing your front doorbell."

"Not cool, man. I already gave you the thumb drive."

Mahegan said nothing.

"But okay." Nathan pointed to a window above the fence. "That's my room. I've got my own entrance. I'll be up there and back down. Don't squeeze me if it's twenty minutes. This stuff takes time."

"Fifteen. Front door."

Demonstrating surprising athleticism, Nathan was over the fence in record time. On the return trip he didn't bother coming all the way over but simply climbed the fence halfway and chucked Mahegan an external drive.

"Everything I got. Peace out."

Mahegan removed the data card from the GoPro, then stuffed the small external drive, about the size of a wallet, into his back left pocket and made his way through the side gate toward his car.

Out of the corner of his eye, he saw two men talking near the side of the house, behind a square brick chimney. He recognized one from his Army days and the other from the pictures in the house. Sam Blackmon, retired Army colonel, was talking to Brand Throckmorton, lord of the manor. Blackmon wore a leather coat, a black turtleneck sweater, and black dungarees. The bulge under his coat indicated he was carrying a pistol. Throckmorton was wearing a blazer, an ascot, a button-down shirt, and neatly hemmed dress slacks that fell atop expensive Italian shoes. Evening wear. They had triggered a motion-sensor light, which shone on them like a theater spotlight. It seemed that Blackmon was mostly listening, though, as Throckmorton gesticulated wildly with his hands.

Mahegan had served with Blackmon on different missions, but the colonel had always been higher up the food chain and had never had more than a passing interest in Mahegan, who respected Blackmon. He had heard Blackmon's retirement had led to a position as CEO of a private security company. He guessed it was the one owned by Throckmorton. Mahegan could envision Blackmon getting a late-night call to come to the scene of a crime to help sweep up the shattered glass of the evening.

Mahegan eased through the expansive side yard, using tall holly bushes to block his exit. He registered that Blackmon might be someone he wanted to contact about the case, should he need inside information on Throckmorton. He reached his car without detection, and as he fired up the engine, Nathan Daniels's face was hovering outside the passenger-side window. Mahegan pressed the button to lower the glass.

"By the way, dude, I think you're on the video."

Indeed, Mahegan thought, he was.

"You like living?" he asked Nathan.

"Yeah, man."

"Then keep your mouth shut."

He handed the kid back his GoPro. Pulling away in his Cherokee, Mahegan thought about what he had learned inside the Throckmortons' house on his previous visit. Those memories both fueled his drive to find Gunther and emptied his soul.

It wasn't good.

CHAPTER 7

O N HIS RETURN FROM THE THROCKMORTON CRIME SCENE IN Raleigh, Mahegan stopped at a grocery store and purchased a burner cell phone. Next, he met with Savage's gopher in a late-model, four-door sedan at the Wallaby gas station where he had waited for the black pickup truck that morning. He gave this man the blood sample Griffyn had provided him and outlined the high-level details of Cassidy's disappearance. Afterward, he watched the gopher's taillights disappear down Route 1, toward Fort Bragg, diminishing red specks in the blackness. Then he drove the wooded back way to his apartment.

Sitting in his leased above-barn apartment, he plugged in the burner smartphone, let it charge, and then followed the directions to activate it. Rarely did he deviate from standard procedures, which did not allow communications augmentation, but as he drove, he had stared at the phone number Grace Kagami had written on his hand, hoping not to smudge any of the numbers.

Once he had the phone powered up, he looked at the clock. It was almost midnight. He was tired, but he had a body to find and a nemesis to kill. Lots to do. He shook off his fatigue and followed his instinct, typing out a text and sending it to the number she had given him.

Good to meet you. Any update? H.

Within seconds, a reply appeared on his screen.

Just want info from me, "H"? ;)

Mahegan studied the phone, almost a foreign object to him. The reply was instant, as if she had been staring at the phone, awaiting his, or someone else's, text. His months in and out of combat had dulled his social media skills, but he knew how to communicate rapidly in an operational environment. He recalled himself on one knee, body armor hanging on his shoulders, radio handset in his hand, with decisions to make.

Short timeline. You seemed most competent on location.

Flattery will get you everywhere.

So that means there's something new?

You're bad at this, you know?

I know. Trying.

Try harder ;)

Mahegan paused, thinking. What was she asking for? He visualized her full lips, framing perfect white teeth; her small hand writing her number on his large palm; and the lightness of her touch as she steadied his wrist with her right hand while she wrote with her left. He had felt energy flow like a current. Perhaps she had, also.

Grab a beer?

Bingo. Where r u?

Not in Raleigh.

That narrows it down. Let's quit wasting time. Meet at Irish Pub in Cary. I'll be in the date booth. Not there in twenty minutes, I'm gone. Peace out.

Roger.

Whatev.

Mahegan deleted the conversation, hit the map function on the phone, and located the pub Grace had mentioned. He stopped in front of the mirror and studied himself. Disheveled dark blond hair, a week's beard, blue eyes shot red from lack of sleep, and preppy clothes. He did a rapid change into dungarees, a worn rugby shirt, and work boots. He was looking like something halfway between where he was this morning and where he was an hour ago. He placed Nathan Daniels's external drive in the safe in his floor but put the small flash drive in the pocket of his dungarees.

The phone's map function told him it was eighteen minutes to his destination. He walked down the steps into the barn, dodged a tractor in the darkened space, and climbed into his Cherokee. He quietly navigated his way past his landlords' large home, its half-lidded, darkened windows showing no signs of life. Mahegan made every stoplight and pulled into the nearly empty parking lot of the pub with three minutes to spare. He noticed a familiar car from the crime scene, a sporty Nissan with a peace sign and a DFT2 sticker on the bumper, and figured it for Grace's. While he recognized the COEXIST and PEACE bumper stickers, he had no idea what DFT2 stood for.

Walking into the pub, he smelled stale beer and cooked meat. He saw the usual green shamrocks that came with every Irish pub he had ever frequented. To his three o'clock were restrooms, to his twelve o'clock was the bar, and to his nine o'clock were booths. He went in the nine o'clock direction and found Grace perched on a small stool inside a three-quarters closed-off booth, like an office cubicle, but with dark, lacquered wood.

"Hawthorne, my man." Grace smiled and used quotation marks again.

Mahegan entered the booth and sat opposite Grace, taking in her lightly scented perfume, something citrusy. They were contrasts. She had showered; he had not. When she changed clothes, she had geared up. He had geared down. She was hyped, and he was reserved. She had three empty beer bottles in front of her; he had none. Staring at her made Mahegan think of a recent friend from the Outer Banks, and for a moment he was fixated. His heart skipped a beat, and then he was back with Grace. He focused on the black top with thin straps hanging off her slender, tanned shoulders.

"Speechless?"

"Something like that," he muttered.

"I ordered you a big, manly beer," she said as the waiter brought them two beers. His was something dark. Hers was amber. The waiter reminded them that last call would be in thirty minutes, prompting Grace to order two more in case the waiter was slow on his rounds.

"Thank you," Mahegan said.

"You're welcome. I was at that frigging crime scene all day, and you're the most interesting person I've met recently. So, cheers." She lifted her glass and clinked it with Mahegan's while she stared him directly in the eyes. "Bad luck not to look in the eyes when you toast, you know."

"Heard that."

"You talk like you text."

Mahegan gave a hint of a smile. "Let's just say I'm still taking in the moment. Studying you. Like art."

"Hmm. What do you see?"

"You're not unlike me. I'm Native American. You're Asian American. We both have a permanent tan, shall we say. You're petite. I'm large. Point being, we're both uniquely sized. You're analytical. I think I am, too. And the area where we differ, quite frankly, is that you're strikingly beautiful."

She winked. "Like I said, flattery will get you everywhere."

"Everywhere?"

"Well, maybe not everywhere," she whispered, looking away. Mahegan interpreted the change in diction as an indication that he had inadvertently touched on a sensitive area, her love life.

"What makes you think Hawthorne is not legitimate?" He tried changing topics.

"You're an Indian. Pardon my directness. Why would someone name you that?"

"Ever hear of Roy Hawthorne, the code talker from World War II?"

Grace's demeanor changed again. She placed her hand over her mouth and gasped. "I'm so sorry." She dropped her head, placing both of her hands on her forehead, as if to summon a more worthy apology. "I saw that movie. Yes. How insensitive of me. Built-in defense mechanism. I caught so much grief as a kid for being the little 'oriental' girl. Sorry."

Mahegan reached his hands across and slowly removed hers from her face. "Don't sweat it. Let's drink some beer." This time he toasted her and looked directly into her copper eyes.

"I get awkward when I'm nervous," she said.

"Why are you nervous?"

"Here you are, practically the Marlboro Man, right in front of me, and I have exactly one thing on my mind, and I just can't keep myself from talking."

"What's on your mind?"

Mahegan watched as she placed her beer on the stained coaster, which had seen thousands of glass bottoms. Grace pursed her lips, as if kissing air, flipped her straight black hair off her forehead, took a deep breath, and said, "Slow down, woman."

"It's been a long day." Mahegan thought about the wait at the Wallaby, Papa Diablo and Manuela, the black pickup truck, Scarface, James Gunther and Sons Construction, the fence posts, the posthole digger, the crime scene, Nathan Daniels, and now Grace Kagami. Busy day, indeed.

"That it has. And I'm coming out of a bad breakup. So let's change the topic. Why were you so late getting to the crime scene?" she said. Grace seemed more relaxed now, as if she had reined in whatever emotion she was feeling.

"Late notice. Our concern is the location of Captain Maeve Cassidy." Mahegan paused, scanning Grace's face. "How long have you been here?"

She leaned back against the wall of the booth and sighed heavily again. "I've had a couple. This stuff gets to me, you know?"

"I know." Mahegan thought of his best friend, Sergeant Wesley Colgate, blown to bits by a roadside bomb in Afghanistan. He knew better than most. "So what do we think about Cassidy? Does anyone know anything?"

Grace leaned forward, drained the rest of her beer, and grabbed the next one as the waiter appeared with the second round, like a quarterback handing the football to a running back. Perfect timing.

"I've got a secret," Grace whispered. "But I can't tell you.

Griffyn said he would 'crush the nuts of anyone who leaked classified information.' "

"Well, you're safe, then," Mahegan said. "Being a woman and all."

Grace flipped her eyes up at Mahegan and smiled. He noticed the small gold hoop earrings dangling just off her slender neck. She had long eyelashes, which remained remarkably still as she held his gaze. Her skin was flawless, smooth, and silky.

"You're funny, Hawthorne." Then, "Maybe I can tell you. But there are two things I know for sure." She drained another half of her beer. Mahegan had drunk barely a third of his.

"What's that, Grace Kagami?"

After another pause, processing, Grace said, "I like that. Grace Kagami. The way you say my name. It's nice."

"Nice name."

"The first thing I know is that Griffyn is a first-class douche bag of the highest order," she said. "A misogynistic, sadistic dickwad. Thinks women are idiots."

"You shouldn't be so obtuse."

She stared at him with deadpan eyes.

"Seriously. I agree. I'm sorry you have to deal with someone like that."

"The second thing is that I'm in no condition to drive, and douche bag wants me at work at six frigging a.m. Can you believe that?"

"I can give you a lift. Maybe we should stop drinking?"

"Again, you're a funny guy, Hawthorne," she said. "And I forgot. I know a third thing. Which I think I also forgot." Grace finished her beer and snatched Mahegan's from his loose grip. "Since you're driving, thank you very much."

She drank the beer as if it were a thirst-quenching sports drink, slammed the empty glass on the table, and snatched her purse from the back of her chair. She stumbled into Mahegan and then pulled him in her wake, saying, "Let's go, Marlboro Man."

A minute later they were outside, the air cool and fresh, a pleasant change from the musty pub. Grace had both hands wrapped around his left arm.

"Holy frigging smoke," she said. "These are some guns, dude."

"Where's your car?"

"I thought you were driving."

"I am. I'll drive you in your car and then walk back here to mine."

She studied him.

"You'll need your car early and won't have any time to waste. I'm not coming in. I'll get you to your door and then leave."

"Damn. Just when it was sounding good."

Mahegan nodded. "It will get good at some point, but not tonight. You've had too much to drink. But I do want one thing from you."

They drifted lazily to her car. He was right. It was the Nissan with the bumper stickers. She dug in her purse and pulled out a jumble of keys that included a pepper spray bottle. Mahegan opened her door and guided her into the small vehicle. He slid into the seat after racking it as far back as it would go. Still a little tight, but he could get her home.

Grace flipped her head toward Mahegan and said, "Sorry."

"About what?"

"Being a lush. Bad day. Not normally like this." Then a pause. "Well, I've been drinking a lot lately. Stupid boyfriend breakup garbage. This place is close to my apartment, and the date booth is where we met."

Mahegan understood. Relive the date. Take him home. Have sex. Momentarily forget about the pain. Random sex would be salve for the wound. He wasn't having any part of that.

"Address?"

She reached up and fumbled with some touch-screen buttons on the GPS display until she was able to hit HOME. The map lit up and showed they were less than two miles away. He followed the directions, and as they approached their destination, he said, "So what's the third thing you know?"

Grace was half lucid but heard him. "I know that you should tuck me in." She smiled. She was definitely beautiful and sexy. Her left breast was nearly hanging out of her black top as she leaned toward him. "And then I can tell you my big secret."

"I guess it will have to wait," Mahegan said. "Because I'm not taking advantage of you."

With mock anger, Grace asked, "Who are you to say that you shouldn't take advantage of me? Maybe I want you to have that advantage taken."

Mahegan chuckled. "You're not even making any sense now, Grace."

"Grace. Full of Grace. Amazing Grace. That's what he used to call me. My boyfriend."

"Well, he's a first-class idiot for breaking up with you. What's his name? I'm not doing anything between midnight and five a.m."

"Ha! That's funny. Theodore Throckmorton. Aka Ted the Shred. He surfs like a wild man. You gonna go scare him for me? I don't love him anymore, anyway."

Mahegan's mind computed the name. Ted the Shred was the son of Brand Throckmorton, whose house was now a crime scene involving Captain Maeve Cassidy. He immediately understood her disquieting nature in the pub.

After a few turns on suburban roads, he was upon the complex. The building was upscale, with an empty guard shack and an open gate. A thick forest of pine trees provided a cordon of privacy along the parking lot. Crape myrtles stood atop boxwood hedges. The headlights of the low car cut across the swimming pool and the clubhouse.

She said, "Here," and he parked as close as he could to where she had indicated. Then she said, "One-twenty-four."

He walked her past the BMWs, Mercedes, and Audis, and while handing her the keys, he saw a yellow Lamborghini parked near apartment 124. Then he saw a tall, broad-shouldered man wearing designer jeans, a fitted Italian shirt, a sport coat, no socks, and Sperry Top-Siders.

"Amazing Grace," the man said. "Here I was, thinking about having a conversation about our relationship, and you've gone and found this . . . refined gentleman."

Mahegan pulled up short, holding Grace as much as she was holding him. He sensed her fear and could feel her shaking, either in rage or panic. He figured panic.

"What are you doing here, Ted?" She spoke with startling clarity, Mahegan thought, given that fifteen minutes ago she was at least acting drunk. He felt her stand up straighter, bringing her head to just below his scarred deltoid. She tightened her grip on his left arm, a silent cue not to leave her alone with him.

"I'm here to talk. I got your texts and your e-mails and your voice mails and your snail mails. You're upset. I'm here to console you." Throckmorton smiled with a crooked grin that dimpled on the left side. His wavy light brown hair was tousled, but Mahegan thought it had that "intentionally arranged to not appear arranged" look.

Mahegan and Grace were two steps below Throckmorton, who was leaning against the door to her apartment. Mahegan gauged his size and strength, placing him a couple of inches shorter than him and about thirty pounds lighter, but by no means a pushover. Throckmorton filled out his designer sport coat with a bulk that indicated he would at least put up a fight. Mahegan considered that he might have a weapon, a gun or a knife, stowed away on his person. Mahegan had also done some surfing in his childhood, and he knew the strength and endurance that were required to be a waterman.

Still, never one to shy away from confrontation, Mahegan stepped up and pulled Grace behind him with his left arm. He'd thought about leaving her below, but he wanted no separation for Throckmorton to be able to get between him and Grace. He locked eyes with Throckmorton and saw a glint of humor, as if he were saying, "Let's go."

Ted the Shred, Mahegan thought. *A surfer. Scrappy. Competitive. Fearless. Tough. Athletic. Strong.*

Mahegan pulled up three feet in front of Throckmorton, continuing to guide Grace behind him with his left arm. She followed his cue.

"Big one you got here, Amazing Grace. You just going to bang him for a night? A week? What? What's the timeline? We've been down this road. You always come back to me, right?"

"You should leave," Mahegan said, locking eyes with Throckmorton.

Mahegan took a step toward Throckmorton, who squared up but still didn't acknowledge his presence and kept talking past Mahegan to Grace.

"Big hands, big feet. That how you gauge them? Just walk into the bar and look for the biggest—"

Mahegan put a hand around Throckmorton's throat, slammed his head into the red apartment door, just below the numeral 2 of 124, and began to lift him off the ground. He sensed Throckmorton's quick hands going for something in his jacket. He was right. Throckmorton's right hand was pulling at a snub-nosed revolver in the interior pocket of the sport coat. A clean grab and he might have gotten off a shot. As it was, the hammer snagged on the lip of the pocket, and Mahegan used his other hand to put a vise grip on Throckmorton's wrist, focusing the pressure on the socket where the forearm met the hand, the articular disk. It was that gap between the two forearm bones where the radius and the ulna met the carpals.

He immobilized Throckmorton's hand, causing the pistol to hang loosely from the jacket, then fall to the concrete with a scratching noise that sounded like sandpaper. Mahegan was squeezing the man's neck hard and felt some of the fight leave him, but he didn't discount the possibility that Throckmorton had another weapon. He banged Throckmorton's head against the door hard enough to cause a concussion, but not hard enough to crack his skull. He didn't want to damage Grace's door.

As he was squeezing Throckmorton's neck and wrist, his mind slipped to another place and time. It was his worst memory and the one thing that haunted him most: men treating women badly.

He was seeing the pockmarked face and greasy hair of James Gunther, who was standing over his mother. So he kept banging the head and squeezing the neck and the wrist until he felt something snap in his hand. He also heard screaming and realized it was Grace.

"You're going to kill him! Stop!"

Her voice brought Mahegan back to the moment, and he found himself staring at the white face and blue lips of Ted Throckmorton. He looked down and saw that he had snapped the man's ulna, the smaller wrist bone. A hematoma was already forming and puffing. He released Throckmorton slowly. The man was gasping for air, and his good hand immediately came up to his throat, which was making a wheezing sound, like a steam valve opening a fraction.

Mahegan studied the man with detached objectivity. He could kill him at this very moment, but the crime hadn't demanded that punishment. At least not that he had seen, but the contempt with which Throckmorton had spoken to Grace reeked of abuse, either verbal or physical. He was a man used to getting his way, to luxuriating in the excesses of wealth. It was hard for Mahegan not to land a killer blow to the head as the man slid down the door. There were multiple options. A forearm to the face could snap his neck. A roundhouse kick to the larynx could collapse his windpipe. A head butt to the face would certainly break his nose and possibly shut off the remaining oxygen flow to the man's lungs. Ted Throckmorton most likely deserved any one of those fates, but he would not receive any tonight.

Mahegan grabbed the man by his shirt collar and belt, lifted him like a sack of flour, and heaved him onto the hood of the Lamborghini. The man instinctively put out his hands to break his fall, and the full weight of his large frame landed on the shattered wrist. His howl was the plaintive yelp of a severely wounded dog.

Mahegan turned and picked up the pistol, then pocketed the weapon. He looked at Grace, who was frozen in place, and asked, "Keys?"

She handed them back to him, her hand shaking and her eyes shifting between him and the nearly unconscious Ted Throckmorton, splayed on the hood of the race car like an art exhibit.

Mahegan opened the apartment door after trying the third key, knowing better than to ask Grace, who looked catatonic. He escorted her through the doorway, stepped inside, flipped the locks, and pulled the chain across the runner. He moved Grace, still frozen and hugging herself, to the kitchen, where he looked out of a small window and saw Throckmorton sliding off the hood of the car. He was holding his wrist and grimacing. He looked at the apartment door, as if thinking about attempting to enter, but quickly dismissed the thought. He fumbled with his key fob, managed to get the car door open, and after a minute backed out and sped away.

Mahegan turned and looked at Grace. "I can stay or go," he said. "If I stay, it's down here, standing guard."

She nodded. "Stay."

"Has he hurt you before?"

Grace looked away.

After a long silence, he said, "Not my business. But I'll stay tonight."

She nodded again and said, "Stay."

Mahegan studied the kitchen. Organized, neat, clean. Everything in its place. She was a fastidious woman. The insecurity she had demonstrated at the Irish Pub was a manifestation of her breakup, and now, on the rebound, she saw him as willing prey. Nothing wrong with that. There was a brief period of time when he had considered it, before the beers and the fight, but not now. His fight-or-flight instinct was telling him to defend and protect.

"It's okay," he said. "I understand."

"There's a sofa. I'll be upstairs. If I leave before you—"

"You will."

"*When* I leave before you, you can use the guest bathroom upstairs and to the right. There are clean towels. I've got food in the refrigerator. Depends on what you like."

"I'm good. You okay?"

Grace was halfway up the stairs. She stopped and turned around to look at him. Mahegan could see family pictures lining the wall of the staircase. Asian parents, smiling. Siblings playing at the beach. College friends in fancy dresses. A wedding.

"Yeah. I'll be fine," she said. "But can I ask you a question?"

"Sure."

"You could have killed him." Not a question, but a statement, like a certainty.

"No. If I had wanted to, I would have. I just beat the life out of him. He comes around me again, I'll do the same."

"He's a powerful and dangerous man, Hawthorne. Be careful."

"Nothing I haven't dealt with before. Now can I ask you a question?"

She tried a half smile, but it quickly faded. "Sure. After everything I've put you through."

"You don't owe me anything. But if you were dating Brand Throckmorton's son, what the hell were you doing at the crime scene? Isn't that a huge conflict?"

She shrugged. "Griffyn specifically requested me. I recused myself, but he calls the shots."

Mahegan nodded. "What was the third thing you know?"

"Well, I know a third and a fourth thing now. But the third thing is that Maeve Cassidy's husband might be someone you want to talk to. I'm told he's on his way to pick up his kid from the babysitter. He'll probably be home in the morning, if we're done with him at the station already. We do think he's involved in something called an EB-Five program. Something to do with legally selling visas to the highest foreign bidder. Might be a good place to start."

Mahegan thought of Petrov's green card. It said "EB-5" on the back. "Okay. And the fourth?"

"Ted will not stop until he hurts you bad. He and his family play for keeps."

Mahegan nodded. "So do I."

"Yes. I can see that. The only difference being that Ted would have killed you, and since *you* didn't kill him, now he will have his daddy fix it."

"If I need to kill Ted Throckmorton or anyone else that deserves it, then I will. There's an old Croatan saying. 'Old age is not as honorable as death, but most people want it.'"

Grace looked away, thought about it, and said, "Sounds Japanese. Like the kamikaze pilots."

Mahegan shrugged. "Probably lots of cultures embrace the idea of a noble death while fighting for something you believe in, as opposed to a life of avoiding danger and getting old."

"Probably."

"I don't say that to scare you. I just need you to know that you can go upstairs and sleep soundly."

"I understand. I will try to sleep."

With those words, Grace slipped quietly upstairs. Mahegan walked to the back of the apartment, which was framed in standard fashion with a combined living and dining room that led onto a concrete slab patio. He stepped through the sliding glass door, stood outside, and listened, hearing nothing but the distant hiss of light traffic. He looked up and saw a deck leading from what he presumed was the master bedroom. He saw a light turn on and go off. There were no stairs, but it would be an easy enough climb for someone determined to get onto the balcony and into her bedroom.

He reentered the apartment, slid and locked the door, placed the bar inside the sliding door frame, and climbed the stairs. He knocked lightly on Grace's door and said, "Grace. Do you have a bar in your sliding glass door in there?"

The door opened, and she was standing there in a UNCW T-shirt that barely covered her below the hips. "Yes. I lock it every night," she said.

Mahegan studied her. She seemed drugged and withdrawn. He had witnessed it before in combat. She was experiencing post-traumatic stress. Whatever Ted Throckmorton had done to her, it had been serious. He nodded and began to turn.

"I'd like for you to check it," she said.

Mahegan turned back toward her and stepped into the room. She moved, but only marginally so that he was forced to brush against her. In response, he held up his hands and lightly touched her shoulders as he slipped by. Her hand came up and touched his as he continued moving. The shock of her touch distracted him. The king-size bed and the walnut chest of drawers slipped past him. He studied the lock on the sliding glass door, tried it. It was solid. He unlocked the door and tried to move it against the bar in the well of the slider, and the door held. He closed and locked the door, tightened the curtain, and turned.

She was standing behind him, an apparition in the dark. He could see her mouth parted slightly and her hair falling on her neck. Her arms were slender yet strong. Her legs were toned. Everything was perfectly in place. But this was not the place for him.

"You're secure. I'll be downstairs."

"You don't have to be," she whispered.

He hesitated. "Actually, yes I do." He walked quickly, her scent reaching out like a long arm, pulling him back. But he was strong. He knew desire could be fulfilled another day, when it was right.

Tonight he had to protect her, this woman he barely knew. Mahegan determined that she needed him in that way more than she needed him in any other.

CHAPTER 8

M AEVE CASSIDY PACED FIVE STEPS ACROSS AND FIVE STEPS BACK, then repeated the process for the 157th time. She was odd that way. She did the math. Her stride was greater than three feet, so she was walking over fifteen feet across each time. She knew plywood came in four-by-eight-foot sheets typically, so it was most likely sixteen feet across. Her cell was four sheets wide and two sheets deep. The deep sheets were end to end, while the wide ones were side by side. Sixteen by sixteen feet.

A single trip across the plywood box was a sortie, as the military called it. One hundred fifty-seven sorties at sixteen feet each equaled 2,512 feet, which wasn't much, not even a half a mile, but it was enough to help her burn some nervous energy.

With each hour that passed, her mind shifted from confusion to clarity . . . and fear. She raced between three thoughts: Piper, danger, and her cheating husband. She held close the precious few minutes she had spent with her daughter, Piper, after arriving at their home yesterday afternoon, before heading out in search of her husband. Not *their* daughter, but *her* daughter. Pete Cassidy was not high on Maeve's priority list right now. He had always seemed to be a good husband, but the shocking image of him with another woman, coupled with a year at war and what *she* had done, erased any memory of the before picture.

Pace, pace, pace. More sorties, more steps. Absently, she clutched her reddish-brown hair, which was oily and sticky. Her mind spun from Piper to the second of the three thoughts, which was the danger she suspected was bearing down on the United States. Her knowledge of what might lie ahead was dangerous for her and her family.

Maeve had left the only clue she could safely leave behind: a half-used bottle of henna extract. Henna, a plant that grew in Afghanistan and that men there used as makeup, for example, lining their eyes or darkening beards with it, was her big clue. *How stupid*, she thought to herself. Who could help her? But that simple bottle of henna extract that sat perched on the top of Piper's chest of drawers was her only hope . . . and perhaps the only hope for several cities along the East Coast.

Pace, pace, pace. Had she done enough? In the darkness, she looked at the outline of her crumpled uniform jacket in the corner of her cell, had an idea, stashed it away, touched the wall, walked to the other side, touched that wall, and continued her regimen.

She tried to stay focused on Piper with every step, but her alternating strides brought images of her frenzied departure from their home in Cary, the candlelit room in Raleigh, her husband groping an attractive woman, and the sheets twirling, as if spun by a dervish, which was the third thought that haunted her. Then she was back to Piper, who was hugging her mother, most likely not entirely remembering her, which hurt. Maeve remembered inhaling the scent of the fine blond hair, freshly bathed with baby shampoo. The clean, innocent smell of her child was offset by the wicked scent—oils and lotions—of her husband's infidelity. The fear of a catastrophic attack on the East Coast, using liquefied natural gas, or LNG, which she had helped steal from Pakistan, then overrode everything else.

Maeve stopped walking and sat in the corner that diagonally faced the door. She wanted a full view the next time the door opened. This time she would be prepared. After some fitful sleep with only a threadbare blanket, a few bottles of water, and a bucket to pee in, she sensed that morning was approaching. Even though she was less than two days into her redeployment from nine and a half time zones away, she sensed the dawn approaching like a distant siren.

As her anxiety began to spin out of control, she turned to her comfort zone, teaching. She visualized herself preparing a lesson plan for her geology class at North Carolina State University. Organizing her thoughts, connecting the logic: her husband, Piper, and the clue she had left behind. There was more, though.

It all came down to the clue, the henna and what she had done with it.

Calming her mind, as she had trained herself to do in combat, she synthesized the information—Piper, the danger, and her husband—as best she could. Someone had figured out, she assumed, that she harbored secrets that only a few people knew. Her top secret clearance was augmented by several compartmented, need-to-know layers of authorization, like additional encryption. While she had perfected state-of-the-art lateral drilling techniques in Afghanistan, she was not proud of the fact that she had essentially stolen millions of cubic feet of Pakistani natural gas.

Yet she had done so. And now there were ships full of liquefied natural gas steaming from Karachi, Pakistan, of all places, to multiple ports along the East Coast. Initially believing that the natural gas was part of a joint Pakistan-Afghanistan agreement, she had uncovered documents suggesting otherwise in her handler's office near their Spin Boldak border outpost. Based on those documents, she was convinced that these ships might be used as weapons, dirty bombs, against the United States. Boston, New York City, Newark, Baltimore, Washington, DC, and Norfolk all were in danger.

So she had left the clue, the henna, in Piper's room, next to a picture of her and Piper.

The documents involved three sets of numbers. Her handler, Jim, had departed the remote forward operating base in Afghanistan one evening, leaving her alone with the small security force that guarded the mouth of the mine shaft. She had gone looking for their next, and last, mission folder. The missions always came into the top secret fax in his plywood room/office, and as she was thumbing through those documents, the machine had whirred to life, delivering a page with numbers, an amount of money, and some basic directions.

She had memorized the three sets of numbers and the dollar amount, one billion. As she ruminated on what to do with the information, the machine had spit out another page. Shocked, she had covered her mouth and backed out of the room, retreating to the relatively safe confines of her room. She knew that the Central Intelligence Agency and the U.S. Army monitored or collected every computer keystroke she made, every Web site she visited, and every piece of paper she possessed during her tour of duty. She hadn't dared write down the numbers, but she'd been concerned she would confuse or jumble them upon her redeployment. So she had improvised.

Now, sitting in the corner of her cell on her second day back in the United States, Maeve lifted her shirt and looked at the fading diagram she had etched on her stomach with henna. Unaware that henna tattoos were all the rage back in the United States, Maeve had designed her own immediately after finding the information, disguising the numbers inside a triangular diagram that somewhat resembled the pyramid on a dollar bill. The numbers were latitudes and longitudes. As a geologist, she was adept at map reading and thought that the numbers represented locations on the East Coast of the United States. But that was as far as she'd gotten.

Now, betrayed by her husband, worried about her daughter, and fearful of possible imminent attacks on the East Coast, she hugged her knees and rocked softly against the hard walls of her confinement. She felt much the same way here as she had in Afghanistan, locked up in a compound near the Pakistan border. The Taliban fighters had swirled past their underground redoubt like a river current slipping past a boulder. The enemy had never detected their location, and her handler, Jim, had made sure she was well fed and secure. He had catered to her basic human needs of food, shelter, and water. There were other needs, though, which she chose not to think about.

Looking at her stomach in the dim light provided by the glow of the backlight of her Army-issue wristwatch, Maeve thought that now the pyramid tattoo and its fading clues couldn't disappear fast enough. Not only was she concerned that her captors would learn that she had smuggled the information out of Afghanistan, but she felt that the symbol was a visual reminder of the twelve-month grind of combat she'd endured.

When she returned to Fort Bragg two nights ago, she'd felt an immediate sense of urgency to let someone know about the liquefied natural gas container vessels. But she hadn't known whom she could trust. Everyone, her commander, her peers, had seemed to be staring at her as she went through the out-processing routine of medical checks and equipment turn-in. But she'd remembered her CIA briefing and the documents she had signed, which required her silence and discretion. The questions that so alarmed her, that caused her to flee the small building in a remote corner of Fort Bragg, had challenged her commitment to those secrets.

Rocking, rocking, rocking. Her mind reeled.

They had briefed her at CIA headquarters in Langley that her mission was of the highest importance to national security. It was all about future energy independence. She would help perfect hydraulic fracturing techniques in a combat zone where there were no legal requirements or restrictions. Upon her arrival in Kandahar, she had linked up with a tall, handsome man who would become her handler. He had said to simply call him "Jim." During her Army training she had heard that all CIA operatives had three-letter names and that none of them were real. There were lots of Bobs, Dons, Rons, and Jims in Afghanistan, she'd been told.

They had flown in a small propeller airplane called a CASA to a dirt runway in Afghanistan, along the Pakistan border. Just across the border in Pakistan, she had seen a massive, shiny new fracking well and a natural gas conversion plant. On the approach, she'd been able to see the beehive of activity in between Quetta and Spin Boldak, maybe ten miles from the border.

She and Jim had landed, disembarked from the airplane, and immediately got in a Hilux pickup truck, which was baking from the desert heat. They had driven due east toward the Pakistan border and had parked in a cave at the base of a large foothill. Inside the cave was a door that led to a state-of-the-art drill operating room, like a command center. Two smaller rooms were on either side. These were the sleeping quarters. It was all plywood and electronics, in contrast to the dusty, barren hills above them.

Maeve looked at Jim and asked, "This is where we do it?"

Jim smiled, a slight dark beard covering his face. "Yes. This is where we do it."

Back then Maeve had not fully understood the meaning of Jim's smile or comment. For the next year, though, she diverted fracked natural gas from Pakistan, through the plant's liquefying process, to the port of Karachi via a pipeline. She operated the drill that snaked through miles of Pakistani desert and mountains north, east, and south of their position, using a software override program that Jim had installed in both the Pakistan refinery and the actual control station just across the border in Afghanistan. She was in effect stealing a small chunk of Pakistan's seventeen trillion cubic yards of natural gas reserves.

Her days were spent operating the drill like a video game. She sat at a console, with four computer monitors facing her. Like a fighter pilot, she had a joystick, and she remotely steered the depleted uranium drill bit through the layers of earth, seeking the most porous veins of gas for ease of movement. Using a crew of military contractor roughnecks to do the heavy labor, she targeted a dozen prime fracking locations, one a month. Study, prep, drill, inject water and chemicals, capture the gas, liquefy, pipe, and load aboard a ship in Karachi, Pakistan.

At first, she didn't know where they were going when the ships departed Karachi. Maeve knew only that they carried about 260,000 cubic yards of liquefied natural gas apiece, which was about 162 million yards of gaseous natural gas. The liquefying process condensed the gas by a ratio of ten to one. Even twelve shipments would amount to less than two billion cubic yards, a small dent in the trillions available to Pakistan. That was how she rationalized what she was doing. The mission was important to her country. She was a patriot. Every soldier had to do his or her duty.

Then, gloriously, the last day came. She walked into the bright sunlight, noticing the construction that had begun around the small hillock that had been her home for the past year. She walked to the vehicle, turned, and for the last time saw the sign hanging loosely on the entrance to what was now a fully operational forward operating base in Afghanistan. She remembered thinking it was odd that the U.S. construction company was advertising to its inhabitants that this base camp was their construction site.

JAMES GUNTHER AND SONS CONSTRUCTION, INC.

The airplane flew in and retrieved her, and tears of joy streamed down her face.

Now tears came again, as she remembered. Huddled in the corner of her prison cell somewhere in North Carolina, she silently rubbed her outer garment above her fading tattoo. And she prayed that the right person, or people, would look in Piper's room and find the clue. Her trembling hand found the bare skin beneath her T-shirt, and she absently raked her fingers across the tattoo on her abdomen. Its message and what lay beneath it were secrets she had carried home from Afghanistan.

Thinking of the threat that she believed the nation faced, she removed her Army-issue wristwatch, set the minute hand to three minutes before twelve, and pulled the crown out so that the time would freeze in place. She then stuffed it in the corner with her nametape.

Maeve's head jerked up at the sound of a hasp rattling. The door opened slightly, slowly, and the first things she saw were a pistol and a flashlight.

Then she heard a familiar voice.

"Hey, Maeve. So good to see you again," CIA Jim said. "Ready to do it?"

CHAPTER 9

Wᴴɪʟᴇ ʜᴇ ʜᴀᴅ ʀᴇᴍᴏᴠᴇᴅ Nᴀᴛʜᴀɴ Dᴀɴɪᴇʟs's ʟᴀʀɢᴇʀ ᴇxᴛᴇʀɴᴀʟ drive from his jeans, Mahegan had placed the small flash drive in his jeans pocket. As he listened to Grace close her door, he sat down in the computer alcove she had pointed out. She used an exercise ball as a seat instead of a chair. He couldn't make that work, so he unplugged the MacBook Pro and sat down at the kitchen table with it.

While the laptop was powering up, he noticed the neat row of pans hanging above the sink in descending order of size. The appliances were brushed chrome and black. Yellow curtains covered the bay windows in the breakfast nook, where he sat. The monitor went straight to the home page without asking for a password prompt. Either Grace was lax about security or Throckmorton routinely went through her files. He seemed like the type.

After plugging in the flash drive, he clicked on the icon and the media player instantly displayed a frozen image of the back deck at the Throckmorton mansion, zoomed out to capture much of the back of the house in grainy relief. Mahegan heard a dull thud in the backyard, like the sound of a sack dropped on the ground. Or two feet leaping over a fence. He withdrew Throckmorton's pistol from his coat pocket and hustled silently to the sliding glass door. Moving the curtain slightly, he saw two men standing on either side of the patio, motioning to one another, like a room-clearing team.

These men were young, solidly built, and sporting close hair-cuts, like military. But there was something ethnic about them, per-haps foreign. Their noses and the planes of their faces reminded Mahegan of Slavic soldiers he had met on a mission in the Balkans. They looked like cage fighters. He briefly wondered what their connection to Throckmorton might be when one of the men formed a cup with his hands and the other placed his foot in the cup to gain a boost onto the deck above.

Mahegan needed to rapidly disable the bottom man. He fig-ured the top man was putting about two hundred pounds of pres-sure on the bottom man's flexed knees. A hard, flat strike against the lateral collateral ligament, the outside of the knee, would im-mobilize him but not prevent him from reaching for any weapons. Mahegan needed a two-part strike on the bottom man before he would tackle the top man.

Mahegan crouched and quietly removed the protective bar from the well of the slider. *Slow is smooth. Smooth is fast*, he thought to himself. The blinds were vertical slats, so he stayed low, flipped the lock, and opened the door in one quick motion. The plastic blinds chattered in his wake, but he was already on the lower man in two quiet steps. The man climbing to the deck was blocking the line of sight of the man doing the boosting.

Mahegan felt the heel of his Doc Marten boot crunch into the side of the man's knee, ripping the ligament and collapsing the femur onto the tibia. Hearing the bone to bone crunch before the man's agonizing scream reassured Mahegan that his next step, a slight movement to the right, was the proper move.

The bottom man spun away to the left, then rolled onto the ground like a gymnast. Mahegan heard the top man whisper loudly, "Ne oluyor!" (What the hell?)

Turkish, not Balkan. Mahegan's time in the mountains of north-ern Iraq, working with the Kurdish resistance, had taught him plenty of Turkish phrases, especially slang ones.

Mahegan kicked the bottom man's head as if he were Beckham bending a soccer ball during a corner kick. He pivoted and saw the top man hanging from the balcony, undecided. *Bad move*, Mahegan thought. The man could have been over the balcony railing and onto the deck, possibly through the glass door to use Grace as a hostage. Or he could have been level with Mahegan, better able to square up against him.

Instead, he was in a vulnerable position. As Mahegan approached, the top man kicked out with his legs. Mahegan caught one in midair, like he was catching a football. He used both hands and snatched the ankle from mid-flight. He rotated his body and twisted downward, feeling something give in the top man's leg. He felt the man's body torque against his own handhold on the balcony railing until one of the railing posts snapped and the man fell on top of Mahegan. As if executing one of his high school wrestling moves, Mahegan fell backward onto the concrete and crushed the man beneath his massive frame. He felt the wind leave the man's diaphragm with an audible "Oomph."

Mahegan quickly spun and placed his thumb on the man's windpipe, crushing it inward while catching the knife-wielding hand that was arcing toward him. The light from a distant streetlamp played off the man's knife. He could see that it had a long blade, perhaps six inches, reinforced by a stiff leather handle. It had seen plenty of use, and with every second that passed, Mahegan knew he was dealing with hardened killers. He ratcheted the man's arm outward, twisting the forearm against the shoulder socket's normal rotation. He felt the man kicking more from a lack of oxygen than from the intention to fight. Mahegan had never understood this reaction, as it simply wasted oxygen and effort.

He heard the knife fall to the cement and released the pressure on the windpipe fractionally. With both arms occupied, Mahegan centered himself and head butted the man's face, flattening his nose. Blood sprayed all over Mahegan and the concrete slab. He let go of the windpipe and the arm and grabbed each side of the man's head and slapped it into the patio with enough force to make him unconscious.

Mahegan stood, glad he had stayed. He wondered who else might come and what the reporting window might be for these two. Had these two been a diversion? Was someone waiting in a car? He scanned the area, alert. The entire episode had taken less than a minute. But it was a minute that had determined Grace Kagami's fate, for the better, as far as Mahegan knew.

His combat mind was racing. He needed to interrogate the two intruders after securing them inside. He needed to defend against near-term future threats. He needed to make sure Grace Kagami was still safe.

He quickly raced into the house and up the stairs. He placed his hand on the bedroom doorknob and turned it. Pushing open the door, he immediately saw Grace lying on the bed, curled in the fetal position, knees tucked under her chest, hands together, as if she were praying. He saw the steady rhythm of her breathing, as indicated by the rise and fall of her UNCW T-shirt. He walked to the sliding glass door and rechecked it. All secure. On his way out of the room, he noticed the bottle of sleeping pills open on the nightstand. He lifted the bottle and saw that the count was thirty. When he looked inside, there appeared to be at least half that many. A suicide attempt would have drained the bottle. She needed help sleeping, and so she had taken a pill. Satisfied she was safe, Mahegan left the room and closed the door quietly.

With the priority one box checked, his mind focused on the two men outside and whether there was another immediate threat. Back in the kitchen, he withdrew the pistol from his pants pocket and tugged the curtain to one side so he could peek into the parking lot. There was a dark SUV parked at the far end of the parking lot. It had not been there when he had tossed Throckmorton onto the Lamborghini, and it appeared empty. With the priority two box checked, he tested the front door locks, returned to the kitchen, and found a box of trash bags and a roll of duct tape in the pantry. Again, he noticed everything was obsessively neat—dress right, dress—like in the military.

Returning to the back patio, he saw both men were still unconscious and idle. The apartment next door was soundless. Grace's clock had registered 1:30 a.m. He didn't relish dragging these men into the home they were invading, but he had little choice. With Grace secure, and with no apparent immediate threat, priority three was to interrogate them. He believed there might be a nexus between the attack on Grace, the party at the Throckmortons' house, and Maeve Cassidy's location.

He bagged both of their heads to prevent blood from staining Grace's carpet. Mahegan then dragged both men into the living room, positioning them between the white sofa and the fifty-five-inch, flat-screen TV hanging from the wall. The neutral carpet would most likely not go unscathed, but he had no options. He stood and stared at them, and they reminded him of dead bodies on the battlefield. Mahegan turned and closed the slider, locked it, and then re-placed the bar and shut the blinds.

He peeled back the white trash bags from each of their heads, as if they were wearing burial shrouds. He frisked both men, land-ing two more knives, a smartphone, one Glock 17, and two wal-lets. He placed the items on the glass-topped coffee table in front of the sofa. For the first time, Mahegan noticed the large painting above the sofa. Depicted was a ninja, stealthy and covert, facing off against a samurai, official and obvious. This contradiction in-trigued Mahegan and perhaps could help him understand Grace Kagami better.

He took the duct tape and secured their ankles and wrists and then bound them together at the knees and the chest area. He put a strip of tape across each of their mouths. The man with the sev-ered knee ligament had regained consciousness, and Mahegan could see tears streaming down his face. Mahegan figured the pain was unbearable, especially with the additional torque the tape was adding.

He sat on the sofa, facing the two injured and bound men. In less than three hours of having a beer with Grace, Mahegan had seriously injured three men. He pored through their wallets and found two identical identification cards showing green banners across the top that read PERMANENT RESIDENT. The cards also listed the men's names and their country of origin, Turkey. Stamped on the back was the alphanumeric sequence EB-5.

Mahegan recalled that Grace Kagami had mentioned some-thing called EB-5, which involved visas and investments. He pored over the other documents in their wallets, surprised that the home invasion team had not sanitized themselves prior to the mission. One of the men had a smartphone, and it showed three missed calls from a 910 area code number, which, Mahegan knew, covered the area from Fort Bragg to Wilmington. He removed the battery and the SIM card from the phone prior to pocketing the device.

As the other man began to awaken and struggle against his binds, Mahegan looked up. He had sufficient information to begin questioning them. Though he would have preferred to have them in separate soundproof rooms, he didn't have that option. He stood and pulled the tape off the mouth of the man nearest him, the climber.

"Seni kim gonderdi?" Mahegan asked. (Who sent you?)

Big brown eyes looked at Mahegan. The man was shocked perhaps that he knew a small amount of Turkish or scared that they had been so thoroughly defeated. The other man's eyes came to life, as well. In the darkness, the eyes glowed, like small lights in a dark forest.

"Kimse." (Nobody.)

Mahegan looked at the balcony climber's injured arm, put the heel of his boot directly on the man's shoulder, and slowly let his weight shift onto that one point. The man screamed loudly, pain obviously ricocheting through his body. Mahegan stepped away and knelt next to the balcony man's head. He reached over, picked up one of the knives from the coffee table, and placed it against the neck of the man who had done the boosting, then stepped over and crushed the booster's injured knee under the same boot heel.

Mahegan asked the same question again as he came back to the balcony man. The booster was writhing in pain, and with each movement, the duct tape pulled and stretched his already severely damaged ligaments and tendons.

"Sana söyleyemem!" (I can't tell you!)

Mahegan had run out of patience, and perhaps the man could see that in his eyes. He lifted the knife and placed the tip against the man's larynx. He said in English, "If you won't talk, I'll make it a permanent condition."

Mahegan could see the man understood the words. He immediately coughed out, "Shred. They call him Shred."

Ted the Shred. Ted Throckmorton. Mahegan had kicked his ass, and he'd called his goons to go after a woman.

"I told you he plays for keeps," Grace said.

Mahegan looked up and immediately put the duct tape back across the man's mouth. Grace was standing at the far end of the combination dining and living room. Her arms were crossed, but she seemed more aware than before.

"And I told you I did, too. They were coming after you, not me." She paused. "I guess I'm glad you stayed."

"We need to get you out of here. Go pack a bag. Now."

"Where are we going?"

"Just do what I said. Now."

She nodded, then looked at the two men, then nodded again, as if to acknowledge that she understood on all accounts. She understood that her ex-boyfriend had sent them to get her. She understood that Mahegan had disrupted their home invasion. And she understood that Mahegan would protect her until further notice.

Mahegan cut the duct tape binding the two men, grabbed the attackers' car keys, and lifted one man onto his back. He carried him to the black SUV he had spotted earlier, opened the back, and dumped the man onto the carpeted surface, ensuring that the man hit his bad arm. He repeated the process with the other man, dumping him knee first into the cargo compartment. He drove the SUV to the pub, performed a minimal wipe down to remove his prints, and then drove his own car back to Grace's apartment. That took fifteen minutes.

When he returned, Grace was waiting for him with a backpack.

"I locked the back door and cleaned up. Here's your flash drive, and here's all their stuff, each piece of evidence individually bagged."

Mahegan stared at her.

"I'm a forensic tech, remember?"

In the melee perhaps he had forgotten. His protective instincts had made him circle the wagons. His skills were most useful then. Hers could be useful now.

"I remember. It's clean?"

Grace rolled her eyes. "You've seen my place, right?"

Indeed. He believed she had tidied up nicely.

"Where we going, Hawthorne?"

"The only safe place I know of right now."

They got into his Cherokee and drove to his apartment in Apex. In his apartment, she dumped her backpack on an old rocker that had come with the place. He watched her assess the random furnishings and the relative tidiness.

"Hey, thanks," Grace said, looking at Mahegan. Then she smiled. "But I'm not seeing where you're sleeping."

Mahegan smiled. There was only one bed and no sofa. "Sleeping bag. On the floor, by the door."

Grace grinned. "Yeah, okay, Kemosabe."

"That would be you. You're Kemosabe."

Grace shrugged. "Let's fire up that flash drive," she said, yanking her MacBook Pro from her backpack. She set it on a small wooden table, where Mahegan ate his meals. Two wooden school chairs were on either side of the table.

"You sure? It's the last couple of days of footage of the Throckmorton house."

He watched Grace Kagami's mind spin, come to a conclusion, and register the answer in her eyes. "Sure."

"It's almost four a.m. You certain you don't want to rest?"

"I'm okay," she said. "Look. Again, thanks. The last thing I expected was to be involved in some kind of frigging 'missing person, sex party' scenario. It's a shock to the system, for sure. And then a home invasion ordered by my ex? There's some serious stuff going on here. So, I'd rather start investigating than sleep."

She retrieved the flash drive, inserted it, and shifted the MacBook so that they both could see the screen. She clicked on the media player, and they sat down and watched. The video started two days before the party, and she fast-forwarded through much of that.

Mahegan watched as the images spun across the screen at eight times the normal speed. Nathan Daniels had had HD-quality cameras, possibly GoPros, focused on the master bedroom, two of the guest bedrooms, and the large sunken family room. The cameras must have been mounted in the top corners of windows, with the exception of the one on the tree branch Nathan had fallen from.

"Stop," Mahegan said.

Grace shifted and looked at Mahegan. A few seconds later, she stopped the video.

Mahegan nodded at her, lightly removed her hand from the track pad, and rewound the video until they were looking at a panoramic view of the back deck off the master bedroom. It was nightfall; some lights were on in the house, showing dark images of people standing around and drinking wine or beer. It was like looking at a shadow box. Mahegan pressed PLAY, and he saw a darkly clad figure approach the steps to the deck from the backyard. It was a woman, small and agile. The time stamp on the video put them about an hour out from when witnesses reported hearing a gunshot. Mahegan stared at the grainy image and thought he saw a pistol in the woman's hand.

As the video continued in slow motion, the woman turned her head prior to ascending the steps, as if to ensure she wasn't being watched. As the head turned, eyes looked directly at the camera. Both in real life and on the video, Grace Kagami was staring directly at Mahegan. The morning sun was edging over the horizon, casting dull plumes of light through the windows, as Mahegan leveled his hardened gaze on Grace.

"I can explain," she said.

CHAPTER 10

MAEVE BALKED AND TURNED AWAY WHEN JIM OPENED THE DOOR to her cell and shined the flashlight on her face. She felt pinned in the corner, as if the light were a restraint holding her in place. She went from anxious to frightened.

"Don't worry," Jim said. "Piper is safe."

Then the bottom dropped out of her soul. They had Piper. Maeve screamed, "No!" Not the only thing she even cared about anymore. This was beyond surreal. Her only child was in the captive hands of the men who had detained her? She would fight hard, Maeve determined. But she needed to use her mind and get control of herself.

"Where is she, you bastard?"

"Safe, Maeve, safe. That's the truth."

There it was, the consoling warden's voice that had manipulated her in Afghanistan.

"Where. The hell. Is my daughter!" she screamed.

"Jesus. I didn't want to do this."

Jim shot her. The voltage from the stun gun caught Maeve in the upper chest area, easily penetrating her T-shirt. She rode the current, fighting it, until she blacked out.

Later, Maeve was reasonably aware of movement and noise. She awoke to a dreamlike vision of staring at the feet of three men. She heard voices talking, the sounds unintelligible to her so far. They were deep voices, men talking about natural gas and pipelines and ships. She smelled a musty scent, like that of alcohol, probably scotch. The words floated through her fuzzy mind, as if disconnected from the sentences to which they belonged.

"Just a few million for the LNG . . ."

"That's peanuts, hardly worth the risk. . . ."

"Nothing compared to what we can do here . . ."

"The market is perfect. . . ."

"The pipeline was genius. . . ."

"Where's the ship now . . . ?"

"Have to get her to work immediately . . ."

The fragments of sentences circled around her brain like race cars lapping the infield. Then with renewed clarity she remembered Jim had mentioned Piper's name and said that she was okay.

Piper. Her daughter. She shifted against her restraints, suddenly awake and focused.

"I see our rainmaker is alive and well," a raspy voice said. Not Jim's voice. This voice sounded older and gravelly, perhaps from years of cigarettes and bourbon.

"She's feisty, so watch out, Dad," Jim said. She would never forget his voice.

"Well, Jimmy, you had that woman all to yourself for an entire year. Don't you think it's time to share?" the first voice said. Dad? Jim was talking to his dad?

"I think it's time to get her into the control cell and get her moving on tapping these veins, like we discussed."

Jimmy was indeed CIA Jim, and he was talking to his father, Maeve concluded.

"I know what I'd like to tap," a new voice said. This one was higher pitched, sounding subordinate and wanting.

Maeve strained to see the men from her vantage point on the floor. She saw hardwood tongue-and-groove flooring, a Persian carpet with vegetable dyes, dark hardwood walls, a stone fireplace, the legs of chairs, work boots and casual shoes propped on the bottom rungs of high-top table chairs.

"Let's go then," Jim said.

"Go get Petrov first. I want to know how he got his ass kicked by a bunch of Mexicans."

"He's down the hill with the rest of the crowd. We'll get to him after we get Lady Cassidy in place," Jim said.

"The rest of the crowd? Those my people. Don't be so rude. Do I need to remind you about who contributing to this project?" another new voice said. This one was thick, with a reedy accent. Maeve placed it as something Asian. Harsh and throaty. Chinese, perhaps. She wasn't an expert but had been exposed to enough Asian languages through both her university work in geology and her Army Reserve career.

Maeve tried to fill in the gaps. How had Jim, now Jimmy, come to be her captor here? What was the endgame? Was Piper's kidnapping blackmail so that Maeve would do whatever they asked her to do?

"We get it," Jim said. "It's your money. But we got you the visas."

"You think this is about visas? That's where you're wrong. This is about the one billion dollars, let's not forget."

Maeve thought back to when she found in the fax machine the piece of paper with the numbers and "one billion dollars" written at the top. There had to be a connection. Her hand touched her stomach, where the fading pyramid held the clues. Were they going to steal one billion dollars in natural gas? At fifteen dollars per cubic yard, natural gas prices were high, but the cost of production was high, also. The gas had to be drilled, fracked, piped, liquefied, and stored. All of that required infrastructure and processing, both of which cost money.

As if echoing her thought, Jim said, "One billion is going to be a tough get, but we will try, as promised."

"Then you should start. Now," the Asian voice said.

Maeve heard the thud of footfalls on the floor and saw the feet coming toward her.

"Just do as we say and Piper will be fine, Maeve," Jim said. He removed the tape from her ankles, then lifted her and walked her through the doorway, along a hallway, down a set of stairs, and into a tunnel, like a mine shaft. They passed several doors and finally made a left at an intersection. He stopped her at a door that opened into a small room, not unlike the control room from which she had operated in Afghanistan. Before stepping in the room, she pushed back against him.

"Where is Piper?" she asked. Her words were slurred, as if she had been drinking. "Did you drug me?"

"Just a bit. Didn't want to overdo it. First thing you need to know is that everything you say and do is recorded on cameras in every corner. Understand?"

Maeve processed what Jim was saying. "Yes. I understand." She nodded.

"I'm serious. I want you to look at the cameras and understand what I am saying to you. Plus, there will be a guard on this door at all times."

She watched Jim's eyes, then looked at the cameras in each corner of the room, then back at Jim. "I said I understand." She nodded.

"Good. We've got to have you at the stick. All you're going to do is exactly what you've been doing. What you trained in Afghanistan a year to do."

"You mean steal natural gas for other people? That's what you kidnapped me for?"

"*Kidnap* is such a harsh term, Maeve."

"It wasn't supposed to be like this, Jim . . . Jimmy. I did my duty in Afghanistan."

Jim chuckled, ran his thumb across Maeve's dry cheek, stained with salt from the tears. "And now you will do it here, dear Maeve."

Maeve shuddered.

He still had the shallow beard. He was over six feet tall and wore combat-style clothes: tight-fitting Under Armour shirt, cargo pants, and combat boots. He was strong, she knew. His muscles were honed and firm. She had not noticed any fat on him during their time together in Afghanistan.

He pushed her into the room, removed a knife, and cut the tape binding her wrists. "Let's just do this. We all answer to some-body, Maeve, so let's get this done."

Maeve stared at the monitors. She saw the one with the planned drill route that she was to follow. Someone had already mapped it out for her. All she needed to do was navigate the drill bit through the labyrinth without making a wrong turn, which could collapse the vein and forever seal off the possibility of retrieving the gas, like closing the opening of a cave. If she fouled up the mission, she could only imagine what her captors might do to her. Or to Piper.

The next monitor showed the wellhead, an open field of dirt surrounded by hills on every side. This was where the drill and the pipes were located. She saw the water tanks necessary for the injection of chemicals and water, which separated the shale deposits to release the gas. The monitor was a thermal night-vision camera and showed her everything in a shade of green. Maeve could discern several men standing near a few pickup trucks, most of them smoking cigarettes. The scene looked like many of the combat bombing videos she had viewed. One minute there would be a bunch of Taliban talking among themselves, AK-47s strung across their chests, and the next the entire screen would go white from an explosion.

The third monitor was blank, until Jim turned it on by quickly typing in a password. Even though she tried to follow his fingers, she couldn't keep up. The screen flickered briefly and then showed a room with four-year-old Piper sitting in the middle of a playpen.

"Piper!"

"She can't hear you, Maeve. I told you she's okay."

"What the hell are you doing!"

"She's fine." As if to convince her further, he said, "For the record, Piper was not my idea. If that matters."

Of course it didn't matter. All that mattered was that Piper was being held hostage, she thought. Maeve looked up, and a young Asian woman picked up Piper and held her, as if on cue. She smiled and kissed the child on the forehead. Maeve felt nauseous and began searching for a bathroom.

"Right over there," Jim said, pointing.

Maeve scrambled into the latrine and retched into the toilet.

She heaved until there was nothing left to give. Slowly, she pushed herself up from the commode and flushed it. She washed her mouth in the sink and looked at herself in the mirror.

She saw her drawn features, almost unrecognizable, staring back at her. She pushed back her hair and studied herself. Feeling as though she was looking at a stranger, Maeve got lost in her eyes. They were vacant. A year in hell had sapped most of her strength, and now that hell just kept going. There was exactly one thing that mattered to her. She would do anything to get Piper back, even if it meant stealing a billion dollars' worth of natural gas from North Carolina's reserves.

That was the quid pro quo.

Maeve walked back into the room with something gnawing at the back of her mind. It was the part of her that had dueled with this man for months in Afghanistan and had also skirmished with the Taliban. Her survival instinct was in high gear. She sat down at the controls and looked up at Jim, who was perched with his ass on the table.

"Finished?" he asked.

"What do I have to do?"

"Now we're talking." Jim smiled. "See that vein there? That's the Durham sub-basin of the Triassic Rift—"

"I know what it is, you psychopath. Just tell me what you want me to do!"

"There are almost two trillion cubic feet of gas in there," Jim continued.

"Why are you telling me what I already know? You want the gas. I'll get the gas. That's the deal, right? I get the gas, and I get Piper back, right?"

"Right. There's just two additional safeguards."

Maeve looked at the screen showing Piper. Jim toggled a switch, which changed the image from Piper to a split screen showing two nuclear power plants.

"This screen on the right shows the Maguire Nuclear Station. What you can't see is a small, unmanned aerial drone that is rigged with explosives at a dirt airfield in Gaston County, just miles away. If you deviate from the path or stop the drill bit from moving forward without my permission, you trigger a sensor that launches the drone, which is programmed with a flight path into the pipe of the cooling tower. The drone is rigged with enough explosives to implode the facility. Can you say, 'Bye-bye, Charlotte'?"

Maeve put her hands on her face, wanting to cry, but knowing she had to remain cogent. She muttered, "You bastard."

Jim nodded and continued. "On the left is the Brunswick Nuclear Plant, near Wilmington. You can see that at the bottom of the screen, in the Cape Fear River, is an LNG ship turning into the waterway leading up to the plant. It is rigged with explosives, and if you deviate from the plan or slow the drill to a stop, it will detonate with several kilotons of energy, like a small nuclear bomb. Of course, the nuclear plant will then have a reaction, which could reach two miles up the road to the military ammunition depot, where thousands of bombs are stored. You will in effect destroy much of the Eastern Seaboard between Wilmington and Charleston, South Carolina. And all of this is traceable to you, Maeve. You filled that ship with gas, and we have records we can release that implicate you in this attack, should it come to pass."

Maeve leaned back in the chair. Wilmington and Charlotte, North Carolina, were two of the coordinates she had engraved on her stomach with the henna.

Steal the gas, or cause nuclear Armageddon in North Carolina and along the Eastern Seaboard?

"Now, down to business. We've already had the men, the roughnecks, get the drill to the first kickoff point. This is where we need your deftness, your surgeon's touch. You need to take it into the shale, to the designated point. Then, when you're done with that, there's another vein you will drill. The second vein is angled slightly to the south from the main kickoff point, and then there's another kickoff point, at which you'll have to drill straight up."

"Another one? Fracking uses just one turn. You go down vertically and then get horizontally into the deposit, insert your casings, and then send down your perforating gun and explosive charges. Why a second turn?"

"It's a superrich vein that, my geology team says, we can better tap this way."

Maeve shook her head, not understanding. In a flash, she had gone from feeble hostage to strident geologist. "That makes no sense."

"It's what my team is telling me."

Maeve processed the information. As she stared at the screen in front of her, she saw the image of the drill bit resting at a depth of three thousand feet, shallow by fracking standards. The aquifer was just above this level. Setting off explosives just beneath the drinking water was unsafe, to put it mildly. She studied the path Jim had directed her to follow. The kickoff point was the turning point from the vertical drill line. The image showed her going to the northwest about ten thousand feet, almost two miles and significantly farther than any horizontal drills had ever gone in the United States.

But it was less than the distance at which she had been drilling in Pakistan. She guessed that they went shallow to save drill length for the horizontal push and for whatever the second kickoff point was all about. In the Afghanistan-Pakistan experiment, they had used specialized titanium drill lengths and depleted uranium drill bits to bore at extended lengths. The reinforced drill parts allowed for more power at the bit after the turn, which had been a problem for conventional drillers.

"You'd have to have the classified materials we used in Pak to make this turn," she said, pointing at the diagram on the monitor. Common drilling equipment would not be able to withstand the torque or stress at such distances.

Jim smiled. "Let me worry about the materials. You just need to try to avoid blowing up Charlotte and Wilmington, dear Maeve."

"Who programmed this route? You, of all people, know I program my own drill routes."

"We've got a guy. Like I said, don't worry about it."

She shook her head again. "Have you checked it? Made sure it's clear?"

"Our guy is the best programmer in the business. Now, let's get to work."

Maeve stood. "I need to use the restroom again. This time for something other than puking."

"You have two minutes. Then we get to work. We're on a time-line. Need to crank her up."

She walked into the bathroom. The bottom line was that she was helping Jim Gunther steal shale gas from his neighbors. She could do that, get her daughter back, and then build a new life somewhere else, away from the military and Jim Gunther.

She closed the door, did her business, and washed her hands and face.

If I don't start the bit, Charlotte and Wilmington are not in play, but Piper is. I have no idea where she is, but if I can break out and take a hostage, I might get a trade. No, that's stupid. Use your skills, Maeve. You will think of something.

She knew her thoughts were desperate as she studied herself in the mirror. *Oh. The glass mirror.*

Maeve reached her hand up and opened the medicine cabinet, which was empty. She studied the weak hinges that held the mirror. *One, two, three,* she thought. *One, rip the mirror off the hinges. Two, shatter the mirror against the toilet. Three, grab the largest chunk and use it as a weapon against Jim.*

She removed her ACU jacket and her T-shirt, then replaced her top. She wrapped the T-shirt around her right hand, which she would use to hold whatever weapon the shattered mirror provided her.

Then she ripped the mirror off its hinges.

CHAPTER 11

"THEN EXPLAIN," MAHEGAN SAID TO GRACE.

Mahegan stood, took three steps, and sat on the floor, leaning his back against his bed. He liked the place because it vaguely reminded him of some of his austere accommodations in combat zones, though he never recalled having a kitchenette or a breakfast table. A cot and some plywood walls were the best he had done, if he was lucky. Other times, communal living arrangements were the norm. Regardless, he liked the independence from the trappings of society. No house to maintain. No vehicle on which to pay insurance.

He looked out the window and saw a pale gray sky edging over the horizon like a battleship ready for combat. The sleepless night before recalled dozens of missions playing out at precisely what sailors called "before morning nautical twilight." He had a mission. Savage had told him he had about twenty-four hours to find Maeve Cassidy. He didn't know what the "or else" was, but if Savage was involved, he knew it had to be significant.

Grace stayed in the chair and turned toward him. "I'm a conservationist. I started dating Ted Throckmorton to get inside the Throckmorton Energy cabal. I don't think his father, Brand, ever trusted me, though he did try to have sex with me many times. Ted was a different story. I could see the conflict in him. He is a rich daddy's boy and is completely beholden to the man. Wants to please him like nothing you've ever seen. But he also has a different side to him, the real side, which would come out if he wasn't so obsessed with pleasing his father."

"Not so unusual," Mahegan said. He thought of his mother and his mission to kill Gunther. As long as Gunther was alive, that windmill would be there for him to charge. Redemption would not come, but justice would be served. And that was important to Mahegan.

"You with me?" she asked.

"Yes. Continue."

"You spaced out on me."

"No. Just focused a bit . . . things falling into place."

"Good. Well, anyway, by day I am a crime-fighting lab tech. By night, I help organize a group called Don't Frack the Triangle."

"Catchy."

"DFT-Two for short. There are about twenty of us, most from Chapel Hill. We don't want the chemicals and wastewater in the aquifer. We don't want the earthquakes. It's serious business they're talking about doing. They're going to drill two miles into the core of the earth and suck out gas and other by-products through concrete sleeves they shove in the ground after they drill. Like those will hold. Two years ago the power company dumped tons of coal ash into the Dan River. The concrete pipe broke. The same thing can happen here. But Ted is all enamored with how much money he is going to be bringing in. Millions. Maybe billions. Those guys in Texas are frigging billionaires from fracking."

"So what were you doing with a pistol on the back deck of the Throckmortons' house?"

"He's got some big investors. From China, Russia, maybe even some of those other countries in Asia. Scary dudes."

"Like Turkey?"

"Maybe. It's through the Employment-Based Immigration–Fifth Preference program, like we talked about. They donate at least a half million dollars to a project, and then they get a free visa for their family. It's happening everywhere."

"I've heard of it. Foreign direct investment. The Afghans were starting to get into the game. Some were getting rich off U.S. government contracts and wanted safe places to put the money and their families. No safer place than the United States when you're in Afghanistan."

Grace nodded, stood, and then sat in front of Mahegan, with her legs crossed in a lotus yoga position. Her movements mirrored her name, Mahegan thought. She was graceful, and her legs slipped into position without any effort.

"I want to be looking you directly in the eyes when I tell you this, Hawthorne. Ted came by, drunk, about three nights ago. I made him meet me on the patio. I wouldn't let him into the house. It has been over six months since we've been together, and all that frigging BS about me e-mailing him and so on was just that, BS. He's a stalker of the highest magnitude. Like that old football player O. J. Simpson. Plus, I prefer women, most of the time. That probably freaks you out, but I don't care. Ted was bad for me in many ways, but we had some good times down in Wilmington, where I would sit on the beach and watch him surf. He earned that nickname, Ted the Shred. He was happiest there in Wilmington, when he was away from the reach of his daddy."

Mahegan nodded, urging her to continue, ignoring the comment about her preferring women. He didn't care.

"So Ted told me something about what they called Operation Isosceles."

"Like the triangle?"

"I guess. Brand, his father, worked with the state department of commerce, and they named all their projects different code names—like Penguin for an ice company or Dining Room for a furniture company. Ted said he was nervous about this because he felt the investors were running the show, not Brand."

"Who is in charge of the investors? Whose project is this?"

"Someone named Johnny Ting is working with a construction company. I'm told that Ting is calling the shots, with Brand Throckmorton and the head of this construction company as their little triumvirate."

"Gunther and Sons?"

Grace snapped her fingers. "How'd you know?"

"They're the biggest in the state." Mahegan hid his urge to kill Gunther.

"But, anyway, there was supposed to be this big meeting two nights ago, and it's this big orgy. Ted calls me up, nearly hysterical that all these EB-Five women have been shuttled over from Throckmorton's compound slash lodge in western Wake County to have sex with the fracking workers, and there's a big orgy at his dad's house. I don't think Brand Throckmorton's tastes run in that direction."

"He's gay?"

"Brand is bi. Ted will never tell you. He has a trophy wife for 'inside the belt line' parties. Apparently, she never gets any, so she is probably the biggest sexual deviant you've ever met."

"Wouldn't be saying much," Mahegan said.

"Regardless, I got a text from Ted, whom, I have to admit, I'd been ignoring, that said, 'Help.'" She showed him her phone. There it was. Sent about an hour before Grace arrived on video the night of the party. "He has *never* sent me anything like that."

"So what happened? You get in there and do what?"

"I slid in through the back door, which was unlocked. Pete Cassidy, Maeve Cassidy's husband, was making out with Sharon Throckmorton, Brand's wife and Ted's mother. He looked reluctant, almost as if he were there against his will."

As Grace spoke, Mahegan tried to recall the layout of the house from his two visits, one semiofficial and one off the books. Mahegan's mind clicked, a gear caught, and he held the thought.

"They didn't notice me, and I slipped through a series of walk-in closets and into a guest bedroom, where I saw a fairly recognizable local politician with one of the EB-Five women. I was looking for Ted, so I kept going. Everyone was so into his or her own scene, it was like walking through a live porno theater. I found Ted in his room at the other end of the house. He was by himself and freaked out. He was sweating and pacing back and forth, mumbling something about ships and natural gas. I have to admit I was surprised. I saw about ten gorgeous women in that house, and they were there for one reason—to have sex, like it was a political payoff."

"Might have something to do with that pipeline to Morehead City. Other than some good blackmail material, how is this relevant?"

"Ted had been threatened by some of the EB-Five guys. There's a Russian named Maxim Petrov. Has a big scar on his face. Also some Turks and Chinese guys. The 'family visas' are being used to ferry in muscle and prostitutes. Enforcers and entrappers. Ted tells me his father has pictures of the chairman of the state Mining and Energy Commission tied up, with a gag ball in his mouth, being whipped by a naked Serb playboy bunny. Something like that, anyway."

"So you brought the pistol because you thought there was danger from the EB-Five crowd?"

"Yes. And that's why Ted had his. They told him if he didn't cooperate, there would be trouble for him specifically. So that's what I'm saying. Ted's dad and Gunther are supposed to be in charge, but Ted was so scared, it's clear that they're not calling the shots."

She was staring him directly in the eyes. Grace had a soulful presence, like a yogi. She spoke softly and with conviction, but not in harsh or argumentative ways. Pleasant and soothing, like a counselor speaking with a patient. Mahegan could see how she could be committed to protecting the environment from fracking, while not crossing the line into hostile territory. He doubted she protested, and was convinced she most likely spoke at public hearings and organized letter-writing campaigns and the like. Good for her. Mahegan had no opinion on fracking. It actually seemed reasonable to him, but he admired the pluck of someone who cared enough to do something to fix what she felt was wrong.

"And then what happened?"

"I was in Ted's room, talking, when the shot went off. After that, all hell broke loose, and I left as quickly as I'd come. Then I raced home, showered, put on my lab stuff, and waited for the call."

"Why the big act at the door with Ted the Shred? He was bowing up on me, and you seemed genuinely scared."

Grace shook her head. "It wasn't an act. Ted is insanely jealous, and he sees Marlboro Man escorting me to the door? Honestly, I'm surprised it went so well."

Mahegan thought of Ted's broken body splayed on the hood of his Lamborghini. "Not so much for him. So what is Isosceles?"

"Not even Ted knew. He told me about his dad's plan to siphon natural gas from parts of Wake and Chatham Counties where the Durham Triassic Basin has rich shale deposits. With horizontal drilling, if you get your drill in there first, you can steal everyone's gas before they know it, and there's no way to tell."

Mahegan ran his options through his mind. Take a four-hour nap, with Grace resting in the nook of his arm, her head on his chest. Go after Pete Cassidy and interrogate him as to what he knew about Maeve. Or find out more about James Gunther's role in this.

"I'm going to have to get to work in a couple of hours. Any way to catch some shut-eye before then?" Grace asked. "I texted Griffyn that I couldn't be there until nine a.m."

"Sure. I was thinking the same thing." Two hours would be perfect.

He stood, held out his hand, which she clasped as she did a miniature pirouette as her legs unraveled from their lotus position. She came to him, as if in a slow dance, placed her hands on his chest, and leaned up on her toes, kissing him lightly on the lips.

"That's all you get," she said. "I prefer women, remember."

She pulled him to the bed. Mahegan lay on his back, and she cuddled into his body as if she were custom fitted for it. Mahegan's mind spiraled and slammed shut, attempting to compensate for two nights without sleep. Shortly, they were both asleep.

CHAPTER 12

WHEN MAHEGAN AWOKE TWO HOURS LATER, GRACE WAS GONE. She had left her computer and her backpack, and he assumed she had gone to work. Stumbling out of bed, Mahegan stretched. He peeled off his T-shirt and studied the lightning bolt shrapnel scar on his arm, a physical reminder of agonizing loss. While he wanted to run and swim, he had a mission to accomplish. The workout would have to wait.

A note was propped on the kitchen counter. All it said was, *I trust you ;).* He fished through his pockets and found his burner cell phone. He had three text messages, all from Grace, who was the only person with the number.

Walked a mile and Uber got me. You sleep peacefully ;)
Be "home" about 5:00 p.m.
Super-weird vibe at crime scene!!!

Mahegan was not accustomed to unsecured communications, and he began to wonder if someone had tapped Grace's phone. After listening to Grace explain why Ted the Shred was nervous, and knowing the Chinese were involved, it would not surprise Mahegan if these EB-5 commandos, as he decided to call them, had handheld International Mobile Subscriber Identity scanners. The devices were the size of a walkie-talkie and could intercept nonsecure cell phone communications. Mahegan had used an IMSI device called a Stingray in combat to intercept enemy communications. He understood the risks.

He removed the battery from the phone and stuffed them both in his pocket, hopeful that no one had drawn a bead on his location yet. He showered and washed away some of the grogginess. While he had adapted to a life of little sleep and high adrenaline missions, he couldn't deny the wear he felt on his body at the moment. He dressed in cargo pants, a lightweight fishing shirt, and a heavier coat that had pockets for secure and unsecure phones and for one of the EB-5 Turk weapons, the Glock 17. He didn't like the thought of using a weapon he had not personally zeroed or shot, but he could quickly adapt. He checked the action, saw that a round was chambered, and pocketed the pistol.

Next, Mahegan pulled out his Zebra smartphone and clicked on the GeoTech Map app, which showed latitude, longitude, and granular detail at least as good as Google Maps did. He had access to real-time, live streaming satellite feed if he needed it.

He thought about the information he had gathered so far. There seemed to be a nexus between Gunther, Throckmorton, and Cassidy. That could work out well for Mahegan. Two birds with one stone and all that. Still, though, his primary mission was to retrieve Cassidy. Savage had told him precious little beyond Cassidy's off-the-books mission involving shale gas in Afghanistan and Pakistan.

His secure phone buzzed with a message from Savage.

Reports of asymmetric attack against nuclear power plants in Southport and Charlotte.

Southport was just below Wilmington on the Carolina coast, and Charlotte was the state's largest city, with over one million people, and was home to the largest financial center outside of Manhattan.

Roger. What do you know about James Gunther or son, James Jr.?

James KIA your mother. Junior in Afghanistan with Cassidy.

Where is Junior now?

You tell me. Cassidy had classified information and skill sets. Why we need her back. Connection to nuclear threat?

Roger. Talking to Pete Cassidy this morning, then will find Ted Throckmorton and Junior.

Roger. Charlie Mike.

Charlie Mike. Continue mission. As if he had any choice. Even if the threat went away, he would continue with his pursuit of Gunther. Staying in North Carolina until he had resolved the Gunther issue was a precondition of Mahegan's deal with Savage. While they had a testy relationship, Savage understood, as indicated by the text message.

James KIA your mother.

It was both a statement of fact and an acknowledgment that his boss knew his true motivations. Savage was a practical man. He knew Mahegan was one of the best, while at the same time he understood he was haunted by the death of his mother. Mahegan had sought and achieved justice for Sergeant Wesley Colgate's death, and he believed that Savage would let him pursue this personal endeavor.

Mahegan caught a movement out of his periphery and walked to the side of one of his two windows. One faced south and provided a view of his landlords' home. The other, which he was standing next to, faced east and provided a view of the dense forest. Mahegan often saw deer and black bears roaming in the area.

This time he caught a whiff of an anomaly, a hard outline against the jagged contours of the forest. The sun was edging over the treetops, pushing through a foggy morning. The density of the trees could provide someone plenty of concealment, unless another someone was watching him from above, as Mahegan was doing now. Mahegan nudged the curtain aside to provide a better view. Actually, there were two men focused on his landlords' home. Maggie and Andy Robertson and their two young children would either be sleeping or just waking now. Maggie was a teacher in the local school system, and Andy worked as a banker in Raleigh.

Their kids were in elementary school, and right now all Mahegan could imagine was that his or Grace's unsecure phone had led two assailants to this location. They either had employed an IMSI tracking device, such as the Stingray, or had retrieved the phone number from spyware on Grace's phone, then pinged his number with tracking software to get a general location. Had Mahegan not removed the battery from the burner cell phone, the team would be focused on his above-barn apartment, as opposed to the luxury home nearly fifty yards away.

Mahegan figured that these two men were like the two men he had fought the night before. These were the EB-5 commandos, the recipients of visas for foreign direct investment. It fit with what Grace had told him earlier, that Throckmorton or Gunther had created an army to enforce and operate their fracking operation. Grace had become a liability when Ted Throckmorton gave her information she didn't need, and now they were tracking her here. There must be a centralized command and control, Mahegan thought, where Throckmorton or Gunther dispatched these home invasion teams to do the wet work.

Mahegan kept a long gun in his apartment. It was a 7.62 mm x 51 mm, custom-built, long-range, suppressed interdiction rifle. *Slow is smooth. Smooth is fast,* he thought. Moving with deliberate speed, Mahegan secured his rifle and knelt at the window. He softly eased the latch and used his thumb to push the window up about six inches, just enough space to get the rifle onto the ledge and to look through the 5-25 x 56 mm scope. He really didn't need the scope at fifty yards but used it to study the two men.

They were military-aged males, as the Army had taught Mahegan to call them. Under twenty-one years of age. Dark hair, broad shoulders, black coats and pants, like Maxim Petrov. These guys could be Russian, Mahegan thought. Or they could be Afghans or Turks.

What he needed to see before he pulled the trigger was a weapon. His patience was rewarded when the far man knelt behind a tree and slowly aimed a long rifle at the home. Mahegan looked away from his scope and through the adjacent window to see the garage door opening. He didn't know the precision with which the EB-5 commandos could operate or what their orders might be, but he couldn't risk having his innocent landlords in jeopardy.

He placed his cheek on the buttstock of the weapon and sighted on the man with the long rifle. The man's head was large in the scope optics, the crosshairs placed directly on his temple. There would be very little wind or drop at this distance. He went through the sequence in his mind: *Pull the trigger, shift to the second man, aim, pull the trigger, and then wait for others, if there are any.*

Fog drifted across the lens, but Mahegan maintained a steady site picture. He heard the car backing out of the garage, saw the man tense, his grip tight on the weapon, and begin to pull back on the trigger.

Mahegan had set his rifle's trigger weight at three and a half pounds, a tad heavy for most people, but he was larger and stronger than most. He felt the release of the sear, the snap of the trigger, and the cough of the suppressor. And he saw the hole in the side of the man's head. The man slumped, and the weapon fell to the ground. Mahegan heard the sound from his perch.

His site picture was already on the man nearest the barn, who was looking at his partner, wondering what had happened. Mahegan blew the back of his head off with a second shot. An eruption of white brain matter shot into the air as the man fell into the underbrush.

Mahegan continued to scan the wood line to determine if there were more than two. Since yesterday he had encountered two teams of two. His singleton encounters had been with Scarface and Ted the Shred. Keeping the rifle trained on the dead men, Mahegan pulled away and scanned with his eyes. Nothing.

He saw Andy Robertson's Mercedes back out. Maggie came running from the house, smiling, and handed him something through the window, probably his lunch. She was dressed and ready for work, also. Wearing a light blue dress, Maggie leaned in and kissed Andy. Mahegan saw two girls at the door, wearing jeans and pink sweaters and carrying backpacks. The Robertson family was rolling at eight o'clock in the morning. What Mahegan knew was that the teacher mom usually took the kids to school with her.

He waited another thirty minutes, and then the rest of the family was away from the house, doing their daily routine. Moving swiftly down the steps, Mahegan opened the barn door and backed his Cherokee into the driveway, about parallel to the man with the rifle. Mahegan did a quick search of both men and found their wallets, flush with EB-5 green cards. These men were Russian.

Probably buddies of Petrov. Either they were seriously stupid or were highly concerned about being stopped and questioned by the police. Or both. Perhaps their mission briefing did not include the fact that they might run up against a former soldier who had skills. He found a key fob for an automobile and a smart phone. He quickly removed the batteries and the SIM card from the phone.

Mahegan knew that Petrov's crew had suffered enough setbacks that they would now take a threat seriously. He pulled out a general-purpose tarp he kept in the back of his Cherokee, spread it out over the cargo space, and then lined up the bodies side by side. His body count was increasing as this operation continued. Two dead and four wounded, counting Petrov and Ted the Shred. The Shred might not be a terrorist, but he was still an asshole.

He drove the bodies along a firebreak to Jordan Lake. One at a time Mahegan carried the bodies to a thirty-foot drop-off where the stream ran narrow through a tight gorge. There logs were piled up, and a beaver was working on a dam. Two boulders leaned against the stream, and the trees lining it were dense. Two hundred yards from the firebreak, the best he could do given the circumstances, he tossed the bodies over the ledge. The animals would get to them before nightfall. He thought about what they might have done to Andy and Maggie and felt no remorse. In fact, he felt pretty damn good.

What didn't feel good was that he was no closer to Maeve Cassidy, though intellectually, he thought he understood part of her captors' plan. He returned to the barn, swept his apartment for brass, placed the rifle back under his bed, got back in the Cherokee, and trolled for the most likely parking spots where the men would have ditched a vehicle to crawl through the woods to the Robertson place. On his third pass he found a stray car parked along a feeder road to the old highway. He tried the key fob and saw the lights flash.

After parking behind the late-model pickup truck—another theme with the EB-5 commandos—Mahegan stepped out of his Cherokee and entered the pickup from the passenger side, away from the road. The truck cab was relatively clear of debris and information, but the registration showed the vehicle was part of the fleet registered to James Gunther and Sons Construction, Inc. He found a mounted Garmin GPS device, which he dismounted and pocketed. He also grabbed a second cell phone from the center console. His sensitive site exploitation, or *search* in civilian terms, complete, Mahegan backed out of the truck and locked it. He performed the same drill with the battery and the SIM card of the other phone he'd discovered.

As he turned, he saw a police cruiser pull in behind his Cherokee. After walking quickly to his vehicle, he leaned in and retrieved his Army CID credentials from the passenger seat, then flipped them up in the face of Raleigh detective first class Griffyn, who had climbed out of the cruiser. The daylight accentuated the man's ruddy complexion.

Raleigh native all my life, Mahegan thought, remembering.

"A little bit out of your jurisdiction, aren't you, Detective?"

"I was getting ready to ask you the same thing, Hawthorne."

"And so here we are," Mahegan said.

"What were you doing in that vehicle?" Griffyn asked.

"I was driving by and saw it parked on the side of the road. I thought there might be a distressed motorist, but upon further inspection I found it abandoned. Probably just some kids fishing in one of these farm ponds." Mahegan waved his hand across the open land on either side of the road.

"Your fingerprints are on the sliding glass door of the Throckmorton home. We need you to come into the office for some questions."

"You saw me put my hand there, Detective. Talk to the Army."

"We have a way to determine the difference between a new print and an old print. The oils were different. Grace did an excellent job of differentiating the old prints and the new prints." Griffyn smiled, indicating he knew something of Mahegan's interaction with Grace. "And we did call the Army. Seems no one really knows who you are."

"Then keep calling," Mahegan said. He took a step toward

Griffyn, towering over the reedy man. Mahegan's sheer bulk dwarfed Griffyn's rail-thin presence. A slight wind blew a few wisps of hair on top of the detective's balding head. Sweat beaded and began to trickle. Mahegan sensed he had won this brief chess move, but the match was far from over.

"I'll do that. Next time I'll have a warrant. I promise," Griffyn said.

Mahegan looked over his shoulder at Griffyn's Crown Victoria, the pickup truck, and the road that stretched beyond. Then he looked over Griffyn's head at the empty road stretching in the other direction, like an unused runway. His anger began to boil. Whether this was an intentional effort to block his pursuit of justice or merely a bureaucratic machination, Mahegan didn't have time for a modern-day Javert chasing his Valjean.

"Tell you what, Detective. I'll come in and participate in your investigation, even answer your questions, once you get clearance from the Army."

It was exactly the opposite of what he wanted to say, but he chose to play nice given his time constraint.

"I'll see you soon," Griffyn said. The detective gave Mahegan a confident nod and stepped into his Crown Victoria.

Mahegan watched Griffyn drive along the lonely stretch of road and wondered how the detective had tracked him there. Or if Griffyn had been tracking the EB-5 commandos.

He stashed that information as he climbed back into his Cherokee and drove past the entrance of the Gunther and Sons construction site where he had pinned Maxim Petrov to the ground with a posthole digger.

Parking his Cherokee a mile away to the east, Mahegan decided to walk through the waist-deep swamp to approach the property. The day before, Petrov had disappeared over the eastern ridge for some time. Trudging through the swamp, Mahegan saw water moccasins coiled tight, basking in the morning sun. Two foxes eyed him warily, and a small herd of deer splashed through the water.

Emerging from the water, he stood up tall and saw a construction crew working on the northeast corner of the fence they had been installing. The outer fence with all the security sensors did not reach the eastern side of the hill yet. It appeared that Petrov, or whoever, had secured the necessary labor to continue the job. Mahegan wanted to see inside the bowl where he had seen the fracking drill, the water and chemical tanks, and the pipes.

There was a small ridge that gave him cover if he stayed to the south side as he worked his way west. Mahegan stayed low for two hundred yards and then caught another anomaly. It was a flat surface against the rounded shape of the hillock. Inspecting it further, Mahegan saw that it was a wall, painted with the camouflage colors brown, tan, and green. It was a respectable job, but not great. He noticed two locked hasps and suddenly got hopeful.

Cassidy had been kidnapped ostensibly to perform some type of fracking mission. Was this her cell or just an equipment shed?

Mahegan found a rock the size of his palm and approached the wooden structure. The sun was up now, almost 9:00 a.m. The work crew was about four hundred yards away, doing the posthole and cement job for the fence. He smelled the new paint and the fresh wood and got even more hopeful. If she was in the cell, he could extract her and retreat quickly to the woods. Her rescue would allow him to transition back to his Gunther mission.

But the warrior in him told him it wasn't going to be that easy. With a couple of powerful swings, he smashed the rock on the hasps, and both of them swung free. Pushing the door inward, he climbed into the structure, still holding the rock high as a defensive measure. He found a blanket, some combat rations, and a few bottles of water. After a quick search, Mahegan found a standard issue army wristwatch and a piece of cloth stuffed in the corner on the floor behind the piss bucket. He instantly recognized the cloth as a Velcro-backed Army combat uniform nametape.

It read CASSIDY.

CHAPTER 13

T HE BATHROOM DOOR BURST OPEN BEHIND THE WEIGHT OF JIM
Gunther's considerable frame.

Maeve Cassidy felt the sharp edge of the jagged icicle of glass
she had snatched from the shattered remains of the mirror. Her
weapon was about eight inches long and three inches wide. In all,
she couldn't have hoped for a better result.

She had weighed the possibility of waiting until Jim wasn't present to create the weapon and then using it on him when he was
distracted. She didn't know, however, the reality of the threats
against Charlotte and Wilmington, much less the threat posed by
the other liquefied natural gas container ships, and didn't want to
take any chances. If she slowed the pace of the drill or left the controls long enough for it to deviate, would she trigger the threats that
Jim had described? Maeve wasn't willing to take that chance, and so
she took the only real chance she saw.

Plus, she knew the threat against Piper was real and visceral.
That shouldn't have been part of the bargain.

"What the hell happened?" Jim shouted. Maeve was pleased to
see that his face was distorted with surprise and perhaps with that
1 percent of knowledge that he had allowed this to happen. He
had let her go into that bathroom unattended.

Maeve staggered, took a footstep toward him, and muttered, "I
just fell from the drugs. Overcome." She gasped for air, her hand
wielding the glass knife, which was discreetly tucked behind her
back.

"Are you okay?" Jim asked. He looked around at the shattered glass and perhaps a second too late understood.

"I fell. Looking for aspirin—"

The shiv was arcing upward into Jim's gut. Maeve felt the blade slice through his shirt, then gain purchase in the hardened muscles of his abdomen. She placed the bottom of her left hand beneath the butt of the blade, cushioned by her T-shirt, and used it to propel the sharp leading edge forward while her right hand guided it into his abdomen. Her left shoulder muscles screamed with agony as she pulled upward with all her might, like in a dead lift, trying to drive the glass fully into him. Rewarding her efforts was the presence of blood soaking his cotton shirt.

The momentum shifted, though. Jim's hands were pushing her elbows down. He had the leverage of height and strength, but she had determination. Her progress, measured by the growing plume of blood, slowed and then stopped immediately.

She kneed him in the balls as hard as she could. It wasn't the first time she had performed that maneuver on him. He gasped with an audible "Oomph" and released a bit of the pressure on her arms. The shiv had come free of his abdomen as his arms pushed and he backed away. When his head lowered in pain, she head butted him with her forehead, then high kicked him in the throat. He stumbled backward into the door and landed with a thud. His arms were splayed outward, as if he were lying on the ground, making snow angels.

Maeve charged him with the shiv and raised it high, going for the throat. She thrust downward with the ferocity of a baying animal. The bloody tip of the mirror shard stopped inches from Jim's throat. His hand clasped her wrist with the quickness and force of a rattlesnake. He peeled her arm away, and she knew the tide had shifted again. One of his hands controlled her wrist; the other was around her throat. She was gasping for air as she felt her wrist being bent backward, almost to the point of snapping. Jim lifted her by the neck against the bathroom wall so that her feet were inches off the floor. She felt herself losing consciousness from a lack of oxygen to her brain.

"Please," she whispered into his ear. His face was directly in front of hers. She could see the thick eyebrows and the dark beard. The menacing brown eyes, which had gone half lidded, the way they always used to do in Afghanistan.

"Just like Afghanistan, dear Maeve. Always liked it rough."

Her bloody T-shirt fell to the floor with the shiv, making a soft click.

"I would absolutely satisfy you right now, but I'm sorry," he said. "We've got a mission to complete. We need to get to work."

Jim lowered her to the floor, keeping one vise grip hand around her neck and the other around her wrist. He had closed the distance between them so that she could not get any leverage to knee or kick him. He leaned over and kissed her full on the mouth, his tongue braving a quick dart into her mouth before she could bite it, though she tried. A hollow click of the teeth mirrored her despair.

"You are going to sit down, and you are going to move that drill bit the way you moved it in Pakistan. You are going to take it farther than you have ever taken it before, and on the second hole you will perform an unprecedented second kickoff point. Then you are going to submerge the perforating charges, and you will detonate when and where you are told. Is that clear?"

Maeve nodded. Her throat was so constricted that she couldn't speak just yet.

"And then, if you behave, you just might see your family again."

The hollow pit in her stomach grew as she thought about Piper. Her only hope was that her young child was being well cared for by the Asian woman and that Piper would soon forget this experience, as if it were a vacation gone wrong that she would never understand.

Maeve limped to the chair in the control room. She placed her bloody hands on the joystick that controlled the drill. She looked up at the monitors. The McGuire and Brunswick nuclear plants were on a split screen. The drill path was etched in 3-D on another screen, and it showed the drill bit turning from the current point and passing under Jordan Lake for almost two miles at an azimuth of 298 degrees, northwest by north.

Deep breaths weren't enough to calm her nerves. She pushed back from the controls and looked at Jim, who had removed his shirt and was dressing his wound with her T-shirt.

"Close," he said, nodding.

"You're an asshole," she said. "And you've gotten yourself in way over your head."

"Nobody's as bad as people want them to be, and nobody's as good as they hope they can be. We're all about the same, dear Maeve. Maybe one degree of difference, but that's not so much, is it? Your line in the sand is just a notch higher than mine. Does that make you a much better person than me?"

"You shot me . . . and did other things to me. Yes, I would say that makes you a bad person."

"You just stuck a broken mirror in my gut. If it wasn't for my rock-hard abs, you might have succeeded. Good thing I didn't miss my Pilates workout this week. So are we really that different?"

Maeve said nothing. Her mind was cycling through ways she could beat him. The starting center for the NC State soccer team during her college days, Maeve had an unapologetic drive to be the best at everything she did. Her competitive nature was overshadowed only by her genuine love of her family and her country.

"We all do what we have to do when we are backed into a corner, Maeve. You saw that in Afghanistan as well as anyone else. You participated in it. I know you're not proud of what we did over there, but we did it, nonetheless."

"Shut up," Maeve whispered. "We swore we would never discuss that."

"And we shall not. It would be troublesome for all of us and our country if word leaked of our transgressions."

"I said, 'Shut up.' Stop it. I'll do what you need me to do. Steal some gas. No big deal."

"Now we're talking." Jim had tied her T-shirt in the knot around what amounted to a deep flesh wound. He had staunched the bleeding for the most part. He stood next to her and pointed at the drill screen. "The water is ready. The power is ready. The kick-off point has been prepped. Now you need to guide us to this shallow but very rich gas field."

"It's just below Jordan Lake? Aren't you worried about the aquifer?"

"We are not concerned in the least about the aquifer, because we have the very best drill handler doing this job," Jim said. "We waited for you, and now you're here. So let's get to work. Once I flip this switch, the nuclear threats go live. Ready?"

Maeve looked at the screen that was showing the 3-D view of the drill path, like a slice of cake with its different layers. She saw the shale formation that they were going to rob. It looked dense and rich, full of gas deposits and maybe even oil. The Durham Triassic Basin was notorious for its shallowness and proximity to drinking water. Something about the map did not seem right to her, but she couldn't place it. She felt as if she was looking at a satellite shot from the wrong angle, and it was challenging to get her bearings. Her drilling in Afghanistan had always had a certain rhythm to it.

Then she looked at the live streaming video of the crew at the drill location. Maeve had no concept of whether she was on loca-tion or miles away. The remote drill techniques they had per-fected in Afghanistan could place her up to fifteen miles away from the actual drill. Oddly, she didn't notice any pipe for the natural gas once it surfaced. Certainly, they could seal the well-head, but with the number of veins they were talking about tap-ping, the pressure would be enormous, too much for any single wellhead to handle. It would burst, and the gas would be lost. She had heard murmurs at the party about celebrating a new pipeline to Morehead City, but her camera angle did not show where that might connect to the wellhead.

Then she saw the rest of the picture. In the corner were several containers. While natural gas usually required substantial refine-ment to eliminate impurities and liquids, her work in combat had resulted in the development of containerized natural gas process-ing plants. She recognized the mobile containers, mirror images of the ones they had perfected in Afghanistan. The only question now was, where was the pipeline? What did they intend to do with the gas? Maeve was an engineer, and these questions came to her naturally. Despite the stress she was enduring, her analytical mind calculated the end-to-end system and recognized that something was missing. Once refined, how were they going to get the gas to market? Not her problem, she knew, but the answer could provide insight into her predicament. Maybe it was the pipeline to the port of Morehead City, on the coast?

Jim flipped the switch. She continued to stare at the live feed of the work yard, where the drill cable and water lines went stiff. The drill head would spit out water to cool the bit and help with the drilling process. If he had stolen the equipment they had used in Afghanistan, there would be a five-pointed titanium-uranium mix drill bit connected to composite drill lengths, which made for faster and more accurate drilling.

Maeve sighed and focused. Nudging the joystick forward, she watched the icon on the screen move toward the vein. She eventually became one with the stick and the drill, moving along the path as if she were down there herself. Like a pilot, she began flying the drill bit around the obstacles represented in the 3-D image.

But she knew that she was not a pilot and that this was not a game.

"Don't stop. That's all I'm saying, Maeve. This is serious business. And in case you get any more ideas, I've got all my notes from Afghanistan. The ones where I overheard you speaking with our interpreter, plotting these terrorist attacks and stealing natural gas in North Carolina."

"What!"

"Be quiet, please. I'm trying to protect you from yourself. You're in this neck deep, Maeve."

Maeve controlled a sob as she pressed the drill bit forward. She closed her eyes and tried to feel the power, the way a fighter jock became one with his machine. She continued, seeking the best path forward toward the finishing point, staying within the margins of error calculated by Jim's "guy."

We've got a guy.

What was going on? she wondered. Why all the secrecy? She imagined that Throckmorton Energy Company was out in front of the state regulations, probably didn't have their permits, and might not own any land with mineral rights. If she was reading the map correctly, Throckmorton's property was right on the edge of Wake County, and not in Chatham County, where the true reserves waited to be tapped.

Millions of dollars of gas lay below the surface, but was the juice worth the squeeze? Jim and his father were committing the felony crime of kidnapping a woman and a child for natural gas. Something didn't seem right. The crime was too small for the punishment that would surely come their way.

Staring at the monitor, she wondered about the conversation she had overheard when Jim drugged her. The Chinese voice had seemed to be the most authoritative of them all. Were the Chinese in charge of this operation? she wondered.

Since she had just returned from Afghanistan, geopolitics was not lost on her. She knew that the United States was nearly a trillion dollars in debt to China.

We've got a guy.

Was she the only hostage, she wondered, if China was indeed running this operation?

CHAPTER 14

MAHEGAN HELD MAEVE CASSIDY'S NAME TAG IN HIS HAND, A TANgible clue that she had been there. It had been well hidden, as if she had purposefully left a sign.

He followed the ridge to the swampy area again, noticing the workers had made decent progress. There would be no going back to the detention cell in the daylight. Sadly, Petrov, or whoever was in charge, would most likely blame the workers for breaking into the cell. Their fate would most likely not be good.

Mahegan followed the stream north, walking parallel to the fracking location where the workers were completing the fence. He found an isolated spot about a quarter mile north of the saddle with the drill head, where he had fought Petrov, and noticed a full drilling rig was standing tall, like a mini Eiffel Tower. It took some effort to see it, but it was there. He saw the iron roughnecks connecting the drill pipe as the drill bored into the ground. The machinery lifted and fell in rhythmic grunts, guiding the drill into the ground. The operation was under way.

With afternoon clouds drifting lazily overhead, Mahegan decided to follow his unsuccessful assassins' GPS to the address listed as "home." He navigated his way through the forest lining the stream until he saw that he was approximately parallel to the GPS street address. There were no visible roads, but he was below any reasonable sight line. He knew some of this terrain from his runs to Jordan Lake along the firebreaks. Except for the stream to his rear, the land rose in all directions. The hilltop to his ten o'clock was large and, he suspected, the most likely candidate for an operation of this size.

Stepping through the dense underbrush, Mahegan dodged a few timber rattlers and unsuspecting foxes. He was surprised at the number of quail he saw flocking near the edge of the forest. He spotted several doves that were darting low and fast, their angular bodies slipping through the air like stealth jets. No matter his domain, he fancied himself an apex predator, yet he maintained an immense respect for wildlife.

It was usually the humans he had the most issues with. His mother had taught him to respect nature, which was consistent with his Native American lineage. Every animal was to be respected, even if he had to kill it for food. He thought about the red wolves with which he had bonded in the Alligator River National Wildlife Refuge when he first returned from combat. He missed them like he missed family.

Hearing the rumble of a vehicle to his twelve o'clock, he followed the sound as it moved from his right to his left, toward the big hilltop. *Never a good idea to conduct reconnaissance in the daylight,* he thought again. He mentally recorded his location, then retraced his steps back to his vehicle. That trek took him an hour, putting him into the late afternoon as he drove back toward the town of Apex, where he lived.

He pulled into a shopping center and placed the battery in the burner phone. He had three text messages from Grace.

Need to talk asap.

Where r u???

Call me!!!

Mahegan typed in a short note.

Date booth. 5:00 p.m.

Instantly Grace shot back a text.

Okay!!!

Mahegan plugged the directions to the Cassidy home into his classified smartphone GPS and followed them through multiple suburban neighborhoods. Mahegan was glad that he did not have a life that required living somewhere like this. He was too damaged to settle into such an everyday rhythm, though maybe someday he could.

His goal now was to have a brief conversation with Maeve's husband, Pete Cassidy, and then meet Grace to warn her about her phone. As he was following the last direction of the GPS, he noticed Griffyn's Crown Victoria speeding past him, the tires smoking and squealing beneath the sharpness of the turn and the vehicle's acceleration. He did not believe the detective had seen him, but he couldn't be sure. Mahegan slowed his Cherokee and watched as the car snaked its way out of the neighborhood.

Processing what he had just seen, Mahegan parked his vehicle in front of a respectable brick-veneer colonial in the suburban neighborhood. There were similar homes packed in tight around it. Yards were small but well kept. He noticed there were few trees and guessed this had been farmland at one time. The driveway was empty, but the windowless two-car garage door was closed.

Walking up the driveway and stepping onto the brick and cement porch, Mahegan listened as if he was in combat, with a lull in the shooting, sensing what might come next. He couldn't hear footsteps, a television, or a radio. The intermittent squeals of children playing in the neighborhood rang through the air like birdcalls. In contrast, this house was deathly quiet. Mahegan would have expected a police cruiser or ongoing protection, given Pete's wife's status and the fact that they had a daughter together. Maybe that was Griffyn's duty. Or maybe he had driven by and noticed there was no protection, so he was racing off to coordinate a detail. But that didn't make any sense to Mahegan, because the smart play would have been to remain in place and sync the detail over the radio.

He pressed the doorbell, which chimed loudly. He heard no movement and pressed again. Looking down, he saw a seam between the door and the jamb. When he pulled open the storm door, it was obvious to him that someone had crowbarred the front door open. Mahegan immediately thought of the EB-5 home invasion teams. They were crude and basic. A crowbar would have been their tactic.

Mahegan removed his captured Glock 17 from his coat and pushed his shoulder against the freestanding door. Looking left, he saw a dining room, which led to a kitchen. To his front was a stairway that led upstairs. To his right was a family room with a television. Nothing seemed immediately out of order, except the door that had been jimmied.

Clearing the first floor was quick. It was a small house. In the garage he saw a blue Chevrolet Malibu. He stepped forward and placed his hand on the hood. Stone cold. Turning back into the mudroom, he found a stairway that led to a playroom over the garage. The floor was littered with stuffed animals, other toys, and children's books.

And Pete Cassidy's dead body.

Cassidy had a hole in the center of his forehead, and he had fallen backward when he died.

Next to Cassidy were a blanket and a stuffed animal. Three books were on the near side of his feet. Plastic toys were scattered on the far side.

Mahegan looked down and saw large footprints with the cloverleaf imprints of combat boots. Mahegan had the horrible thought that Pete Cassidy had been holding his daughter when a competent marksman shot him in the forehead. The child would have fallen to the floor and most likely would have cried as the home invasion team scooped her up.

Mahegan had to admit that the EB-5 commandos were omnipresent and kept the pressure on like a basketball team's full-court press. Everyone associated with this operation was being pushed, and only where Mahegan had intervened, as far as he knew, was there success in breaking down the security.

What is Maeve Cassidy's secret? Why is she at the center of this thing? Mahegan wondered. He cleared the remainder of the top floor, including two guest bedrooms, a guest bath, and a master bedroom with a large bath. He saw Maeve's gear spread all over the bed, dumped and searched by the invasion team, no doubt. The items were familiar to Mahegan: T-shirts, uniforms, boots, helmet, body armor, and knickknacks to remind a soldier of home, such as family photos.

A four-poster rice bed was the central piece of furniture, and it was complemented by a matching dark-wood bureau and a chest of drawers. They weren't rich, Mahegan thought, but were doing okay. He pawed through the gear, noticing multiple rubber bands, and saw that the clothes had once been professionally rolled and packed for the tightest possible fit.

He sat on the bed and thought about Maeve Cassidy. Who was she? he wondered. *A geologist, a soldier, a mother, and a wife.* She had found her husband in bed with another woman, which indicated to Mahegan that perhaps the problems had begun prior to her re-deployment. After a year in combat she had most likely had her fill of geology and rocks and shale formations. Their daughter, Piper, would be who she missed the most and would be the most significant point of leverage that anyone could bring to bear against her.

Was the child kidnapped, also, as insurance? Mahegan wondered.

The bedroom nearest the master was the child's room. Each wall was painted in a different pastel color. A twin bed ran across the far wall, beneath the window, and a white chest of drawers faced the bed from the opposite wall. An open chest full of toys and games sat next to the closet door. Pictures lined the night-stand next to the bed, as well as the chest of drawers. The word *Piper* was spelled out on the wall above the bed in twelve-inch stuffed cloth letters that alternated pink and purple and hung askew.

Mahegan studied each picture, as if to determine when and where it might have been snapped. Most were of Piper at various stages of her infancy and youth. Some included Maeve and Pete.

Only one included just Maeve and Piper. The picture must have been taken immediately prior to her deployment, Mahegan thought. Maeve was forcing a smile, while Piper was obliviously grabbing at her mother's ear. He studied the woman for a moment. She had auburn hair, soft eyes, and a warm, reflective smile. Mahegan also saw toughness in the countenance, which perhaps others might miss. The child's pink and blue outfit contrasted sharply with the olive digitized pattern of Maeve's Army combat uniform. She was a soldier preparing to do her duty, and that counted for a lot with Mahegan.

He noticed the picture was slightly scored and bent, while also being too small for the frame, which was also marred.

In his early days as a paratrooper, Mahegan had carried a picture of his mother in his helmet. Many soldiers did this so that they were only a quick flip of the hands away from home, and it was not uncommon to see someone staring into the middle of a helmet, as if it were a time travel portal. Once his missions became highly classified, he had sanitized his entire uniform, tacking his mom's photo on the wall of his locker in the base camp.

To Mahegan, this picture looked like a helmet photo. He carefully removed the backing, which he could already see was improperly placed in the frame, as if done in a rush. He used a fingernail to lightly remove the waffled cardboard piece between the stand and the photo. As he withdrew the photo from the frame, he saw the handwriting and knew it would be significant.

Turning the photo horizontally, he saw the faded outline of a drawing that looked similar to the pyramid on the back of a one-dollar bill, complete with floating eye. It was a rough sketch with no detail, a draftsman's outline. Beneath the base of the pyramid was the phrase *PiperCub2012*. The ink was more recent than the photo. The letters and lines weren't smeared, and they seemed to have been drawn on top of the smudges and the minor stains on the back of the photo paper.

He pocketed the photo, unsure of its relevance, if any. But to Mahegan, it seemed like a deliberate clue. He recalled the name tag he had found earlier, stuffed in the corner of that cell. Maeve Cassidy was trying to signal something to someone.

Next to where the picture had been was what Mahegan recognized as a soldier's shower kit, open and obviously pawed through. He pulled apart the opening and studied the contents: toothbrush, nearly empty tube of toothpaste, stick deodorant, disposable razor, tweezers, and two tampons. Next to the shower kit was a small bottle labeled HENNA. He lifted the henna bottle, unscrewed the top, and saw that it was powder extract from the plant. Mahegan knew that tribal leaders in Afghanistan often used henna to darken their beards or line their eyes, much like women applied make-up.

Mahegan also pocketed the henna, realizing that he had burned too much time in the house with his Cherokee parked out front and a dead body in the playroom. He put the picture frame back together and slid it into a bureau drawer after wiping it down with one of Piper's small shirts. He folded the shirt and replaced it in the bureau. Mahegan traced his steps out of the house, wiped down the doorknob, returned the door to its original position, and walked down the steps, where an attractive woman with a small child in tow was awaiting him.

"Anything going on in there?" she asked.

Mahegan flipped his badge and showed her his creds. "Just a routine check," he said.

"Ain't nothing routine about what I'm hearing. Swingers' parties, wife swapping, and all that." She eyed Mahegan. "You involved in any of that?"

"No, ma'am, and I have to get moving. You have a wonderful day."

Mahegan heard the little boy ask, "Mama, what's a swingers' party?"

Mahegan drove to the Irish Pub, retracing Griffyn's route out of the neighborhood instead of his own entrance. He found himself on a parkway that ran parallel to his original route of entry. Seeing nothing, he doubled back toward the pub, thinking.

As he was navigating from the shattered remnants of the Cassidy home, Mahegan cycled through his thoughts. Reasonably certain that the EB-5 commandos had killed Pete Cassidy, Mahegan wondered if Griffyn had found the body. And if he had, why hadn't he established a crime scene? Also, who had taken Piper, and where was she?

He saw Grace's car in the parking lot, shut down his Cherokee, and walked into the dimly lit pub.

"You go first," he said.

"Nice to see you, also," she replied. He forgot that she had an anticipation of social pleasantries, despite the mission at hand, even under pressure. Perhaps, especially under pressure.

"Yes. It's good to see you." And it was. She seemed relaxed and confident. She wore a black V-neck top that accentuated her slender neck. "How was your day, dear?"

"Much better, Hawthorne. You're trainable."

"Seriously, in about five minutes two foreign men are going to come through this door and attempt to kill us. This thing has gone completely off the rails. Your phone is tapped. Ted or somebody put a locator on there, and they've got spyware. They found my apartment because I was curious and left my phone on. They also have a Stingray, which basically let them see the texts between us, find my number, and then find a way to track my phone. That part I haven't gotten figured out yet. So we need to get moving."

"You're serious." Grace's face had gone pale.

"As a heart attack."

"Which you're giving me. My big news was that Griffyn thinks he's got something on your fingerprints on the door. He'll try to lie to you about the time difference, but it's all smoke and mirrors."

"Even more the reason to get moving. I just saw Griffyn, by the way. He's a complicated man. Hand me your phone."

She slid it across to him. Mahegan twisted it with his bare hands, snapping it in two. He pulled the SIM card from the slot and yanked the battery out of the chassis. Walking out of the pub, Mahegan tossed the detritus in a Dumpster. They had both parked in the back of the pub, and as they rounded the corner, he saw another black pickup truck nosing into the same part of the parking lot.

"Down," he said. Fortunately, they were near the Dumpster, and Mahegan pushed Grace into the wall, shielding her with his body. He had an oblique view of the action, and as he had expected, two Slavic men stepped from the truck and walked hurriedly around the far side to the front of the pub. Mahegan said, "Stay here."

He walked to the pickup, opened the driver-side door, popped the hood, and ripped the wiring harness for the spark plugs from the engine. He shut the hood and then quickly moved to the outside back corner of the pub, with his back to the wall.

Mahegan let the first man pass and clotheslined the second one with a linebacker-style tackle. He felt the man's windpipe give a bit. By the time the first man turned around, Mahegan was on him. Two straight rights across the man's face stung him. Mahegan spun him around and slammed his face into the hood of the truck, denting the metal. Shifting his attention to the second man, Mahegan lifted him on his back and threw him into the bed of the truck. He grabbed wallets, cell phones, and GPS devices. He lifted the other man into the back of the truck, and they both lay there, unconscious but not dead. Mahegan would have preferred dead, but they were in public. He hoped he wouldn't regret his decision.

He raced to the other side of the building, saw Grace huddled in the corner by the Dumpster, grabbed her hand, and hustled her into his Cherokee.

"What the hell is going on? It's like that zombie movie. They're everywhere."

"No. They're very specifically focused on people who can interrupt their operation. Look at these wallets," Mahegan said, handing them to Grace. "Here's the deal. You follow me in your car to my place."

"I thought you said your place was compromised."

Mahegan stared at her a minute. He had never said the word *compromised*. *Compromised* was a military term meaning "unsecure." He found it unusual that she would use that term, but let the moment pass and said, "Yes. They found my place using your phone. Whoever is in charge dispatched a team, but they're no longer with us."

"What the hell?"

"As long as we keep batteries out of phones, we can breeze

through my place and then keep on the move. I need to secure some equipment."

She quickly perused the wallets. "You're right. EB-Five from Serbia."

"I have a theory which we can discuss tonight. Get in your car and follow me."

Grace jumped out of the Cherokee and slid into her own car. Mahegan gunned his SUV. He wasn't sure, but he didn't think anyone had seen the two minutes of action in the back parking lot. It was still early in the evening, and unless a cook was on a smoke break, which was entirely possible, they were clear.

Fully expecting Griffyn to be either following him or waiting for him at his apartment, Mahegan was relieved that no such confrontation was imminent. Grace pulled her vehicle in next to his in the barn, and he shut the swinging barn doors. They ascended the interior steps to his apartment, where he unlocked the door. Several of the anti-intruder devices were still intact, such as the Scotch tape across the door frame, the thin string at ankle level, and the combination lock on the door.

He swung the door open, and they entered his apartment, which was untouched from when he had left it earlier. He locked the door, removed the rifle, ensured it was loaded, and sat on the bed.

"What have we gotten ourselves into?" Grace asked. She sat next to him on the bed.

Mahegan stood and moved the breakfast table next to the bed, along with both chairs. He spread all his booty on the bed and the table. In one bag there were the cell phones with the extracted batteries and SIM cards, the wallets, and the weapons from the Turks who invaded Grace's home. He also had a GPS device from Petrov's vehicle and his Blackberry. He laid out the smartphones, wallets, and GPS device from the two men he had shot this morning, as they were approaching the Robertson household. Next came the equipment from the two men he had just knocked unconscious in the back of the Irish Pub. Removing the identification cards from all of the wallets, he laid them out on the table like a blackjack dealer.

"Two Turks. Two Russians. Two Serbs. All hit men. All twenty-one years old or under. All relative amateurs, but with enough balls to try to do the job. Glock 17s, disposable cell phones, and GPS devices. Tools of the trade and indicators of their mission—to enforce. They enforce with the weapons, communicate with the phones, and find their way around unfamiliar territory with the Garmins. The Garmin GPS devices all have a spot on the Wake and Chatham County borders as their 'home' location. I was at that location today. They're digging a fracking well."

Mahegan watched Grace, studying her for a tell, or a sign that she already knew what he was telling her. Instead, all he noticed was a mixture of fear and confusion etched on her worried face.

Mahegan stood and said, "You said my place was compromised. That's a military term, not a civilian one. It was an odd thing for you to say."

"Is that a question?" Grace countered, standing.

"It's a statement. The question is, can I trust you?"

"I've been wondering the same thing about you. I've given you information that is helpful to you personally and to this case. I've jeopardized my job to help you. What have you done for me?"

"Other than save your life, not much," Mahegan said.

Grace's defensive posture softened, and her body went slack. "I'm so used to fighting with Ted that I automatically attack instead of talk. I'm sorry. You did save my life, and I'm grateful for that. You defended me when you barely knew me. That counts hugely." She walked to the window and looked into the fading evening. Through the window Mahegan saw the sun setting into the line of trees beyond the Robertson house.

"So my place was compromised. It's a true statement, but a military one, not a civilian one."

Grace turned from the window and walked toward Mahegan. "I'm a forensic expert. Evidence gets compromised. Crime scenes get compromised. It's a common term in the business. You have your language. We have ours. Sometimes the terms overlap."

Mahegan studied her face. She looked him directly in the eyes as she spoke and gave no signs of parsing or dishonesty.

"Okay. I had to ask."

"Your antennae are way up, but I understand," Grace said. She was inches from him, inside his personal space, which he didn't mind. Not at all. But he also didn't need the distraction of an alluring woman. She was exotic and beautiful. *Not fully Japanese, but more Polynesian*, Mahegan thought.

"Roger. Can I see your wallet?" Mahegan asked, pointing at her backpack.

Grace paused, then laughed. "You're serious?"

"I'm serious."

"Why didn't you just go through it when I wasn't here? I left everything except my car keys."

"Wasn't my place to do so. I'm a straight shooter. If we can't talk like this, then we have no business talking at all," Mahegan said.

Grace walked over to the kitchenette, picked up her backpack, and dumped it on the bed with the EB-5 bounty.

"Toss me in with the rest of them, though I was born in San Francisco and moved here with my parents, who work in Research Triangle Park."

Mahegan opened the purse he found in the backpack and pawed through the licenses and other identification cards. She had a North Carolina–issued driver's license and all the appropriate badges to allow her into the Raleigh Police Department headquarters. She seemed legit, but she was glaring at him.

"You can get mad. Doesn't bother me," Mahegan said.

"Well, this sure as hell bothers me!"

"I'm sure it does, but I have to do it. I go with my gut, and I got hung up on the term *compromised.* Just one of those things. You're legit. My bad."

"That's it. You're bad?"

"We need to talk about all this," Mahegan said, waving his arm across the bed and table. "Minus your stuff."

Grace had crossed her arms and shifted her weight so that one foot was forward from the other, a thinking pose.

"What about you? Let me see *your* stuff," she demanded.

Mahegan paused, thinking *fair enough*. He went to his desk drawer and removed his full pack of "Hawthorne" credentials he had removed from his safe this morning. They were in a manila folder and included an ersatz passport and birth certificate.

"She pawed through the folder and Mahegan realized, a second too late, that he had placed in the folder that picture of his father he had taken from Throckmorton's house two weeks ago.

"What's this?" Grace asked, as Mahegan firmly removed the folder and picture from her hands.

"My credentials," he said.

"No, the picture. That's what I mean."

"That picture is none of your concern," he said. "But this one is."

Mahegan withdrew from his pocket the photo he had removed from Piper Cassidy's room and showed it to her, happy to change the topic away from the Throckmorton photo of his father. "Here."

She stepped forward and took the picture from Mahegan. "This is her? Maeve? And her baby, Piper?"

"Yes, but the important part is on the back. And her husband is dead."

"Dead? As in killed dead? Or heart attack dead?"

"Murdered. Shot in the forehead. Probably while holding the child."

She looked at the image of Maeve and Piper Cassidy, mother and daughter. "My God. And now her husband and her father is dead," Grace said, pointing at each face.

Both mother and daughter had chestnut hair. Piper's was still in the reddish-brown phase, while Maeve's had taken on a darker shade. Their facial features were similar, especially the eyes: copper irises flecked with thin bands of amber, which made them look alive with excitement. *Electrical* was the word that came to Mahegan's mind as he stared at the images.

"Okay. You're frigging forgiven. I understand the stakes here, I think," Grace said. She pushed at Mahegan and said, "Asshole."

Mahegan turned to Grace and said, "Look at the back. The picture she drew."

Grace studied the drawing and said, "It's kind of random. The dollar-bill pyramid with the mystical floating eye."

"The term below that is what has me intrigued. It's like an e-mail address, but not quite." Mahegan pulled the bottle of henna extract from his pocket. "Found this in Piper's room, next to the picture and a shower kit."

"Henna? Like the tattoos?"

"Never thought of that. It's mostly used to darken men's hair and beards in Afghanistan."

Grace lifted her wrist with the Latin phrase *Esse quam videri* written in small cursive letters. "Remember? In two weeks I'll replace this with some famous Hawthorne quote, I'm sure, but this is henna."

"I do now, but maybe she was trying to dye her hair? To run away if she felt she was in that much danger? It was in the child's room, so perhaps she was doing that for both of them."

He watched Grace process his theory. "She changes her hair, she's still got the same issues. Someone is after her, and she has to care for Piper. A disguise doesn't buy her much."

"I found this, also," Mahegan said, removing the nametag and handing it to her. "In a wooden cell on the Chatham County line."

Her eyes darted from the cloth strip to Mahegan's eyes and back. "She's alive."

"Not necessarily, though I believe that. All this means is that her uniform was in that cell. But you're right. It's a good sign."

"And something else," Grace said. "This tells me she leaves clues. She's trying to communicate. Work with me, but this is what I do. I study evidence and draw conclusions."

"Okay."

"Henna is all the rage for tattoos nowadays. The drawing is a clue. The *PiperCub* phrase is a clue. So we need to think through what she's saying. What is she telling us?"

Mahegan looked out of the window. He saw treetops, the rooftop to the Anderson home, a long winding gravel driveway, and steam lifting from the Shearon Harris Nuclear Power Plant in the distance.

"*PiperCub2012* obviously refers to her daughter and the year she was born," Grace added.

Mahegan could see Grace was on another azimuth.

"Yes, that's clear, but what about this user name?" She went to the laptop and typed in a common address lookup function, then typed in "PiperCub2012." The search engine spun for a few seconds, and then she proclaimed, "One result in Cary, North Carolina!"

Mahegan watched her fingers click across the keyboard. Raising her hands in triumph, as if she'd scored a touchdown, Grace proclaimed, "Bingo! It's an Instagram account, according to this investigation account I use."

Mahegan knew that Instagram was an application where people could upload pictures, but that would require a password. Recalling the picture, he lifted it and looked at the back. There was a line underscoring *PiperCub* and an arrowhead pointing to the left.

"On Instagram now," Grace said.

"I think it's this simple," Mahegan said. "Try *PiperCub* spelled backward."

Grace looked at him, he showed her the back of the photo, and she nodded.

"Worked. We're in. Oh my God."

Mahegan leaned over Grace's shoulder and looked at the image on the screen.

"It's like a dollar-bill pyramid," Grace said.

"Numbers along each leg of the triangle," Mahegan said, pointing.

"She makes a henna tattoo with a clue or series of clues in it?"

"Her mission was sensitive. They probably checked everything but the one thing they really couldn't check, her body."

"She's got some rockin' abs," Grace muttered.

The picture was obviously a selfie. The angle of the camera, probably a smartphone, was askew, but the quality of the photo, Mahegan had to admit, was good. Even her handiwork was precise, and Mahegan was reminded that she was a scientist, accustomed to neatness and order. The dark orange tattoo was a rough facsimile of a pyramid, with neatly drawn bricks inside the triangle upon which the floating eye rested. Along each of the legs of the triangle was a set of numbers.

"Write these numbers down. Here," Mahegan said, pointing.

Grace scribbled each of the numbers on a piece of paper, then went to work on the keyboard. "I'm changing this password to make it harder to do what we did," she said.

"Print the picture, too," Mahegan directed.

She quickly hit PRINT, and his printer whirred to life via bluetooth, then spit out a fair-quality photo of the tattoo.

He retrieved the picture, studied it for several minutes, and then placed it in his safe.

"I'm guessing numbers. Numbers are usually things like safe combinations, phone numbers, building addresses. That kind of thing," Grace said.

"Addresses," Mahegan said.

"Three ten-number addresses?"

"She's a geologist. Try latitude and longitude."

Grace sat down and punched the Google Earth button, then typed in the first ten-digit number. They watched the globe spin until it provided an overhead view of the Brunswick Nuclear Plant, just south of Wilmington, North Carolina.

"Oh, damn," Grace muttered.

She typed in the next number, and the globe spun a short distance to the McGuire Nuclear Station, located just north of Charlotte, North Carolina.

"Double damn," she murmured.

"I can already tell you the third, but type it in, anyway," Mahegan said. He walked over to the window, looked at the steam drifting skyward. "Shearon Harris?"

"Shearon Harris. Triple damn."

The map coordinates were for North Carolina's three nuclear power plants.

"That explains the watch," Mahegan said. He pulled the watch he had found next to the nametape in the holding cell.

"What do you mean?"

"Three minutes to midnight." He showed her the face of the watch with the minute hand stuck three clicks from the twelve o'clock position. Grace shrugged.

"Every year the nuclear scientists get together and move the minute hand on the nuclear Armageddon clock based on their assessment as to how close the world is to nuclear disaster."

"Is three good or bad?"

"The closest it's ever been."

CHAPTER 15

Brand Throckmorton sat with his two partners in over-size burgundy leather chairs in a semicircle that faced the river-rock fireplace. Though the hunting lodge on his family property in western Wake County was the size of a small mansion, Throckmorton considered it a cozy place for them to enjoy the occasional cigar, scotch, or woman, whichever they preferred. He ensured there was an ample supply of all three. The fireplace faced them like a gaping mouth. It was over ten feet wide and was long enough to fit whole tree trunks, which it often burned. Clearing the rig site a half-mile down the hill had provided ample wood fuel supplies for years to come.

Throckmorton had decorated the place in a Civil War theme, given that there was an old Underground Railroad warren located on the property. An original 1853 Enfield three-band musket hung over the hearth, like a sentry keeping watch. One of Throckmorton's work crews had found the muzzleloader in a stream, and one laborer had attempted to pirate the treasure. Throckmorton had secured the rifle while dispatching a team to make sure the day laborer never returned.

Confederate flags dangled on either side of the mantel, which was made of wood he had refurbished from two carriages of twelve-pound Civil War cannons. The painting above the musket showed Sir Walter Raleigh with his boot on the neck of a Native American. Throckmorton rarely brought visitors to the lodge, so his decorating faux pas and historically clashing artifacts and art-work persisted without challenge. Neither of the Gunthers cared about the decorating as long as the cigars, booze, and women were available.

While there were no slaves burrowing their way to freedom on the property, there were a fair number of indentured servants working the land and anything else Throckmorton demanded. The problem with Throckmorton's family property was that none of the Durham sub-basin was directly beneath it. But Throckmorton had devised a plan. The Department of Commerce had approved a jobs scheme for him and then he had received approval for an EB-5 program for the gas well. Originally billed as an energy project to create three hundred jobs in Wake and Chatham County, Throckmorton's plan had pegged his target at twenty-five million dollars. He needed just twenty-five international investors to pony up one million dollars apiece or—and this scenario was less desirable—a greater number of investors to give five hundred thousand to one million dollars each. Of course, there was a 10 percent markup on each contribution, which equated to a cool two and a half million dollars at the outset.

The U.S. State Department had then issued the visas to whomever the contributors wished, as long as they were family members. "Like Abscam," Throckmorton had once said, "only legal." Abscam was the infamous FBI sting that captured U.S. politicians taking bribes in exchange for securing visas for Saudi Arabian nationals. It was such a good idea that today it was a formal program that incentivized foreign direct investment.

Throckmorton had courted a special clientele that could secure his compound, including this hunting lodge; women who could provide special "services"; and men who could manage the gas well. His goal was to steal every bit of the Durham sub-basin shale deposits and move the gas along the newly constructed pipeline within the North Carolina Railroad right-of-way, all the way to the port of Morehead City, where Petrov would have Russian tankers waiting to ship the gas. The only real issue was the low price of natural gas in relation to other energy commodities.

Throckmorton's study of fracking in Texas had proven that perseverance and cutting corners paid off. If he could go shallow with the drill on the edge of the shale formation, then he would go sideways into the vein, moving the drill in and out at ten-degree intervals. He would use the explosives to fracture the shale in multiple locations across the miles of compressed fossil fuels and then suck all the natural gas out from under the property owners in Chatham County.

Thinking of the drilling made him think of Maeve Cassidy, their expert driller.

"So is she doing what we need her to do?" Brand Throckmorton asked Jim Gunther. Throckmorton pulled at his ascot and looked at the others in the room. He considered himself a man of refined tastes, and his partnership with James and Jim Gunther had challenged that notion. He viewed them as ruffians, but nonetheless appreciated their skills.

"Adds new meaning to the term *wildcatter*," Jim said, rubbing his stomach where Maeve had cut him.

Throckmorton had seen Jim stumbling out of the control room and had ushered him quickly to the makeshift infirmary, where two of the nurses were cooling their heels, dressed more like the prostitutes that they were than the professionals that they wanted to be. Counting all the injured—the two Serbs, the two Turks, Petrov, and now Jim—Throckmorton knew that the medical team had used their learned skills more in the past two days than they had in the two months that they had been in America. And there were still two missing, causing him to wonder about the reliability of his crew. They had stitched and bandaged Jim's gut cut, which in the end looked worse than it actually was.

"Kick your ass, did she, boy?" James Gunther, Jim's father, said now.

Brand Throckmorton looked at Jim, who was rubbing his stomach.

"I'll be okay."

Throckmorton looked at the father-and-son team, thinking about his own son, Ted. Throckmorton liked to think of himself as the first North Carolina energy wildcatter and wanted to leave a grand legacy for his family. He had studied the oil barons of Texas along with George Mitchell, who had unearthed natural gas from the Barnett Shale north of Fort Worth. Throckmorton had grand visions of his name being linked to the Durham sub-basin in similar fashion. Mitchell had used a new trial-and-error technique called slick-water fracturing. Thanks to Jim Gunther, and now Maeve Cassidy, Throckmorton had his own Department of Defense–tested technique, complete with ill-gotten materials and outlawed special chemicals. Well, Throckmorton thought, they were okay for use in Pakistan and Afghanistan, but not in the United States. No biggie.

Executor of his family land along the western edge of Wake County, Throckmorton had asked himself, *How can I make a billion dollars?* He had found a way, he believed. Tired of being a mere millionaire by inheritance and now plagued with debt from lousy investments, Throckmorton had thought to couple the EB-5 foreign direct investment scheme with the burgeoning penchant for fracked natural gas in North Carolina.

He had needed labor and know-how, which was where James Gunther and Sons Construction came into play. Acquaintances at first, Throckmorton and Gunther had become business partners at Throckmorton's urging. The recession had been kicking Gunther's ass in the road-building business, and he had been sending Jim to score government contracts overseas. Suddenly, a generic request for proposals from the Department of Defense for an exploratory natural gas mission in Afghanistan had come through. In advance of submitting their proposal, Gunther had hired an African American veteran and had put him on their Web site. Then he'd filed with minority, small business, and veteran advantages. They had quickly drilled a few wells in Lee County to demonstrate "expertise" in the energy business. Loathe to choose Dick Cheney's Halliburton, the president's administration had steered the contract toward a business in North Carolina, where they needed the votes in the next election.

Throckmorton and Gunther won the Afghanistan contract,

and later Throckmorton code-named his endeavor Operation Isosceles, a cute moniker for fracking in the Triangle of North Carolina. They learned the cutting-edge trade secrets in Afghanistan first and then imported them back to North Carolina. The Department of Defense could put a lot of wind behind the sails of an effort if it wanted to, and without knowing, they certainly helped Isosceles.

Throckmorton took a long drag on a Cohiba cigar, looked at Jim, and asked, "Where's my son?"

Jim spun his baseball cap around so that it was facing backward on his head and kicked his leg over the arm of the worn burgundy leather chair. They were all drinking scotch and smoking cigars that had been imported directly from Cuba via one of the EB-5 clients.

"Heard he went surfing down at Wrightsville. Hurricane Muriel is churning in between Bermuda and the Bahamas, so it's supposed to be kicking up a decent swell."

Throckmorton looked at Jim and then at the fireplace. He felt his neck turn red all the way up past the ascot to the finely tapered layer of his black-dyed hair. His ascot covered his anger, but his words still held some bite. "We got all this going on right now, and he's surfing?"

"Sport of the kings, they say." Jim chuckled. "Me? I'm too worried about them giant sharks to do that crazy stuff."

"Can we get him over to check on the Morehead City port? That operation needs to come off without a hitch. We're putting about two million dollars into that sumbitch, so those boats need to be on time, or this whole thing is screwed."

"I can call him, but I'm not sure he's fully on board with all of this, to be honest with you, Mr. Throckmorton. Me and the Shred have had a few conversations, and he seems a bit squeamish."

Throckmorton stood, cigar in one hand, with an inch of ash, whiskey tumbler in the other. Its copper liquid leaned like the fluid in an off-center level.

"I cashed every chip I have. I blackmailed three board members of the North Carolina Railroad to get them to vote for the pipeline to Morehead City in their right-of-way. It is built. Everything is done but the connection from the railroad to here. So don't tell me my son's not on board!" The cigar ash fell to the floor like an exploding dot to an exclamation point. "He's staying on my yacht in Masonboro Inlet, banging UNCW chicks and surfing. Meanwhile, we are up to our ass in alligators, trying to manage all these workers Ting brought in, not to mention running the security company!"

"You put it that way, Mr. Throckmorton, I might drag my ass down to Wilmington," Jim said.

"Shut up, son," James Gunther said. A man of few words, the elder Gunther could still a room the way a corporate CEO could quiet his staff upon entry to a conference.

Throckmorton looked at Gunther. Unlike him, Gunther had a presence. He was a large man, over six feet tall. His shoulders were broad from shoveling tar and asphalt for decades as a line worker, then a manager, then as the owner of his company. Throckmorton knew that Gunther still worked his contracting jobs, paving, building, and fracking with his men. His face always carried a three-day stubble, which made him look beyond his sixty years. Gunther was the hick to Throckmorton's playboy.

Throckmorton had chosen him as a business partner for two reasons. First, he was adept at processing Immigrant Petition by Alien Entrepreneur applications for the EB-5 program. Second, his construction company could easily pivot to the fracking business. Gunther had drilled some vertical wells in Lee County.

For the EB-5 program, all Throckmorton had had to do was send Jim and Ted around the world with a tin cup, touting the fracking project. It was an easy sell. A *New York Times* bestselling book had just been released on the new billionaires in energy, and everyone wanted in on the action. Instead of American companies looking overseas for energy deposits, foreign investments were seeking to ride the new wave of energy in America.

Ted and Jim were a natural sales team. Both tall and handsome, Ted was the more refined executive, while Jim gave the appearance of a knowledgeable hands-on journeyman. Throckmorton had rehearsed them on their shtick, Ted as the marketer and Jim as the drilling expert. They had recruited talent from Russia, Serbia, Afghanistan, China, Japan, Turkey, and Saudi Arabia.

Throckmorton had taken three years to put his plan in place. He had collected the money, purchased some extra land for access to the railroad, and obtained for the "alien entrepreneurs" their EB-5 investor green cards. While the purpose of the EB-5 program was to create U.S. jobs, Gunther had been using illegal immigrant labor for so long that he was solely focused on importing healthy men to work the rig and do the necessary construction.

Throckmorton had decided that healthy young females might also prove useful. His son and Gunther's were agreeable, also; however, Ted had weakened. What Throckmorton didn't know now was if Ted was out of the picture altogether or just in one of his melancholy moods. He knew his son ranged from adrenaline seeker in the ocean during the day to author and poet by night. He had fallen for a woman who would not provide an agreeable bloodline for a family with their prominence. Unaccepting of Grace Kagami as a potential daughter-in-law, Brand Throckmorton was not opposed to her presence in general. She added to the ambiance of his soirees, not unlike the Balkan girls from the swingers' party the other night.

As if reading his mind, James Gunther Sr. asked, "You ever get out from underneath Griffyn and those dick wads?"

"They're scrambling all over the mansion, but I think I've got them under control. It's Ted I'm worried about."

"The Shred will be okay, Brand. Just let me work on him a bit," Jim said.

"*The Shred*," Throckmorton said as if he'd smelled dog shit, "is not focused. Banging that slope and writing poetry. He should be like you, working with his hands. Going to Afghanistan and vesting himself fully in this operation. You want to be part of a billion-dollar enterprise, you gotta put in some sweat equity."

"About right," James Gunther said. The elder Gunther ran a rough-hewn hand across his weathered face. His gray hair was cut close in an old-fashioned butch cut. He wore ten-year-old dunga-rees with oil, tar, and mud stains on them that wouldn't wash out. He filled out his flannel shirt, and at the V in the neck, a white crew-neck T-shirt was poking out. James Gunther Sr. was old school.

"I got this, Dad."

"Son, I have to agree with Throck here. He knows of what he speaks. Just like I would know if you was a damn pussy. So some-thing needs to be done about him. He thinks he's in for an easy one-quarter cut of this thing. But he ain't contributing. Sumbitch needs to contribute." He said the last word as three distinct sylla-bles: *con-tri-bute*, with an emphasis on the long *u*.

Jim fought back in an unusual display of opposition to his fa-ther. "He was always the one who was going to connect us from a logistics standpoint. The railroad pipeline and the trucks. He's working all that, to the best of my knowledge. And he helped get all the EB-Five guys. He was out there, all over the damn world, shaking down these guys."

"Damn fool is surfing today. He ain't working anything," Throck-morton said. "Ted the Shred my ass."

The elder Gunther stood, picked up his shotgun, and said, "I've had my share of fun. I'm going to check on them crazies down there by the rig and make sure they're behaving. Son, you need to get back down there and make sure that psycho does her job. We need all that basin fracked and flowing our way. To hell with a bunch of mineral rights." He spat tobacco from the cut of a new cigar into the fireplace, emphasizing his distaste for the law and anything that might get in his way.

"I got her," Jim said. "She's drilling."

"Make sure you ain't drilling *that* stuff until she's done. Got it? You need to bust a nut, plenty of Throck's green-card sluts are available. And when she *is* done, I got first dibs, you hear? Might get my machinery working again."

Jim nodded and grimaced. "Understood."

As Gunther started walking toward the door he stopped and said, "Hell's he doing here?" Then spat, "And with that other troll."

Throckmorton and Jim turned their heads and looked through the large bay windows. They saw a tall Asian man walking briskly to the front door, hands stuffed into the pockets of a black Windbreaker. Dark jeans covered lanky legs. Black hair fell across the man's forehead like a stringy mop. Behind him was a stocky man. They reminded Throckmorton of the old film *Skinny and Fatty*, except these two were Chinese, not Japanese, not that he cared. The heavyset man followed the taller man with short, squat steps that pushed outward, in contrast to the long forward strides of his companion.

"He knows better than to come up here without asking," Throckmorton said. "Especially to bring Chun with him."

Jim was up and moving toward the front door when it opened.

"Hey, man. Hold on now," Jim said, holding up a hand.

"We have serious problem," Johnny Ting said. Ting stood in the doorway. Chun stood behind him, hands stuffed in his pockets, like he didn't want to be there.

"You're damn right we do," Gunther said, leveling the shotgun at Ting.

"You no shoot me. I control twenty workers and ten women. We missing two workers, and four come back beat up. I bring Chun because he do the math, numbers guy. He did drill-path software. Now he do calculus on workers and schedules."

"Beat up? They get in a bar fight? Trying to go after some white snatch?" Gunther asked.

"Yes. Fight at bar. Irish bar, they say."

"Well, there you go. Four got their asses kicked, and two are hungover somewhere."

"We find empty truck on road. Everything missing. Two Russians nowhere to be found. Two Serbs and two Turks got ass kicked. All four, everything missing. I send them after woman, like you tell me," Ting said, looking at Throckmorton.

"So a woman kicked their ass? Kagami? I just wanted them to scare her so she did what Griffyn told her to do," Throckmorton said.

"Two missing. Four hurt bad. Down to fourteen. With drilling starting, we are not good."

When Ting spoke in his thick Chinese accent, Throckmorton could see his triangular tattoo jump above the neckline of his jacket. He wasn't sure what the symbol stood for, but he generally dismissed all tattoos as random mistakes that the owner wished he or she could erase.

"Can any of the women help out?" Jim asked.

Throckmorton coughed. "Let's not get crazy here, Jim. We have certain requirements."

Gunther spoke. "Take two of the women. Leaves eight for you, Throck. One a day, plus a backup. Like baseball. A designated hitter."

Ting's voice got excited. "Missing big picture. Someone hurting my men. My biggest, strongest men are gone. Chun has work schedule." Ting turned toward Chun, who nodded sheepishly.

"Work schedule not good without twenty men. Can get by with sixteen, but not fourteen. And Petrov is hurt," Chun mumbled. He spoke softly, almost in a whisper. The wind carried his voice inside the room, the words circling like a whispered warning.

"Give it twenty-four hours, Ting. Then we'll get worried. For now, nobody knows jack about what we're doing. Kagami was probably hanging with some dude, and your guys got stupid," Throckmorton said.

"My guys not stupid! Something going on! We follow phones to location in Apex, just up the road!" Ting pointed his finger at the ground. "Operation will stop if we don't stop it. Chun has numbers!"

Throckmorton sighed. "We don't need the drama right now, Ting. We'll look into your problem. We got them all green cards. They have phones and guns and GPS devices."

"And cash," Gunther added.

"And cash. That's right. We're paying them well."

"What I'm saying . . . everything gone. Even with the Russian. Petrov. Everything gone."

Throckmorton saw Gunther lower the shotgun. Behind Ting and Chun, he watched the sun dip into the hills west of Jordan

Lake. "So you're saying you're missing two men. Four have been badly injured. And then Petrov. So that makes seven."

"That's what I say. Almost half have been hurt," Ting said.

"Tell you what," Gunther said to Ting. "Have Petrov go find those Mexicans that helped him." Turning to Jim, he said, "I told you we didn't need the Mexicans, that we shoulda just used the green cards for the cell."

"Too much work to do, getting the rig ready, Dad. Plus, Petrov was the only one we felt we could bring in on that aspect of the project. You know that. The Mexicans were easy."

"Ain't nothing easy about nearly half our labor hurt, son."

Throckmorton felt waves of fear begin to rise in his stomach. Everything had been smooth sailing so far. Not a hitch. The hard part was over. Now he was losing his green-card workforce?

"Get the Mexicans," Throckmorton said. "All three of them."

"Only two Mexican," Ting replied. "Petrov said one was giant. White but not white."

"What the hell does that mean? Giant. White but not white?" Throckmorton countered.

"How he tell it," Ting said.

"Well, go find all three. Bring them in. Maybe they're the problem," Throckmorton replied.

"All three. I will go with Petrov. He scared." Ting turned on his heel and walked briskly toward the rig site a half-mile down the hill. Chun followed as best he could with his short steps.

Throckmorton thought about Petrov, who was big and powerful. The man had the flat eyes of a rabid dog. They had vetted him. He was former Spetsnaz, Russian Special Forces, and had also been an Olympic middleweight boxer for his country. After he'd earned a bronze medal, the Russian president had awarded him a small energy pipeline business guaranteed to provide him financial security. Petrov had grown that business in the face of competition from the monopolistic titans of Russian oil, until he woke up one day and found his financial security revoked. The president had given, and he had taken. Still, Petrov had received a green card from a blind-trust donor in Russia. Throckmorton figured it was one last favor for the mighty Russian boxer and Special Forces hero. Regardless, he was their go-to guy. He knew the energy business, he knew security, and he knew wet work.

Petrov scared? How could that be? Who could scare Petrov? Throckmorton looked at the two Gunther men. They didn't look concerned, so he tried not to show his fear. But this time his ascot could not conceal his emotions.

"Don't get your panties in a wad, Throck. We'll take care of this."

Throckmorton nodded. He certainly hoped so.

CHAPTER 16

"WHAT DOES THIS MEAN?" GRACE ASKED. THEY WERE SITTING on Mahegan's bed, staring at her MacBook Pro. She was leaning her shoulder into his arm to maintain her balance while she typed across the keyboard.

Mahegan was keenly aware of her scent, light and citrusy, like fresh air.

"I just got about ten texts from my group, telling me the rig is up and drilling is going on at the Throckmorton property," Grace said, looking at the screen of her iPhone.

"You have spies?"

Grace rolled her eyes. "What? You think you're the only one who can frigging pull off a combat mission? We've got people, most from the Chatham County side, who are looking at this thing. These are my girls. And before you ask, yes, I dated one of them. Anyway, they saw the rig stand up and are hearing drilling sounds. It's happening."

Mahegan liked the feel of Grace against him. Processing the intelligence he was receiving from her environmental group conflicted with desiring to wrap his arms around her. As always, though, the mission took precedence. Maeve Cassidy was being held captive, possibly to run a drill on Throckmorton's property. The left-behind nametape proved that she was there. She had drilled for a year in Afghanistan. Why else would they need her? What did the nuclear plants have to do with the entire affair? Why was the watch frozen at three minutes to midnight? And where was Piper Cassidy?

"How do these things connect?" Mahegan asked, nodding at the screen.

The monitor was showing three Google Earth latitude and longitude locations, indicating the three nuclear power plants. The McGuire Nuclear Station was just outside of Charlotte, which two million people called home; the Brunswick Nuclear Plant was just outside of the Wilmington area, where one million people called home; and the Shearon Harris Nuclear Power Plant was a mere fifteen miles south of North Carolina's famed Triangle Region of Chapel Hill, Durham, and Raleigh, where another two million people resided.

Five million people—that was half the state of North Carolina.

"My friends in the DFT-Two group think Throckmorton wants to provide more energy than the three nuclear plants combined. Look here." Grace pulled up a Web page that showed the oblong shape of the Durham sub-basin of the Triassic Rift that slashed diagonally across North Carolina's Piedmont. The entire rift ran over a hundred miles from Granville County in the north, along the boundary between Wake and Chatham Counties in the middle, to Moore County, north of the golfing town of Pinehurst. "This is the entire Durham shale sub-basin. If you can get the gas from this, you will be a rich man. Billions. Just like the Barnett Shale in Texas. Almost the same size as the natural gas section of the Barnett, as they call it in Texas."

Mahegan was not a student of energy production but had studied fracking to prepare for his day laborer job two days ago.

"Maybe Throckmorton sees the nuclear plants as competition that must be defeated," Grace continued.

Another gear caught in Mahegan's mind. Competition was something he understood, but his view had more to do with market forces.

"You make money from drilling for gas, retrieving it, storing it, and getting it to a refinery, or whatever they call it, for someone to buy, right?" he said.

"Essentially. Those are the basics. Yes."

Grace looked at him, her face inches from his. He saw the soft flutter of her eyelashes as she blinked. Her skin was perfectly smooth. Thick black hair fell in waves around her face. She smiled.

"What?" Mahegan was unusually distracted, but she was an unusually distracting woman. "Let's just try to finish this case up as quickly as possible," he said.

"That's it? No 'Your eyes are like shimmering moonlit ponds?'"

"No. More like the gateway to hell. Now, let's think this through."

She playfully shoved him with her shoulder, its firmness catching Mahegan on the defective ripped deltoid of his left arm. She noticed his wince.

"Did I hurt the big, strong man?"

"No. War injury. That's all." Mahegan refocused on the computer.

Grace rolled up his shirtsleeve, and he saw her stare at the eight-inch lazy Z scar left by Sergeant Colgate's vehicle blast. Above that was his black and gold Ranger tattoo.

Her hand came to her mouth. "Jeez. I'm such a screwup. Challenge your name, 'Hawthorne,' and then make fun of a no kidding war injury," she said. Her finger traced the marbled skin where the doctor had removed the metal from his shoulder. The Z cut into the deltoid, the biceps, and the triceps. He had been swimming to keep the shoulder in shape, but he knew it would never be 100 percent. It was just something he would have to deal with for the rest of his life.

At least he was alive, Mahegan thought. Grace's focus on his scar took him back to a place he didn't want to go: the hunt for the American Taliban, the capture of a bomb maker named Commander Hoxha, and the roadside bomb that had killed Wesley Colgate, his best friend.

"You're not going to tell me about that picture of your father, are you?" she whispered.

"No. Not right now, anyway."

He felt her lips on his arm, full and moist. She kissed the bottom of the scar, then the middle, and then the top. She ran her tongue along the arc of the Ranger tab tattoo.

"And we should concentrate," Mahegan said without much conviction.

"Yes, we should," she whispered. Her lips moved to his neck, and he felt her hand closing the MacBook and sliding somewhere behind them. Artfully, she slid her left leg over his pelvis and straddled him, now kissing him fully on the lips. "I'll convince you to one way or the other," she said in a hoarse voice.

He reached his hands behind her and pulled her body into his so that he could feel her heat on his abdomen. She worked her lips and tongue into his mouth in a slow, sensual manner. She *was* like art, Mahegan thought. Every sense came alive: the feel of her soft lips against his, the sweet taste of her tongue, the clean scent of her hair, the rapid sound of her breaths and moans, and the stimulating sight of her hands quickly removing their clothes. Every dimension and sense collided. While Mahegan knew he didn't have time for a romantic interlude, he gave in to the seductive pull of the moment.

Afterward, they were both breathing heavily and sighing from the release of the sexual tensions that had been building. Lying in bed, staring at Grace's face as she rested on his chest like a small animal warming on a river rock, Mahegan said, "Nuke power and gas don't really compete. One provides electricity, and the other provides heat. Your gas bill in the winter is higher than your electric bill. Conversely, your electric bill is much higher in the summer from pushing your air conditioner. Natural gas only indirectly competes with nuclear power."

Grace traced a finger on his chest and batted her eyes up at Mahegan. "You say the sweetest things," she whispered. "Makes me just a bit teary eyed. Truly."

Mahegan smiled as she rolled on top of him and did a push-up so she was staring him in the eyes.

"Yes?"

"Seriously? You want to talk about your light bill after the monkey sex we just had?"

"If you're going to call what we did 'monkey sex,' then yes, I would prefer to talk about my light bill. But if you're going to say, 'Hey, that was good. Let's do it again,' then I'm happy to talk about whatever you want."

Grace laughed, her lips pulling back against her perfect teeth. "You're a piece of work, Hawthorne." She kissed him again. "Rain check on round two. I have no doubt you're up to the challenge, so to speak. But we've got a tattoo to interpret and a mission."

They each pulled on various pieces of clothing, flipped over, and lay on their stomachs, staring at Grace's MacBook.

"Drilling has started. Cassidy is a geologist and is probably on their property, doing that drilling. Throckmorton doesn't have a permit to drill yet. He's got these EB-Five commandos enforcing and acting as roughnecks, working the drill yard. He has millions in foreign direct investments. They've most likely kidnapped Piper Cassidy. They're trying to kill you. And Maeve Cassidy memorized the numeric coordinates for the three nuclear power plants," Mahegan recounted. "And left them as a clue."

"One of which is just down the road from the fracking site," Grace said. "But really your point is a good one. They don't compete directly."

Grace's iPhone pinged.

"Elaine from Chapel Hill. She's my best friend," Grace said, looking at her phone. "Oh my God."

Mahegan looked at Grace, their eyes meeting.

"It's a link to an article about a town in Pakistan where hundreds of people have died from fracking chemicals in their groundwater. The town is along the Afghanistan border. The girls in DFT-Two have got this big conspiracy theory that the military was fracking in Afghanistan and Pakistan. We see all these LNG ships—that's liquefied natural gas—coming into the Wilmington and Morehead City ports, but they're not from the usual places. These are from Karachi."

Mahegan wrestled with the notion of telling Grace the information Savage had provided him during his brief call two days ago. That, in fact, Cassidy had been drilling and fracking along the Afghanistan-Pakistan border. But the operation was classified, and even though he now knew her intimately, that did not equate to trusting her with national secrets. Though, she seemed to have a good feel for the open source information available. Mahegan had seen the line between classified and unclassified blur over the years, particularly with the release of the WikiLeaks documents.

"What kind of chemicals?" Mahegan asked.

"All the standard fracking by-products," she said, continuing to read the article. She scrolled with her thumb, sliding the page up the screen every few seconds. "Hydrochloric acid, glutaraldehyde, ammonium persulfate, methanol, ethanol, boric acid, you name it. There are over fifty chemicals, and most companies won't tell you what they use."

"They pump that into the ground?"

"Yes. There are dozens of documented cases where those solutions have leaked into the aquifers of other states, the water tables where we get our drinking water."

Mahegan processed the information. His crash course on fracking, coupled with what General Savage had told him about Cassidy's mission, came together in stunning clarity. Cassidy had been working with a new chemical compound designed to ease the drilling and hold open the fractures in the shale wider and longer so that the gas would more readily flow into the pipes. That had been the Holy Grail all along for the energy wildcatters. The geologists knew where the shale was, but getting the oil and gas from the deposits had proven either impossible or exorbitant in cost. If there was a new, more efficient way to loosen the shale and extract the gas, the United States might never have to rely on imported gas again.

Energy independence. No more wars over oil. The Middle East would be relegated to the second tier of foreign policy concerns.

"Start at the beginning, Grace. Walk me through the process," Mahegan said.

Grace sat up and pulled the sheet over her lap. She wore just her UNC T-shirt and a lacy thong. She spoke in animated fashion, using her hands to outline her points.

"Obviously, you start with a known area of trapped natural gas. Conventional vertical drilling methods, like they do for oil, won't release this gas, because the gas runs horizontally, in veins that are parallel to the crust of the earth. Most oil and gas come from deep pools that you could drill straight into, like sticking a soda straw into the ground. Then you just suck the gas or oil out of the ground until it's empty. As those pools began to run low, wildcatters began exploring other techniques to get at known reserves that were not proving fruitful.

"The Barnett Shale is probably the most famous. George Mitchell tried for thirty years and finally figured out that if he drilled vertically, then kicked off horizontally, he could ride into the veins. Even that didn't work great, so they started going in vertically, kicking horizontally, and then adding depth charges that would rupture the shale, releasing the gas. That was the big payoff."

"Depth charges?"

"Perforating charges," Grace said, using her fingers to form quotation marks. "They're bombs under the ground to break up the rock to release the gas into the pipe they've created as they've drilled. Then there is a complex series of stops placed behind each bombed area until they've exploded everywhere they want to. The stops block the gas from getting ahead of the next area they want to bomb.

"Obviously, they start at the very end of the pipeline, bomb, block, move forward, bomb, block, move forward, and so on, until they've created enough fissures to have the gas rush into the pipe. When they remove the last stop, the gas comes blowing out of the well and they have to cap it, because it is screaming out of there at a high psi rate. Enough to blow out your eardrums."

"I knew some of that. Interesting. So you think Throckmorton's play is to steal as much of the Durham gas as possible, using Maeve Cassidy as the driller? And that Piper is the quo to that quid?"

"Has to be. Throckmorton is into this fracking thing using foreign direct investment. He needs to get the capital moving now. He's moving without a permit. Throckmorton is old Raleigh, big money, and he has all the politicians in his back pocket. I'm thinking a missing permit is not going to be a big deal for him. Meanwhile, he becomes a billionaire by stealing gas."

"But what's he do with it? How does he make money from it?"

"That's the hard part. We're seeing some new equipment on the field where they're drilling. And we know that the natural gas pipeline from Louisiana cuts through North Carolina, with an offshoot into Raleigh. The party at Throckmorton's was to celebrate the state's completion of a pipeline along the railroad from Durham to the coast, that is, to Morehead City."

"Where there's a port." On Mahegan's several military deployments, he'd sometimes had to use the roll-on, roll-off facility at the Morehead City port.

"Which would mean exporting the gas. Oh my God. You're a frigging genius."

Mahegan nodded, then looked up, concerned. He rose from the bed and pulled on his black cargo pants and a black Under Armour T-shirt. After gathering all the phones, GPS devices, and identification cards on the table, he sat down in front of them.

"I need you to stand watch. Just sit in the chair over by the wall, where you can see east out of that window," he said, pointing at the opening where he had rested his sniper rifle to shoot the two EB-5 commandos that morning. "And you can look south out of that window."

Grace positioned herself perfectly so that she could see but would not be seen by anyone from the ground.

"You can see the house. You might see the Robertson family coming or going. That's normal. Anything else isn't."

"Why the sudden security?" she asked.

"I shot two men down there this morning. I told you that. Even though I've pulled the batteries and SIM cards from every phone, they may just be looking for their two men at their last known point."

"You sure everything's off?"

"Yes. Remember, they're after you, not me," Mahegan said.

Mahegan stood and tossed all the stolen weapons and some of his own personal equipment into a duffel bag, calculating what he would need for the evening's mission. He placed the SIM cards from each of the phones into a Baggie, which he would give to Savage's guy. He then began using a mini USB port and cable attached to his government-issued smartphone to upload SIM cards that would show text, call, and location data of the EB-5 commandos. The information would automatically transfer via a secured wireless connection to Savage's team, which was the part Mahegan was worried about. Despite the encryption, the information carried identifiable ping data, which active scanners could recognize. He was tempted to do the link analysis himself, but Mahegan figured they had about an hour, maybe less, before one of two groups appeared: Griffyn and the Raleigh Police Department, or the EB-5 commandos. Both would be hostile, but only one overtly so.

He had the eight phones arrayed on the table, all of them similar models except the older BlackBerry. Two were from the Turks he'd injured while they were invading Grace's home. Two were from the Russians he'd shot this morning on the Robertson property. Two were from the Serbs who had come looking for them at the pub and who were very much alive and could most likely identify him. The last two were from the first Russian, Petrov, with the scar on his face. He was wounded and probably lethal.

He retrieved his government-issued smartphone, opened the Zebra app, and typed a message to Savage, relaying everything he knew about the case. His big thumbs caused multiple typos and errors, and he lost time by going back and correcting them.

"Okay, ready?"

Grace had managed to get fully dressed in her jeans, T-shirt, and pullover sweater, which she had brought in her backpack. She wore hiking boots and looked ready for whatever Mahegan threw her way.

"Yes, sir," Grace said. She saluted Mahegan.

Mahegan shook his head and said, "Let's get out of here."

He swept all of the phones into his duffel bag, which he clasped in his large hand, as they exited his flat, and Mahegan spun the combination lock on the door.

"This way," Mahegan said. He gripped her hand and pulled her down the steps, into the barn room below his apartment. After sliding an iron bar through the barn door handles, he turned and guided Grace through the back door.

They stepped lightly into the woods, close to where the Russians had been that morning. Mahegan still smelled the blood on the ground. He stopped behind a fallen oak, its root base providing ample cover, like a firing port in a castle. As they knelt, Mahegan could feel the soft pine straw and the deadfall beneath his kneecap. His senses were alive as he listened to the distant rustle of a squirrel in a tree. He heard water from a rill running toward Jordan Lake. He thought he recognized the sound of a deer rubbing its antlers—a constant *scrape, scrape, scrape*—against a hardwood, probably an oak. The hooves were on the ground; the antlers, against the tree. The buck was marking his turf as mating season began.

"Snakes?" Grace whispered.

"Animals are your friends," Mahegan said, meaning it.

"Snakes aren't animals. They're reptiles."

"Reptiles are animals. Now be quiet. Look," Mahegan said, pointing.

A single car raced into the long driveway, passed the Robertson house, which was dark, and pulled all the way up to the barn. This was not the EB-5 commandos. It was Griffyn.

Grace's tight clutch on his arm indicated to Mahegan that she understood what they were seeing.

Detective Griffyn, tall and balding, with tiny eyes, stepped from his car and looked around the unfamiliar, dark expanse, trying to find his way. Mahegan could see him thinking, *A barn?* He could also see the pistol in Griffyn's hand. It had the square, boxy look of a Glock, but he couldn't tell for sure at thirty meters. Mahegan put his hand on Grace's shoulder, silently communicating for her to stay calm.

He was thinking, *Two options.* One, he could take down the detective and question him to determine his role in the scheme, if any. The downside was that Griffyn might have no role, and Mahegan would then be charged for assaulting a police officer. Who knew? There could be some kind of charge for attacking the man with the closest bloodline to Sir Walter Raleigh. Mahegan's second option was to steal Griffyn's car and drive some distance toward the fracking site and carry on with his original plan. Both options provided some element of risk and reward.

Mahegan's style was to gain as much operational intelligence as he could and then to move swiftly, staying inside the enemy's decision cycle. He believed Throckmorton wasn't aware of him yet, but that could change very quickly. Like military dead space, the enemy knew you were out there; they just could not see you. Throckmorton was missing valuable men, and if Gunther was involved financially, if the man had anything on the table at all, Mahegan knew that Gunther would do whatever it took to stop the bleeding.

Mahegan decided his most valuable play was to detain Griffyn, question him, and then carry on with his mission. He watched the man survey the barn doors, which Mahegan had locked from the inside after Grace and he had parked their cars. Griffyn looked over his shoulder at the Robertson home and then looked back at the doors. He pulled on them without success.

Griffyn slowly began walking directly toward Mahegan and Grace, then turned left, toward the back of the barn. When he made the next left and headed toward the back door, Mahegan took Grace's hand and they moved toward Griffyn's car, gingerly avoiding twigs and branches and making as little noise as possible. He opened the front passenger door of Griffyn's Crown Victoria and whispered to Grace, "On the floor," as he handed her the duffel bag. She would fit better in the compact space.

He slid into the backseat, then eased the door closed with a click. Mahegan did his best to hide his large frame in the foot well on the passenger side. Griffyn was a relatively tall man and had the driver's seat racked back a good distance. Fortunately, the Crown Vic was a large car. He noticed Griffyn was not an exceptionally neat man. There were food wrappers and newspapers on the floor and on the backseat. Those would make it harder to keep quiet when he sprang, so he adjusted them while he could, sliding some of the wrappers into the other foot well. He risked a peek up over the middle console and saw that Grace was tucked in a tight little package, like a kid doing a cannonball off a diving board.

He heard Griffyn walking quickly, feet crunching on the drainage gravel Mahegan had placed around the barn to help with some of the water issues Andy Robertson had discussed with him. The gravel was also an early warning system for him. Griffyn stormed into the Crown Vic, opening the door with fury and then slamming it with equal counterweight. Mahegan heard something thud onto the passenger seat, and he guessed it was the gun.

Bad move.

He felt more than heard Griffyn's weight shift to the passenger side as he inserted the key fob into the slot. There was also the sound of metal clicking, like a handset being removed from a sleeve. He heard the tick of a dial being turned and then the random voices of police chatter.

"We have a ten-twenty-three and need a ten-nine immediately. . . ."

"Wilco. Address please . . ."

He was listening to the chatter, and wondering why Griffyn wasn't making his call, when he heard, "What the hell?"

Mahegan came up quickly with his pistol to the back of Griffyn's head and wrapped his arm around the man's thin neck. Looking to his right, he saw that Grace had Griffyn's pistol and was aiming it at him. She had taken a scarf from her pocket and had draped it across her head and face, making her look like a Muslim terrorist.

"Start the car and drive," Mahegan said. "I've killed two people in the past twenty-four hours, and I've got no problem with a third."

"Hawthorne?"

"I said to drive, Griffyn."

"Where to?"

"You know where I want to go. Show me where Maeve Cassidy is being held."

"How would I know that?"

"You've got two weapons aimed at you right now. You really

want to play poker? I'm the stable one here. That one in your front seat . . . Who the hell knows?"

"I'm out here on official Raleigh Police Department business. You have no business—"

Mahegan had had enough. He rose up and struck the man on his temple, knocking him unconscious. He dragged the man over the front seat and into the back, then pulled some plastic flex cuffs from his duffel bag and used them. He used Grace's scarf to gag Griffyn, securing it tightly enough to make him appear as if he was grimacing constantly. With the man's hands secured behind his back and his mouth gagged, Mahegan climbed into the front seat as Grace unwrapped the scarf from her face and sat in the passenger seat. She looked over the headrest at Griffyn.

"You don't know how many times I wanted to do that," she said.

"What? Aim a weapon at him, knock him out, or handcuff him?"

"Pick one. He's such a frigging douche."

Mahegan started the car and then drove the route to the fracking site, only he turned sooner and followed the stream on the east side, sticking to the improved dirt and gravel road that led to the hilltop where he had heard a vehicle driving during his earlier reconnaissance. The forest on either side of the road was thick, making navigation without headlights a challenge. He was trading the idea of stealth for the concept that Throckmorton and Gunther would be expecting Griffyn's vehicle. They would look out the window and see his car and then would go back to drinking whiskey or whatever they were doing.

To his left, Mahegan saw a bank of lights, like a baseball field lit at night. In the middle he saw the newly erected rig, looking like a small Eiffel Tower. He heard the crunch of turning gears and the hiss of hydraulic pistons. Indeed, the operation was under way. Somewhere close by Captain Maeve Cassidy was steering a drill toward the Durham shale and was ready to pump new chemicals into the land so that Throckmorton could steal what the people of North Carolina rightfully owned.

Driving in the darkness without headlights, he felt the curve of the road and knew they were climbing a hill. He looked at Grace and saw that her eyes were wide with anticipation. She still had the pistol in her hand and was fumbling with it nervously. As they crested the hill, he was instantly upon a guarded checkpoint with minimal lighting. He slowed the vehicle, thinking perhaps that there was an electronic signal the Crown Vic would emit to lift the gate arm.

If there was one, it didn't work. From either flank, two men emerged from the woods with long rifles drawn on them. Mahegan turned on the high beams to see if he could ram the checkpoint. It didn't appear so. He did see, however, that Maxim Petrov was standing in the middle of the road.

The Russian was holding a baseball bat.

CHAPTER 17

T HE JOYSTICK TREMBLED IN HER HAND.

"We've got a guy," Jim had said. Someone besides Jim was in charge. The man she had come to know in Afghanistan was evil, but would he design attacks on nuclear facilities? She didn't think so.

Someone else had developed this elaborate plan.

We've got a guy.

Maeve took a few deep breaths and continued to navigate the drill through the earth.

Just get through this, Maeve. Do what you have to do. Anything and everything to save Piper.

The drill had bit through two miles of earth and into the Durham sub-basin. She hated violating this unspoiled resource. As a geologist, Maeve was conflicted about tapping the land for hydrocarbons. Was she a hypocrite for not worrying so much about it when her vehicle fuel was coming from the Middle East? It was a definite conflict. She understood the earth's texture and fragility. What she had endured in Afghanistan had only made her more convinced that the human race had to find a different way to provide energy. There was a balanced menu of options—solar, wind, sea, electric, nuclear, and fossil fuels—and they should collectively power the economies of nations. Right now Maeve didn't like that 80 percent of the world's energy came from hydrocarbons.

That introspection caused her to think about the small percentage of energy derived from nuclear power, which spiraled her right back to her dilemma. The threat that her mistake could ignite an attack on Wilmington or Charlotte was horrifying to Maeve. Wasn't holding Piper captive enough to get her to commit to doing what they need her to do? She was motivated 100 percent. Anxiety circled her throat like a snake tightening its grip. Her hand started shaking. She felt the initial onset of panic coming at her from two directions. First, the nuclear plants. Second, they had Piper! They had kidnapped her daughter, the only thing that mattered to her in this world!

Her eyes blinked, and she felt the slow nod of her head as she began to fall asleep.

Indeed, she was dreaming. *Stop it! Wake up!* she told herself.

She watched as her hand overcorrected and the stick jumped, causing the beeping red dot that represented the drill bit to bounce against the edge of the designated path. A loud siren erupted in the room, like an air raid warning.

Jim came barging into the room, shouting, "You know what that means, right? Damn it! What happened?"

Maeve stared at the screen and saw that the red dot was back within the boundaries and was moving forward on the designated path. Jim flipped a switch to display the drone at an undesignated airfield in Gaston County. The drone must have had a thermal camera in its substructure, because Maeve could see that its propeller was spinning and it was rolling along a grass runway.

To Maeve, the sight was unbelievable. She had triggered this through a subtle error. How could she have been so careless? She was watching an aircraft that was no bigger than a small Cessna airplane but that looked like a small F-117, the stealth fighter with the extended bat wings. She knew what it was. Military defense contractor BAE Systems had made a prototype called the Corax, which was a stealth unmanned aerial vehicle. It carried a payload, such as bombs. She knew that much. What was this one carrying? she wondered.

"What is that?" she shrieked. "I didn't do that. It was just one little mistake!"

"You did that, dear Maeve. The McGuire Nuclear Station will

be melting down pretty soon. Hope you don't have any friends in Charlotte. We're safe, though. Three hours away," Jim said. He had leaned over the back of the chair and had whispered this in her ear. She wished she had a lighter to ignite the air every time he breathed the noxious whiskey fumes onto her neck. She wanted to burn him. To kill him. She wanted to put him on that airplane, which had just taken off from the grass runway.

"Dear God."

"Watch this," Jim said, flipping a switch and showing a split screen on the monitor to the left of her drill path monitor. Despite the frightening sight of the Corax taking off, she kept the drill moving forward within the boundaries of the path, for fear of igniting the second threat, the liquefied natural gas container ship by the Brunswick Nuclear Plant.

"What is that?" But she knew what it was. Someone had placed another thermal camera on the fence surrounding McGuire and had aimed it at the cooling towers. In the greenish hue of the camera, she could make out spotlights crossing the sky above the cooling towers, like for a used car sale advertisement. On the other half of the screen was the image being fed back from the Corax in flight. It was sailing smoothly through the sky, then darting like a bat, perhaps responding to radar stimuli. Maeve wasn't sure.

Soon the static camera that was focused on the two cooling towers showed a black object piercing the spotlights and aimed directly at the top, in an almost vertical suicide attack down the pipe.

"No. This can't be happening," Maeve said.

"It's happening, dear Maeve. Trust me." As Maeve listened to Jim, he sounded as if he might not believe it himself.

"Who put you up to this? You're a bastard, but you're not a mass murderer," Maeve demanded.

They watched both images. The darting bat was now in a complete nosedive, and the image of the cooling towers was growing larger. The ground camera showed the black speck in the sky becoming a larger, recognizable object. It was like a slow-motion fastball coming to home plate, initially barely visible and then suddenly upon the batter in full dimension.

Then something happened that neither of them could have predicted.

Two oval objects the size of small water towers flipped open, revealing what looked to Maeve to be large machine guns, like on the Aegis cruisers in the U.S. Navy. The weapons spat at the diving jet, tracking it as it approached in its rapid descent. A fraction of a second prior to impacting the dome of one of the cooling towers, the plane shredded into small pieces, and a large airburst ignited.

To Maeve, the plane was nothing more than confetti in the sky, while the airburst was an orange and black demon boiling above the nuclear plant.

She clasped her mouth with her left hand, her right continuing to push the red dot forward.

Jim seemed to ease back away from her. She felt him sigh and relax. That was good information. This was not his plan. Perhaps he hadn't even believed that the threats were real.

"Don't mess up again, is all I've got to say," Jim said. He departed the room.

But Maeve's mind was spinning. She had just inadvertently launched an attack on a nuclear facility. She was aiding and abetting terrorists.

And they were holding her daughter ransom.

She had to find Piper, but how could she leave the joystick and the control room? Where would she even begin to look?

We've got a guy.

Maeve stared at the computer monitor and saw that the sky around the nuclear facility was littered with chunks of the drone burning brightly in the camera's thermal retina.

CHAPTER 18

T HE TWO MEN WITH THE WEAPONS CLOSED QUICKLY ON THE VEHI-
cle. Petrov remained motionless, save the slapping of the bat into
his left hand. Mahegan listened to the *thunk, thunk, thunk* of the
bat and visualized what Petrov might have in mind for him, maybe
even for Grace.

The Crown Vic likely had bulletproof glass, Mahegan thought,
and its weightiness indicated some type of ballistic protection.
Mahegan said, "Hang on."

He slammed the gearshift into reverse, held the brake a fraction of a second, floored the accelerator, and performed a perfect Rockford, spinning the car 180 degrees, slamming the gear
back to drive, and aiming the car down the hill like a bobsled.

Mahegan then slammed on the brakes, slapped the gearshift
back into reverse, and used the higher gear ratio to gain traction
and power for the short punch through the metal arm blocking the
road. He could hear the unconscious Griffyn bouncing around in
the back and didn't feel bad about it one bit.

"What the hell are you doing!" Grace shouted, hanging on to
the dashboard while ducking at the sound of gunfire.

Mahegan said nothing. He aimed the car at the metal arm, which
broke easily at the point of impact under the combined weight and
speed of the Crown Vic. The bulletproof glass designed to protect
Griffyn was working just fine as Mahegan pulled another Rockford,
this time aiming the nose of the car at Petrov, who dove out of the
way, losing the bat but grabbing his pistol.

Mahegan throttled the car, and it leapt up the hill inside the compound, three weapons firing small-caliber bullets at the now spiderwebbing rear window. The car actually gained some air as it crested the hill. Mahegan could see the distant lights of the hunting lodge, which looked to him more like a mansion the closer he approached. Sparks flew from the front bumper as the car came back toward the hill, smacked the gravel, and leveled out. In the rearview mirror, Mahegan saw the three men. They ran, stopped and fired, ran, stopped and fired, continuing in their pursuit but becoming smaller and smaller in the mirror.

The front windshield looked okay, and Mahegan saw nothing to be gained by storming the compound any further. He saw two new muzzle flashes from the south side of the lodge and three from the north. Counting the three men at the gate, Mahegan placed their security at about eight people. Based on the numbers of men he had seen digging postholes and during his recon effort earlier, he guessed Throckmorton·had about fifteen personnel on location. Of course, he had injured four and killed two, so the number might be less.

"What. The hell. Are you doing?" Grace shouted.

The closest defender was about a hundred yards away. Not close, but not far for assault rifles. The fire was not well aimed, but Mahegan knew that all it would take was one lucky bullet. He opened the driver's door, stepped out, opened the back door, dragged the bound Griffyn from the backseat, and left him on the gravel, like a delivery.

He shut the back door, heard the distinctive snap of supersonic bullets zipping nearby, and sat back in the car. The teams were closing to fifty yards from three directions. He spotted two weapons in the main window of the lodge, which put the number of guards at ten. Some of the commandos on rest cycle had been awakened, or these were rounds fired by Throckmorton and Gunther, if Gunther was there.

He thought back to Petrov's tactile BlackBerry, which had a calendar entry about Gunther's visit that morning. Perhaps he was still there. Mahegan could feel the man the way a hunter could track an animal. Grace was screaming at him, but everything was in slow motion. He saw the men with the assault weapons closing on his position, but he remained motionless. He stared at the lodge window and saw a head staring back at him.

And he knew it was Gunther.

He could feel Gunther in that house, the same way he had felt the need to come home early on the day he walked in on his mother being attacked. He closed his eyes and visualized pulling Gunther away from his mother and tossing him through the sliding glass door. Gunther was not a small man, but Mahegan had been driven that day by the most primal emotion he had ever felt. He remembered watching a large chunk of glass stab Gunther in the back and thinking, *Okay. He'll bleed out,* as he moved on to the next assailant.

"Hawthorne!"

Mahegan came back to the moment and opened his eyes. Quickly, he assessed the vehicles in the front driveway of the lodge: two pickup trucks and a Suburban. He calculated the response time of the guards and their general professionalism. *Okay, but not great.*

Then he got the hell out of there.

Mahegan heard the footsteps as the bullets continued to smack into the car windows. He reversed course and pulled another 180, this time catching one of the guards with the nose of the Crown Vic. Spitting gravel from the rear tires like a cigarette boat did a rooster tail, Mahegan sped past Petrov, who stood in a perfect shooter's stance, his pistol jacking back in his hand, as the bullets thudded into the car windows, making it nearly impossible to see in any direction.

Mahegan kept the Crown Vic between the ditches as he used his forearm to smash out the shattered driver's side window. Slaloming down the winding gravel and dirt road, he hung his head out the window, watching the edge of the lighter road and keeping the car to the left of the black ditch.

Soon they were near Route 1 and moving northeast, away from the county line. Mahegan drove to a shopping mall that was five miles from his apartment. He parked, grabbed a rag from the duffel bag, and wiped down the car.

Grace stood in the parking lot and watched, her arms crossed, as if protecting herself from the cold. Mahegan knew that she wasn't cold, but angry and afraid. Her boss was with the bad guys. He wouldn't tell her how he knew. Not yet.

Grabbing his duffel bag, he turned to Grace. A parking lot light was shining on her like a stage beam. "That was called a probing attack. I hadn't planned on it, but I hadn't ruled it out. When I saw Griffyn come looking for us, I knew he had either tracked my signal to my boss, which is next to impossible, or talked to the people who had originally tracked your phone to mine. It's the only way he could have known where we were. Period. He's a bad seed. So I left him with his comrades. This isn't the end of it. Probably just the beginning. But I know enough now to find Maeve Cassidy and her daughter. I couldn't give a rat's ass about the drilling, other than the nuke thing. That bothers me. I know you're freaked out, and I don't blame you. Now, walk with me while I get us a hotel room."

"A probing attack?"

"Yes. It's an Army term of warfare. When you don't know anything about your enemy disposition, you probe his defenses and see how he responds."

"They shot at us."

"Which is important information. In fact, there were eight guards outside and two inside. That makes ten, which I put at about half of their entire force, based on the number I saw the first day I was out there, digging postholes. I've hurt or killed six, seven if you count the guy that went flying across the hood. I don't think he's going to be okay. There are three main objectives of a probing attack. First, you want to avoid decisive engagement, meaning you need to be able to get out of there."

"But we almost didn't."

"*Almost* is the operative word. We made it out. Second, you want to gather as much intelligence as possible. They had three vehicles, a house, eight people outside guarding, a darkened entrance below the house and on the east side, like a tunnel or a storm shelter. And the house is stuck out on a peninsula of land that falls away to the fracking site below it, which is about a half a mile away."

"You saw all that?"

"And more. They are seriously invested in this."

"The third objective?"

"It's a bonus if you can injure or kill the enemy on the probing attack. One guy isn't much, but it's better than no guys. We did okay. Plus, we left them your boss."

"What about my job?" Grace was still shaken, still standing in the same circle of light, like a Broadway performer with stage fright.

"What about your life, Grace? Griffyn wasn't at my place to bring you flowers. He was there to kill you. For some reason, you're a liability. I need to know what you saw at that house."

Grace nodded. "There's a Holiday Inn up the road about a mile, on the other side of the mall. Let's walk and I'll tell you what I saw."

She had somehow gathered her composure. Perhaps the reality of Griffyn's duplicity had sunk in. He didn't know. She stepped toward him, unsure initially, but then clasped his arm, with the cup of her hand around his biceps.

They started walking, and Grace Kagami, the beautiful mirror, told him everything.

CHAPTER 19

JAMES GUNTHER STEPPED OUT ONTO THE SLATE-ROCK PORCH OF Throckmorton's elaborate compound and hideaway. The smell of gunpowder hung in the air like a malodorous ghost. The volume of assault weapon and pistol fire rivaled anything Gunther had ever heard, save a few bird hunts Down East, where they had slaughtered anything that moved. Rabbits, squirrels, foxes, red wolves, gators, doves, quails, and coyotes were all fair game, and all decent eating if prepared properly.

He took a step down from the slate porch to the stone steps that led to the circular gravel drive. He saw that his Ford F-150 pickup truck had a few nicks from amateur gunfire. The Keystone Cops had been shooting into a circle. He had never been in the Army, but he knew enough not to form a circle jerk and shoot one another. Clearly, these EB-5 guys were not well trained, and he and Throckmorton were pushing them beyond their limits. He had certainly believed they were quality staff when he hired them. They had had to prove themselves in a rigorous shooting skills test, a course on handling fracking equipment, and a test of their familiarity with Chatham and Wake County topography.

All of that had gone smoothly. He managed the roughnecks, the field laborers who were doing the construction and fracking on the graded valley below the compound. Throckmorton dallied with the women, which was fine, but he didn't have the time or the desire for that anymore, given what had happened at the

Indian's house years ago. Though, one of the concubines down below was his. That was all he wanted. In the partnership with Throckmorton, Gunther could do almost everything he wanted. But while the main shard of glass had sliced into his back, another, smaller wedge had cut his scrotum and everything it held. He had not been protected by pants when Mahegan heaved him through the glass door all those years ago, and now he was essentially a eunuch.

But that didn't mean he didn't take out his aggression on Tessi Slovnik, the tough, beautiful Serbian mechanic. Actually, as his boots had crunched on the gravel and he'd watched the Crown Victoria speed away, he had thought he might need to visit Tessi.

He had seen an unrecognizable face in the splintered windshield of the car. His vision wasn't perfect, but there had been something familiar in the way the man's eyes connected with his. The intent stare, eyes locked, had seemed to suggest something from long past, at least for Gunther. The stranger who had boldly penetrated their defensive perimeter, using Griffyn's car, must have a history. He didn't know what it was, but it was something. There was more to this little gunfight than a man who had made a wrong turn. It was a deliberate psych job. It was an "I'm coming to get you."

Those thoughts didn't unnerve Gunther. He had been dealing with rednecks and ruffians all his life. This was just one more something he had to handle. Throckmorton was too focused on the girls and the money. Somebody had to do the dirty work. His cut of $250 million was a solid cut. He could retire and move somewhere in Down East North Carolina. They could embezzle the money they had, but he was worried about the Chinese guys, Ting and Chun. Something about them didn't sit right with him. They were too . . . in control. They had an answer for everything and were one step ahead of him most of the time. They knew how to drill, and they had all the numbers down pat.

Gunther considered himself a simple man. Before that crazy kid had come in and changed his life forever, he had needed some strangeness about once every other day, and he really hadn't cared where it came from. As long as he could take it forcibly, that was all that had mattered to him. Now he got to do the forcible part without any of the sex. While the freckled blond mother had been a nice piece of ass, she definitely wasn't worth a lifetime loss of sexual ability. And for that, he blamed the kid. The giant Indian kid who had come into the house and had fought four of them like there was only one of them.

Gunther had been in many fights, but never one like that. The kid was a rarity, and he wondered why he was thinking now about a young boy whose name he couldn't even remember. The woman had been a startling blonde, alone in a clapboard home near the right-of-way they had been paving for a new road in Robeson County. They had asked for some lemonade or tea, and she had actually responded by turning her back, smiling, and saying, "Sure, boys." Hell, if that hadn't been an invite, Gunther didn't know what was.

But that day crystallized for him at this very moment, as he walked up to a bound and gagged Griffyn, who had been tossed from his very own car like a sack of seed. One of the commando teams had mounted up in a truck and had sped after the Crown Vic. *Good luck*, Gunther thought. No way they were catching that guy, if it was who he thought it was.

He nudged Griffyn with his boot and said, "Thought they trained you better than that, Detective."

The commandos had performed the outer perimeter circle led by Petrov, who had orchestrated their movements. He was the Russian Special Forces guy. No wonder they got their butts kicked in Afghanistan, Gunther thought.

He reached down and removed the gag from Griffyn's mouth. "Tell me how the hell you got yourself in this position."

Griffyn coughed. "Snuck up on me. Both of them. Dead. I'm arresting them tomorrow. Cassidy's husband is dead. We think the big guy did it."

"The big guy?"

"Yeah. The Indian. Hawthorne. Army special agent."

Gunther rolled this around in his mind. *Hawthorne?*

"What's he look like?"

"A giant. Six and a half feet tall. Massive. Powerful. Blond hair, blue eyes. Probably one of those eastern bands from the Outer Banks or maybe Robeson."

Gunther felt a stir, everywhere except the one place where he couldn't. A buzz coursed through his veins.

"You ain't going nowhere right now, Griffyn. You're a damn liability. That guy figured out you were in with us without even thinking about it. We'll send you down to the nurses and let you rehab, but we can't risk you being out there for about the next twenty-four hours."

"I've got a major murder investigation on my hands, Gunther."

"No. You've got a missing person case. Cary has the murder. Get your facts straight. And technically, the Army has the missing person case. Just another reason to keep your ass locked up tight here, instead of stepping all over other police jurisdictions. Let it cool for twenty-four hours, and then we'll see where we go from there."

Griffyn, who was still bound like a tied hog, nodded.

"Untie his ass and take him into the Underground," Gunther said.

The men carried out his direction. He felt Throckmorton come up on his side. Smelled him, too. Some kind of musky aftershave. The man got on Gunther's nerves, but he was willing to violate a sack full of principles to make a quarter billion.

"What's your deal, Throck? This thing falling apart?"

"Not at all. Miss Cassidy just made it to the first spot, and we're ready to send down some perforating charges to get the natural gas flowing. Thought I'd come up and give you the good news."

Gunther nodded, still staring at the gate a quarter mile away in the darkness, as if he expected the Crown Vic to come barreling back through the opening. If the fourteen-year-old kid was driving it, he was certain that he would already be back, ready to finish what he thought he'd already done: kill him.

But if fifteen years had passed and the kid was now a man and the man was a soldier or a cop, that was a different story. The man would be wiser, more cunning.

Gunther had seen Throckmorton's anxiety when he learned that Petrov was nervous about going to see the big guy who was with the Mexicans. This kid from his memory would be enough to scare Petrov.

"We've got to plan for defending against a full attack on this compound, Throck. If my instincts are correct—and I hope I am flat-ass wrong—we've got someone coming at us for two reasons."

"The first?"

"To get Cassidy and her kid back."

"The second?"

"To kill me."

"Why?"

"That ain't important. What's important is that his daddy found me and died, and now the son has found me, and he will die."

"The Indian? That guy who was chasing you?"

Gunther had hired private detectives to find out what had happened to his friend Tommy Boyd. He had suspected it was more than a meth lab accident, and he had been right. Boyd's throat had been cut from ear to ear with a large knife.

"Remember that Indian? We got a picture of him?"

He watched Throckmorton's Adam's apple bob up and down. He knew the refined gentleman was not thrilled with the dark underbelly of how Gunther survived with his business or life, but they were from different worlds. He had made Throckmorton join him that morning several months ago when he had seen Mahegan's father. Throckmorton had taken a photo. Gunther was sure it was for blackmail or insurance, but he didn't care. He'd kill Throckmorton before it ever came to that.

"Yes, I remember."

"That's his son. I'd bet a paycheck on it. The one who threw me through a sliding glass door."

CHAPTER 20

"A SPOILING ATTACK? WHAT DID WE SPOIL OTHER THAN MY BREAK-fast?" Grace asked Mahegan. They were lying in bed, the Holiday Inn sign casting a shaded green light through the pale curtains that covered the window. She had stripped down to her T-shirt, and Mahegan was naked except for his boxers. After the adrenaline dump, Mahegan knew that they had both experienced a level of physical and mental exhaustion usually associated with the completion of athletic events or combat. The endorphins were rushing.

"Probe. Spoiling attack. Like I told you. I'm just wired that way. Can't explain it and haven't really thought too much about it. I get information, and I go. I process and analyze as I'm moving. You're a forensic scientist. Your job is to study the evidence in a somewhat static environment. I'm a soldier. My job is to kill the bad guys and help the good guys. So I get information, process it, and move before anyone either thinks I have the information or believes they are vulnerable."

"Is it really that simple? Good guys and bad guys?"

"Well, sometimes there are bad women," Mahegan said. He looked at Grace, her head resting on his chest again. She turned her gorgeous eyes up at him and smiled.

"I can be bad," she said.

Mahegan ignored her teasing and said, "You know what I mean. Evil. Poisonous. Men and women. Sociopaths. Harmful."

"And it's your job to stop all that?"

"What I can. Not saying I can stop it all, but I do what I can where I can."

"So you're a vigilante?"

Despite his exhaustion, Mahegan was in an introspective mood, but he let Grace's question hang in the air, unanswered. His mind was replaying the risk he had taken tonight. He had acted on impulse by taking Griffyn hostage and stealing his car. Then he had driven directly through the guarded gate and dumped Griffyn's body on the driveway while they were under fire. He had gathered needed information, but it was a huge risk, maybe even a gamble. He could recover from a risky endeavor if he made a mistake, but if you lost a gamble, you lost it all, Mahegan remembered from his training. Tonight, he decided, he had edged more toward the gamble side of the spectrum. But every time he felt that he had perhaps done something too risky, he was presented with new opportunities that were potentially too rewarding to ignore. Was the slope becoming too slippery to prevent sliding into some catastrophic error?

"We should sleep," Grace said, yawning. Mahegan felt her warm breath on his chest. Her small hand was resting on his sternum, and his left arm was holding her close. She was molded to his body, and he could feel her heart beating on his abdomen. After a few minutes of silence, he felt her body go slack and fall into a steady sleep rhythm.

Continuing to think the next steps through, Mahegan decided to close his eyes, also. He immediately cycled through all the data, wondering what he was missing. Maeve's henna tattoo, which provided a mysterious warning, perhaps, about North Carolina's three nuclear plants; the EB-5 commandos; the fracking; the murder of Pete Cassidy; the kidnapping of Maeve and Piper Cassidy; and the apparent complicity of Detective Griffyn all made for an incomplete puzzle.

But most overwhelming for Mahegan was the sense that Gunther had been there, looking at him through the window. Mahegan found himself at the intersection of professional duty and personal agenda, a street corner with two equally satisfying destinations, but if you chose one direction, you might as well forget about the other. *Wait*, he thought. *There might be a way to do both.*

Could he? Should he focus on Gunther and his personal feelings, he could make mistakes in safely securing Maeve Cassidy, which might also be connected to some large plan with the nuclear facilities.

But he had promised himself that all four of his mother's attackers would die a painful death. He had personally delivered on two of those promises at the scene of the crime, and Gunther was all that remained after his partner's meth lab explosion.

Lying there, with Grace sleeping on his chest, her body curled around him like a cat, he was struck by how her presence made him feel more grounded. Maybe because she needed protection, he felt useful to her. Certainly, his mother's death had been a scarring event for Mahegan, and so his self-satisfaction in protecting and defending, especially women, was most likely connected to the day that Gunther took her fifteen years ago.

Reviewing his early days as a rapidly growing boy in Frisco, North Carolina, Mahegan remembered his mother taking him to the beach every day, completing the short walk from their trailer park to the turbulent waters of the barrier islands of the Outer Banks. There the beaches were wide, and the currents were wicked. Riptides sucked the water through forever shifting sandbars at velocities so high, some swimmers were pulled out to sea so quickly that they were never found again. Samantha Mahegan, though, was a champion swimmer and believed in the waterman's way of life. She surfed, dove, swam, and kayaked in the ocean and in Pamlico Sound, just steps away on the north side of the island.

Mahegan remembered watching his mother surf the hollow tubes off Frisco Pier. Since he'd been a five-year-old, gangly kid, his mother would shred the open face of waves with the best of the men, who respected her abilities and deferred to her when she outmaneuvered them for position on the finest swells. There came a day when Sam took young Jake out on the board, walking him through the minor swells as he lay there, balancing himself, and pushed him into his first wave. He stood and rode the white water all the way to the beach, enjoying the sensation of connecting with nature, being *pushed* by nature.

After that day, Mahegan went on to become a respectable surfer, but by the time he was fourteen, he had outgrown most surfboards' ability to hold his weight, and the previous year his father had made them move to Maxton, in Robeson County. Maxton wasn't anywhere near the beach, but there were jobs there for Native Americans with construction skills. Neither Sam nor Jake had wanted to move, but in Frisco they had barely been able to put food on the table. So his parents had loaded the family Roadmaster station wagon with everything worth taking from their rented trailer a few hundred yards from the beach. After his military discharge, while he was drifting along the Outer Banks last year, Mahegan had learned that the site of that trailer park was now filled with multimillion-dollar homes.

Maxton had been bad news from the beginning, and it had ended in the worst possible way. While the trailer park in Frisco had not been anything for a kid to brag about, it was all Mahegan had known, and it had been home. So when they moved to another trailer park in Maxton, it was no big deal to Mahegan. Trailer parks were what you made them, he figured. And his mother made theirs a home. His father was working a steady job in Lumberton, which was thirty miles away, and the work had him gone more often than not.

On his first day walking back from middle school, thirteen-year-old Mahegan chose a route along the Lumber River that appeared to be a shortcut to his home. Curious, he left the road soon after passing a bridge. When he was level with the river, he noticed a water moccasin basking in the sun on an exposed cedar tree root. The snake was spread across the vertical root like a man might lounge with his leg draped across a sofa.

True to his native heritage and his mother's Outer Banks pioneer lineage, Mahegan had learned to love the land and all her animals, whether they were the red wolves of Alligator River National Wildlife Refuge or a resting snake on a cedar root. Kneeling several feet from the snake, he admired its tan and black scales. Mahegan studied the elliptical eyes and the flickering tongue. The snake turned its head toward him, sensing his presence. They locked eyes, and Mahegan smiled as he continued to study the pit viper.

The shotgun blast startled him, but he didn't flinch. It was as if he was watching the scene in slow motion. He heard the noise, and a split second later he had snake guts exploding on him, along with the shattered cedar root. Then he heard the yelling and hollering of three or four boys, all maybe his age, maybe a little older.

They came running down from the bridge, laughing and proud.

"Damn good shot, Lanny," the tall kid said.

Mahegan studied the kids who were running directly toward him. He had been less than five feet from the snake when "Lanny" pulled the trigger. Mahegan sized up the three boys. One was almost as tall as him, but thin as a reed. Lanny, the shooter, was pudgy and wore camouflage pants and a sweatshirt with the sleeves cut off. The third kid had a distant, hard look about him. The tall one and Lanny were laughing and joking, while the third stayed a step behind and locked eyes with Mahegan.

As they stumbled upon Mahegan's perch on the trail, he stood, towering over even the taller boy. His crimson tan was as deep as ever, since he had just moved from Frisco, where he had had daily bouts of summer sun. With Maxton and Robeson County filled with Lumbee Indians, Mahegan was not surprised when the tall kid said, "What are you looking at, cherry nigger?"

"That's one BFI there, Jimmy," Lanny said, looking at the tall kid.

Mahegan said nothing. He knew that BFI stood for "big fucking Indian." He had heard people call his father that before. He kept watching the intense third kid. He noticed the kid's hands were moving, and as he shifted a little to his right, he saw a switchblade in his hand. Mahegan assessed his situation: Three to one. Shotgun and a knife.

The tall kid, Jimmy, stepped forward as Lanny leveled the shotgun at Mahegan. He was thirteen. They were probably fifteen. He was new, and they had been around long enough to form a small gang.

"Three to one. We've got a shotgun. What's your problem?" Jimmy asked.

Mahegan continued staring at the kid with the switchblade. Without moving his gaze, he said, "You killed my snake."

Lanny and Jimmy laughed.

"That ain't your snake, Shitting Bull. That's a nasty cottonmouth that deserved to die," Jimmy said. He seemed to be the leader.

"How is it you get to decide that?" Mahegan asked Jimmy. The switch-blade kid had moved a step to the side. Mahegan assessed him as a fighter, whereas the other two probably were less skilled.

"Maxton's my town, asshole. You ain't full blooded, so you're just a half-breed buffalo jockey. You don't belong nowhere. We'll give you five seconds to get the hell out of here, or we'll let you visit your friend in snake hell," Jimmy said.

Mahegan watched the fighter and calculated his geometry. He had placed his backpack on the ground. His opponents were still wearing theirs. He would be more agile, though they could be more adept at fighting. His back was to the trail that ran parallel to the river through the thick forest. To his front were the three kids, and behind them by fifty yards was the bridge and the road. It wasn't likely that anyone driving by would think twice about four kids with backpacks hanging out by the river. In fact, they would probably smile and be glad that they were outdoors, communing with nature, instead of playing video games indoors.

"One," Jimmy said.

Mahegan had never been in a true fight before. He'd been shoved and pushed and called names, but he'd endured nothing of this magnitude. The middle school wrestling coach had talked to him today and had invited him to try out as a heavyweight wrestler. Mahegan was tall and powerful—not an ounce of fat on him—from his days as a waterman, diving and swimming. He had broad shoulders and long arms. The swimming coach would probably be talking to him soon, too, the wrestling coach had told him.

"Two."

But Mahegan was a smart kid. His mother had taught him to make quick decisions in the water. Where's the wave going to break? How do you paddle into it properly? Where is that sweet spot of balance on your board? How do you get on the face of the wave and not just ride the white water? What do you do if you see a bull shark coming at you? *That was what Mahegan was thinking about as the kid continued counting.*

"Three."

He had learned that balance and skill were necessary components of any athletic endeavor. While he had to ride the wave as it presented itself, he had learned that you could manipulate the wave with turns and carves and upper-body movements. He knew also when to let the bull shark swim past and when to fight it.

"Four."

As he watched the pudgy kid lift the shotgun, Mahegan did an upper-body turn, making sure to keep his right foot firmly planted, like a pitcher turning on a windup. He wanted to give the appearance of a departure while coiling for a strike on Jimmy, who had made the mistake of stepping in front of the pudgy kid with the shotgun.

"Knew you were a pussy," said Jimmy.

Mahegan's upper body swiveled back in Jimmy's direction, adding force to his punch, as if it was released from a baseball pitcher's windup. His fist hit the kid in the face, moving about eighty miles per hour, he figured, and he heard the distinct crack of the tall kid's nose flattening onto his face. Blood sprayed everywhere, and Mahegan stepped forward and pushed the tall kid into the river with a loud splash.

The shotgun fired but missed Mahegan as he spun into the pudgy kid with a backward rotation. It was a double-barrel, so he knew that the weapon was empty, but he didn't discount the fact that the fat kid might have a few shells in his pocket. His main concern, though, was the knife guy, the fighter, who was using the pudgy kid to shield his movements. Mahegan grabbed the shotgun by the barrel with his right hand, used his left forearm to strike the shooter in the temple, and easily tossed the weapon into the river with the kid still attached to it.

For the first time since their encounter began, the boy holding the switchblade smiled. He flipped the knife a few times in his hand and stepped forward, ready.

Mahegan remained in a fighter's stance, left foot forward. The switchblade flashed against the sunlight as the kid spun toward Mahegan to deliver a roundhouse, leading with a high kick that missed and then quickly following through with a slash of the blade. But it, too, missed. It was a gamble, Mahegan would later recognize.

On the kid's follow-through, Mahegan grabbed his arm and used his momentum to slam him into the cedar tree that bore the shattered root. The kid seemed stunned momentarily, stumbling, with one foot sliding into the water. Mahegan followed with a straight punch to the back of the kid's head. He watched his eyes roll back and heard the kid's ankle snap as his unconscious body fell into the water, his foot wedged between two root sheaths.

Mahegan looked at the three injured kids and knew that he had not seen nor heard the last from them. He didn't care. He had survived his first fight in pretty good fashion. He had learned something about himself, namely, that he was a natural. The same way some people were born to fly fighter jets or invent new technology, Mahegan was born to protect. To defend. If not himself, then others.

Oddly, it was his mother who had taught him the balance needed to survive in any arena, whether it was a childhood playground or an Afghan battlefield. *Balance, Chayton, my son. It's all about balance.*

Mahegan snapped back from the childhood memory to the present, where Grace was still breathing an easy rhythm on his chest. He listened for sounds in the hallway and in the parking lot. He knew he needed to rest. Tomorrow would bring more information and, necessarily, more rapid action.

Balance. No more gambles, unless they were absolutely necessary. Protect the things he cared about and the people who cared about him.

His mother. Protect her memory.

In the end, there was no choice at all. He had to find a way both to accomplish his assigned mission and to defend his mother's honor. Some might call it revenge, but Mahegan called it justice. The world was an unfair place, and it required people like him to make it just a little bit fairer.

That was Chayton "Jake" Mahegan's calling.

The falcon-wolf. The hunter-killer.

And then there was the picture he had found in Throckmorton's house. The one that Grace had glimpsed. He was confident that she hadn't seen the entire picture or who else was on the film. It was a rarity these days, a stock paper picture, but it had been there and had convinced him that Throckmorton was working with Gunther and that the new project in western Wake County was where he would find Gunther.

As he lay there, he tried to isolate the most important detail from the cacophony of activity that had occurred during the past three days. What was he not doing that he should be doing? he asked himself. He thought about the nexus between Throckmorton and Gunther. What was their play? What was their state of mind after tonight's spoiling attack?

Their mission would be to move as quickly as possible to get the gas from the shale and to the market. Cash in and cash out. Let the feds and the state regulators try to figure out what had happened to the previously gas-rich shale deposit once the legal fracking began. It was no different than a bank heist, only more complicated, in that it involved lots of technology and workers. When people were stealing large amounts of money, they worried about security. Griffyn would surely talk and tell them that "Hawthorne" was up in their grill.

Again, while it was a gamble to dump Griffyn there, it was better to know that he was inside the compound than to have him as a rogue double agent outside. Griffyn could trump up all sorts of charges against him and remove him from the chessboard for Throckmorton and Gunther. That would be one of their plays, Mahegan figured. Also, they would go back to the beginning. There had been talk at the Wallaby gas station of a two-man crew from Chapel Hill that had never returned from a fracking job. If they hadn't already, Gunther and Throckmorton would have Papa Diablo and Manuela eliminated as quickly as possible. The plan from the outset had most likely been to kill all three of them.

Mahegan decided that in a few hours, he would drive to the Wallaby and warn the men there not to take the Gunther fracking job.

CHAPTER 21

J AMES GUNTHER SAT IN THE OBSERVATION ROOM AND WATCHED MAEVE Cassidy maneuver the drill out, steer the newly inserted piping into place, and guide the perforating charge into the hole. She followed that procedure by forcing millions of gallons of pressurized, chemically laced water into the shaft. The chemicals cut through the rock and held open thousands of freshly created fissures, which would instantly release gas.

Like a doctor performing remote surgery, she expertly inserted the fracking block, known as a stop, that prevented the gas from coming up the pipe. They had several more fractures they wanted to make in this drill path. All told, Gunther had Chun and Ting program fourteen horizontal paths, which would sap the great majority of the gas from the Durham shale.

The woman had skills, Gunther had to admit. They had made a good decision when they agreed to acquire her talents. For some time Gunther had been unsure about partnering with a prissy boy like Throckmorton. Ever since he and his road crew had killed that blond mother whose son had broken *his* son's nose in a fight in Maxton, down by the river, his entire focus had been on becoming the richest, most powerful country boy in North Carolina. Gunther knew he couldn't screw anymore, but he could acquire wealth and dominate people.

It had never really been about sex to him, anyway. He busted a nut by hurting people and being the top dog. He had come from

THREE MINUTES TO MIDNIGHT   183

nothing and had built his construction business one ditch, one road, one bridge at a time. Suddenly, he'd been winning state and city projects quicker than anyone else. He had bid on projects he couldn't do, but he had still won them and had subcontracted them out to others who needed to work. When he saw the movement toward fracking in North Carolina, that was when he started leaning in that direction. But he overinvested in that, and the bureaucrats on Jones Street in Raleigh were taking their damn sweet time passing laws and regulations. As his balance sheet began to collapse with the recession, James Gunther and Sons Construction was nearly bankrupt.

Then, when they were on the brink of financial disaster, Jim landed the big-time government job in Afghanistan. When Jim told him what he would be doing in Afghanistan, Gunther scratched out a plan. His dealings with most rich people had shown him that they believed they knew how the world worked, and that they were certain their privilege was hard earned, even if handed down over generations. So Gunther let Throckmorton believe the entire fracking and funding scheme was his idea. He went to Throckmorton because he truly needed a loan, but he slipped in a few tidbits about Jim's classified mission in Afghanistan that whetted Throckmorton's appetite.

Gunther looked at the monitor showing the EB-5 roughnecks feeding the drill into the ground. It was a coiled, snaking device that was fed into the sleeve that led underground. Somewhere, miles below, it was connected to the working end that Maeve Cassidy was steering through the Triassic layer of earth and into the Durham shale.

"Everything to your satisfaction, Dad?"

Gunther scratched his face and ran a hand across his bloodshot eyes. He didn't mince words and had no time for pleasantries, even with his son.

"What'd y'all do with Griffyn? RPD sees him missing too long, they'll go ballistic."

"He's in one of the rooms in the tunnel down the way," Jim said, turning his head over his shoulder. "I talked to him. He could be useful if we get more intel on these people watching us. And I had him call the Raleigh Police Department and tell them he's taking a few days of personal leave. Also asked him about this Hawthorne guy. Some kind of Army criminal investigator."

"You see him?"

"Only from a distance. Big guy in the car with Grace Kagami, Griffyn says."

"The Shred's slope? What the hell is she doing in there?"

"There's some connection. Kagami was placed as lead forensic tech on the Throckmorton scene."

"That was a botched operation from the get-go." Gunther coughed. "You were supposed to snag the Army woman when she showed, but you got sidelined by all that commie pussy."

"I got her here, didn't I?"

James Gunther Sr. leveled his gaze on his son, mad that he had not immediately taken Maeve Cassidy hostage when she showed at the Throckmorton home. He knew that his son had the same weakness for women that he had once possessed. While he wanted to cut the kid some slack for being diverted by the EB-5 women, some of whom were rather exotic, he had an operation to run.

"What you got was a major criminal investigation going, and you would be all over the front pages if Throckmorton didn't own part of the newspaper. That's the only thing keeping a lid on this thing. All them big-money folks keep their secrets buried by buying off the newspaper. Hell of a thing, but it's working out for us this time."

"She has perforated the first zone, and all looks in order. She's blocked the gas, and we're lowering the next charges. In a few hours we will start drilling the second vein. All is on schedule," Jim said.

Gunther smirked at his son's effort to change the topic, but he stayed on course. "What are you going to do about Griffyn?"

"I have a plan for him. Don't worry."

Gunther laid his flat black eyes on his son and said, "Don't you ever tell me not to worry, boy. I've been worrying about you and your screwups since you got your ass kicked by that BFI when you was fifteen years old. The only reason you're still alive is that I've spent a lifetime worrying about how to clothe and feed your sorry ass. Now, you get the hell out of here and make yourself useful. Be best to kill Griffyn and blame it on this Hawthorne guy, if that's really his name."

Jim nodded, apparently unsure.

Never lacking when it came to providing parental guidance, Gunther said, "Get your ass moving, son. We need to be done within the week so we can pull down the rig and just have the wellhead there."

Gunther watched Jim walk down the worn limestone steps and into the labyrinth that was this section of the Underground Railroad. He knew it was dilapidated, but this part had served its purposes well.

He stood from his chair and grabbed his shotgun. Done watching the woman drill, blast, and inject chemicals into the shale, he wanted to have a chat with Ting. Looking at the wellhead camera monitor, he saw what looked like a small gathering of animated men at the base of the rig.

"Bunch of jack offs," he muttered. "Wasting time. Wasting money." Gunther left the observation room, followed the dusty, worn path in the tunnel, and shouldered through the door that led to the basement. He turned and walked up the steps to the storm shelter doors. Pushing them up and out of the way, he emerged into the night, brandishing his shotgun. An enforcer. All his life he'd been making men do things they didn't necessarily want to do, and he knew how to complete a job. Force of personality mixed with the right kind of threat usually did the trick.

Instead of driving around the bend and tipping his hand that he was approaching, Gunther picked his way along the half-mile downhill trail. He walked until he was around the eastern side, where the fence wasn't totally complete, past Cassidy's first night's accommodations, and through the tall grass. He approached from behind the port-o-johns that were lined up next to where the trucks were parked.

Gunther stood and listened to the men talking in their native languages. They were wearing an assortment of denims, flannels, and Carhartt Sherpa jackets, which Throckmorton had purchased in bulk. The men stood under a weak bank of lights that centered on the wellhead. Gunther had intended to keep the light weak so that airplanes and adjacent landowners didn't get too suspicious too soon.

Most of the conversation seemed to be between Ting, Chun, and Petrov. Petrov knew some Chinese, apparently, but not much, because Ting and Chun were using animated hand motions to try to communicate with him. Gunther remembered that earlier they had been wearing surgical masks, but those hung loosely around their necks now. The chemical spray required at least that. Part of the reason he was in the control booth when Cassidy shot the chemicals into the earth was that he didn't want a third eye growing out of his forehead.

English was the one language that all the men spoke with some proficiency. Gunther stepped out, the shotgun on his shoulder, and said, "Hell's going on here?"

The three men in the inner circle looked up, startled. Petrov's flat gaze hung on Gunther. Ting and Chun were more animated and continued speaking in Chinese, their high-pitched voices bugging the hell out of Gunther.

"Ting, what the hell are we doing?" asked Gunther. "We've got another vein to start on in a bit and more charges to lower."

Ting turned toward Gunther. "We using too much explosive. Need to use less each blast, Mr. Gunther."

"I thought you guys calculated all of that?" Gunther squinted his eyes, suspicious.

"Yes. What I say and what Chun say is Petrov like a big boom. We want small boom just to hit right spot. Too much create problems and seal off the gas before chemicals get in to hold open for gas to come out."

"Well, damn it, do what you have to do, but do it. Fish or cut bait. Quit talking about it and get moving."

"We moving, Mr. Gunter," Ting said.

Gunther watched Ting and Chun turn toward Petrov, who was still staring at him.

"You got a problem, Petrov? Got your ass kicked by some Mexicans. Now you want me to kick it? I'll kill you right now if you don't get your ass back to work. And get those Mexicans and the 'white but not white' guy tomorrow morning."

Petrov waited a moment, then nodded. "Yes, Mr. Gunther."

Gunther turned and walked back the way he had come, figuring the exercise would be good for him. He broke a sweat on the climb back up the hill, but afterward, he was glad he had done so. He had done some thinking on that climb. Maybe the stress of losing seven workers was causing the crew to overreact. Then again, maybe something else entirely was happening behind their backs. He had to think about that one, but he decided to go down and talk to Cassidy about it.

He retraced his steps into the basement, found the door to the Underground Railroad hideout, and this time walked past the EB-5 female guard holding a Remington shotgun and into the control room instead of the observation room. There he found Maeve Cassidy studiously maneuvering the joystick as she manipulated the next explosive shaped charge into the horizontal cut. He observed her skill by watching the monitor, which was displaying a three-dimensional image of the ground through which they were drilling. It showed the vertical drill and the kickoff point where the horizontal drill began. Gunther saw the layers of the earth and the boreholes, which was like observing a child's worm farm, along with the fractured areas and the newly placed charge.

"What do you need, Jimmy?" Maeve asked without turning around.

"Ain't Jimmy, woman."

Maeve jumped. The joystick slammed to the side, and the monitor showed the explosive had detonated.

"What the hell?" Maeve screamed. "You scared me! Good thing that charge was where it needed to be."

"That's my question. How much explosives you need to do that job? For each fracture?"

"I thought you knew."

"Would I be asking you if I knew?"

Maeve stood and stared at Gunther, who was still holding his shotgun. He could tell she was considering some options outside the purview of answering his question.

"I'm stronger than you think, and I will kill you without batting an eyelash. If you weren't the one helping us with this, I would have already splattered your brains on the television screens there." Gunther pointed the shotgun at the HD monitors.

"Each explosive charge contains two to five kilograms of MDX in shaped containers made with depleted uranium to create maximum fracture," she said.

"Is that too much, just enough, or not enough?"

"It's about right. Maybe a little strong, but about right," she replied.

Gunther had to give it to the woman. She was poised and strong. He liked that about her. Licked his lips, wishing his other parts worked.

"Okay, now tell me why Ting and them would be saying we are using too much explosives."

He watched her think. She scratched her chin and flipped her hair behind her ears.

"No reason that I can think of. All I can say is that this is what we used in Afghanistan. This is what Jim brought back with him. The DU is entirely illegal. Not that anything we're doing is legal, but that part is especially bad. Mixing the new chemicals with the depleted uranium could be deadly to the water supply. Maybe that's what they're concerned about. They may have seen the shape charges and don't want to poison the water."

"They don't give a rat's ass about our water. It's something else. You think about it and let me know if you come up with anything. In the meantime, don't stop working." He flipped the switch, and the fifty-five-inch monitor showed Piper sleeping on her back, dressed in pajamas. She held a small blanket and sucked her thumb.

Gunther watched Maeve gasp and clutch her heart.

"Cry me a river, bitch. Now, get back to work."

He shut down the screen and exited.

On his walk back to the lodge, he was thinking about why the Chinese would want to use fewer explosives than the Russian, who was the expert and was in charge of the drill site.

Could the Chinese be saving the explosives for something else? he wondered.

CHAPTER 22

MAHEGAN WAS AWAKE AT 5:00 A.M. THE SUN HAD NOT YET CRESTED, and Grace continued to sleep in the same position on his chest. He watched her eyelids jump, her eyes moving beneath them, as she dreamed. Not wanting to interrupt whatever story her brain was telling her, he continued to lie there until he felt her move some time later.

She opened her eyes briefly, muttered something, then closed them again. He wished she would wake up, as he needed to slip away. He did his best to slide the pillow under her head without changing the elevation. He had pillows under her leg and head as he gently rolled off the bed, and she continued to breathe in her steady rhythm. He dressed, left her a note, closed the door quietly behind him, and walked back to the shopping mall parking lot to retrieve the Crown Victoria.

He drove to the Wallaby in Apex, where he saw the work line starting to form. Manuela was already there, but as usual, Papa Diablo was probably hiding or having breakfast. Mahegan parked the car in the shopping center parking lot and walked across the street to the Wallaby, where he found Manuela, the big Hispanic man from his fence job three days ago, by himself, pacing back and forth beneath a streetlamp that was competing with the slate gray of dawn.

"*Hola,*" Mahegan said.

"*Hola*—" Manuela stopped short when he saw Mahegan.

"Come with me," Mahegan said.

He led Manuela behind the car wash associated with the gas station. There was a pool of oily water on the pavement where the cars drove through the dryer.

"Bad people," Mahegan said. Manuela stared at him, as if he didn't understand, so Mahegan tried his limited Spanish. "Muy malas personas."

"Sí. Sí," Manuela said, pointing at Mahegan.

"No. Not me." He paused and constructed the sentences in his mind. "Les hombres de petróleo y gas. Muy peligroso. Díselo a tus amigos." Mahegan stuttered through his broken Spanish but thought he did okay.

Manuela took a step back. Mahegan knew he had put these men in danger, but if he had not been there, Petrov probably would have killed them.

"There is talk," the man said in basic English, clearly not wanting to have to listen to Mahegan try his Spanish again. "That day we went. The day before us, a two-man crew never came back."

"I remember."

"What you say may be true. I tell my friends. We not go with those men."

"Take this," Mahegan said, handing a burner cell phone to Manuela.

Mahegan saw Papa Diablo walking quickly across the lot about fifty yards away. That meant one thing: a promising truck had arrived.

"Mierda," Manuela said. "Mierda, mierda, mierda!"

Papa Diablo was already in the back of the same truck in which they had ridden three mornings ago. Petrov was standing outside, looking for someone, most likely him and Manuela. A tall Asian man stepped out of the passenger side of the truck. When they didn't choose any other workers, Mahegan knew that they had come for all three of them. They were loose ends.

Manuela walked toward the truck, which drew the attention of both Petrov and the Asian man. Mahegan watched as Manuela removed his jacket. He was preparing for a fight. While the Asian man appeared more bookish than ruffian, Petrov would make up for him. Mahegan had caught Petrov completely off guard before, and this would not happen again.

Mahegan was taken aback as his military mind ratcheted into gear. *Two of America's most threatening enemies, China and Russia, in the same truck?*

Petrov came around the back end of the pickup, lowered its tail, and gave Manuela a welcoming grimace. "Yes, yes. You did such good work the other day."

Manuela walked up to Petrov and got in two good jabs before Petrov figured out what was happening. Once he did, though, he was the Olympic boxer, leading with his left foot and left hand. He got inside on Manuela and landed three good jabs to the face and drew blood. Manuela, no slacker, scored a few body blows that made Petrov cough. It was the straight right that stunned Manuela long enough for Petrov to get in close and hammer him three times across the face with roundhouse hooks, driven by the pivot of Petrov's right foot and the whirling of his shoulders into perfect strike position.

Manuela was down and then in the back of the truck with Papa Diablo, who had not moved, because, as Mahegan saw, the Asian man was holding a pistol out of sight of the lineup of men, but clearly visible to him and Diablo.

"You. White but not white. Your turn," Petrov said.

Mahegan strode the twenty yards between them with long strides, then veered away at the last second and landed a solid right cross on the Asian man. Mahegan threw the punch from his hip, extending his fist outward, rotating it as it arced through the air, twisting it just as it struck the spot between the nose and forehead, then snapping it back, ready for the second punch. The pistol bobbed in the man's long fingers until Mahegan grabbed his wrist, threw an elbow into the man's gut, and squeezed his hand until the weapon clanked to the ground. He palmed the man's head like a basketball and slammed his forehead into the truck, then turned to find Petrov closing on him.

Having the presence of mind to kick the pistol under the truck, he blocked Petrov's right cross and drove his left fist into the left pectoral, which he had cut with the posthole digger. Mahegan pivoted this time off his left foot, turning his hips to provide extra momentum, and twisted the fist into the injury. Petrov stepped back, stumbled a bit, and Mahegan saw a cloud cross over his eyes. Either he was in intense pain from Mahegan's punch or the man had moved to another place mentally. Mahegan guessed both.

The Russian took up a fighter's pose, while Mahegan enticed him away from the truck. He watched as Diablo and Manuela scampered out the back and hurried behind the drive-through car wash with the rest of the day laborers, who were watching the fight go down. Out of his periphery, he saw that the Asian man was still down and that no one had gone for the pistol. Petrov probably had a weapon, but he could see the man was focused on mano a mano.

He watched Petrov's rhythm. The man rocked back and forth, obviously falling into a pattern he had developed as a boxer. His technique was too good to be anything but professional. He looked uncomfortable moving farther than a few feet toward Mahegan, as if he expected to stay in a square boxing ring. So Mahegan continued to draw him away from the truck, out of his comfort zone, out of the ring. Petrov looked confused, perhaps wondering why Mahegan would not stay in the zone and fight him. Petrov stumbled and lost his bounce but quickly regained his step. One, two. Left, right. One, two. Left, right. Mahegan watched and waited. He stopped, and Petrov kept coming forward, but his steps were out of sync. Mahegan had deliberately stopped when Petrov's right foot was forward, where he had less power.

Mahegan's wingspan was over seven feet wide. He had learned in fighting to create his own internal safe zone, which was a little over three feet. Anything inside three feet and Mahegan could tap, tap, tap it all day long with a powerful jab or a right cross. Those were his two basic punches. Having wrestled in high school, he could also fight close, but he avoided that now. He had learned the hard way that weapons could appear from the most unlikely places.

Petrov stumbled into that three-foot zone, and Mahegan scored a firm left jab on the boxer's forehead. He kept coming inside that zone, though, like a Joe Frazier or a Mike Tyson with no reach, and started going for Mahegan's body. Petrov landed some good blows into his rib cage with a strong right uppercut. Mahegan violated his rule and slipped into wrestling mode when Petrov kept pummeling. He dropped down into a fireman's carry takedown and lifted the man onto his shoulders, absorbing some body blows in the kidneys from Petrov's weaker left hand. But still, it counted.

Mahegan strode forward with Petrov's active weight on his back, like he was carrying a live bear, and flipped him into the bed of the pickup truck with a loud *thunk*. Petrov was up quickly, and they both stared at each other when they heard sirens blaring, as if the round had ended and each fighter had to go to his respective corner. Soon Mahegan could see blue lights flashing from about a half mile away. Petrov leapt out of the pickup bed, pulled the Asian man into the cab, climbed behind the wheel, and sped away in the opposite direction.

Mahegan walked across the street, watching as the police cars fishtailed into the parking lot of the gas station. As he looked over his shoulder, Papa Diablo and Manuela waved and nodded, an unspoken thank-you for most likely saving their lives. The two informal leaders of the group disappeared in the parking lot, like ghosts. Mahegan figured most of the day laborers were illegal and wanted nothing to do with the police. As he walked to his car, he thought again about the plight of these men, who got in vehicles with people they didn't know, went to locations they were unfamiliar with, and worked for an undetermined wage.

There had to be a better way. But he had done his duty, righting a wrong or, if not that, at least protecting those men, who were so desperate that they would have gladly gone back on the job. He also knew that he had removed all doubt that he was the nemesis to Gunther and Throckmorton and their EB-5 commandos.

The battle lines were now clearly drawn.

CHAPTER 23

Hᴇ ᴅʀᴏᴠᴇ ᴛᴏ ᴡɪᴛʜɪɴ ᴀ ᴍɪʟᴇ ᴏꜰ ʜɪꜱ ᴀᴘᴀʀᴛᴍᴇɴᴛ, ᴡᴀʟᴋᴇᴅ ᴛʜʀᴏᴜɢʜ the woods along a firebreak, grabbed his secure smartphone from the safe, and used his Zebra app to send a message to Savage. He pocketed his phone, relocked his safe, backed his Cherokee out of the barn, and drove back to the mall where he had parked Griffyn's car. He walked the remaining mile to the hotel.

As he rounded the bend, he saw a yellow Lamborghini in the Holiday Inn parking lot. Mahegan girded his mind for the worst possible scenario. In the past three days he had killed and fought more people than he had on some of his worst days in combat. His missions were usually designed so that he had to move quickly in and out. This mission, however, resembled his last, involving the American Taliban, in which he fought and killed suicide bombers trained in America and ready for action on U.S. soil.

Here he was, fighting to save the life of an Army officer and her daughter . . . and to avenge his mother's murder.

As he was walking into the hallway of the Holiday Inn from the side entrance, Mahegan heard loud noises coming from his room. Shouts, mostly, and female voices. Leading with his pistol, Mahegan opened the door to the room to find Grace, three other women, and Ted the Shred seated in chairs or on the beds. The Shred had his hands tied behind his back as an attractive blond-haired woman yelled at him. Her hair was pulled back in a pony-tail that fell midway down her back. She wore a black Under

Armour outfit that made her look a bit like a ninja with no mask, Mahegan thought.

"You're part of this, Ted, you asshole, and . . . ," she said, looking at Grace, then at Mahegan, who focused his pistol on her.

"Who the hell is this?" Mahegan asked.

"Elaine, this is Hawthorne," Grace said. Then to Mahegan, "You can put down the frigging pistol, Hawthorne."

"Who let him in on this?" Elaine demanded, turning her attention away from Ted and to Grace, who was now standing between the two double beds. "This is *our* deal, Grace. *We* are taking these assholes down."

Mahegan didn't know Elaine, but she certainly had an edge.

"This guy has, like, saved my frigging life ten times in the past couple of days," Grace said.

"I don't care if he's the pope. We said this was classified. No leaks." Elaine's thin neck showed sinewy tendons as she emphasized her point.

"This is actually my room," Mahegan interrupted. "I'm going to give you a couple of minutes to explain what's going on here, and then I'm going to decide whether or not you can stay."

Elaine looked at Grace and then at the two other women, who wore similar clothes to Elaine's. Black jumpsuits. They were the Don't Frack the Triangle, DFT2, Chapel Hill watch team Grace had mentioned, Mahegan guessed. Besides Elaine, there was a short, stocky woman with a close haircut, looking almost like a man. The other was striking and lean, and she looked at Mahegan with curious eyes, as if trying to place him.

"Like Pink says, 'Just when it can't get worse, I've had a shit day. . . . Blow me,' " Elaine said.

"I think that last phrase is actually from Pink's 'Blow me one last kiss,' " Grace snapped. Then to Mahegan, "Elaine thinks everything you need to know in life can be explained by Pink songs. Study those and we're all good."

Elaine was watching the dynamic between Grace and Mahegan.

"We're all lesbians, so don't get any ideas," Elaine barked.

Mahegan looked at Grace, who shrugged. Elaine saw the inter-action and turned to Grace.

"You slut. You slept with him? *Fuckin' perfect.*"

"Let's focus here, Elaine," Grace said. "We've got Ted here, and Hawthorne can be helpful to the cause. Pink can't help us."

"Why is Ted here?" Mahegan asked. "And who are these peo-ple?" Mahegan waved a hand across the room. "And why are they here?"

"This is Brandy," Grace said, pointing at the stocky, dark-haired woman sitting on the bed, holding a big industrial flashlight. "And this is Theresa. They've been a couple for a few months."

"As *we* used to be," Elaine said to Grace.

"Oh, get over it, Elaine. That was two years ago," Grace said.

"It's been written in the scars on our hearts!" Elaine pointed her finger at her chest as she quoted another Pink song, Mahe-gan guessed. He had heard of Pink, mostly from the female sol-diers talking about listening to her music. She had a large following among the troops in Afghanistan, but he wasn't certain that he would be able to identify a Pink song on the radio.

They didn't look like a couple, but what did Mahegan know? Theresa was lithe and athletic, and she had the silky brunette hair and high cheekbones of a runway model. Brandy was the oppo-site. Grace and Elaine, he could picture. Or maybe it was easier to picture those two together than it was Brandy and Theresa. He shrugged.

"Okay. Not my business. These are your watchers?" he said.

"Grace!"

"Lighten up, Elaine. He knows more than us about this, and we've been watching these guys for three months build that rig at night," Grace said. She walked over to Mahegan, who was still standing by the door, which was closed.

The room had the confused air of a school classroom with no teacher, Mahegan thought. Ted was the dunce in the corner, primitively bound and gagged. The four girls were the students, who were fighting, not knowing what to do. Somehow they had reached an impasse in their decision-making process.

"What about your man there?" Mahegan nodded, trying to move the conversation along.

"I bought a disposable cell at the grocery store next door while you were gone, and called Elaine," Grace said. "Turns out, the Shred was stalking her, trying to find me. Mickey Mantle here slugged him with that flashlight when he stepped in the room. I found some rope in your duffel bag. Sorry." Grace cast her eyes downward.

"In the Army we called this a goat rope," Mahegan said.

"About right," Elaine agreed. "Did my time. Navy." He saw her size him up with an obvious vertical scan, as if he were a bar code, then turn toward Grace. "If you're going back to the dark side, Grace, this one will do. Better than that dickhead." She nodded at Ted the Shred.

"Appreciate the permission, Elaine," Grace snapped. She turned to Mahegan and said, "We were about to question the Shred. Maybe you have some special techniques?"

"Maybe I do. Depends on what you're trying to find out." Mahegan looked at Ted, whose eyes were wide as he listened to the conversation.

"He knows stuff about what is happening at the drill site. So, we figure it's time for him to tell us," Brandy said. She lifted the flashlight and said, "We took his ass down hard."

"Up all night?" Mahegan asked. The three women were amped on something, maybe just caffeine.

"Been drinking that five-hour energy stuff all night long," Elaine said. "We've got a buzz, for sure. Hiding out by our big rock."

"So why don't we all sit down?" Mahegan said. He guessed that was the best way to get a handle on the awkward moment. Theresa sat next to Brandy but kept her furrowed brow stare on Mahegan, and Elaine pulled over a chair from the computer work area, which was standard fare in all hotel rooms. Grace sat on the bed nearest the door. Mahegan remained standing.

"So who tied and gagged Ted?" asked Mahegan.

Brandy raised her hand. "That would be me."

"Did you take the battery out of his cell phone?" Mahegan asked.

The ladies looked at one another.

"No. We pulled it from his pocket, though. It's right there," Brandy said, pointing at the table.

Mahegan saw the blinking light indicating there was a message. He walked over, picked up the cell phone, and crushed it against the corner of the table. He picked at the shattered parts, snatching the SIM card and the battery and pocketing both.

"People were tracking you, Grace. They're probably tracking him. We don't have much time, so let's remove the gag." After thinking for a moment, Mahegan asked all the women, "Are your phones on?"

"Of course," Elaine responded, as if Mahegan were an idiot. Then, "Oh shit."

"Remove your batteries, just to be safe. If you can't, then turn off the power completely."

The women fumbled with their phones. Brandy and Theresa had Droids with removable batteries, but Elaine had an iPhone, which turned off. Grace kept her burner operational.

That task completed, Mahegan thought through his approach with Grace. He had neared a trust boundary where he was willing to share certain information with her, but he knew nothing about the three watchers. He had to make a decision, though, about the women and the information he would share with them, if any.

Brandy had stood and had started walking toward Ted when Elaine said, "Wait a damn minute. How do we know if he's not going to scream or something stupid like that?"

"I'll shoot him," Mahegan said, holding up his pistol. He nodded at Ted, who had clearly heard him and who acknowledged his cooperation with a silent nod.

"Fair enough," Elaine said.

Mahegan briefly pictured Elaine and Grace together. Elaine dominant and in control, with Grace more submissive and tender. He could see it.

Mahegan was also thinking about the high technology tracking devices that Throckmorton and Gunther had used to find and follow them so far. How long did they have before this room would be burned? he wondered. How had Ted found Elaine? If they were holed up in hide positions, watching the drill site, how had Ted found them?

Brandy made quick work of the handkerchief, and Mahegan thought of the old English proverb "In for a penny, in for a pound." He was vested here, and he might be able to enlist the help of the watchers. Sometimes it paid off to hold secrets, and sometimes it was more profitable to share information. While Mahegan wasn't necessarily in a sharing mood, they had captured Ted, and his bounty of information, whatever it might be, was equally their booty, whatever their purpose.

"Okay. I'm going to ask the question here, ladies," Mahegan said. Then to Ted, "How did you track Elaine and find her?"

Elaine snapped her head toward Mahegan and then toward Ted. "Yeah. Good damn question."

"Elaine, please be quiet," Mahegan said. The timbre of his voice was that of a commander issuing orders, but restrained.

He sized up Ted, who was shaking his head, smiling. The man had an arm in a sling from the crushed wrist. His forehead was swollen and red from where he had slammed it into Grace's front door. The ropes crisscrossed his chest and legs, binding him to the second chair in the hotel room.

"You guys are something else," Ted said. "Three dykes, a bi criminal, and a BFI."

"BFI?" Elaine asked, obviously still engaged.

"Big effing Indian," Mahegan said. "I've heard it all before. Now, Ted, I guess you've been in touch with at least your dad, if not some of the others from the fracking operation. You guys are in deep stuff. You've lost six workers, maybe seven, and you know all the other bad things your father and his partners have done. So answer my questions, or I will hurt you even worse than I did the other night."

"Damn. You did all that?" Brandy asked, nodding toward Ted.

"I told you he's saved my life, like, ten times," Grace added. "Now, let him do his thing."

Mahegan saw that the right wrist was in a cast, which could be used as a lethal weapon, if Ted were given the opportunity. He pulled out his Duane Dieter Spec Ops knife and flipped open the blade with a well-practiced turn of his wrist. He stepped toward Ted, who began stuttering.

"Hey, man. Hey, man. What the hell, dude?"

Mahegan lifted Ted's right forearm and slid the knife inside the cast, then sliced through the plaster easily. He removed the cast loop over the thumb and tossed the device aside like a Civil War doctor disposed of severed limbs.

"I'm going to grab this wrist right here," Mahegan said, placing his large thumb on top of the broken ulna. "And I'm going to squeeze until you tell me how you found Elaine. I imagine you think you're tough, but trust me, you aren't."

At the slightest pressure on the weal, Ted howled.

"Wait a sec, Ted. We had an agreement that you weren't going to make any loud noises that might call attention to us. You're violating all kinds of agreements here, which is going to have severe consequences for you immediately, because I'm guessing we've got precious little time," Mahegan said.

"Damn. I'm liking this," Elaine whispered.

"So, last chance," Mahegan said. With a little more pressure on Ted's wrist, tears streamed down the man's face. Having surfed, Mahegan knew that the wrists were crucial for paddling and popping up into position on the board. Ted wasn't going surfing any time soon unless he was an idiot, which, Mahegan figured, might be the case.

"We have a cell phone scanner. A Stingray. I've got numbers, and we've got a GPS tracking system." Ted coughed. "Damn it, let go!"

"We're getting somewhere, but we're definitely not there," Mahegan said. "Where is this system, and who controls it?"

"Man, you guys are in way over your—"

Mahegan applied enough pressure to break the bone, again. He felt it give through the soft tissue that had swollen to protect it and help the injury heal.

"Damn. Damn it!" Ted howled again. Mahegan passively watched him grimace and squeeze the words out of his tightly pressed lips. "Okay. Okay. It's at Dad's compound, but you don't need to be there. You can access it through a computer. That's how I found Elaine. Like that app you can use to find your phone if you lost it."

Mahegan released Ted's wrist. He had more questions, but that was a relevant piece of information. He looked at Grace. "So Elaine's phone number is in that system right now?"

"Too late for that, man. The last known location will show us here." Ted smiled. "So you guys are screwed. Trust me, if these green-card guys see a target-rich environment like this, they'll drop everything. The environmental whack jobs, the BFI, and the lab tech who's supposed to be working the scene from the shoot-ing are too big a bull's-eye to pass up."

"I agree," Mahegan said. "On second thought, batteries back in your phones. You ladies, please go do your thing. Watch. Give me one looking out the window there, one of you at the end of the hallway, watching the back, and one in the lobby. Read a newspaper or something. If you see black pickup trucks and some folks who look foreign, give Grace a call."

"That's half of Apex," Elaine said.

"You'll know the difference. Military haircuts, physically fit, and possibly openly carrying weapons."

"You mean the guys from the fracking site?" Brandy asked.

"Yeah, those guys."

"Hell, we've been watching them and know what they look like."

"Roger," Mahegan said. "Now get moving."

The three ladies moved toward the door. Theresa, who was leading, stopped. Looking at Mahegan, she said, "You were at the drill site. You and two Mexican gentlemen. You worked all day, digging holes and putting in a fence. I saw the fight you had with the guy with the scar."

Mahegan nodded, acknowledging her memory and her profes-sional acumen. "You guys are good."

"He looks meaner every day," she said. "I watch him the most. Him and the two Chinese guys. They're up to something. The rest are just workers, but those two are in charge of something. Maybe the whole thing. Please be careful. I wouldn't want anything to . . . happen to you."

"I agree. We'll talk about that, but first we need to squeeze Ted here like a ripe lemon and then get out of here, if we can."

"Okay," Theresa said with a soft voice. Mahegan noticed the phone in her hand and something rectangular bulging under her spandex ninja outfit. Was that a phone, also? Mahegan wondered.

Before he could follow up, Theresa went into the lobby, Brandy took the hallway, and Elaine took up a post at the window. Mahegan logged his observation of Theresa as he figured that Elaine had stayed in the room because she wanted to hear firsthand the information Ted could provide. She took up a sentry post to the side of the window that looked out onto the street. Mahegan gave her a measure of respect for her tactical skills.

"Ted. I want to know why your EB-Five commandos have been trying to kill Grace."

Again, Elaine's head snapped up. "They've been trying to *kill* you?"

"Elaine, please," Mahegan said.

"They weren't trying to kill her. Just wanted to scare her so she would do what Griffyn wanted on the investigation. Dad doesn't want it getting out that he's got hookers from Europe over here."

"Sex slaves for your dad's highbrow parties?"

"Well, technically, they have their visas, and they have skills. But, yes, their primary job is to have sex with whomever Dad is entertaining. CEOs, congressmen, whoever. My dad has hidden cameras and will blackmail everybody if they don't pass the laws they need. Genius, really," Ted said.

"Yeah, genius," Mahegan replied. He saw that Elaine was standing now and was about to launch on Ted, so he stepped in front of her to block her. "Sit down, Elaine. This is my investigation."

"We captured him," she asserted.

"You'll have your turn to ask him some things. Now, please."

All his life, Mahegan had worked mostly with men, whether it was in the Army or on the odd jobs he held afterward, such as fishing boat mate, landscaper, and bouncer. What he knew professionally about the women with whom he had trained and fought was that they were keenly adept at ferreting out the right information and making sound recommendations and decisions. He preferred, and usually worked with, a female military intelligence analyst named Cixi Suparman, an Indonesian American Army captain who had attended ROTC at the College of William & Mary. Everyone called her Superman, which Mahegan knew she secretly liked. Her two sergeants were female, as well.

In Mahegan's experience, women saw things that men generally didn't see. Maybe it was the hunter-gatherer thing. He did know that the Israeli government impressed females into their military intelligence and border persistent-stare programs because of their better ability to notice anomalies and change. And so his line of questioning was intended not only to get information but also to reveal information to these women, under the general assumption that they would be equally as cognizant as the tested Israeli women or his intelligence analysts in Afghanistan.

"Please just listen to my questions and his answers. I have a method here. I want you to process what he is saying with what you have been observing. You represent an environmental group. I have a very narrow interest that, as luck would have it, coincides with yours. So, let's work this together for the moment," Mahegan said.

Elaine nodded.

Grace looked at Elaine and mouthed, "Thank you."

"Explain the EB-Five thing, Ted."

Ted was rubbing his forearm, above the swollen ulna. "Man, you really messed me up," he mumbled. His sun bleached brown hair and square jaw made him look like something between a preppy and a surfer, a look that didn't quite fit in either domain, to Mahegan. His eyes were cast downward.

"And I will continue to do so if you don't cooperate. There's a lot at stake here. I'm running out of time. People are dying. You're probably not liable yet, but you could be soon. A smart man like you probably wants to find a way to separate himself from what is going on out at the drill site and your lodge. Maybe you already have. So, tell me about the EB-Five guys."

Ted hung his head, shook it, and looked out the window, which was covered with a sheer drape that obscured recognition from the outside but did not block line of sight from the inside.

As he lifted his head, Ted stared at Mahegan and said, "My dad partnered with James Gunther Construction. Gunther had been drilling some wells in Lee County. I knew Jimmy from just being around Raleigh. Bars, mutual friends, that kind of thing. Dad cooks up this grand scheme to do the first fracking well and get as much of the Durham shale as possible before the gold rush starts. So, as these people will probably tell you, they've been prepping for about six weeks."

"What is the makeup of the EB-Five crews, and who is operating the drill?"

Ted stared at him. Mahegan knew the answer, of course, but he wanted confirmation.

"Russians, Chinese, Serbs, and Turks, I think. Dad was very specific. As Jimmy and I went around selling the project, which we called Isosceles, we were supposed to get thirty million dollars from thirty people. Each of those thirty people would get one visa. Dad said to make it a package deal. A million in, we pick the visa from a list of possible recruits, and they get a premium on their return. So we picked ten attractive women and twenty athletes who could perform a variety of drill and security tasks. The pay was good. Labor was easy to find."

Mahegan did the math. He had personally killed two and severely injured five of the EB-5 commandos. Plus Petrov. That put them at fourteen workers/enforcers. Ted wasn't doing whatever he was supposed to be doing to contribute.

"Why did you defect?"

Ted's head popped up like a puppet pulled by a string. "I didn't defect. What are you talking about?"

It was a guess for Mahegan and a good one. His protest and overcompensation told Mahegan all he needed to know.

Ted was lying.

He moved toward Ted's wrist with both hands.

"Please, man," Ted pleaded. "You gotta give me a break here. They'll kill me."

"What did you see? What pushed you away? Made you think twice?"

Ted hung his head, then looked up. "Oh, man," he sighed. "Oh, no."

"Tell us, Ted. We're out of time."

Mahegan could feel his control of the situation slipping away. It was an instinct developed by years of combat. His aura picked up on threatening stimuli the way spider webs caught flies. He went for the wrist.

"It's all in the Underground! I saw it," Ted shouted.

Grace's phone pinged with a text.

"It's Brandy," she said. "She sees a black pickup truck with a topper shell parked across the street, at Starbucks. Nose in toward Starbucks, and the bed is facing us. The tailgate is up, but the window on the topper is open."

Mahegan nodded. *Women. Analysts. Details. Specifics.* They were as good as the Israelis or the Army intelligence operatives. Then he frowned.

"It's all about Sharon—" Ted started to say.

It happened in less than two seconds. Mahegan stepped forward to tackle Ted as he realized what the open topper window meant, but in mid-sentence, right at the word "Sharon," Ted's head exploded in a shower of pink mist and gray matter, which landed all over Mahegan and Elaine, who got the back splatter from the bullet crashing through Ted's skull. There was no percussive sound.

The hotel room window glass had shattered into a million shards when the heavy-gauge bullet crashed through it and then Ted's skull. The force of the bullet had snapped his neck forward, but his body had remained awkwardly stable in the chair.

Mahegan pulled Ted and the chair to the floor, then pivoted and tackled Elaine with one arm while dragging Grace down with the other. Bullets chased them in a line across the floor, like a sewing machine stitching a seam. Lying between the two beds, though, they were out of the direct line of fire.

Even though their opponents' tactics had so far been unrefined, Mahegan knew it would be only a matter of time before they adapted. Every enemy did. In this case, the EB-5 commandos were synchronizing information and tactics. They had geo-located one of the phones, most likely Ted's or Elaine's, and maybe even had a listening device in Ted's phone. He didn't know what the women had said to Ted before he had arrived, smashed Ted's phone, and removed the battery and SIM card. Whoever was in charge of surveillance would have put a locator in Ted's phone if they were worried about him defecting, and clearly he had. He had said as much. The commandos were also being less obvious, in a way, and more tactical. A silenced sniper shot was less discreet than a knife to the throat but more likely to avoid detection than a machine gun.

"Text both of them and tell them to get to the room now. I don't want them roaming around to be kidnapped," Mahegan told Grace.

Grace used her burner phone's voice command. "Get up here now!"

He heard the beep and the whoosh of the text leaving the device. Within a minute, Mahegan heard the women's footfalls outside the door.

"Stay low and watch the hallway!" Mahegan shouted. Then he crawled to the door, opened it, and let them in.

"Stay down," he said. He watched their faces as they saw Ted the Shred dumped on the floor like a store mannequin, but with his head blown apart. Sniper fire continued to pock the walls at a steady rhythm. Mahegan counted as every five seconds a shot blew more of the wallpaper off the drywall, with bits and pieces of wood, chalk, and paper creating a growing cloud in the room. It was suppressive fire.

Bad news, Mahegan thought.

The shots were measured in time to keep them from leaving the room, which meant that there was another element at play. Most likely the commandos had zeroed in on Ted's phone, put the sniper in place to prevent him from revealing secrets, and moved another team in to either kill or capture all of them. Either Brand Throckmorton was a very hard man to have his son killed, or Gunther had made this call.

He looked at the women, all silent, all staring at him, awaiting direction. They had never been under fire, he was certain. Now the bullets kept coming. Some were hitting the door, a kinetic exclamation point denying their exit. The clock kept ticking.

What now, Ranger? He visualized his crusty Ranger instructor laughing at him as he waded neck deep in the Yellow River swamps of north Florida, with a ragged line of tired and hungry Rangers filing behind him, as he led the patrol to a distant objective.

He heard feet running along the hallway, but they were going in the opposite direction and were too light and hurried to be the EB-5 commandos. Probably hotel visitors becoming aware of the situation. Even silenced sniper rifles made a loud whisper as the bullets cut through the air and a thump when they smacked into the walls.

Mahegan was waiting on a cue. He knew it would come in one of two forms. Footsteps, heavy and thundering, would signal an assault force that would breach their hotel door, maybe toss a grenade in. That was a bad-case scenario.

What happened, though, was the second cue he'd been listening for.

It was a siren.

Griffyn.

This was a smoother operation than the other commandos had tried on him, for sure, but it still had flaws. The sniper rifle and the suppressive fire were tactically sound. Even bringing Griffyn in to conduct a faux arrest was a good idea. But to have Griffyn come in with sirens and his *Kojak* light flashing was a mistake. Maybe they had to make it seem official, but it would give him enough time. It was a well-synchronized operation, but he had a small window of opportunity.

"Okay, ladies. Follow me."

Mahegan grabbed his duffel bag, tossed his knife in it, and stayed low as he slowly opened the door. Grace had a backpack, which Elaine had brought from the watch site. The ladies had whatever they had come with—phones and backpacks. The shots kept coming, pinging into the wall just above his head. He cleared left and right and stayed low as he watched the sniper bullets punch through the wall and into the opposite side of the hallway. He crawled to the next hotel room door and then farther, checking every few seconds to see that each of the women was beyond the steel rain of the sniper fire. When he sensed the time was right, he stood, jogged to the exit, and entered the stairwell.

The fire exit took them to the back side of the hotel, which was a parking lot surrounded by a wood fence taller than Mahegan, probably eight feet high. A few random cars were parked in the lot, but nothing that concerned Mahegan. The siren was growing louder, though. It was maybe less than a half mile away.

Mahegan tossed his bag over the fence and cupped his hands. Backpack strapped to her shoulders, Brandy was the first to put her boot into Mahegan's stirrup and let him lift her so that she could clumsily scramble over the top of the fence and fall on the far side. She landed with a loud crash, and Mahegan hoped his gear was okay.

The siren was now directly in front of the hotel, loud and obnoxious.

Elaine had already scaled the fence by herself, backpack and all. Mahegan heard her whispering to Brandy. Something about "hauling ass ASAP."

Theresa grabbed the fence, took the stirrup, and nimbly flipped over the top, full of athletic elegance. Mahegan watched Theresa with suspicion, noticing the outline of two cell phone–size rectangles pressing against her tight spandex. But Grace was next, and he had to continue to focus on the fluidity of the situation. Mahegan lifted her with his cupped hands. Her backpack shifted under the weight of her computer, which held the video files he'd taken from the Throckmortons' backyard. Quickly, she was weightless in his hands as she grabbed the top of the fence and pulled herself over it.

The siren grew louder. Out of his periphery he saw two police cars, one from each direction, bearing down on him. They were different makes and colors. One would be Griffyn, and one would be from either the sheriff's office or the Apex town police. Grace was over the fence. He would not make it, he thought. They would shoot him. He had spent the past ten years of his life making split-second decisions about life and death. He chose life this time, because he knew that Maeve Cassidy didn't stand a chance if he wasn't there to provide her one. "Live to fight another day," as the saying went.

Mahegan said, "Run!"

Grace said, "Not without you."

"Don't be stupid. Go!"

Mahegan made it easy for Grace to quit arguing. He turned and saw four weapons drawn on him. They looked like military-grade Beretta pistols, nine millimeter. The black pickup truck with the topper cruised along the road slowly in the distance. Mahegan raised his hands as he watched a head turn in the window of the pickup. It looked like Petrov. Smiling.

"On the ground. Now!" Griffyn barked.

Mahegan kept his hands up as he knelt. The pavement crunched into his knees, and he felt vulnerable, but he couldn't imagine that the sheriff's officers would be in on the fracking conspiracy, as well. No, Griffyn had taken a calculated risk. Have a partner from the county sheriff's office, keep the town police out of it, and use a bogus warrant to take him into Raleigh Police Department custody. Griffyn's risk was that the sheriff's office would either want to take control or would see the lie in Griffyn's actions.

Griffyn approached from twenty meters away, brandishing a pair of handcuffs as if they were a medieval mace, twirling them around a long, extended finger. To his ten o'clock, Mahegan saw a sheriff's deputy on either side of the dark brown car, doors open, and weapons drawn and steadily aimed. The Raleigh Police Department cruiser was at Mahegan's two o'clock. Griffyn had been in the front passenger seat. The driver was behind an open car door, with a weapon aimed at Mahegan.

Griffyn circled behind him and grabbed each of Mahegan's hulking arms, pressed his hands together behind his back, and ratcheted the bracelets on his wrists as tightly as they would go. Mahegan had tried the trick of flexing his wrists to prevent the cuffs from being supertight, but Griffyn had obviated that tactic. Plus, Mahegan had felt the scar tissue around his left shoulder and deltoid burn as Griffyn used his knees to bend Mahegan's elbows in toward one another. Leaning over and acting as if he was checking Mahegan for weapons, Griffyn whispered, "You will pay, you know that, right?"

Griffyn found the ankle pistol Mahegan carried and held it up like a trophy bass, saying, "Let's make sure we get this on the video, guys!"

"Video is running, Detective," his driver called out.

Mahegan had thankfully left his Spec Ops knife in the duffel bag. He hated to lose the gun, but he had so many in the bag that once he got out of this jam, it would be irrelevant. The knife had been with him in combat. It had saved his best friend's life, and so it meant something to him. He would consider using it on Griffyn if the opportunity presented itself.

Griffyn said, "Get up."

Mahegan struggled but stood, kept his balance, and stared straight ahead, like a proud convict might. He didn't move. He made no threatening gestures. He gave no reason for Griffyn to do anything except steer him toward the Raleigh car. The county guys were window dressing, unknowing participants in Griffyn's scam.

Once in the back of the car, he relaxed. He heard Griffyn say, "Thanks, guys. You might want to call the town police and get them to help you with whatever went down in that room with the broken glass."

"Roger that, Detective," replied one of the sheriff's deputies.

Griffyn slid in the backseat with Mahegan and said, "Drive me to my car." Then he slid the steel mesh and Plexiglas window shut and leveled his pistol at Mahegan.

"You're a dead man, Jake Mahegan."

CHAPTER 24

MAEVE CASSIDY HAD PUSHED THE DRILL BIT DEEP INTO THE second vein that had been charted for her.

We've got a guy.

She was tired, hungry, worried, and pissed off. Plus, she smelled as bad as she had at any time during her combat tour, possibly worse. With her hand that was not pressing the joystick forward, she ran her fingers through hair as greasy as lard. She had no concept of time. Was it daylight or nighttime?

To her front were the same damn monitors she had been staring at for the past forty-eight hours. To her right was a solid rock wall. To her left was the door with the silent guard standing there like a statue in her olive uniform. She had gone from holding the shotgun at the ready to leaning it against the wall. And to her rear was the bathroom. The only downtime she had was when they removed the drill and inserted the perforating charges. That was a sum total of two hours.

For the first vein, she had persistently steered the drill almost perfectly through the challenging virgin shale formation. She had blown the perforating charges, and she had injected the chemical-laced solution into the three miles of rock at a rate of five thousand gallons a minute, creating three thousand pounds of pressure. It was too much for this fragile shale, she knew.

She wasn't sure whether to be thankful or not that Jim had somehow shipped back the radioactive drill bits and had been able to re-create the toxic fracking fluid formula. It certainly made her job easier, but she was growing more uncomfortable by the minute. Her sense of dread hung over her like a lingering storm cloud.

Now Jim was in the room, sweating and yelling at her, "Faster, Maeve. We've got to move that drill faster. We're running out of time."

"Jim, I'm two miles from the kickoff point. Within twenty-four hours I'll be at the perforating point. But I don't understand the upward kick at the end. The first vein was standard, and that one is capped perfectly and ready to go, but this one is different. Makes no sense," Maeve said. She was stressed beyond belief but maintained her outward cool.

This new cut was strange. The joystick and the map were saying one thing, but her feel and intuition were telling her that the drill azimuth was not what was being reflected on the monitor. She initially chalked it up to being tired and worried, but then she saw a granite formation on the screen, and the drill just kept going like a knife through butter. No way that should have happened.

"I'm sure it's just the different equipment. Now keep drilling."

Jim stood there with his permanent half-grown beard and his baseball cap turned backward. He wore a flannel shirt and blue jeans with hiking boots. Maeve noticed that the boots had fresh mud caked around the soles like icing.

"Look at the map here," Maeve said. She pointed at the map of the twenty-mile area surrounding the fracking field. "I'm on this azimuth, going three-point-seven-four miles from the kickoff point. I've been through six depleted-uranium drill bits, doing God knows what harm to the environment, as I bore through the Triassic Sub-basin. I'm actually drilling between Jordan Lake here and Shearon Harris Lake here. The entire Triangle—Chapel Hill, Durham, and Raleigh, which includes two million people—gets its drinking water from Jordan Lake. Shearon Harris is the nuke plant, so they don't use that lake. Plus, the shale's over here, beneath Jordan." She pointed at spots north and west of the wellhead as she talked, bypassing Shearon Harris Lake, which was south and east of the fracking field.

She went on. "Now you've got me going on this azimuth, slightly offset from the first one by about ten degrees. We will use another five or so depleted-uranium drill bits, will destroy more of the environment, and will drop down more of the perforating charges. We will blow more holes in the shale and damage the aquifer."

"And you will keep doing that," Jim said. "Until we're done. Our timeline has moved up considerably. Drill faster. I have an entire stockpile of drill bits for you. Just keep moving. You saw the drone attack on McGuire. The liquefied natural gas boat is still out there in front of Brunswick."

"I need a break, Jim. I need a break, and I need to see Piper. For real. Not on some TV screen. I need to touch my baby. I will drill this, and I will get it there fast, but I need to see my baby girl first." Maeve tried not to have her voice sound pleading, though she was desperately doing so.

"No can do, Maeve. I'm not in control of that boat. It is wired by bluetooth to the drill's computer mechanism right there," Jim said, pointing at the monitor. "If it stops other than to change bits or lower charges or shoot fracking water, then it will trigger that giant bomb of a boat by the Brunswick Nuclear Plant."

Maeve blew air out of her mouth like a shot. She felt her bangs lift with the mini breeze she created. "I gotta see my baby girl, Jim. She's all I've got."

Jim shook his head. "Not yet. Meanwhile, drill, baby, drill, as they say."

Maeve stared at him. She felt her eyes start to water, but she kept it all in check, shutting down her emotions the way a fighter pilot shut down a flaming engine, immediately and without reservation. It was the only way to survive.

She heard Jim leave and refocused on the line she was following. The drill bit was moving. She could feel the thrum of it through the joystick. She let her mind flow downward to the hole she was piercing through a layer of earth two hundred million years old. The shale had been formed after the first extinction event in the Triassic era, when dead reptiles created coal, oil, and gas. Fossil fuels.

Piercing the crust of earth layered over eons, she wondered how she had gone from idealistic geology professor to petty natural gas thief. She had stolen Pakistani natural gas for her country, and now she was stealing North Carolina's natural gas deposits, something tantamount to a bank heist.

How did they believe they were going to get away with this crime? Even they couldn't see what she had seen. No one was getting out alive, but then again, she had to hope. With every bite of the drill bit toward its next objective, she became even more convinced that the Gunthers and Throckmorton had no idea what they had signed up for. She wasn't so much being held hostage with the attack drone on McGuire or the explosive-laden ship at Brunswick. Those nuclear plants were a gun to the heads of Throckmorton and Gunther, and she believed she knew whose hand was on the trigger.

But, of course, hope was elusive, and she powered on through sheer determination. Part of shutting down her emotions required a heavy dose of optimism to take their place. Something had to fill the void. While Maeve's wasn't blind optimism, she was pragmatic and hopeful, even while understanding that hope counted for little when in the maw of an operational mission such as this.

The only real question was, which of the men would be her executioner? Would she be shot and buried in a dirt hole somewhere on the property, worms and maggots soon eating her flesh? Or would she be dumped in the bottom of one of the two lakes she could see on the monitor? Whatever it was going to be, it wasn't going to be pretty. Her only well-placed hope was that they wouldn't hurt Piper, because she was too small to know anything other than the fact that she missed her mother. The notion that Piper would never really know her mother was a heavy boulder on her chest, crushing downward and making it hard to breathe. After a year in combat and now doomed, Maeve would be nothing but a distant memory, fading as quickly as a shooting star as Piper aged. She prayed that Piper would find a good home with kind parents, like her.

She felt the terror build from deep inside her soul and began to panic. She suddenly felt claustrophobic, surrounded by her doubts and fears, which were as tight as a cocoon. Her breathing became rapid and shallow. Her forehead was drenched with perspiration.

She was going to die.

And Piper would never remember her.

Leaning over the control panel, she stood and gasped. Knowing that someone was watching her, she refused to care. Even better. Let them see her have a vicious panic attack on HDTV, or whatever the hell they were watching. She pulled at her hair with her one free hand, her wound biting her with pain, and she so desperately wanted to remove her right hand from the joystick so she could go into full theatrics. Her neck corded into tight, ropy knots as she screamed a primal wail that no one could hear.

There was no one looking for her.

She was going to die.

And Piper would never remember her.

What could be worse than that? she wondered. Her life would count for nothing. Piper would not feel a connection to her mother. No memories, no love passed through the generations. All she had ever wanted in life was to have a family and to be a good, productive citizen. To give more than she got. But now her life, and death, would be a soundless whisper disappearing into a black abyss, forever lost to history.

Then, like a random lighthouse beacon appearing to a ship lost at sea, a notion occurred to her, giving her the slightest sense of direction . . . and hope.

It was a simple thought.

Trust your instincts.

Her instincts were telling her something, perhaps even showing her a way out. *If you're going in the wrong direction, turn around and go in the right direction,* she thought.

Sure, everyone would die at some point, but the thought of Piper not knowing how much her mother loved her was debilitating. It was 180 degrees from the direction she wanted for her daughter. She wanted Piper to feel her love, to thrive, and to flourish in the world. She had to live for that, if for nothing else.

Like a squall moving offshore, the panic slowly subsided from a full-on hailstorm to a light drizzle, which was the best it was ever going to get in her dreary habitat.

Exactly opposite. One hundred eighty degrees.

She looked at her hand, feeling the rhythm of the drill bit.

She looked at the map on the monitor. One lake to the northwest. One lake to the southeast.

Exactly opposite. One hundred eighty degrees.

One lake for drinking water.

One lake for a nuclear plant cooling system.

Exactly opposite. One hundred eighty degrees.

"Oh my God," she muttered, her hand over her mouth.

With her free hand, she narrowed the field of view of the map to just that area that included Jordan Lake, Shearon Harris Lake, and the fracking location. Using the ruler function on the mapping device, she measured the drill line at exactly 3.74 miles. She used the computer touch pad to lift and move the same 3.74-mile line to the exact opposite azimuth, from northwest to southeast.

The line terminated at the cooling towers of the Shearon Harris Nuclear Power Plant.

She lifted her digitized pattern Army Combat Uniform jacket and looked at the fading series of numbers in her henna tattoo. The last set of numbers she had found in Jim's room at the base in Afghanistan. They had been scribbled next to the darkly circled "one billion dollars."

Even though the monitor showed she was drilling northwest, everything in her gut told her that she was drilling southeast, directly toward the nuclear power plant.

The upward drill path after the unusual kickoff point was beneath the power plant, where all the nuclear fuel rods were housed and stored.

This wasn't about stealing natural gas.

It was a terrorist attack.

And she was the traitor.

She backed away from the joystick, causing it to slap back into neutral. The monitor to her left blinked to life. It showed a viewpoint that was from a camera that apparently had been placed in a tree across from the Brunswick Nuclear Plant. The nuclear power plant's unique fifteen-story square-box cooling towers, to Maeve, looked like giant Legos that had been pieced together. The camera feed, if it was live, indicated it was late afternoon, almost dusk. The sun was a golden ball dipping below the trees.

Adjacent to the property was a canal that fed off of the Cape Fear River. The camera showed a channel no wider than a football field, but evidently wide enough for a liquefied natural gas container ship to be parked 150 yards away from the cooling towers. She could read the ship's name, which was painted in large black letters in a square font on the port side: *LNG Labrador.* Maeve imagined that the explosion created by the natural gas tanker, ignited by her failure to keep moving the drill bit, would be like a miniature nuclear blast on its own accord.

The forests would catch fire, the buildings would burn, and the reactors might literally melt down from the intense fire, causing an altogether different and more severe type of meltdown, one impacting the towns of Southport and Wilmington, where close to a million people lived.

She stared in disbelief at the monitor. Nothing had happened. She had a true Sophie's choice. Did she give the son or the daughter away to the concentration camp? Did she destroy Wilmington or Raleigh?

She stepped forward and pushed the joystick. The monitor continued its persistent stare at the *LNG Labrador.* How the ship had gotten past the nuclear plant's security safeguards, she didn't know, but there it was.

Earlier she had determined that if she could keep the drill bit moving, she would be able to find a solution to avoid a catastrophe.

"Hope and optimism," she whispered. But now the words rang hollow, bereft of any meaning, because she knew, realistically, that neither existed.

CHAPTER 25

MAHEGAN RODE IN THE BACK OF GRIFFYN'S CAR, CUFFED AND sore, wondering how the detective had discovered his real name. Griffyn had said he was asking around Fort Bragg, but Mahegan's cover was deep. Savage would never give him up. Mahegan remembered his few scrapes with the authorities in the Outer Banks and decided that the detective had tapped his statewide networks. While it bothered him, it made no real difference, other than that Griffyn knew that Mahegan was not an Army CID agent.

He studied the cruiser. It was the very same style he and Grace had stolen from him the day before. Probably fresh out of the motor pool. This car was clean and litter free. He was sitting in nearly the very same spot where he had hidden and placed a gun to Griffyn's head.

The sun was setting as Griffyn made the necessary calls to keep up his facade of working the Throckmorton case. With Grace missing, he had apparently assigned a new forensic tech to study the evidence, and this tech immediately said that she could not find any of the samples. "Grace must have misplaced them," Mahegan overheard Griffyn say.

Convenient, thought Mahegan. No trace of Maeve Cassidy existed. No clues on her whereabouts. He could see the setup coming like a speeding train barreling through town. Grace would be pilloried in the press and within her department. She would be without a job. Who would hire a woman who was careless with the evidence of a case involving a service member just returning from combat? He began to feel the framework of an elaborate plan that went beyond Gunther and Throckmorton.

Through the windshield he could see the taillights of the black pickup truck that carried the sniper. It was either Griffyn's protective escort or Gunther's insurance that Griffyn returned. Focusing on his predicament, Mahegan thought about the beauty of long arms. His wingspan was nearly seven feet if he were to hold both arms parallel to the ground. He tugged his hands beneath his butt, feeling his left shoulder burn as he ripped and shredded more new scar tissue. Once his hands were beneath his buttocks, he slid the chain of the cuffs along the tight cords of his hamstrings.

The car was bouncing up a road he knew. They were headed to the lodge where he had last seen Griffyn, dumped on the gravel like the trash that he was. He felt the left turn and then the right and knew there was a series of potholes coming up that would rattle Griffyn's teeth. He felt the front right tire slam into a sharp-edged hole, heard Griffyn mutter, "Damn," and acted like he had been knocked over.

On his back in the rear seat, Mahegan brought his knees tight into his chest, like he was doing a cannonball dive, strained with his long arms, and felt the chain snag on the heels of his Doc Marten boots. With effort, he backed off with his hands and tried it again as the car hit the full field of potholes. He grabbed the heels of his boots with his hands, pulled his knees farther into his chest, and rolled his shoulders forward. His hands were now in front of him. Griffyn did not have a protective shield in his car.

"Hey, sit up back there," Griffyn hollered over his shoulder.

"Roger that," Mahegan said.

He wrapped his hands around Griffyn's neck and violently crossed his arms, as if he were punching a face in each direction. His right fist shattered the left passenger window, which was good, because it gave Mahegan more leverage to try to snap Griffyn's neck.

The car swerved hard to the right and skidded toward a tree

not ten yards off the road. Mahegan braced for impact, and Griffyn struggled with his hands to loosen Mahegan's grip. The car slammed into the hardwood, and the air bags inflated with a loud pop. Mahegan felt the back end go up a bit and then settle. All he could hear was the ticking of the engine and the hiss of fluids leaking and spraying, released from their hoses and housings. He pressed his fingers against Griffyn's neck. The man was still alive. A weak pulse, but still there. Still a threat. Yet Mahegan could spare no time.

Already the sniper truck had stopped. He could see the bright red taillights and braking lights. Then the white lights indicating reverse came on thirty yards away. The truck was quickly backing up. He heard the topper window slap up and saw the sniper sliding into position.

Knowing the back doors of the police car would not open, Mahegan rolled into the front seat and pulled the key from the ignition. The first bullet was close, but the sniper had misgauged because the truck had not stopped moving. He found the handcuff key, undid his manacles, and bolted out the passenger door. Two sniper shots ticked behind his ears as he slid around the back of the car.

Mahegan was quickly in the woods, moving toward the fracking site. The slope of the hill made it challenging for the sniper to get a shot, for the moment. He knew the terrain was difficult as it led west, and he believed he could escape through that land better than through the sparsely populated woods to the east and near New Hill. Plus, he didn't want to have fire aimed at the town, where stray bullets could injure innocent civilians. He crashed through the thick forest, the land sloping downhill toward a creek he remembered from his earlier recon and had studied during the first day's fence work. The creek would be a good place to hide until he could find Grace and the other watchers.

Mahegan had survived combat by thinking multiple moves ahead of his enemies. Already knowing he was going to hide in the creek, he began considering where the watchers might be. He recalled his day along the top of the ridge where he had seen the entire operation and the terrain surrounding the fracking field in all directions. He had done a reverse intelligence analysis, as his intelligence chief, Cixi Suparman, had taught him to do. As he was thrusting the blades of the posthole digger into the ground, he had been scouting the distant ridgelines and high ground, asking himself the question, *Where would I watch from?*

He thought he remembered seeing a large boulder to the west, which could be the same one Grace's watchers were using. He remembered seeing the clearing to the north that was the beginning of the sloping backyard of Throckmorton's lodge. Beneath the lodge he had seen some rock crevices in the low ground toward the east. Were they caves and tunnels? Ted the Shred had mentioned something about the underground. Might that be what he was talking about? Yes. The creek, then the rock, and then the caves. That was his plan.

He heard them behind him, coming hard. At least two, maybe three shots rang out. He could hear the bullets zip past, but they weren't close. It was random fire. He used to hear about the "mad minute" in Vietnam, everyone shooting randomly in the bushes at dawn, just in case the Viet Cong had snuck up on the base camp and were lying in wait.

Even with a bright moon, it was difficult to see. The forest canopy was thick. He felt the ground level out and get soft very quickly. He was in the low ground that was a swamp most of the way to the south. They would expect him to go south or north, downhill and away from the lodge or to the lodge, but not west and into the muck of the swamp.

So he stuck with his plan and went west. Quietly.

He waded into the center of the creek, where the cool water reached his chest. He continued to lower himself in the middle of the creek, until only his nose was above the water. He grabbed some mud from the bottom of his shoe and smeared it on the exposed parts of his face. The water tasted musty, like dirt. Bullfrogs barked a rhythmic night hymn like bass players. The fetid scent of fish-spawning beds filled his nostrils. The water was about the same temperature as the air, about sixty-five degrees, Mahegan determined. He could last for a while before hypothermia set in.

The flashlights crisscrossed the hill he had just descended like prison yard spotlights during a jailbreak. He heard them crashing down to the base of the slope and stopping just thirty yards from where he stood perfectly still in the water. A snake of some variety wove its way atop the water, inches from his face.

He could hear their voices, loud and accented.

"Which way?" a man asked.

"Wait," Petrov said. After a full minute, Petrov added, "Let's go back to the truck and secure the compound. Things are moving fast. But first, shoot in each direction."

There was another "mad minute" to the south and the north, during which bullets whistled through the forest, all eventually either hitting a tree or yielding to gravity eight hundred yards later.

They took a few steps, and he saw Petrov turn around and say, "That way, too."

Both men held their rifles with the buttstocks in the well of their shoulder and fired three-round bursts into the swamp. Some of the rounds plunked into the water close to Mahegan. Luck was on his side, though, and the men turned and scampered up the hill. They were circling the wagons tonight. Things were moving fast.

He waited another ten minutes, until he heard the truck roar up the hill. He listened for Griffyn but didn't hear anything. Perhaps Griffyn had already left the scene when Mahegan was racing down the hill. A common tactic, though, was to feign that you had departed, when actually you had an ambush lying in wait.

So Mahegan waited another ten minutes. He listened to the bullfrogs and the quick scamper of squirrels and rabbits. He knew these sounds and was listening for the anomaly. The man-made sound.

His patience was rewarded.

Petrov and now Griffyn had circled back near the base of the hill. Griffyn was limping and rubbing his head. They were quiet, though. They waited in nearly the same spot that Petrov and his sniper had waited in before, and they looked out from there.

"No sign," Petrov said.

"He's got to be here," Griffyn countered. He kept rubbing his forehead.

"We will find him tomorrow. He will come to us, and we will kill him."

Petrov's thick accent didn't mask the clarity of his words. He was a serious man, and Mahegan had beaten him now three times. Mahegan was good, but that run of luck would never hold. He needed to move soon and keep the pressure on these men, instead of hiding in the creek. He willed them to move, but they stayed.

"Have you been paid?" Griffyn asked Petrov, as if he was killing time.

"Not enough," Petrov grumbled.

"Me neither. We need to talk to Throck and Gunther."

"Talk isn't working," Petrov countered. "One more try, but then action is required. You know them. Have a big conversation with them. Tell them you are risking everything. Your career. Your life. Look at you. This man almost killed you. This was never part of the plan."

"I damn sure am. That stupid party he had the other night . . . I was lucky enough to be awake when Throck called. If it weren't for me, Dudley or Franks or one of the other dicks would have gotten assigned to this case. They don't care who Throckmorton or Gunther is."

"You care, yes?" asked Petrov.

"Of course I care. Why?"

"Because you are serious man in serious trouble. You have big Indian chasing you. He will kill you next time, unless you take proper steps. You must do this."

"What kind of steps?"

"Your family," Petrov said. "Get them out of town somewhere. Or put them in hotel. I would assign one of my men to you, but we are running low on men, thanks to this guy."

"That's not a bad idea. I can move my family for a bit."

"Okay. Let's go. Enough of this crap."

The two men walked more quietly up the hill, perhaps hoping to surprise him as they did so. Mahegan waited another ten minutes and heard the truck come back to pick them up, do a Y-turn on the narrow road, and rumble up the hill.

Turning west, Mahegan strode slowly through the creek, which eventually led to the swamp, which eventually led to mud and firm terrain. He found the newly finished fence, complete with sensors and cameras. The day laborers had worked fast. He wondered if any more of them had been killed at the end of the workdays.

He turned left, walked along the fence line, crossed the road with the sign that said JAMES GUNTHER AND SONS CONSTRUCTION, INC., and then angled to the northwest. He was wet and cold, but his body reheated after he walked two hours up the steep hill. He stopped and looked at the fracking site. There were a few men doing menial labor, but they were focused inward, on their task at hand. Mahegan guessed that the security perimeter would be tightened around the compound that protected the lodge.

He continued walking and found a minor trail, most likely from deer or bears. He saw a large boulder fifty meters up the hill and caught a small glimpse of a human figure hiding behind a tree. He thought it might be one of the watchers, so he approached deliberately under the darkness of the forest.

Then he heard a voice say, "Stop right there."

It was a woman's voice, firm and assertive.

"Elaine?" Mahegan asked. He spoke in a tight whisper. "It's Hawthorne. I saw you from twenty yards back."

"No way," she said, stepping out from behind the tree. She had lowered her voice to match his pitch.

"It's a decent spot, but my angle was good to see your outline."

Mahegan knelt next to the tree and pointed to the work site. It was about three hundred yards away to the east and downhill. They were on a rock outcropping that was covered with dense maple and birch trees. The ground was hard, dirt mixed with the shell of the rock that lay beneath. Elaine placed her hand on his shoulder as she knelt next to him, then used both hands to look through her night-vision device.

"You've got to be careful about your profile. They can see you, too, if they're looking," Mahegan told her.

"No one has seen us yet," Elaine countered. "But thanks."

"No one that you know about," Mahegan said. "If Ted had your phone number programmed into their tracking system, they could be onto you right now."

"We learned our lesson. We went to the store and bought burners after all that stuff went down at the hotel. I left my phone on at Grace's place, since it has been compromised. Thanks, by the way."

"For what?"

"Helping us escape. You sacrificed yourself for us. That counts," Elaine said. "I know I was unreasonable back at the hotel, but I don't trust easy. Anyway, how did you get away?"

"Long story, but they're looking for me and probably all of you. Where are Grace and the others?"

"Grace has security on the north side. Theresa and Brandy are . . . resting."

Mahegan ignored Elaine's opening to pursue the fact that Theresa and Brandy were together. He had never been one to think too hard about politics or social issues. He had always believed that being thrust into the crucible of fire together made you a team, regardless of anything that made you different or the same. *Pull your weight, and you're okay. Slack off and be useless, and you're dead weight, regardless of who you were or where you came from.*

"You said you did your time," Mahegan said. "Right. Navy."

Elaine looked at him. "Yep. Up in Norfolk, Virginia. Went for the college option and ended up with two sexual assaults."

"Did anybody pay?"

"Damn straight." Elaine leveled her green eyes on him. They looked more like jade in the moonlight.

He nodded, leaving it at that. She could mean that she reported them and they were prosecuted or that she slit their throats. Either option was fine with him. "Text Grace and tell her to meet us here," he said.

Elaine pulled out her phone, and a few minutes later, Grace appeared. She hugged Mahegan. He could see her bright smile, and he was surprised that this elicited a smile from him.

"Be careful with that smile. You'll get us all killed, lover girl," Elaine said.

"How did you get away from Griffyn?" Grace asked.

"Long story, but Griffyn survived."

"That's unusual for you," Grace said.

"What can I say? I was running out of time and needed to come find you all."

They scooted behind the boulder, which served as a shield from the drilling action below. Mahegan was positioned between the two women, who continued talking in loud whispers. The incessant clanking of steel hammers hitting metal, the errant shouts of people's names, and the loud screeching of the drill echoed through the still evening like lost cries for help. With his back to the boulder and the noises echoing through the valley, Mahegan felt his adrenaline dump. He could use some sleep, also. Grace's body next to him felt warm and comfortable.

He thought about last night, remembering her warmth draped across him like a blanket. He had stayed awake, on watch. She had slept well, had even dreamed. He wondered what Grace dreamed about when she slept. As sleep gathered around him, he felt safe and well guarded, his mission focus fading. For now he was with the watchers, women who cared about the earth as much as he did and who were fighting for something in which they believed. That mattered to him. He wasn't sure what their plan was, but he did know that they were good at what they were doing.

"I need a couple of hours of shut-eye," Mahegan said. "We good up here?"

"Get some rest," Elaine said. "Grace, go ahead and join him. I've got this."

"We need two to watch, though," Grace said to Mahegan. "Can't violate our tactical rules. And with me working the crime scene or being with you, I haven't been able to help. So the girls need their rest."

Mahegan tried closing his eyes. The questions he'd asked Ted were coming back to him. If Ted the Shred had indeed defected, what was his issue? Why had he done so?

With his eyes shut, the wall of granite a hard mattress behind his back, Mahegan whispered, "Was the Shred really that much of a dick?"

Grace paused, then said, "No. He always had this gentle, artsy side and even supported some of my environmental concerns. He had anger issues, sure—mostly trying to be like his daddy—but nothing severe until the past few months. That's when I dumped him for good."

"I told you the Shred was a loser from the start," Elaine said.

"Do you have a key to the Shred's place?" asked Mahegan.

"No. Why?"

"I'm wondering if he's got something in there that could help us," Mahegan said. "He had to have uncovered something that didn't sit well with him. Maybe something about new fracking techniques being harmful to the environment?"

Grace shrugged. "Eh. He supported me, but I can't see him shooting a frigging bottle rocket over that. Money was numero uno to him. And control. He was a control freak, for sure."

"Where does he live? Can we get into his place?"

"In a condo near the sports arena. I could get us in."

"Car's a mile from here," Elaine said. "Here's the key. Go exactly one hundred and twenty yards north, and you will hit a firebreak. Take a left, walk down the firebreak a mile, and you will see a small black SUV parked on the right-hand side as you're facing west. There's a small depression there. We always pull a few tree limbs over it to break up the outline. Your bag's in the wheel well."

Mahegan took the key and nodded. "Thanks." Then to Grace, "You stay here. Tell me where and how to get in."

She told him, and he was up and moving. As he took long strides, he counted his paces and found the firebreak at exactly 120 yards.

He kept counting as he walked the mile. The night air was still and tinged with moisture. Animals scattered in the leaves as they sensed him moving. An owl hooted repeatedly, communicating to a distant brother, he assumed, before the nightly hunt. The moon hung clearly overhead, and as he walked, he heeded the owl's clarion call.

Like the owl, Mahegan was on the hunt.

CHAPTER 26

"YESTERDAY AN UNMANNED AERIAL SYSTEM WAS LAUNCHED FROM this airfield to attack the cooling towers at the McGuire Nuclear Station," Sam Blackmon said, pointing at what looked more like a grassy road in Gaston County. Blackmon was the CEO of Best Brand Security Solutions, BBSS, which was one of many Brand Throckmorton subsidiaries.

Throckmorton yawned and leaned back in his Italian leather chair, upset at being woken up and called to an emergency management meeting in Raleigh after midnight. He had overheard the two Gunthers arguing about the Army investigator named Hawthorne. He had escaped again. His mind wandered from Hawthorne and the havoc he had wreaked at the lodge last night to the fact that Cassidy had cut the first vein and their plan was working. He would leave Gunther to deal with Hawthorne while he luxuriated in "my riches with my bitches," as he liked to opine. He had been in the middle of a particularly tantalizing encounter with one of the EB-5 women deep in the bowels of the Underground Railroad, which was adjacent to his property, when he got the call from Blackmon.

He was not in a good mood.

Throckmorton had personally picked Blackmon as the CEO of this company after the colonel had retired from the military. Throckmorton had based his decision on two things: Blackmon had a reputation as an aggressive commander and the NC State

University graduate had the respect of both the local and the defense communities. Based on Blackmon's bona fides, Throckmorton had fronted the company ten million dollars as a start-up when the Iraq and Afghanistan wars were in full bloom. Situated just up the road from the Special Forces and Airborne center at Fort Bragg, BBSS, or "Double BS," as it was affectionately known in the military contractor world, was positioned to capture talent departing the military and offer them double the salaries they made as soldiers.

Those salaries had been cheap, as the company had grown tenfold on the rising fortunes of defense companies during the wars, yet now it was on an extreme downswing. As the wars had evaporated, so had the profits. Security gigs at nuclear plants and school systems were the best bets now, but not nearly as lucrative as the Defense Department during a time of war. In his search for more business, Throckmorton had learned that electrical power companies were raking in the big bucks now and were taking extra precautions, especially around nuclear facilities. Throckmorton had used his contacts and some blackmailing to get the three contracts at the North Carolina facilities.

"Okay. But our systems shot it down, right? What's our liability?" Throckmorton asked.

Blackmon shifted his large body. A former Special Forces officer, he was tall and broad. He shaved his head every morning and wore a trimmed goatee. His voice was a baritone against Throckmorton's tenor. "Yes. Our radar picked up the threat at exactly two and a half miles to the west by northwest. Here," Blackmon said, pointing at a large monitor that was showing a video replay of the drone attack. The small airplane was nothing more than a speck on the screen. "Our Aegis system deployed at exactly the right moment, tracked and shot down the invasive aircraft." The video continued, showing the bat-wing drone coming into full view, diving for one of the cooling towers, then disintegrating into a million pieces, which littered the sky like confetti.

"We have an investigation team on the ground collecting the debris to put it back together as best they can. The Nuclear Regulatory Commission has a team on the ground, also. Right now this is top secret within the Department of Homeland Security and the Department of Defense. The airplane was so close and was moving so fast that there have been a few UFO sightings by citizens, but that's all. We thought so, anyway. Until this showed up," Blackmon said. He punched a button and a smartphone video that had been shot by hand and showed the drone, in full downward attack mode, being shredded by the Aegis guns began to play on the monitor. "Fox News just aired it a few minutes ago."

Throckmorton nodded. "Okay. I'm guessing this is why we're having an emergency meeting at 'oh dark thirty.' "

"Well, there's that. But also, a liquefied natural gas container ship got past the gate that we man at the mouth of the Cape Fear River and floated to within two hundred yards of the reactor at Brunswick."

"Say what?"

"Yeah, that's what I said."

"How did it get past the gate? What's our liability?" Again with the liability. He was always concerned about the downside risk to him personally.

"We're assessing that now. Dirk Brownlee is the guard who was on duty at the time. He's obviously not there at his guard post. We checked with his wife. She says he went to work this morning, and she hasn't seen him since. His truck is still in the parking lot. So either he found a ride out or he's catfish bait at the bottom of the river. This natural gas boat adjacent to the nuclear plant is a no kidding terrorist threat just sitting there, like a queen checking a king in chess."

"So what's our move? Or the country's move?"

"Obviously, if you blow up a ship full of natural gas near a nuclear site, it will have the same effect as if the terrorists blow it up. Melts the entire structure. We're talking about two hundred thousand cubic meters of liquefied natural gas. We have to work on the premise that it is rigged with explosives. Just the threat of it there is almost as devastating as if it were to blow up."

"How so?" Throckmorton asked. But he knew.

"Unlike the drone attack on McGuire, this big ship next to a nuclear reactor is hard to miss or misinterpret. Pilots have called it in. Boaters have called it in. Employees at the nuke plant have called it in. Media is swarming on this thing like ants at a picnic. And so, coupled with the release of the smartphone video of the drone attack at McGuire, the media is piecing this together as an attack on nuclear facilities, at least in North Carolina, if not throughout the United States. The European stock markets are crashing through the floor. All energy stocks are plummeting, except those that deal exclusively in natural gas. If there's a nuclear facility in their portfolio, the company is tanking hard. If it's a pure gas or oil play, it's rising."

Throckmorton drummed his fingers on the cherry conference room table, pulled at his lip, and said, "U.S. stock futures?"

"All down dramatically. It's all over the news."

Throckmorton thought some more. Nodded. This was good. He was going to be a richer man.

"So why just those two? Why not Shearon Harris, right down the road?"

"Homeland Security has deployed teams to defend along the NRC buffer zone. They've dropped boats into the lake. Snipers on the rooftops. Hunter-killer teams roaming the premises. There's no way for whoever is attacking these facilities to complete the triangle and hit Shearon Harris."

"Didn't they say that about Pearl Harbor? I mean, we're in the meltdown zone for Shearon Harris, Sam."

"Homeland feels good about our defense of McGuire. They're trying to figure out what to do about Brunswick. And they feel good about Shearon Harris. They're focusing their efforts and resources here."

"Shearon Harris only has one tower. That should be easy enough to defend."

"Not so fast, boss. The Shearon Harris Nuclear Power Plant has the largest collection of spent fuel rods in the country. The facility was originally plumbed for four cooling towers, which would provide the ability to power the entire Triangle and Triad regions. But they only built one. That means it has three empty pools for storing spent fuel rods, which are shipped routinely to Shearon Harris for storage."

"So we have the country's largest collection of fuel rods right next door to two million people?"

"We do."

"But we also have airtight security, right? We've got the Aegis system. We've got our own ground patrols and security. We've got the Homeland guys. Right?"

"Right. And the governor has mobilized the National Guard. They have Humvees patrolling outside the buffer zone here at Shearon Harris and riverboats around the LNG ship at Bruns-wick. But again, that chess piece is in place. Not sure how you get rid of it. We don't even know who is running this show."

"No clues? No leads? Nothing?"

"Nothing. The drone is nothing but a bunch of pieces now. We shot it, and it blew up, so we might be able to find some of the ex-plosives and start a trace, but it's not looking good. This boat, on the other hand, came from Karachi. That we do know. The ship's captain is a guy named Mohammed Massoud. Here that's like Tom Smith. He said he has gone to the coordinates given him."

"Who gave him the damn coordinates? Who's talking to him?"

"Homeland is talking to him. They say it's connected to some drilling operation in Afghanistan. They are searching for a Cap-tain Maeve Cassidy, who was the lead geologist on the mission. She redeployed from Afghanistan three days ago and immedi-ately disappeared. Her husband is dead, shot by her service pistol. Word is they think she has gone rouge and has hatched a plot to cash in on the gas she pumped from Afghanistan and has paid off enough people to have Massoud steer this boat next to the reac-tor. Barring that, I don't think they know who he works for yet. The ship is flagged out of Liberia, left Karachi, Pakistan, full of liquefied gas, and somehow got through the outer gate at the mouth of the canal. That's what we know. We're reviewing our tapes, but they are sketchy around the guard post."

"Okay," Throckmorton said, thinking. "Captain Maeve Cassidy?"

"That's right."

"Where was she last seen?"

"Babysitter says she stopped by the house, kissed her daughter, Piper, who is also missing, by the way, and went to find her husband at a party. No one has heard from her since."

"Here's what we do. Focus on Shearon Harris. Let Homeland have Brunswick. Make sure we don't forget about McGuire, but make sure Shearon Harris is well protected. Let me know if you hear anything else about Cassidy. She could be the key to this thing. Hardened combat veteran like that, she's probably got a screw loose."

Blackmon shrugged, clearly uncomfortable. "I'm a hardened combat veteran, boss."

"You are. We're talking about a geologist here, not a snake eater like you." He saw that Blackmon let it go.

"Roger that," Blackmon said. "Anyway, we're hearing that F-fifteens have scrambled out of Seymour Johnson and are flying CAP. AC-one-thirty gunships are flying right now, using their optics to tell whether there are intruders. They've got that awesome one-hundred-five-millimeter cannon, which can create some damage. We used it quite a bit in Iraq and Afghanistan."

"Okay. We take our lead from Homeland and cover our ass in every respect. We did well at McGuire. If our man at the gate is found dead, then I think we're off the hook there. And if we can hold down the fort at Shearon Harris, our liability is limited."

"Not to mention that we prevent a major nuclear attack from happening," Blackmon added, not without a bite to his words.

"There's that, too," Throckmorton said.

He was tired. This was all very interesting. The most exciting news was that natural gas prices were going to skyrocket and that he had shorted all the right energy stocks.

Perfect timing, he thought. Now they just needed to get their gas to market and sell into a rising market.

It was almost enough to make him forget about the lovely Serb he had waiting for him in the tunnel.

Almost.

CHAPTER 27

MAHEGAN FOLLOWED GRACE'S DIRECTIONS TO TED'S TOWN house. He had left the car in a small park about a half-mile away from the town house and had set out on foot. As he walked, he thought of Grace, Elaine, and Maeve Cassidy. All three of them seemed to show the kind of strength his mother had, and he could relate to that. His bent on serving in the military, at the end of the day, had come from his mother's subtle but persistent re-frain to *always make a difference*. Grace and Elaine were making a difference, and they were helping him. His natural inclination was to protect them, but he wondered if it could go both ways. They had said they would be there for him, but trust was a diffi-cult concept for Mahegan.

He had trusted that his mother would be safe in their home, but he remembered how quickly that trust had been brutally vio-lated by four men, three of whom were dead and one of whom he intended to kill, soon. The movie reel started to play in his mind, whetting his appetite for Gunther. The burn was always there, like a pilot light, but now the flame was cooking. He would deliver jus-tice upon James Gunther and, if necessary, his son.

Mahegan was careful to avoid the streetlights as images of his mother flashed in his mind like in a photo slide show, her face ap-pearing, then her smile and laughter at the beach, then her pen-sive, chewing-on-a-fingernail look as she studied his homework at the kitchen table. She was there in the water, holding his surfboard, and she was on the beach, taking pictures. She was cooking dinner, repairing a leaky faucet, and doing laundry, usually with that beautiful smile on her face. These weren't chores; they were life. Sam Mahegan had been both mother and father most of the time. His father, while a good man, had rarely been home. His mother had silently pined for his father, but she had focused her abundant positive energy on Chayton, as she had always called him. In Frisco, Mahegan remembered, she had been known everywhere and loved by everyone.

Maxton was different than what everyone had expected. While his parents had thought that they would quickly blend into the population in Robeson County, given their Native American status, the opposite happened. His father was pushed away on distant construction jobs around the state, while his mother was left to carve out a new niche in a new town. She was a beautiful woman, and good-looking women in small towns usually got noticed, which she did. That was when Mahegan started hearing the catcalls and the whistles as men from all walks of life chased after his mother. But mostly, it was the wealthy men in the town who wondered what man in his right mind would leave a woman like Sam Mahegan alone. They decided that she must have untended needs and desires and that they were the right people to quench her hidden thirst.

Mahegan began a ritual of walking with his mother whenever he could, to protect her to the best of his ability. It was a tall order for a thirteen-year-old kid. They would meet after wrestling practice in the school parking lot. She would be coming from the elementary school, where she had found a substitute-teaching job; he would be coming from the gym showers, his hair still wet. They would sometimes eat in the Main Street diner, where businessmen in their suits and ties gave her long, hard stares. Mahegan guessed the diner's business improved significantly, as he and his mother ate there a few nights a week. She was trying to meet people in the community. One night he ordered his usual cheeseburger and fries, while she ate a salad. A man came over and introduced himself, sliding right in the booth, next to Mahegan, so he could look at his mother directly.

"Noticed y'all are new in town," the man said. "Appreciate you taking up teaching at the school. Parents are already raving about you and your reading lessons. We've got a little barbecue going on this weekend we'd like

to invite ya to. Here's the address. No pressure. Just being friendly and all."

Young Chayton turned his head and sized up the man the way a boxer looked at his opponent before they touched gloves. The man wore a thread-bare blue blazer over dungarees and a flannel shirt. Mahegan had seen him before. He was one of the ones who had come in after they had eaten in the restaurant a few times. Word had spread: a good-looking woman and her son were in the diner. His alarm bells were ringing loudly, and for the first time in his life, he spoke above his mother.

"We have plans that day," Mahegan said.

"Well, young man, I haven't even said what day the party is."

"Doesn't matter. We have plans. Thank you kindly, sir." Mahegan made eye contact with his mother and nodded, as if to say "I've got this."

"My son has asked me to help him with his schoolwork this weekend. And I've got chores to do, as well. You know how moving into a new town can be. We appreciate your kind invitation, but perhaps we could join your group another time."

Mahegan nodded again, as if that put an end to it. Expecting the man to leave their booth, Mahegan began to slide back to reclaim his spot in the middle. But the man didn't move, and Mahegan bumped into him.

"Pardon yourself, young man. Can't you see I'm talking to the lady?"

"This lady is my mother, and my father wouldn't appreciate you talk-ing to her like this," Mahegan said. He looked at his mother again, com-municating that he wanted this one.

"Well, that's part of the issue. None of us have seen a father. And what in the world is wrong with inviting newcomers to a party this weekend?"

"You're talking to my mother because she's beautiful. You don't care the first thing about us being newcomers. Now, please leave her alone." His mother had taught him how to do this, how to stand up for himself.

The man ignored him, as if he didn't exist; he hadn't heard him. He looked at Sam Mahegan and smirked. "You clearly have no idea who I am, young lady. If you want to work in this town, teach in this town, live in this town, I suggest you get this half-breed under control. We have pro-tocols here—"

"Chayton, we're leaving," she said, standing. She flipped her salad

*into the man's face and followed it with her iced tea. She hurriedly pulled
a twenty-dollar bill from her pocket and tossed it on the table.*

*But Mahegan couldn't get out of the tight booth without pushing the
man out of his way, and he felt grown up enough to do it. As he pushed,
he felt something hard on the man's waist. It was a pistol, which the man
had his hand on.*

*"I own most of this town, and you have just made a terrible mistake,
ma'am. A terrible mistake. I determine who gets money and who doesn't.
Who gets protection and who doesn't. You should think about that. A terrible mistake . . ." Mahegan saw the man shake his head when he stopped
talking and start leering at his mother. "But I will let you make it up
to me."*

"Please move so my son can come with me," Sam Mahegan said.

*The man stood, brushing bits of food from his clothes. Wiping his fore-
arm across his wet face, he turned toward Mahegan's mother. "No man at
home and you don't want a man from town? You banging your son?"*

*Mahegan was on his feet. It was the first time he hit a full-grown man.
He unleashed a solid right cross as if he were executing a wrestling move,
twisting his hip, following through, feeling the man's unshaven face
scrape across his knuckles, and watching his black eyes flutter, as if powered by a dying battery.*

And that was the first time he met James Gunther.

*When Mahegan looked up, his mother was aiming a snub-nosed re-
volver at the man's face. "Come near me again and I will kill you," she
said. Turning to her son, she slid the weapon into her purse and commanded, "Let's go."*

Mahegan neared Ted the Shred's town house. It was an end
unit in a gated community. It was bigger than most houses he had
visited, even bigger than General Savage's quarters on Fort Bragg.
He tucked aside the freshly stoked memories of Gunther, if only
for the moment. Focusing on the task at hand, Mahegan slowed
his pace and walked quietly through a wooded park to the back of
the town house.

It was a large, hulking brick beast with windows like giant eyes,
which watched him move in the shadows. Grace had said that
there was a sunken stairway to the basement, that the last step was

actually hollow, and that Ted had always hidden a key in there. Mahegan found the last concrete step and pulled at its heavy over-hanging lip, and sure enough, it popped up on hinges. He saw a few dead bugs surrounding a shiny gold key, which he inserted in the door. After letting himself in, he immediately went to enter the code for the alarm, which Grace had given him, but saw that it was off, which meant one of two things.

Either Ted had not turned the alarm on the last time he left his house or someone was in the house and had disarmed the alarm. The basement was not a basement at all, but a bottom floor with a sports pub that included a wet bar, a foosball table, a pool table, an air hockey table, a dartboard, and full taps for beer, brand-name labels and all. The large-screen television was at least ten feet by ten feet. He saw a quiver of surfboards racked vertically in a homemade stand.

Mahegan stood with his back to the door and listened. The house was quiet. It didn't seem as though anyone was home, but it was three levels and big, so he couldn't be sure. He silently moved through the bottom floor, checking the two full bath-rooms and the guest bedroom adjacent to the sports pub. Certain the bottom floor was clear, he removed his pistol and ascended the oak tongue-and-groove stairs, staying on the balls of his feet to deaden the noise. At the top of the stairs was a door to the kit-chen, which was three times as large as Grace's but equally as or-ganized. Grace might have had something to do with that. In the darkness Mahegan saw that everything was dress right, dress—in its place, squared away, and neat.

He cleared to his left and found that the kitchen opened to a breakfast nook, which looked out over the lawn he had crossed to get to the "basement." He rounded the corner into what appeared to be a home office, leading with the pistol, and in the dim light cast by the streetlamp, he saw a head leaning against the back of a chair.

"You that big Indian they keep talking about?" It was a woman's voice, one he had not heard before.

He guessed. "Mrs. Throckmorton?"

"The one and only," she sighed, standing. "Well, certainly not the only, but the one. Call me Sharon."

Mahegan could see that she had been drinking.

She slurred her speech as she balanced herself against the chair. "I heard my son was shot. They are blaming it on you. I assume the cops are looking for your ass. But I figure if you were the guy who did it, you would be long gone by now," she said. She turned toward him. She was crying. "I loved my son. Do you know what that's like?"

"You lost a son. I lost a mother," Mahegan said. "So, yes, I do understand part of what you are saying."

"They're making you and Grace good for the whole thing. I came here to be with him. To just sit here, where we used to talk and laugh. And now he's gone. Just like your mother, I guess." Then, after a pause, "I'm sorry. That's got to hurt."

As she stepped toward him, the dim light allowed him to see that Sharon Throckmorton was a beautiful woman. She stood about five feet nine and had striking red hair, which framed the most perfect face a plastic surgeon could create. But still, Mahegan saw natural beauty beneath the scalpel's work. She had probably had the surgery because she could afford to. Who knew? Maybe it was the only avenue to fight against her husband's peccadilloes.

"I was with your son when he was shot, but I didn't shoot him," Mahegan said. "The men working for your husband did. I'm not sure if he knew anything about it or not."

"Well, I'm damn sure not going to put up with it anymore!" she shouted, brandishing a Taurus revolver. "Ted was all I had, the only one I cared about anymore! All the sex. The lies. The drugs. The whores. It's all bullshit!"

"Easy now, ma'am."

"Don't you 'ma'am' me, you asshole. I could screw you for hours. I can compete in this world!" She pointed her gun at the floor to emphasize her point.

Mahegan got it. Her husband's affairs and sexual desires had driven her to believe she was competing in a sport, except the season was year-round. The younger players were always being groomed, and they graduated into the arena. A powerful man like Throckmorton wielded money the way a fisherman used a lure, to attract the biggest fish possible. But if it was a competition for her, it would be no different than any other sport, Mahegan thought. Players got older, and they retired. Except marriage wasn't supposed to be like that. He hadn't gotten the full picture as a child, but he knew his mother had loved his father dearly. Mahegan had learned enough from his parents to know the importance of family.

"We're not competing here, Mrs. Throckmorton. Nobody's competing," Mahegan said.

"Who are you kidding? Hot body like you gets laid all the time. I already heard you were knocking on Grace. And you're a man, to boot. You get *better* with age, apparently." She sighed. Mahegan saw tears streaming down her cheeks, cutting a path through the makeup.

Mahegan walked toward her and reached out his arms. As he stepped to her, he placed one hand on her wrist, locking down her hand with the Taurus, and another on her back. Then, pulling her close, he said, "It's okay. Ted seemed like a good man. And he can still help us."

The Taurus dropped onto the Persian carpet with a dull thud, and the echo was soon overtaken by Sharon Throckmorton's sobs. Twice Mahegan's age, she cried like a baby into his chest, gripping his shirt with well-manicured fingernails and gulping for air every so often.

After a few minutes, Ted's mother went limp. He picked her up and cradled her in his arms, then laid her on the sofa, her red hair fanning out like exotic coral on the white pillow. Tears continued to race down her face, and Mahegan felt intensely sad for her. While Mahegan didn't have children, at one time he had had a mother, whom he had lost in a similar fashion—to violence. What made the situation worse was that events were unfolding rapidly, which would only heighten her pain when she realized the full extent of her husband's complicity.

Mahegan wished he could do something that would reduce her feelings of loss. But he knew from his own past that nobody could do that. Violence had defined his life, he realized, from the moment he'd thrown three older kids in the river when he was thirteen to this very moment. No matter how hard he had tried to avoid it, his world had been a kinetic tornado. Gunther in the diner. Fights in the juvenile system after killing two of his mother's attackers. Then the military, where he had excelled because of his intellect and strength. Yet, somehow, he had not lost the compassion his mother had cultivated in him through her love.

And so he gave Mrs. Sharon Throckmorton a moment to mourn her son and the lifestyle she had lost. Mahegan pocketed the Taurus and sat in a leather chair at a small desk beneath an HD television hanging on the wall. To his back was a sliding glass door that led to an overhanging deck that looked out onto the wooded park. He stood, slid the curtain closed, and sat down again.

His hand bumped a remote-control computer mouse that was sitting alone on the desk. Its silver body and red LED button gave it a futuristic appearance. The HD television screen blinked and came to life with a reel of a surfer dropping down the face of an overhead wave, tucking into the pocket, and letting the lip cover him until he was finally spit out of the tube in a blast of spray as the wave crashed into the ocean.

The ten-second video was on a loop and replayed continuously, like a giant screen saver. Mahegan realized on the third loop that the surfer was Ted, who was actually shredding what was a nice barrel of a wave. In the background he recognized Crystal Pier in Wrightsville Beach. Mahegan had worked on a deep-sea fishing boat out of Wrightsville Beach more than a year ago and knew the small tourist village. He saw from the GoPro video that the pier was new, its wood still a light tan, the color of sand. The video could be as new as last week or from five years before, when the new pier was completed after a hurricane had wiped out the old one.

"What's that?" Sharon asked.

Mahegan turned and saw that she was sitting upright, running a hand over her skirt.

"Just a screen saver, I think," Mahegan said.

Sharon stared at it. "That's from two weeks ago. He was proud of that. He rarely got covered up at Wrightsville." She wiped at both of her cheeks, stood, and walked toward Mahegan. "I'm sorry."

"Nothing to be sorry about."

"Lots to be sorry about," she said, sitting in a chair opposite him.

"Let's work in the other direction. Let's try to find something to be thankful for," Mahegan said.

"I already offered that up to you, and you shot me down." Sharon laughed a tinny, hollow laugh, as if she might be a little crazy. Mahegan realized she was embarrassed.

"You're a beautiful woman, but I don't go where I don't need to be. Plus, I've got a mission to complete, and I think you could help me."

"Help you? How?" She leaned back in her chair, interested.

"I know who shot your son. I can give you a measure of . . . justice." He thought about that word. Revenge was too simple. The complicated emotions that washed over him every day were more than that. Revenge was about the avenger. Justice was about righting a wrong, bringing order to the universe, and setting things straight.

"You said it was someone who worked for Brand?"

"That's right. What do you know about these EB-Five folks?"

"Oh, Lord, don't get me started on that. All these buff nineteen- and twenty-year-old chicks with those men. Once I saw Brand had his own harem, I freaked. He didn't have just one mistress. He was like an Arabian king."

"To what end, though? Think about that, can you?"

"I don't need to think about it. It's all about getting that natural gas before anyone else does."

Mahegan nodded. It was more than that, he knew. "Did you believe Ted to be a good man?" he asked. "At the end of the day, was he the man you raised him to be?"

"He was," she said. Sharon paused, looked at Mahegan. "He tried his best to be a prick like his dad, but he was too much like me. Kindhearted. In the end, though, Brand corrupted him and me. Sex, drugs, money, you name it. Grace even came to me crying once that Ted had hit her. I thought, 'No way,' but she showed me the bruises. I love Grace, and I believed her. She's kind and good-hearted. But Brand had beaten me, and Ted had to be like his dad, I guess. When I came over here to talk to Ted, I found him in the bathroom, crying and puking his guts out. He kept saying, 'I didn't mean to do it.' So, it happened, for sure. How someone can actually make you a different person than what you know yourself to be . . . I don't know." She shook her head solemnly.

"What happened the night of the party? Why were you with Pete Cassidy?"

Sharon looked away, then down at the Persian carpet. "How do you know about that?"

"I just know," Mahegan said. He wasn't going to turn on Grace or on Nathan from next door.

"Brand invited him over. He had been working some kind of small deal with the guy. He was a banker, a nobody, but someone Brand apparently had met somewhere. It might've even been LinkedIn. Knew his wife was a fracking expert. Anyway, he wined and dined him and brought him home that night, drunk. Meanwhile, Jimmy shows up with a van full of nineteen-year-old Russian and Serbian girls and some of his buddies. Brand disappears—I presume with one of the hotties—so I said, 'Screw it. This guy's drunk and hasn't been laid in a year. How bad could it be?'"

"Who's Jimmy?"

"Jimmy's bad. That's who Jimmy is. Big man Gunther's son."

As soon as she said it, Mahegan knew, almost like when one experienced a flash in the mirror before getting rear-ended, that this Jimmy was the same Jimmy from the fight at the river when he was a child. He could sense now, without knowing how, that something in his life was coming full circle.

All the violence of the past fifteen years, the kinetic tornado that had been chasing him all this time, had begun with a move he and his mother had never wanted to make. He had often wondered about the path his life might have taken if they had stayed in Frisco. Would there have been peace? Had he left his natural habitat behind as a child in a way that would keep him always at odds with the universe? He thought about a Croatan maxim: "When a man moves away from nature, his heart becomes hard."

Frisco had been his natural habitat. His nature. And now he was a hard man. He had tried returning to Frisco after leaving the Army, but he had kept drifting along the coast, restless and out of bounds, maybe not with a heart of stone, but with a heavy heart, one full of guilt and grief. Frisco hadn't worked without his mother there. Once she had died, Mahegan realized, there was no home, regardless of where he lived. Mahegan held his father's memory close, too, but he wasn't prepared to confront what he had learned just a few weeks ago. Instead, he thought about who had started it all.

Jimmy. Jim. James, Jr.

The kid who had told his dad about the big Indian who had kicked his ass. The dad who had hit on his mother in the diner. The dad who had killed his mother. Jimmy. The spark that had ignited the flame.

Jim and James Gunther.

Gunther and Sons.

"You okay, mister?"

It was Sharon, bringing Mahegan back to the present from a place where his mind was spinning like a dervish.

"I'm okay. What's Jimmy got to do with all of this?"

"He's the one who's been out selling this program, getting those EB-Five applications, selecting the prime beef women and the young men to do their chores."

"Is he the one who shot Maeve Cassidy?"

Sharon nodded. "Yes. I had my Taurus, which I see is in your pocket right now."

Mahegan nodded. "It's your gun. How bad was she hurt?"

"I don't know. Initially, I didn't know who she was, and saw she was packing under that uniform, so I kept my pistol up. Hell, I *was* banging her husband, and she'd been gone in war for a year. Kind of a dynamic situation."

"What happened next?"

"I ran naked down the hall while all hell broke loose."

Mahegan could figure the rest out, though. Jim probably cold-cocked Pete Cassidy while he cleaned up Maeve. She was the prize. He took Maeve to the cell where Mahegan had found her name-tag and watch. Now she was drilling, using the tools and techniques learned in Afghanistan.

"One thing didn't make sense to me," Sharon said. "The guy's wife knew Jimmy. She said, 'What are you doing here?' And he called her 'dear Maeve.' Strange."

"How could they have known each other from before?"

"Jimmy was gone overseas for several months. Nobody would ever tell me where, but I suspected Afghanistan, because I kept hearing Brand talk about making Pakistan's natural gas liquid. He also kept mentioning a ship. Ted would meet him sometimes. I never liked it."

"What did Ted do mostly?"

Sharon shrugged. "He was a list guy. He made lists of stuff and people that they needed."

"Do you know where the lists would be?"

"He had a MacBook Air, so probably on that."

Mahegan slid open the desk drawer with his large hand. Lying in the center of a neat roll-out, fold-down computer tray was a MacBook Air laptop, a cooling vent beneath it. He powered it up and turned to Sharon. "Password?"

He was mildly surprised when she said, "Shred-four-twenty-two. April twenty-second was his birthday."

After he typed it in, a large image of Ted getting barreled inside a different wave came up on the screen. His hair was slicked back, and he had a huge smile on his face as he held up his hand, making the Hawaiian "shaka" sign, thumb and pinkie finger thrust outward.

"Did your son have a conscience?"

"He did. Yes. Why are you asking these questions?"

"I think he found something out. I think he defected."

"If he found something out that was illegal, he would."

"Well, it's illegal to hit women, but I think he found out something worse than that."

Mahegan scrolled through the Finder function in the software and began typing words in the Spotlight function, scanning for what he thought he needed. When he typed in the word *Chinese*, he received multiple hits for several files. He began to scan the files and saw what he feared most. Then he typed in *Russian* and again found information that chilled him to the bone.

Mahegan didn't scare easily, but what he had just learned was larger than Maeve Cassidy, bigger than anything that he could have imagined.

"You look like you've seen a ghost."

"I think I have," Mahegan said.

He shut the laptop and turned to Sharon.

"No man ever has a reason to hit a woman. So I won't say he was a good man, because he wasn't. But once he realized what this is all about, he took himself out of the situation, probably to think." Mahegan nodded at the surfing video loop on continuous replay. "Went surfing. And then he came to the right conclusion."

"What was that?"

Mahegan reflected on what he had seen in Ted's files, on what General Savage had told him, and on what he had personally observed over the past three days.

"This is a terrorist attack."

CHAPTER 28

M AEVE WAS CURIOUS ABOUT THE SUMMIT MEETING THAT AP-
peared to be taking place in the observation room just beyond
her control room. In the reflection of the monitors she could see
four men huddled over a small tiled breakfast table.

The drill bit was at the second kickoff point, ready to begin
boring upward into what the map showed was a rich vein of shale
gas deposits. Her gut told her the bit was resting exactly 180 degrees from that azimuth, directly underneath the Shearon Harris
Nuclear Power Plant.

As a geologist, she had studied nuclear power only as it related
to other geothermal types of energy production. She was not an
expert on the topic but knew enough to understand that a nuclear facility's most vulnerable spot was its cooling pool where
spent fuel rods were stored.

She heard a noise, but didn't dare turn her attention away
from the screen. Someone had entered the control room.

"Hey, Cassidy. We're going to give you a break," James Gunther
the elder said. "We need to know how to fix an operational snafu."
He was wearing his usual overalls and white thermal underwear
with long sleeves and a small square pattern.

"What about the drill bit?"

"They're lowering the concrete casing right now. It'll be a couple of hours before you can drill again. This is the primary vein.
The first cut was to test your skills. This cut is the biggie."

"I need to see Piper. I promise I will do whatever you need, but I need to know my girl is okay." Maeve tucked her oily hair behind her ears. She felt like a baying animal, cornered, with no recourse.

"Maybe if you give us some good answers, we can work something out," Gunther said. She watched him flip a switch that connected her drill pulse to the detonator on the *LNG Labrador*—theoretically, anyway, she now knew. "Now, move your ass."

Maeve stood and followed him, feeling her weary body groan and ache with the days of sedentary but mentally exhausting work. She half shuffled up the three steps to the observation room, where more televisions and computers blinked and scrolled information. Helicopters and boats along the Cape Fear River were swarming around the *LNG Labrador*. It was prime-time news. She leaned against a chair, depleted, and struggled to sit.

Jim sat across from her, wearing his trademark backward baseball cap. He grinned and rolled a toothpick across his lips from side to side. That look confused her. Her loneliness and despair could do that to anyone, she guessed. But what had happened in Afghanistan was her cross to bear. Brand Throckmorton was at the end of the table, overdressed for the early morning meeting, as if he had just come from another, more important discussion. Gunther pushed her down into a chair.

"Here's the deal," Gunther said. "The Russian and the Chinese guys are arguing over how much explosives to put in the perforating charges. We'll be ready for that by nightfall today. In case you're not aware, it's three a.m. right now. This is a critical blow. The critical blow. Once we get the gas flowing from the first two wells, we're ready to push this along the new pipeline. But shale is different in different places. You're a geologist. Why is Ting doubling the amount of explosives for just this very first perforation in the second drill line?"

We've got a guy, she thought. *Well, why don't you go ask the guy, you assholes?*

Maeve coughed. Her throat was sore. She ached inside. Hunger had come and gone. She was dehydrated. Needed water.

Needed to see Piper. Food could wait. She knew the answer but was loathe to tell them.

"It is not unusual to use more explosives on the first charge, as it is the one farthest away. I'm assuming they've done all the density testing and formulas to calculate how much they need?" It was a question. Her voice croaked as she talked. "Water, please."

Jim slid an unopened water bottle across to her. "Drink up."

Maeve debated whether to tell them her theory. *Assess and act.* She couldn't forget what had worked for her so far. She was assessing. Why were they asking these questions? Because they didn't know, which meant the Chinese or the Russian or both were the de facto leaders of this operation. Her assessment led her to believe that she had information that they did not have. That could give her a strategic leverage point. *Could* being the operative word.

"Have you seen the density testing of the area you've got me drilling into?" she asked Jim.

"I've studied it, Maeve. Calls for two kilograms. They're putting in ten kilograms in each charge."

"That's too much," she said. "I don't care where you're fracking. That's just too much. Have you just asked them?"

Throckmorton looked bored. James Gunther looked at Jim.

"I have," Jim said. "They said their calculations show a need for more explosives."

Of course. If you were going to drill through the bottom of four nuclear power plant cooling pools, you were going to want to do two things. Drain the water, which would get sucked back through the shaft she had drilled during the fracking process and dumped into Jordan Lake, and jumble the secured fuel rods so that they touched. She knew that much about nuclear energy. If the rods touched one another, a meltdown was guaranteed. With its hundreds of spent fuel rods from all across the country resting in four twenty-yard-deep Olympic-sized swimming pools, Shearon Harris was a prime target. No amount of aerial or aboveground security and reconnaissance could prevent this attack.

"Maybe they're right. No one has drilled this shale deposit before. What kind of readings did we get from the first shaft?"

"Normal. Everything was normal. Perfect, in fact," Jim said.

Maeve said, "So just tell them to use five kilograms, which is on the high end, anyway, instead of ten kilograms. Take charge of them the way you take charge of me."

She hoped they would understand the insult. Three men ordering around a woman, yet being told what to do by male investors.

"What are you saying?" Gunther asked, rubbing his gray stubble.

"I'm saying that you three men take the path of least resistance. Seduce my husband and kidnap me and my baby while you let these international rogues run all over you. Bow up to them, not me." She nodded emphatically, directly before James Gunther's backhand caught her across her face, twisting her neck to its limits, the tendons and ligaments straining to protect the vertebrae. What little spit she had left dribbled out of the right corner of her mouth as the welt began to form immediately.

"Go for it. See if any of those others can drill as fast or as accurately as me." She spit out some blood onto the table. "You think I care? You're going to kill me, anyway, so why should I even play in your scam?"

Gunther paced the room. Jim stared at Maeve, thinking. Throckmorton smoothed the lapels on his suit coat.

"Because of Piper," Jim said. "She lives."

"And I die? Is that the trade?"

Gunther spoke over his son. "There is no trade. You do what you're told to do. Or your precious little girl and you die. There are no deals here. All my life I've been working hard. Honest wage for an honest day's work."

"So what's my wage? Right now I'm slave labor. Illegally held. If I promise not to go to the police, can we agree that if I keep your secret, you'll help me disappear? Quid pro quo?"

"Maybe if you leave the country," Throckmorton said, speaking up for the first time. "Maybe if you get us through this little hiccup, finish the rest, we will buy you a one-way ticket to Mexico or some Caribbean country. How about that?"

Maeve processed the comment. It was the first time that any of them had offered any shred of hope. It was much better than nothing, which had been her thin gruel for the past few days. Now there was hope, as fragile as it was.

"Okay," she said. "I'll take that deal." Maeve had her hands on the table and felt them weaken. Her arms were trembling, as if she had no control. Her eyes fluttered up into the top of her eyelids as she passed out.

She awoke to the sound of heart monitors and to multiple restraints across her arms and the rest of her body. She looked to the left and saw three men in body casts, grimaces frozen on their faces, the result of some terrifying industrial accident or worse. To her right were two more men, one whose monitor had just quit beeping and was spitting out the shrill indication of a stopped heart, like an off-key instrument in a symphony.

The nurses rushed to his side, all young and beautiful, applied the paddles, yelling, "Clear!" about five times, but with no luck. The man had died.

In the mayhem, Maeve heard two nurses talking.

"He was hit by the car right outside. That madman."

"I know. Maybe he can help us."

"We don't even know who he is. But he has hurt many of our people. Now be quiet. The microphones will hear you."

The second nurse looked at Maeve and then turned to whisper something in her partner's ear. She was about five feet eight inches tall and wore stilettos, white fishnets, and a white nurse's outfit. She had beautiful black hair.

The woman walked over and cast her large brown eyes upon Maeve. She looked Balkan to Maeve. The nurse checked her IV bag, replaced it, followed the intravenous tube all the way to the arm, and slid her hand down to Maeve's hand. Maeve felt something resting in her palm. She didn't dare give a tell to the cameras that were watching. The woman looked at her and nodded.

"You are very good patient. I am Sabrina from Bosnia. I will be back in a moment."

Sabrina from Bosnia departed, and Maeve took that as her cue to look at what she'd placed in her hand. It was a note. She began coughing, holding both hands up in front of her face. She flipped open the folded note with her thumb and saw the writing.

I can get you to Piper.

She stopped her faux coughing fit and lowered her hand into the sheets. Sabrina moved quickly, palmed the note like a Vegas card trickster, and pulled the sheets over Maeve.

Mauve rested her head on the soft pillow and felt the fluids nourishing her body. She also felt another bud of hope. A deal for her and Piper? A helpful nurse? A renegade vigilante wounding the foreigners. There wasn't much time for all of it to come together, but she could hope.

As she felt the pulse of optimism, the nurses and other women all came scuttling back into the makeshift infirmary, frightened looks on their faces. An air raid siren was bellowing in the distance. Bells were ringing. Across the expanse of the infirmary, she saw three men standing in the doorway. She recognized Jim, but not the two Asian men.

Jim Gunther was arguing with one of the Chinese men. "Ting," she thought she had heard. They both held pistols. Ting got his up under Jim's chin.

"Where's Cassidy? Why you stop?"

"She was sick, Ting. Give her a break."

Ting looked at the beds. Maeve saw his eyes calculate the damage to his team members, who were in various states of injury around her. His intense stare focused on Maeve.

"You!" Ting said. "Up and to the drill. Can't do it ourselves. Need your expertise. Now, get to work."

"She needs to rest. Damn it, Ting," Jim said. Maeve was oddly touched that Jim was fighting on her behalf.

"She no work, she die," Ting said. "You die, too."

"I can do it." Maeve coughed weakly.

Jim and Ting turned toward her.

"See? She ready to go."

Maeve watched Sabrina turn and undo her leather restraints. Then she helped her stand. A bit dizzy, she gained her balance and walked with Chun into the control room. When she walked past Jim and Ting, she saw fear in Jim's eyes. He nodded at her, as if to say, "Thank you."

"Up from there," Ting said, pointing at the second kickoff point. "Straight up into that vein."

Maeve was too scared to challenge Ting. She had measured the drill length. It would push the bit to within twenty yards of the earth's surface, about where the spent fuel rods were stored, she guessed.

Nodding, she sat down and began to assess the situation. As the Chinese men leaned forward and their shirt collars slid lower, she saw dark ink triangle tattoos with lines and curling notations covering about four inches of both their necks. *Triad*, she thought. These men belonged to the Chinese underground mafia called Triad. So this was an attack by Chinese terrorists?

"We at last concrete sleeve. You can drill at same time. Now start."

Ting stood over her. She pushed the stick forward, then backed it up, tilting the drill bit perpendicular to the horizontal drill line. This path would take her six hours, maybe eight if she stalled. Once the drill bit began to churn through the reinforced concrete and into the cooling pools, the nuclear attack would begin. She presumed that they all felt safe down here in the Underground Railroad habitat, but she couldn't see why. The death and destruction would be severe within twenty miles of the nuclear power plant and significant within forty miles. Durham, Chapel Hill, and Raleigh were going to be under the dome of the radioactive meltdown. Two million people.

The Chinese men have a way out, she thought. They had to have an escape plan.

Then she thought, *I can get you to Piper.*

If she and Piper were going to die in a nuclear meltdown, then she would be holding Piper. What she had learned in Afghanistan was that no one ever beat the system. If this was her penance for her one-time misdeed with Jim, then it was a heavy price to pay. Maybe she still had some element of control. She was, after all, the one pushing the drill. Could she disable it and snatch Piper before they were able to accomplish their underground attack? Six hours, maybe more, maybe less.

Would the vigilante save their lives? She inexplicably visualized him as a distant, silent hawk soaring above the terrain, searching for his prey, ready to pounce once he spied his quarry.

CHAPTER 29

M AHEGAN STOOD, READY TO MOVE. HE HAD OVERSTAYED HIS welcome. Looking at Sharon Throckmorton, he saw something register in her eyes, like an acknowledgment, but not in a good way.

"Big, strong man responds to tears every time," she said, removing a small pistol from her purse. "You'd be amazed. I had a speaking role in one of those comic book movies filmed down in Wilmington. Ted actually helped me get the part. He was always so connected."

Looking at the gun aimed at him, Mahegan considered his options. It was a baby Glock 27, efficient enough at ten feet, which was the approximate distance between them. She was talking like a woman possessed. Either she was an adept actress, which she had just acknowledged, or she was a tough woman, used to moving from one bad situation to the next. He felt the weight of the Taurus in his pocket, as if it were urging him to use it. If this had all been a play, then he was certain the Taurus was not loaded, which left him the Russian Glock in his other pocket.

"I know about your mother. Dead mother, loving son. Loving mother, dead son. We're not so different. I knew you would let your guard down, especially after I gave you the password. Who cares what Ted has on his computer? It's going to burn."

"So Ted the Shred, your son, was just another pawn in your own personal retirement plan?"

"I loved Ted. Him dying wasn't part of this scenario. We were splitting the two hundred fifty million dollars. Half of that's enough for anyone, don't you think?"

Mahegan first thought about the $250 million, trying to push away the thoughts of his mother. That money would have been Ted's cut. Then there was Brand, James Gunther, and Jim. A billion total. To do what? Siphon gas from the Durham shale and pump it where? Overseas for the Russians? Lots of logistics. Lots of risks and empty promises, in Mahegan's view. Perhaps that worked for the Russians, but where would they get a billion dollars?

He continued to consider his options. Did she have the guts to shoot him? He wasn't interested in finding out. She seemed just crazy enough to shoot if he made a quick movement.

"So what's your endgame here, Sharon?"

"Me? There's a big-ass bounty on your head. Anyone with information leading to the arrest of Jake Mahegan, former Army officer, will receive a one-hundred-thousand-dollar reward. I don't care about the reward, but I am interested in removing you from the equation."

"So take me to this Underground," Mahegan said. "If you don't prevent what is really happening, that two hundred fifty million dollars is meaningless."

Mahegan heard a truck stop outside, its engine a low rumble in the quiet night.

He had killed or injured several of the commandos, and now a fifty-something woman was pointing a gun at him, holding him in place, like a bishop checking a king's move. She might not be a great shot, but then again, she might be an expert. Mahegan's rule was to always give the enemy credit. He realized that his Achilles' heel was his memory of his mother and his desire for revenge, but he needed to find a way to embrace that memory as fuel, instead of viewing it as kryptonite.

"Well, enlighten me. You said 'terrorist attack,'" Sharon said. "What's that mean?"

"You're dealing with international terrorists. Chinese Triad. The Russian just wants to get the natural gas and sell it on the market.

The Chinese guys are terrorists. Your deal is probably with the Russian. Right? The others are terrorists."

"And what kind of 'terror' are they bringing our way?" Sharon mocked.

"My guess is that it has something to do with all these nuclear reactors. There was a drone attack on McGuire. There's a giant bomb sitting outside of Brunswick. And nobody knows, except maybe two people, what's going to happen to Shearon Harris."

"Who's that?"

"I'm sure they will make me and Maeve Cassidy good for it."

"Then we've got no worries."

"You've got plenty to worry about," Mahegan said. "Unless you're leaving the country in the next hour or so."

What he had seen in Ted's notes had clarified the entire mission. He had found an Excel spreadsheet filled with names and countries of origin. The only two from China were Ting and Chun. They were direct investors to the tune of a million apiece, which gave them visas. The others were the children of investors, which was the original intent of the program. Jim and Ted had been careful as they flew around the world with their shopping list. They needed young men and women who could run a fracking operation, as well as do the things Brand Throckmorton wanted done. As Mahegan had clicked down the list of names, he had noticed that each of the men had prior experience in oil or gas extraction. The women, too, had useful skills. Some were nurses, auto mechanics, or interpreters. There were eleven women, not ten, as Ted had said during his interrogation. Why had Ted lied? Or did he mean there were ten in the Underground?

Immediately he thought about Grace.

And Theresa. As in Theresa Kostrzewa, whose name was listed on the Shred's spreadsheet. If Theresa was a double agent, this was a slicker operation than Mahegan had suspected.

Also, according to his notes, Ted had grown suspicious of the Chinese investors. In his notes, he referenced a split between him and Jim over the plan to threaten nuclear power to make the commodity price of gas rise.

"It's one thing to steal the natural gas from the Durham shale, but entirely another thing to even hint at threatening the nuclear power plants," Ted had written in what he'd thought were secure e-mails. And Ted had written something about Maeve Cassidy that had piqued Mahegan's curiosity. "Jimmy and Maeve have issues."

It got him thinking about the bonds he had forged in combat and the talk that had sometimes buoyed the spirits, lifted hope. He thought about the time that he and his friend Colgate had planned to take some of their combat pay and buy a house together in the Outer Banks. They had wanted to make an investment not only in real estate, but also in their lives and in their partnership as combat buddies. War begot isolation. It caused people to seek solutions, to find partnerships and friendships, and to unlock possibilities that had previously seemed impossible.

Mahegan heard a key slip into the front door. He looked over and saw a tall man, about his age, wearing a baseball cap backward and lifting a long rifle from his side. Mahegan immediately recognized the firearm as an Arma bean-bag nonlethal weapon. He had familiarized himself with them during his Army days but had dismissed the concept of "nonlethal" as useless in a weapon. If someone was worth fighting, they were worth killing.

"Hey, Jimmy. 'Bout time you got here. Look what I found," Sharon said gleefully.

"Had to work through some issues," Jim said. "Good find."

A few nights ago these two individuals had aimed weapons at Maeve Cassidy, and now they were aiming at him. Had Jim really shot her? he wondered.

"So you two are a couple?" Mahegan asked. "Teammates?"

"You might say that. She's older, but she has some endearing qualities, don't you think, Mahegan?"

"Certainly is a beautiful woman, if you like plastic surgery," Mahegan said.

"You don't remember me, do you? You was down there, about to pet that damn cottonmouth, and we shot it."

"I remember." It was the incident that had forever changed his life's direction. He visualized the three kids approaching him, taunting him, slinging racial slurs like they were arrows intended to wound him.

Jim approached Mahegan, careful to stay in between Sharon and Mahegan.

Over his shoulder Mahegan called to Sharon, "You really think he's going to go for a woman your age? Think about what he was doing in Afghanistan and who he was doing it with."

He heard Sharon Throckmorton rustling in her handbag, and as if on cue, he felt the bite of a Taser on his back and the thud of Jim's Arma bean bag on his rib cage. They each struck him for a different reason, he figured. Sharon struck out of anger; Jim to shut him up. As he rode the electrical current to the floor, he was vaguely aware of Jim standing over him.

As Jim reared his foot, in a steel-toed boot, back, he said, "Fifteen years ain't such a long time, buffalo jockey."

The boot connected with Mahegan's head, and everything went black.

Elaine handed Grace the high-powered night-vision goggles. "Look at that truck over there, lights out, winding up the road on the east side of the wellhead. I see three heat signatures. Confirm."

Grace took the goggles and held them to her face, steadying her elbows on the boulder. She caught glimpses through the trees of three figures, two in the front seat and one lying down in the backseat of the four-door pickup truck. "Confirmed."

"Looked like a big guy in the backseat," Elaine said.

"No way they got Hawthorne."

Grace looked at Elaine, who said, "Have to consider Pink, you know?"

Grace rolled her eyes. "Enlighten me."

"Hit the town brass knuckles . . . I hope I don't end up in jail, but then again I don't really care."

"What are you saying?"

"We're going in if they got your man."

Grace nodded. He had "gone in" for her several times. It was only right that she do the same for him. "I'm in. Wake the girls."

"We're awake," Theresa said. "And we're not going anywhere."

Theresa held Brandy's neck by the crook of her arm and had a pistol to her forehead. Theresa shoved her toward the other two women and tossed her a length of rope. "You did such a good job with Ted the Shred. Show me what you can do here. Tie them up, or you get the first bullet."

CHAPTER 30

MAHEGAN AWOKE WITH HIS HANDS TIED BEHIND HIS BACK AND HIS feet taped together with what seemed like an entire roll of duct tape. There was no light. The room felt cold and musty, like an underground tunnel. Perhaps he was in the belly of the beast, which would be just fine with him.

He lay as flat as possible and then rolled across the floor until he hit a wall. His feet hit it first, so he laid his back flat against the wall and rolled seven times, until he hit another wall. His night vision had always been superb, but he couldn't see any distinctions in the blackness. The doctors at Fort Bragg had found that his retinas were an anomaly, in that they had a microscopic layer resembling a hawk's tapetum lucidum, which enhanced his night vision. Yet night vision required that at least some light reflect back through the retinas. He could safely assume he was in complete blackness.

Instead, he counted. One full roll was about five feet. His math put him in a room that was thirty-five feet wide. He moved his feet perpendicular to the wall and rolled until he hit another wall. Then he measured from that wall five complete rolls. The room was wider than it was deep. He reached out with fingers to assess the texture of one of the walls. It was stone. He was lying on dirt. He scooted until he had gone around the entire room. It seemed impossible to him, but there was no door that he could find.

He found a corner and used his shoulders to rock back and

forth so he could raise himself. He stood awkwardly and pressed his hands into the stones where two walls came together. As he was extending his back and pushing off the balls of his feet, his head hit the ceiling before he was fully upright. Unfortunately, the part of his scalp with a laceration from Jim's steel-toed boot hit the ceiling first. He winced at the pain. His ribs had taken a pounding from Jim and his high-velocity bean bag. Plus, Mahegan's back had absorbed ten million volts of electricity.

He hopped around the cell for about ten minutes, using his head to feel for any type of opening or panel. In the far corner, he gained an extra two inches of height and could almost stand completely upright. He tapped the back of his head against the structure above him and determined it was a steel panel, perhaps a trapdoor.

He used his neck muscles to press his head against the recessed panel. It was heavy, like steel, but it shifted slightly. The neck muscles weren't the strongest muscles in the body, not by a long shot, but Mahegan's were solid. As he flexed, his traps flared like a cobra's hood. He pushed with the back of his head, avoiding the spot where Jim's boot had connected with his scalp. After some effort, he pushed up on his toes and raised the panel enough to get one of its corners away from the lip of the opening the panel covered. He shuffled his feet and turned, using his neck and head to keep pressure on the metal panel, until he felt one of the other corners fall beneath the edge of the lip. He kept turning and then hopped out of the way as the heavy panel dropped into the darkness and landed with a muted thud on the dirt floor.

Light began seeping in from somewhere, perhaps three or four times removed from its original source.

As he sat next to the metal panel, his fingers felt sharp edges of cut steel. The edges had not been ground out and sanded.

He spent the next fifteen minutes maneuvering the steel panel to the farthest corner from the opening in the ceiling to minimize sound carry. He positioned the panel so that it was standing and leaning slightly into that corner of the room, thus forming a triangle with the juxtaposed walls and providing a sharp edge.

Using his left leg to hold the panel in place, he knelt, as if preparing to pray. He worked his wrists over the serrated edge of the metal, feeling the duct tape tear and loosen. His left shoulder gnawed at him, reminding him of the pain of Colgate's loss and everything associated with losing people he loved. After a few minutes he had worked his hands free. He ripped the tape from his arms and then opened and closed his fingers to get the circulation going again. Next, he carefully unwrapped the tape from his legs, spooling it so that he could use it again if he needed to.

He stood and paced the length of the room several times to work out the soreness. The cut on his scalp was deep, but he could feel it drying. The blood was mostly caked, which he took as a good sign. Lifting the steel panel, he estimated its full weight to be over fifty pounds. He shoved it diagonally through the opening in the ceiling and then pushed it along the floor above him. Wedging his arms into the opening, he pushed himself upward until he had straightened them, as if he were performing a gymnastics stunt on parallel bars. Sliding his buttocks onto the edge of the opening, he assessed his environment.

There was complete blackness in all directions, except directly ahead of him, which he calculated as north. There he could see a slight variation in the shade of black, like from midnight to onyx. It wasn't so much that there was any light, but that there was a break in the pattern of complete blackness. Though he had escaped from the cell, he still was not outside.

He lifted the steel panel and eased it back into place. It was not an easy task, but he figured it was worth doing, as anyone checking on him would likely just inspect to make sure the panel was still intact. Mahegan walked to his right and his left, feeling the walls. They were curved and sloping. He was in a tunnel. The Underground.

Heading in the only direction that was not pitch black, after perhaps a hundred meters Mahegan found a locked iron gate at the end of the tunnel. It was shaped like the tunnel itself: half-moon at the top and straight down on the sides. The iron bars were sturdy and intact. He felt for a lock or a hasp and found a smooth metal keyhole on the exterior.

He heard the hiss of tires in the distance and the gurgle of a creek nearby. Stray noises, neither entirely woodland nor urban, clashed like the instruments in an off-key orchestra. A bird's whistle was answered by a car's horn. A frog's croak by an emergency vehicle's distant siren.

And then he heard a voice approaching. Whispers. One of the watchers.

CHAPTER 31

TING CROSSED HIS LONG LEGS AS HE WATCHED FROM THE OBSER-vation room. He noticed with amusement that Maeve Cassidy would occasionally look through the window at him with nervous eyes. He guessed that she knew what he was forcing her to do.

Drilling through the largest collection of spent nuclear fuel rods on the East Coast had been Chun's idea, but Ting was the vanguard, the operations officer responsible for the mission. Chun was the mountain master, the leader of Triad's U.S. division. Similar to a multinational corporation, the Chinese terrorist organization had its own organizational chart, complete with positions and duty descriptions.

Economic competition was a prelude to asymmetric warfare. The Employment-Based Immigration: Fifth Preference program had legitimately allowed billions of dollars of foreign direct investment from China into the United States. Ting had used some of that money to pay off money-hungry Jim Gunther. The money had clouded Jim's judgment to the point that Ting wondered if he understood what was truly happening. Likewise with Brand Throckmorton, the sexual deviant. His desires were easy enough to placate with the workmanlike efforts of their bevy of sex workers.

The challenge was always going to be the elder Gunther, whom Ting respected. The man was a crafty and a worthy adversary. There was no pretense, and his nefarious nature permeated everything he did. Ting always knew where he stood with Gunther, as did everyone. Ting and Chun had needed Gunther's operation in order to drill. They had needed the female American soldier in order to use the classified drilling materials and techniques. Ting had maneuvered Gunther to secure price-fixed contracts with the Russians. And Ting had shown Petrov how to exploit the natural gas boon. Petrov had ships sailing to begin the transport of liquefied natural gas from Morehead City, North Carolina, to Saint Petersburg, Russia. They had a daisy-chain express of ships steaming toward North Carolina.

There would be no gas for them, though, Ting knew. Petrov and Gunther would be sorely disappointed. He had only to keep the soldier from talking, because he could see it in her eyes that she had figured it out.

The orders were clear, though, and Ting was a good soldier, also. The Sino-American conflict would begin to take shape the same way that surrogates on remote battlefields fought the Cold War. The meltdown of the nuclear reactor would kill hundreds of thousands of Americans and would wipe out the economic center of the Southeast. It would poison agriculture; would cut critical overland interstate arteries, such as I-85 and I-40; and would destroy the water supply for millions of people.

Those events would trigger the next phase of the operation, which Ting knew was more severe and more crippling than his portion. He was the lead, the true vanguard. He took pride in the fact that his prominence in the Triad organization had led to his selection by the prime minister for this classified mission. Years of unclassified trade missions and EB-5 exchanges had worn down the Americans' sensitivities to China's true intentions: dominance and recognition.

Staring at a video feed to his iPad, he watched the drill bit approach the concrete subfloor of the nuclear facility. The head was spinning at a thousand revolutions per minute. Depleted uranium and titanium were melting the earth in front of it like warm butter. This was for his eyes only. Chun had programmed the routes and had written the code to fool the soldier into thinking she was drilling in one direction, when in fact she was drilling in exactly the opposite direction.

Now that she knew, Ting could see that holding her daughter as ransom—Gunther's idea—was brilliant and, it had turned out, essential to the mission. He could see her motivation in her determination to get the drill path just right, to avoid another attack on a remote nuclear facility while, ironically, perpetuating one on this facility.

Jim had ultimately proven useful by capturing the renegade who had been disrupting their plan, which was to drill the first cut, open a vein of gas, and distract Gunther and Throckmorton, by having actual fracked natural gas flowing, while Cassidy drilled through the nuclear cooling pools.

Staying on schedule would be critical. As soon as the drill punched through the cement floor and the water from the cooling pools began draining out through the newly bored cavity, Ting and Chun would be rolling to a private Triad jet parked at Raleigh-Durham International Airport. Meanwhile, the nearly two million residents of the Triangle would be unknowingly breathing in high levels of radiation. As soon as the jet left U.S. airspace to the east, the Chinese prime minister would call in his country's one trillion dollars in U.S. debt instruments, such as bonds. The prepared press release would cite the instability in the energy markets and the domestic terror threat from U.S. service personnel returning from combat.

"She's about to break through the final layer," Chun said.

"I will get the truck ready, Mountain Master," Ting said.

Chun nodded, a man of few words. They had rehearsed this plan and had survived even the unanticipated threat of the crazy man driving through the checkpoint gate. The drill was moments from breaking through the concrete, a feat that would spark nuclear Armageddon for the southeastern United States.

Ting stood and took one final look at the woman, whom he had finally grown to respect. She had done her duty for her child.

Too bad she would not live to enjoy any benefit from that effort, he thought.

As he stepped into the Underground, he heard the echo of a distant scream, like a banshee's wail, barreling through the tunnels.

CHAPTER 32

M AHEGAN CROUCHED IN A CREVICE FORMED BY THE NATURAL contours of the tunnel, which could have been an old mine shaft and appeared to empty into a creek or a stream near an interstate or a high-speed controlled-access road. Now that he had escaped the cell in which Jim must have dumped him, he imagined a labyrinth behind him in the musty tunnel system. Passageways and crevices probably gave way to parts of the fracking operation.

He clearly recognized Theresa, the athletic brunette with a slight accent. She used a key to open the gate and then pushed each of the women through the opening. She, or someone, had tied the hands of Grace, Brandy, and Elaine. Theresa Kostrzewa, perhaps Polish, maybe Russian, definitely East European. Probably Petrov's partner or lover or both. He remembered her agility when she was escaping over the hotel fence. Lithe and agile, she was like a leopard, springing from his cupped hands up and over the eight-foot-high boards. He also remembered her two cell phones. Most likely, she had provided directions to the strike team that had killed Ted Throckmorton.

Now, clearly a turncoat, she held a weapon to the backs of the three women. She also carried his duffel bag; its heft caused her to list to the left. Mahegan steadied his breathing, waiting and watching. He prayed that none of the women would see him, or if they did, that they would ignore his presence. Moving as they were from the night, with its ambient light, to the pitch blackness of the tunnel, they stumbled past him, coming within feet of his still body. The women could probably feel the heat from his core, which he was working hard to control. Turning his energy inward, away from the captives, he observed everything: the black ninja spandex suits, the dark running shoes, the mouths gagged with tape, the wide-eyed fear, and the focused determination of Theresa Kostrzewa.

Like a conquering general, she wore an arrogant smirk. She had her left hand cocked over her left shoulder, the fabric handles of the duffel bag looped through her fingers, while she simultaneously held a flashlight in the same hand. In her right hand was the pistol.

Mahegan guessed that she had been waiting days to pull the trigger, figuratively and perhaps literally, on this operation. Bringing in the watchers had to mean one of two things: either the ladies had figured something out or the operation was coming to a close. Based on what Mahegan had seen in Ted the Shred's notes, he believed it was the latter. It was also clear that Theresa knew she was one person in charge of three hostages. Mahegan knew from experience that things could go badly wrong in this scenario, even with bound and gagged hostages. He watched as Theresa stopped.

"Hold on, ladies," she said. Her voice echoed down the long tunnel.

Mahegan gauged the distance from the gate to the cell where he had been held to be about one hundred meters. He ran several calculations through his mind on how best to attack her. He watched her rhythm. She quickly turned and locked the gate and was back on task within two seconds.

"Okay. Keep moving, ladies. We don't have much time."

Not much time. So he had been right. The operation was culminating. The confirmation was unsettling. He had too many adversaries to quell in too short a time. Retrieving Maeve Cassidy had taken a backseat to preventing the disaster he believed she was being forced to cause.

Should he follow Theresa into the lair or kill her? Should he set the watchers free or keep them contained? Should he follow Theresa through the tunnel to its logical conclusion, where the Chinese and Russians were most likely controlling the operation?

At the moment of decision, he had no choice to make. Theresa was scanning with the flashlight in sweeping arcs, as if she were painting broad strokes on a canvas, left, then right, then left again. He watched her rhythm, got into the sync, and saw that the next left arc was going to land almost precisely on him. The light cast by her flashlight moved from its zenith on the right and began to cut toward him across the backs of the legs of the three women in front of Theresa.

"Stand up, Grace," Theresa hissed. The flashlight beam stopped a foot from Mahegan's hide position. He was pressed into the crevice in the limestone wall, looking like a piece of high-relief artwork. Grace had stumbled, and Theresa had reacted by focusing the light on Grace as she clumsily attempted to stand again. Mahegan knew this was an act. Grace was an excellent athlete. She was providing him this opportunity.

He struck with fury, taking one lunging step away from the jagged tunnel wall as he chopped down with his left arm across Theresa's right hand, causing the pistol to fall to the tunnel floor. Mahegan's right hand was over her mouth, but not before she shrieked, "Help!"

He grabbed her neck with his open left palm, pulled downward, and snatched her heel—a wrestler's ankle pick—to pull her legs out from underneath her. He quickly flipped her on her stomach. The duffel bag thudded onto the dirt next to her head. She put up a fight, her legs flailing and kicking at his back, but with little effect. Grace had come around to his front and was leaning in his face, offering the tape on her mouth to him. Pressing one knee into Theresa's back and keeping a hand over her mouth, Mahegan ripped the tape from Grace's face and worked it across Theresa's mouth. She continued to push against Mahegan's heft as he quickly undid the knots around Grace's hands and used the rope to bind Theresa's wrists instead. By the time he was finished securing that knot, Grace had her legs untied and was sitting on Theresa's legs, facing away from Mahegan. They were back-to-back.

"Okay, done," Grace said.

Mahegan stood as Theresa flopped on the tunnel floor like a fresh-caught tuna on a boat deck. Quickly, Mahegan and Grace had Elaine and Brandy untied, and they used some of the excess ropes to further tighten the binds on Theresa.

"Thanks," Mahegan said.

"Saw you. Nowhere to hide," Grace said.

They were standing in the tunnel, in near pitch blackness. He said, "You sensed me. We have that."

Elaine whispered, "You two can get a room after we figure out what the hell is going on."

"I know what's going on," Mahegan said. "Follow me."

He had a plan for using the watchers to help him. Digging into the duffel bag, he distributed weapons and phones, a few of which still had battery life once their SIM cards were replaced. He pocketed the key to the gate from a coiled, springy key chain on Theresa's belt. He carried Theresa deeper into the tunnel.

"Lift that. It's heavy," he said, pointing at the access panel.

Grace and Elaine managed to remove the steel panel covering the opening to the cell he had been held in. He slid Theresa through the opening feet first, then dropped her, listened for a thud, and didn't care if she broke her neck. He replaced the metal panel, took a length of rope, and tied it across some anchor bolts on either side of the opening. Why Jim had not done this, he had no idea, but he was glad the man had been careless. He turned to the women, they all knelt on the dirt, and he quickly sketched out the plan and what was at stake.

"You've got to be kidding me. This is a nuclear attack?" Elaine said.

"Yes. And if my calculations are correct, we don't have much time."

Like a football team, they broke their small huddle. Mahegan gave Elaine a quick hug, and two of the women went one way, while Mahegan waited with Grace as they prepared to stride into the belly of the beast.

CHAPTER 33

MAEVE'S HAND WAS SHAKING AS SHE PUSHED THE JOYSTICK FORward, inching the drill bit through what she suspected was the last thin layer of concrete. She had sweat through her Army combat uniform, which now clung to her skin like a wet suit. She was feeling the drill the way a dentist did when gouging out a cavity.

The Chinese men in the observation room were pacing back and forth, talking to one another. She was unable to hear them, not that it would have mattered. She didn't speak Mandarin.

Where had Jim gone? she wondered. Her heart was breaking for Piper. She wanted to kill Jim.

Not only had he forced himself on her in Afghanistan, but she also carried his child. When she had drawn the henna tattoo, she had found herself subconsciously scraping her womb. He had commanded her in Afghanistan, in every sense of the word, and now his dominion over her continued with the threat of telling her husband. She hadn't figured out what she intended to do about the baby, but her desire to kill Jim remained.

He had shot her and then indentured her, condemned her to servitude in this hellish pit, where people would die at her hand, because of her actions.

She wondered where her husband, Pete, was right now. How he was doing. What he was thinking. She closed her eyes briefly, feeling entirely alone, without spirit and without support.

Sitting at the controls and having figured out the endgame,

Maeve wanted nothing to do with this terrorist plot. In Afghanistan what Jim had talked about was diverting some gas and paying her a good, honest wage, not stealing gas for a billion dollars. And certainly not destroying nuclear facilities. In the underground bunker along the Pakistan border, the idea had been tantalizing, almost surreal. She understood now that the Chinese men, who were now pacing back and forth, had played them all.

Under the threat of Jim's blackmail about her pregnancy, she had agreed to play the victim for the cameras, for the Chinese, and especially for Jim's father. Fatherly approval had been the driving force behind all of this for Jim.

How foolish she had been.

The drill bit was inches from the line on the map, which she knew was the bottom of the cooling pools for the spent fuel rods. She said a short prayer, asking for forgiveness of her sins against her husband and her child, not to mention what she was about to unleash on mankind. Under the watchful eyes of the Chinese men, there was nothing she could do to stop the momentum. She was frozen with fear. In her mind, from 3.7 miles away, she could hear the high-pitched whine of the drill as it screamed its way through the earth and the concrete.

The joystick stopped. The monitor indicated a glowing red-hot drill bit, worn to the point of uselessness. The link between the drill bit and the joystick was automated, controlled by computers and electronic circuitry. She had replaced over ten drill bits, counting the previous cut she had made. Like a race car driver nearing the finish line but low on fuel, Maeve had to stop and replace the bit. There was no other option.

She signaled to the Chinese men, who came racing into the room. The computer automatically calculated when the drill bit was shorn and could not proceed. A flashing red light indicated that she should stop, but she didn't dare. The Chinese men understood and shut down the circuitry that would supposedly explode the LNG ship. Ting shouted into his cell phone, apparently to have the crew replace the drill bit. Like a pit crew, they would have it done in less than an hour. Pushing away from the joystick,

Maeve stood. Her back hurt. Her vision was blurred. She watched the images on one of the monitors in disbelief. Helicopters hovered over the *LNG Labrador*. Rangers rappelled down ropes, lifting their weapons to eye level, at the ready as they swarmed the ship.

Maeve looked up at the ceiling, almost wishing that Army Rangers were descending upon her location right now, though she doubted that was the case. They were hidden underground in the middle of the state, far away from Wilmington.

"I need a nurse," she said to Ting, who stood before her, tall and reeking of garlic.

"No stop. Chun fix in ten minutes. Override the controls."

"Ten minutes. That's all I need. Nurse."

Chun looked her up and down, evaluating her medical condition with a quick scan. "Ten minutes." He nodded. After stepping out of the control room, he told the guard to escort her to the infirmary. "Ten minutes."

I can get you to Piper.

In the infirmary she found Sabrina the nurse, dressed down in designer blue jeans and a tight T-shirt with the word *Golden* written in sparkling glitter across the front. Her raven hair was swept back across her forehead. Sabrina's large eyes flicked from the guard to Maeve. She put down a magazine and stood.

"What?" the nurse asked harshly.

"I'm not well. I need special medicine. That you can get me to?"

The guard appeared bored and returned to her post.

The nurse waited until the guard had walked beyond the doorway, and whispered, "Five minutes."

She escorted Maeve to the back of the infirmary, beyond the suffering wounded. Maeve counted seven men in the beds, one with a sheet over his face, and shook her head, thinking, *There really has been a battle here.* Through three doors they walked, each one a layer beyond the next, like in a set of Russian nesting dolls.

In a small room she recognized the young Asian woman she had seen on-screen from the control room. The woman was holding her daughter, Piper, who looked directly at her.

And didn't recognize her.

Who would never remember her.

"Oh my God," Maeve whispered. "What have I done?"

"You are wasting time. Go hold your baby," the nurse ordered as the Asian woman set Piper down.

Maeve stepped forward and knelt before Piper, who was holding a small Barbie doll, playing with its attire. Her face was screwed up in a question mark, as if the outfit didn't match. She was wearing the same blue corduroy pants and print sweatshirt she had had on four days ago, when Maeve briefly stopped by their home.

"I'm your mother," Maeve said. "I was gone for a long time in the Army. I left when you were three, and now you're four. Remember I came home and saw you a few days ago?"

"I'm Barbie's mama," Piper replied. She stared her mother in her face, a dawning of recognition descending upon her. "Mama!"

Piper's arms were around her neck in a flash. From stranger to hero in an instant. It was nourishment for Maeve's empty soul. The one thing worth living for had reconnected with her and given her a reason not only to live but also to thrive, to find a way out of this predicament.

As she squeezed her child tightly, the lights went out, and everyone started screaming.

James Gunther Sr. stood in the den of the hunting lodge, impatient and curious. He turned to Throckmorton.

"What the hell them Chinese up to in there?" Gunther asked.

"Something to do with the second cut," said Throckmorton. "It's not going how it should, apparently. You guys know anything?" Throckmorton turned to his wife, Sharon, who sat idly in one of the overstuffed leather chairs. She was smoking a cigarette and looking at Jim, who was chewing on a toothpick, his hat on backward.

Looking back at her husband, Sharon said, "We caught the Indian. Isn't that enough?"

Throckmorton turned away from her caustic comment and

looked at Gunther, who shook his head as if to say, "Can't you control your own wife?"

Jim shrugged and said, "Well, it's true. We did. Good teamwork. Them roughnecks been trying for days. Sharon and me trapped him."

"I appreciate that, son. I do," said Gunther. "But bringing him into the Underground was a bad idea."

"Why's that, Dad? He don't even know where he is. We kept him alive, like you asked. Everything will have his prints on it. We'll let Griffyn take him in."

The elder Gunther nodded. "We sure it's the same guy?"

"He recognized me from the river, fifteen or sixteen years ago."

Gunther nodded again, then looked at the monitor that showed the wellhead. Men were kneeling over the cable and removing one basketball-sized object and adding another. Gunther recognized that they were replacing the drill bit.

"Okay. I'll go rough him up in a while," he said. "In the meantime, they're changing the drill bit now, and I see they've got double the explosives loaded for this blast. This is not good, Throck. I'm thinking we need to take charge of these guys, give them a little less rope."

"You have always worried too much, James. It has been the hallmark of your career."

"Worry is what has made me successful. I've got a construction enterprise over five states along the Eastern Seaboard. I employ over two thousand people. I get things done. And I'll be damned if I'm going to let a bunch of Chinese and Russians tell me how to suck the egg. We were doing just fine until Mahegan showed up. Now that we've got him in the bag, we can cruise along, get the gas into the pipeline down to the port, and have Petrov sell it for us. What the hell we need the Chinese guys for?"

"They have all the computer programming," Jim said. "All the equipment."

"It's more than that," Gunther said. "We're going to have to duke it out with them here pretty soon. I can feel it. Get your weapons and get Griffyn. Let's round up the crew after they change the drill bit and have us a powwow."

Throckmorton stared at Gunther. "You're serious. You think this is going to hell in a hand basket?"

"I don't *think* it is. I *know* it is. I can feel it like I can feel a bad summer cold front. We're going to have us a good old-fashioned shoot-out if we're not careful. The only good thing, like I said, is that my son and your wife took that Indian off the playing field. One less thing to worry about."

Throckmorton walked to the door leading to the Underground operation. He tugged on it and looked at Gunther. "They've locked it."

"Well, get the key. Don't we have it?"

"No. What he's saying is that they've locked it from the inside," Jim said. "Only way in there is through the tunnel about a mile from here, where we dumped the Indian."

"Or to blow it," his father said. "We got explosives."

CHAPTER 34

MAHEGAN WHISPERED TO GRACE, "NO TALKING," AND THEN they moved toward the gate, where Mahegan could get satellite reception.

Picking through his duffel bag, Mahegan secured a flashlight, his government cell phone, a burner phone, two pistols with four magazines, and his knife. He gave a pistol and a flashlight to Grace, who already had her burner cell phone. They sat against the wall of the musty tunnel, listening to dripping water that sounded like sonar or radar pings in the distance. The gray relief that marked the opening to the tunnel was too far in the distance to be discernible. Mahegan's secure government-issued phone showed one message from Savage. He read it and digested it as it disappeared before his eyes in usual Zebra message fashion.

The attacks on Brunswick and McGuire were decoys. The natural gas ship had no explosives and a confused captain. The drone that had been launched at McGuire was impotent, a mere test of the facility's defenses. Mahegan figured that Throckmorton could say that they were running defensive maneuvers to ensure that their security status was up to par. Meanwhile, though, the energy markets had crashed, except for natural gas and oil, which had acted inversely to the companies with large nuclear holdings.

Mahegan typed a note back to Savage, giving him an update on his status and what he believed to be the real threat. To his surprise, Savage responded immediately. Savage's message was ominous.

No time to lose. Drive on.

It was exactly what he had thought and said to the watchers. He powered down his government cell phone and tossed it in the bag. If someone tried to open the phone with the wrong password, the device would completely zero out its contents and become a useless piece of plastic.

With the knife strapped to his calf, he placed a pistol in each front pocket of his black cargo pants, and two magazines in each of the rear pockets. Brandishing the flashlight like a saber, Mahegan moved cautiously deeper into the tunnel, inspecting the walls, looking for doors and hidden passageways. Grace followed quietly. The tunnel had been used to support the Underground Railroad, an escape route for slaves migrating north as they attempted to flee the ravages of their masters. Mahegan had felt hash marks on the walls of his cell, and the tunnel that showed signs of hope and despair beneath the weakening beam of light. A diagonal slash through a set of four vertical hash marks indicated that someone had counted and waited for their fate to change.

Instead of escaping from the tunnel, though, Mahegan was walking into its darkest depths. Evil had existed here before—slaves had been trapped and murdered for attempting to escape—and a foreboding surrounded Mahegan, like a python slowly wrapping itself around his body, squeezing his lungs, dimming his senses, and stripping him of his sensory powers.

He was on his hands and knees now, the tunnel rapidly closing in on all sides. He found another gate, half the size of the first one. On his knees, he wrestled with Theresa's key, and it worked. As he pushed the gate, it squeaked on rusty hinges. The tunnel walls began to close in again, and he was wondering if he had missed the entrance to the drilling operation. It had to be somewhere along this azimuth.

He had studied the compound from his position in the front

seat of Griffyn's vehicle as he had performed the spoiling attack, memorizing it like a battle plan map. The house was the center-piece, and the tunnel spanned beneath it and to the left, when he looked at the house from the front. That would put north to his back, as it was now. He was moving south, toward the tornado shed doors on the side of the house. His mind mapped out where he thought he should come out in the house, which was about one-third on the left-hand side, the side that he believed Gunther had been watching from the window when he had conducted the spoiling attack.

He looked back at Grace, who nodded in the darkness. She was good to go.

Then he found it. Looming before him was a small ladder, and it led to a door on the tunnel's ceiling that looked like a manhole cover. He could sense people above him, milling about. Feet padded quietly, as if the floor was insulated. He heard the low rumble of voices speaking unintelligible words. Some were shouts, and some were whispers. He could hear the hushed tones of those trying to stay safe, along with the harried pitches of those who were wor-ried about something. Stampeding boots and shoes loosened dirt from above him, the grains dancing along his back like thousands of tiny spiders.

He could find no light at the gaps in the manhole cover and thought he heard the words, "Power out!" The watchers, Elaine and Brandy, must have shut down the electricity, their first task. While he suspected that any respectable industrial operation would have backup generators, shutting down the power lines coming into the Throckmorton property would give their enemies one more thing to do while he tried to find a way to stop the drill and the rest of the operation.

He held up a hand in front of Grace's face, indicating for her not to follow him. This was her position, and he would come back to her. She nodded in understanding. Mahegan leaned forward and placed his back against the manhole-sized door and pressed against it, as if pushing up from a power-lifting squat. He felt the cover give, heard it squeak, and finally felt it lift free. It must not have been opened recently, as rust flakes fluttered in front of his eyes. He immediately saw feet darting in both directions. Chaos was brimming, which was always a good time to make an entry.

Mahegan pushed up from the tunnel and into the blackness. There still was no ambient light. Shouts echoed back and forth, mostly cries of concern from women. These must be the sex workers, Mahegan thought. He had seen eleven female names on Ted the Shred's EB-5 list. His guess was that Piper was located somewhere with this group and that one of the women was in charge of the child. The men were animals, but Mahegan didn't think they had it in them to kill a child.

The bulk of the shouts were coming from his right, so he moved to his left, where he figured the child might be. In the darkness, he was just another confused denizen roaming the labyrinth, seeking safety.

According to Mahegan's last hearing test, he ranged in the top 1 percent of humans, putting him near the range of the owl he had spotted the other evening. In elementary music class his teacher had told him he had perfect pitch, meaning he could recognize any musical tone without having heard it before. He also could distinguish between the slightest differences in tones. Mahegan's ability to discern pitch and tone explained his later ease with Asian languages, such as Mandarin. Since it featured differing pitches and inflections, Mandarin was a challenge for the most earnest student, yet Mahegan had mastered it easily.

Knowing that part of combat was leveraging his innate abilities to his advantage and to his opponents' disadvantage, he listened as he walked. Listening was a skill, one requiring him to shut down other stimuli. His mind locked in on his audible capabilities, and he listened for tonal differences, listened for the cry of a child. He brushed past smaller people, mostly women moving in each direction, some with purpose and some without.

One woman stopped him and grabbed him, asking, "Where should we go?" in a thick Russian accent.

Mahegan said nothing and guided her slightly in the opposite direction.

After he had taken exactly twenty-four steps from the manhole-cover door, he heard the distinct whine of a young girl.

"Mommy, I'm scared!"

The voice was coming from his two o'clock, at a distance of about fifteen yards. It was muffled, and most likely, the child was behind a door or a wall.

"Please, Mommy, don't leave me."

"It's okay, baby. I'll be back. I love you."

Mahegan knew intuitively that the voices belonged to Maeve and Piper Cassidy. It was a stroke of timing that he had found them together.

From a distance to his rear came an Asian male voice.

"Bring Cassidy back! We have generators up in five minute."

Mahegan placed the dialect as from either northeastern China or Beijing, but most likely Beijing.

"Come. Now!" This was the voice of a woman about ten yards ahead of Mahegan. He determined that Maeve most likely had a guard or an escort if she was visiting with her child.

Task number one, then, to Mahegan, was to kill the guard. He pulled his Duane Dieter Spec Ops knife from its sheath as he walked toward a shape in the darkness. In stride, Mahegan clasped his hand over the woman's mouth as he pulled the knife across her throat. He didn't relish killing a woman, but she was not on his side. Lowering the dying guard to the ground, Mahegan distinguished an open door.

"Bring the child," Mahegan said to Maeve, who was inside a room.

There was a pause. Then, "Mommy. Yes. I want to go with you."

Then, "Who is that?" in another female voice.

Mahegan stepped into the room, immediately doing the friend-or-foe calculation. Two friends, the mother and child to his right, and a possible bogey to his left. He reached out to the one he believed was Maeve Cassidy, placed his hand on her arm, and said, "Bring Piper. Now."

"Where?" she asked.

"Who are you?" the third voice asked. Mahegan detected an East European accent, most likely Bosnian.

"No time. Let's move, Captain," Mahegan said, pulling rank.

He guided Maeve and Piper from the room and into the diminishing chaos. The disorganization following the power outage had led to the almost acceptable rhythm that, Mahegan had noticed, followed all chaotic situations. The fear led to people seeking and finding some type of certainty, which led to calm, which eventually gave way to forward thinking and momentum.

"Where Cassidy?!" It was the same voice that had been behind him before, but it was closer this time. Definitely, a Beijing dialect of Mandarin.

"Wait. Take me," the female East European voice called out from behind.

Mahegan had Maeve, who was holding on to his arm while she was tugging on Piper.

"Mommy, where are we?"

Mahegan whispered to Maeve, "Tell him you're coming."

"I'm on the way," Maeve shouted to the Chinese voice up ahead.

"Hurry up, Cassidy. Where Kosovic?"

Mahegan figured Kosovic was the guard he had just killed. He picked up his pace until he was five yards in front of the Chinese man. Still holding the knife in his hand, he flipped it into the broadest area he could distinguish in the dark and heard the blade penetrate the man's chest. Mahegan closed the distance quickly and snapped his neck, then quietly laid the man on the ground. He noticed the man was fleshy and overweight. Not especially tall, the dead man was either an accountant or a programmer for the operation. Mahegan figured it was either Ting or Chun, as Ted's list had only two Chinese names. The dead man was different than the hired muscle Mahegan had been fighting for days. Mahegan retrieved his knife with a wet, sucking sound.

He turned to the second woman, who was still with Maeve. "You have five minutes to round up every one of your friends, including the wounded in the beds, and lock them in that room where Piper was being held. If you do that, you can come with me."

"Not my friends, but I do it." There was a hint of desperation in her voice. She moved swiftly back into the tunnel, barking commands, "Everybody. Emergency. Into baby room. Now!"

Satisfied that the woman was making progress, Mahegan stepped up to the manhole cover, raised it, fed Piper down the hole, felt Grace take her, and then stopped Maeve.

"I don't know how deeply you are involved in this scheme, and I don't really care. What I do need to know is how bad the situation is," he said.

Maeve hesitated. He saw her look over her shoulder. "Not here," she said. "In the hole. Wherever that goes. With Piper."

Mahegan lowered Maeve into the hole, and Grace was quickly upon her, placing a strip of tape across her mouth and a pair of flex cuffs from Mahegan's bag around her wrists.

Remaining on one knee above the manhole cover, Mahegan counted in his head to five minutes, but he never reached the number before the woman returned.

"Done," she said. "I go with you now."

"Why?" Mahegan asked.

"I'm not like the others. I want freedom in America."

That was good enough for Mahegan.

"Got another one," Mahegan said as he lowered the East European–accented woman into the hole. Mahegan followed her and closed the manhole cover.

"You've got five minutes to give me the layout and tell me how to stop this nuclear attack." He removed the tape from Maeve's mouth, but left the cuffs in place for the moment.

"So, you know?"

"I know everything except for how far you've gotten," he said.

"The drill bit burned out. I was torqueing it at the highest RPMs, trying to buy some time. I'm not in on the nuke thing. I was in it for the money, but it's not what you think."

"How's that working out for you?"

"Not so great. But I can make amends."

"In part. If you tell me. Now talk," Mahegan urged.

"You need me to do this. I can go back in there and act like I'm going to finish the job. The two Chinese guys locked everyone else out. They're in the final phase. They have an airplane waiting to take them out of RDU before the radiation happens. They're Triad."

"I know who they are."

Maeve paused. "You're the guy. The Indian."

"That's me. How does the drill work? Can anyone do it?"

"It's at a point where a chimp could get in there and push the drill forward until it breaks through the concrete pools. I'm sure that's what's happening. It's all electronics. The Chinese have wired it, and I'm sure they have backups. They also made it look like I was drilling northwest, when the drill was actually going southeast. But they've got to either change the worn drill bit or override the sensor that automatically prevents the bit from exploding. They've got perforating charges ready to go, also."

"Explosives? How much?"

"Ten kilograms. It's more than enough to drain the pools. That's like five explosive formed penetrators you saw in combat."

Mahegan processed everything she was saying. They might not be changing out the drill bit. He considered the possibility that they could lower the perforating charges and blow a hole in the concrete.

"Could they lower the charges without finishing the drill?"

Maeve stared at him. "It's possible, but risky. If you want to guarantee you're through the concrete, the drill will do it. The explosives are to create havoc after the hole is punched. I'm certain. Punch a hole in the pool, let the water drain, and then set off explosives that rupture the casings for the fuel rods. That's tantamount to a nuclear detonation."

Mahegan nodded. "Where's the Russian? Petrov?"

"He's at the drill site," Maeve said.

"And Gunther?"

"Just on the other side of the door from the control room. Gunther and his son, Jimmy."

Mahegan felt a buzz run through his veins. *Gunther and Sons.* He thought about his mother and the love that he still carried for her. He looked at Piper and back at Maeve, daughter and mother.

"You go with Piper. I'll figure the drill out. Grace, take them to the rally point. Tell the watchers I'm going in. And make that phone call."

Maeve shook her head. "I need to make amends. I can help you stop this thing. I trust your friend to take care of Piper. And if we don't stop it, then we're all dead, anyway."

"Your call. I can do this, but if you can help, I can use it."

Grace intervened. "She's the expert on the drill and geology."

To Maeve, Mahegan reiterated, "Your call, but we need to move now."

"I'm in," Maeve said. Can you cut these off?" She nodded at the flex cuffs.

Mahegan used his knife to slice through the plastic. Maeve leaned over to hug her daughter. Maeve said, "Baby, go with this nice woman. She will take care of you. And I need you to be a big, brave girl, okay?"

Piper, scared, nodded. "Big, brave girl."

"That's right, baby. BBG. Just like we talked about before I left for Afghanistan. You did so great then, and you'll do great now."

"Big, brave girl."

Grace lifted Piper when the mother was done hugging her daughter. "I've got her," Grace said. "Help Hawthorne."

"We need to move," Mahegan said. He wanted to tell Grace his real name, thought she deserved to know at least that, given the skin she was putting in the game. They were out of time. "Don't forget," he said instead. "Make that call."

Mahegan turned and pushed back through the manhole cover

that led from the tunnel to the operations area above as Grace led the Bosnian woman and Piper to the gate at the other end of the tunnel.

Emerging from the tunnel into the hallway, next to the dead Chinese man, Mahegan felt Maeve behind him, nimble and quick. He heard a loud whine, like from a turbine engine spinning up, as the lights came back on.

CHAPTER 35

Rᴇᴛɪʀᴇᴅ Sᴘᴇᴄɪᴀʟ Fᴏʀᴄᴇs ᴄᴏʟᴏɴᴇʟ Sᴀᴍ Bʟᴀᴄᴋᴍᴏɴ ᴡᴀᴛᴄʜᴇᴅ the monitors at the Shearon Harris Nuclear Power Plant. As was his style, Blackmon had moved to the location of the threat. He paced the floor of the command center in the Shearon Harris nuclear facility. Giant HD television screens displayed dashboards full of charts and systems information. All systems were green, which was good. The outer perimeter was secure. The fence had not been breached. The patrol boats were scanning with night-vision devices. The Aegis machine guns were ready for another aerial attack like the one at McGuire. He even had a drone flying with night-vision optics that piped information back to the command center.

Crossing his muscled arms, Blackmon looked at the display monitors that provided a persistent stare through mounted cameras at the most vulnerable aspect of the plant's operation: the spent fuel rod cooling pools. At nearly one hundred yards long each, they looked like giant swimming pools. Four cameras showed four pools connected by a quarter mile of circulating water that flowed seamlessly along directed currents. The spent rods were stored vertically in racks, like architectural columns, with ten rods to a container. Blue underwater lights gave each pool an eerie glow, as if the intent were to make the scene look as though it was radiating nuclear energy.

To attack the pools, the terrorists would have to get through several layers of defense over land, over lake, or from the sky. Blackmon felt he had all of that covered fairly well. Thankful that the other two "attacks" appeared to have been ruses, as reported to him by his contacts inside the Department of Homeland Security, Blackmon had to believe that the lack of activity at Shearon Harris was not a good sign. The overt attempts at the other two facilities were hands quickly played. Here, there was something missing.

The Fukushima, Japan, disaster in 2011 had left over thirteen hundred fuel rods primed to create the worst nuclear incident in history. Only Herculean and surgical cleanup efforts had prevented the fuel rods from being exposed to the atmosphere, where they would have ignited on contact with the air. The protective layers that Blackmon had built into the security here, coupled with the design of the nuclear plant, essentially ruled out any possibility of nuclear disaster.

A tsunami had created the Fukushima situation. A lack of maintenance and engineering had led to the power surge and the subsequent fires that created the Chernobyl, Ukraine, disaster in 1986. Both were accidents, not the result of terrorist activity.

As he paced the floor of the command center on location at the nuclear power plant, Blackmon stared at the cooling pools again. He began thinking about how someone might attack the place. He thought about inflated boats over the lake and quickly dismissed that notion. They could parachute onto the roof and use explosives to breach the facility, but his security teams would have time to react. Plus, he had increased the sensitivity on the Aegis systems so that they would detect anything larger than five feet long descending from the sky. There were no real options over the land, unless someone planned on a Pickett's Charge into the teeth of his defenses. *Bring it on*, he thought.

He thought about tunneling options and stopped pacing. An insurgent attack from underground was something he had not really considered before. It had never seemed likely, and still didn't, but neither had drone or ship attacks. He paused, looking at the monitors, and spoke into his headset.

"Stix, come see me ASAP, please."

Blackmon had called Roger Stickman, his security specialist for this location. The two men had served together in Iraq and Afghanistan. They were friends and trusted one another. Hiring and working with people he trusted was the only way that Blackmon operated. A few minutes later the muscled African American man walked into the command center.

"Hey, boss. What's up?"

"Tell me more about the capacity of our sensors or protections against someone tunneling into the facility."

"We have seismic indicators on the perimeters that would pick up any earth disturbed down to fifty feet below the ground. The remote sensors are in a circular pattern and are spaced fifty feet apart all the way around the outer fence line, which is about a half mile from the facility. No way a tunnel operation could get through there."

"Unless it was deeper than fifty feet, right?"

Stickman hesitated. "Well, sure, boss, but this is the industry standard."

"Since when did we care about industry standards, Stix?"

"What are you thinking, sir?"

"Nobody in their right mind would come at this thing on land, over the lake, or from the air. But they could come underground."

"It'd have to be a big-ass operation, and there'd be a lot of dirt piling up somewhere."

"Could be done."

"Possible, but not likely."

Just then, the two men turned and looked at the cooling pool monitors. Red lights were flashing on the screen showing cooling pool number two.

In all, seventeen hundred spent fuel rods were in the water there. Blackmon stared at the screen, wondering exactly what might be happening.

"What the hell?" Stickman's eyes were wide with concern. He began tapping on a keyboard, bringing onto the five-foot display monitor a blueprint image of four cooling pools. Immediately, they saw the small, red, pulsating dot at the breach point beneath pool two.

More tapping of keys brought up a split screen, with the new half showing the water level in the pool. The indicator was showing that the level was beginning to fall.

"Somebody's draining the pool," Stickman said.

"How is that possible?"

"It's not. Unless someone's drilling from China. This is the equivalent of a nuclear explosion. Those rods touch the combination of oxygen, argon, and nitrogen that we call air, this place burns down and we get mega Chernobyl. Everybody in the Triangle region will be getting chemotherapy, whether they want it or not."

"I'm aware of all that, Stix. But this has to be a leak, right?"

"No way. Someone drilled or dug their way into that spot."

"What are we missing?"

Less than four miles away, Johnny Ting sat at the control panel, tired of waiting on Cassidy. He had watched her enough to know that it was a fairly simple process once she had navigated through the layers of igneous and metamorphic rock, preserving the precious depleted-uranium drill bits. With one bit remaining, Ting had Petrov retrieve the miles of cable at the wellhead, remove the worn-out bit, replace it, then feed the cable back into the previously drilled hole. Now that it was done, he didn't even need Cassidy anymore. Ting could now clumsily navigate the path himself.

Cassidy and her kid were nowhere to be found, but he didn't care now. She had done her duty and provided them a real fracking well that was ready to pump gas, deluding the American proprietors into believing this was a legitimate operation.

Watching the high-definition display on his screen, he manipulated the bit straight down the three-thousand-foot-deep pipe, hit the kickoff point, and pushed the bit southeast 3.74 miles through the previously drilled channel. Then he hit the next kickoff point and followed the path up three thousand feet. Using the directional drill required concentration and focus, which Ting had to spare. But he could see why they had needed Cassidy for most of the work. He was an impatient man, he knew he had an airplane waiting on him, and he knew that the Chinese government's plans to call in their debt hinged on his ability to create a real-world nuclear disaster here in the United States.

The drill had trouble climbing the three thousand feet from the second kickoff point since it had no rock and sediment to bite into and pull against. It was like trying to turn a screw in a worn-out hole. But he finally got it to the base of the concrete pool, where the drill worked best. Its sharpened and hardened edges made easy work of the cement.

Soon he felt the bit move more quickly and knew that he had punched through the bottom layer. The camera at the end of the cable, behind the drill bit, was flooded with water, which was a good sign. He retracted the drill bit and punched it through the pool bottom in a few more places, like making air holes for a pet in a shoe box. He let the drill climb through the pool like a Hydra and bang against the racks holding the fuel rods, cracking their bindings, so that the rods began to tumble on the floor of the pool.

Once he was able to get the explosives into the cooling pools, he would show America that China was the true superpower.

CHAPTER 36

THE ONE TEXT MESSAGE MAHEGAN HAD SENT FROM HIS GOVERN-ment smartphone needed to work. He also needed the watchers to follow through on their mission. Without those two components to his plan, the entire region was going to be a nuclear wasteland. He knew that once the spent fuel rods came into contact with the air, they would be like struck matchsticks, igniting from spontaneous combustion inside the reactor.

The way he saw it, he had two of three problems to solve. He had to find a way to stop the drill and the explosives Maeve had described to him. Or, if they had already breached one of the pools, then he had to plug the hole to prevent the nuclear wastewater from draining into the earth and to keep the fuel rods underwater. Independent from those two issues was the fact that Gunther could not leave the premises alive. Technically, Mahegan had done his duty in securing Maeve Cassidy, but he knew that was a moot issue now. The looming nuclear disaster overrode any obligations Mahegan had to keep secret Cassidy's Afghanistan mission, as General Savage desired.

He turned to Maeve as they stood at the door leading to the command center and observation room. It was a standard heavy metal door that could be locked with a key from either side. Looking over his shoulder, Mahegan saw men lying in single beds, with intravenous fluid bags hanging from nails punched into the stone walls. He recognized some of the wounded as those he had fought. He could see that the tunnel was a combination of centuries-old earth and recent efforts to create living quarters for the EB-5 workers.

In for a penny, in for a pound, Mahegan thought to himself again as he looked at Maeve. He didn't trust her and wasn't sure what her angle was, but if he could get her on the drill, they had a chance. He noticed her sunken cheeks and hollow eyes, which accentuated the narrow planes of her face. Her hair was slick from days of sweat and oil. She still wore the uniform that she had on the night she came back from Fort Bragg. Her visage and aroma reminded him of combat . . . and reminded him she was a soldier.

"I can make amends," she had said.

He believed she needed the opportunity.

"I see your wheels spinning," Maeve said. "You can trust me. Let's just knock this out. Then you can figure out what to do with me."

Mahegan nodded. "Can you kill Jimmy if you need to?" he asked.

That was the rub, the real test.

"I can." She nodded. "It's all I've thought about for months. He raped me, knocked me up, and made me complicit in his scheme. The question is, can you stop me?"

Mahegan nodded. "Fair enough." He paused. "Pete is dead. Jimmy or one of the commandos killed him."

Maeve's hand came to her mouth. Tears snuck out of the corners of her eyes. Mahegan had deliberately given her the information now so that she wouldn't be shocked if they got into a situation where Jim or someone else told her in an effort to make her pause.

"No."

"Yes. I saw him on the floor of your playroom, with a bullet hole in his head. After dumping you in the wooden cell—"

"You saw that?"

"Yes. I found your name tag and watch. Regardless, Jimmy probably circled back to your house after your husband had picked up Piper from the babysitter's, either that night or the following morning. Then he shot your husband and kidnapped your child to extort you into stealing natural gas for him and his father."

"I can kill Jimmy."

"Thought that might help clarify the situation," Mahegan said. "Now the hard part. The guys who were questioning you when you returned? They work for my boss, Major General Savage. They let you get away, hoping you'd lead them to the Chinese. They picked up on some cyber exchanges between this location and Beijing. The texts were encrypted and hard to decipher but mentioned your name and fracking in the same sentence," Mahegan said.

Maeve's eyes narrowed. Her mouth twitched. The hands that were wiping tears now became fists, which she flailed at Mahegan.

"You used me as bait!" she hollered.

Mahegan lightly grabbed her wrists, which continued to pump like pistons.

"You know what this is. You've known all along," Mahegan said.

"How the hell would I know?"

"The watch. Three minutes to midnight. You may not have known precisely how, but you knew that this was a nuclear event."

Her arms stopped flailing. Her countenance shifted from one of fury to that of recognition. Mahegan felt her go slack.

After a moment she cast her eyes up at him.

"Yes. I knew."

"I thought it was fair I gave you both pieces of information. I believe in informed decision making. And Maeve?"

"Yes?"

"If General Savage had not wanted you to escape the compound, you never would have."

"I get it. Now I know. Let's go."

He went over the plan with her briefly, then pulled open the door and stepped into the hallway leading to the observation room. Maeve pointed at the back of Ting's head, which was looking at the monitor.

Maeve pointed through the wire mesh window at the back of

Ting's head as the Chinese man looked at the monitor. Mahegan opened the door and with five quick, silent strides Mahegan was on the Chinese man. After wrapping a powerful forearm around the man's neck, he squeezed until his adversary passed out. Mahegan laid Ting on the floor facedown. Removing some flex cuffs, he zip tied Ting's hands and feet, then pulled a section of rope between the cuffs so that he was effectively hog-tied. He removed the man's wallet, saw that his name was Johnny Ting and that he was here on an EB-5 green card.

Maeve was already in the seat where Ting had been and where she had spent the past several days. "Look at that," she said, pointing at the display.

It was a video image of the drill bit spinning in the nuclear fuel rod pool, like an alien monster erupting from an embryonic hibernation. The bit was smashing into racks of fuel rods, breaking them open, and shattering the metal rods into millions of radioactive shards, which littered the water like snow in a globe. The camera behind the drill showed the spinning bit to be an artificially intelligent terrorist bent on destroying everything in the pool.

"Can you pull it back?" Mahegan asked.

"I think so, if no one has jacked with the controls."

She maneuvered the joystick and began retracting the drill cable, pulling in the slack. The drill bit spun and actually faced the camera, as if to question the motives of its operator. Through the camera Mahegan could see dozens of fuel rods stacked on the bottom of the pool, free of the racks. They looked like cut timber in a cleared forest. It was difficult to gather much more information, because the drill bit kept moving the base of the cable, but he had seen enough to know that as soon as the water drained from the pool, the fuel rods would create an enormous radioactive fire.

"I've got it," Maeve said. He could see she was pulling the drill bit back through the hole. Water was coursing past it, drowning out the image.

"How do we stop that leak? It has to be at least four feet wide, based on what I saw."

"I'm thinking. It's impossible to block it at the base of the pool. The nuclear guys will not have prepared for this contingency. A minor leak, sure, but not this. They have divers that go down and check the rods on a regular, frequent basis, but the water at the bottom of these pools is as radioactive as it comes."

"And it's now rushing into our hole and will come shooting out of the well just down the hill, like newfound oil," Mahegan said.

"Hadn't thought about that."

"Where is the channel the most narrow between the pools and the well?"

"You're a genius," Maeve said. "The second kickoff point. I can lower the drill and try to make the channel collapse on itself."

"What about the explosives? You said something about perforating charges. Can you use the fracking explosives to collapse the well?"

"Yes. One-two punch. Let me get the drill to try to make the rock and earth block the channel. Then we'll pull out the drill and put in the explosives to collapse the vein."

"You need the workers in the yard to do that, right?" Mahegan asked. "Where Petrov is?"

"Yeah. He has been handling the operation down there. They are short on people to do the heavy lifting now . . . thanks to you, I guess."

Mahegan turned to Ting, who was now conscious. Using his knife to emphasize his point, Mahegan put the tip under Ting's chin and said, "You are an enemy of my country. You're a terrorist. I have full authority to kill you. Now, tell me, what were your last instructions to Petrov?"

Ting shook his head. "You kill Chun," Ting said. "He the one in charge. I am low-level foot soldier."

"Then I guess I don't need you," Mahegan said. He lifted the knife, pulled back Ting's head, exposed his throat, and placed the knife's razor-sharp edge near the carotid artery. "I did kill Chun, and I didn't even think about it. In fact, I had already forgotten about him, until you just reminded me."

A personal radio in Ting's pocket came to life with a Russian voice. "We are commencing retraction of the cable and preparation of the explosives."

Mahegan pressed the tip of the knife next to the Chinese man's larynx, pushed it in and drew blood, then pushed it in a little more, until the man screamed.

"Okay. I'm going to grab this radio, and you're going to say, 'Hold at kickoff point. Then pull back.' "

Ting shook his head, until he realized he was making the gash in his neck hurt worse with the knife still in an inch there.

"Say it once for me so I know you've got it," Mahegan said.

"Stop at kickoff point. Then pull back," Ting said in his thick Chinese accent.

"Okay, so I'm going to press this button, and you say it again. If you say anything else, I will cut your throat, and you won't say anything ever again. Understand?" He pushed the knife another half inch into Ting's throat. Blood was pooling on the floor.

"Understand."

Mahegan pushed the button, and Ting shouted, "I am not—"

Those were the only words he was able to say, because Mahegan cut his throat and shut off the radio in a simultaneous motion.

"Petrov's pulling the cable back. I'm going to have to fight him at the kickoff point," Maeve said.

"I speak some Mandarin," Mahegan said. "I know Ting's accent is Beijing Mandarin. I can probably replicate it once, so let me know when you need me to do it."

Mahegan stood behind Maeve as they watched the drill bit head fall through the channel under her direction. Water sluiced past the camera, drowning the image.

CHAPTER 37

S AM BLACKMON COULDN'T BELIEVE WHAT HE WAS SEEING. THERE was a drill bit the size of a basketball spinning wildly in the bottom of the pool and eating through the fuel rod racks. The water in the pool was draining fast.

"Have we opened the floodgates in the lake?" he asked. The idea was to have water coming into the pool as fast as it was flooding out.

"We're trying, sir," Stickman said. "But we're on standby, waiting for a permit from the state."

"To hell with that," Blackmon said. He had been under fire many times and wasn't going to lose his cool. But he did feel fear boiling in his stomach. "Open those gates all the way. I'll take the heat for this."

Less than five miles from Sam Blackmon, Grace linked up with watchers Elaine and Brandy in the parking lot of a major shopping mall, behind which the Underground Railroad emptied into a tributary in Durham County. They were anonymous in the mostly vacant lot, and so they stood in the cool evening air. Piper's small hand was cradled in Grace's slender fingers as Grace explained the situation.

"This is the kidnapped kid, Piper Cassidy. Hawthorne rescued her and the mother, but the mother went back in to help him with the drill."

"Guy's amazing," Elaine said. "Enough to make me want to go over to the dark side."

"Let's not go overboard," Brandy said.

"This is serious business," Grace said. "These guys are drilling up through the nuclear power plant. Hawthorne knows you were in the Navy, Elaine, and figures you at least know how to use a rifle. He wants us to go up to the boulder and start picking off the workers when he gives us the signal."

"You're kidding?" Elaine asked. "I haven't shot a rifle since basic training."

"You've probably never shot his kind of rifle. It's got a silencer and everything."

"Well, if he needs the help, we'll give it to him," Elaine said.

"Agreed," Brandy said.

"You've got to take care of Piper, Brandy. Plus, I've got a bound and gagged Bosnian in the back of my car. Take Piper to Elaine's place and chill until we come get you."

Brandy nodded. "Got it." She took the keys from Grace's hand.

Elaine popped the hatch on her SUV, and Grace heaved Mahegan's bag of tricks from the trunk. They all hugged, and then Grace knelt in front of Piper and told her it was going to be okay. Brandy reassured her and then put her in the front seat of Grace's car. Grace leaned into the backseat and stuck her finger in the captive woman's face.

"Don't you dare try anything crazy," Grace said, whispering out of Piper's earshot. She pointed at Brandy in the driver's seat. "This woman here is just out of jail for murder."

They watched Brandy pull away in Grace's car, then hopped into Elaine's SUV. Grace made the phone call Mahegan had asked her to make. The Wallaby gas station was practically on the way to their destination. In the parking lot she saw a Buick Electra idling low to the ground. Elaine pulled up so that Grace's door was on the driver's side of the Buick.

"Diablo?"

"Sí."

"It's time. I see you've still got the phone Mahegan gave you. Can you do this?"

Diablo nodded. "I'll try to find Manuela."

"*Gracias,*" Grace said.

Elaine then pulled out of the parking lot. The drive to the fire-break took about thirty minutes, and it would take them another twenty to get set up behind the boulder. The night sky was cloud-less, with a sliver of a moon, like a haunting smile. The women trod softly through the forest paralleling the firebreak. They took turns carrying Mahegan's duffel bag, which carried the equip-ment they would need. They tried to be careful, aware that their cover might have been blown by all the activity.

"Elaine," Grace whispered.

"Yes?"

"If we get discovered, just know you can count on me."

"Never a doubt," Elaine replied. "And likewise."

"I mean, don't doubt me. Okay?"

"I won't."

Upon their arrival at the boulder, Elaine reached into the duf-fel bag and extracted an M4 carbine, with its night optic scope and silencer. Grace grabbed a pair of night-vision goggles, held them against her eyes and focused the lens.

"Lots of activity down there," Grace said.

"I don't know a thing about this rifle, Grace. It's like a small M-sixteen, which I did shoot a couple of times."

"How hard can it be? Just put the bullets in it and aim it," Grace said, turning toward Elaine. She removed the night-vision goggles and watched her friend fumble with the weapon.

Elaine found a box magazine with shiny metal cartridges that held bullets and slid it into the well of the M4 until Grace heard a click. Elaine pulled on the charging handle and chambered a round more loudly than she meant to. She thumbed the safety to off and sighted through the scope.

"All black," she said.

"Turn the scope on," Grace said. She watched Elaine feel for an on-off switch, find the knob, and flip it.

"Much better. Bright green. I can see Petrov at the wellhead. Some of those idiots are smoking cigarettes. The lights actually help," Elaine said. "Let me give this thing a test run."

Through the night-vision goggles, Grace watched Elaine spin to her left and pick out a target beyond the drill rig, a small Eiffel Tower–like structure.

"Truck tire. About six feet tall. Just below the trailers. Shooting at it ought to tell me whether I can hit anything with this. It's about three hundred yards."

Grace knew that at one time Elaine had been a reasonable hunter. She had learned to hunt with her father near the farm where she grew up. Not a particularly rich family, they had actually had to hunt for provisions. Her parents had stocked the freezer with deer, bear, and birds. She knew that Elaine's love of nature had fueled some of her opposition to the fracking.

Grace heard Elaine flick the safety lever to the single-shot position. Elaine leaned the accessory rail against the boulder, steadied her aim, and pulled back on the trigger with the pad of her index finger. Grace heard Elaine exhale slightly; then she jumped at the cough of the weapon as it fired. She settled down quickly enough to put the goggles to her eyes and find the tire. It had deflated with a pop, which she'd heard above the din of turbines and shouting at the wellhead. Grace watched the workers at the wellhead for any sign that they had heard the shot. The men continued to push and pull at ropes and pipes, apparently none the wiser.

"Pretty easy," Elaine said. "Tell Hawthorne I can do it. And I see five workers down there, including Petrov. And I see your idiots smoking cigarettes. I'll just aim at those, and it's not a problem to shoot them if he really wants me to, but I would prefer he deal with them."

"Conflicted, are we? These guys are about to create a radioactive fire inside the Shearon Harris Nuclear Power Plant. We're all toast if that happens."

"I said I will do it. Just text him and tell him we're ready."

Grace worked her thumbs across the smartphone, letting Mahegan know their ready position and the status of the wellhead. She also sent a note saying that she had met with Diablo, but Manuela was present at the time, so the Mexicans were not a sure thing.

As both women watched Petrov and his men extract the drill cable, Grace's phone vibrated with a text from Mahegan.

In a minute I will give word to shoot Petrov.

As the message came in, Grace and Elaine used the optics to scan the far wood line. A car was snaking its way up the road.

"Car coming up the road. Maybe it's the Mexicans," Elaine said.

"Let's hope so," Grace said.

Grace relayed the information to Mahegan.

"Okay," she said, turning back to Elaine. "We're good to go, as Mahegan would say."

"Too bad he's not here with you," said a third voice.

Griffyn had found them.

Grace spun upward and faced off against her boss. Her stomach dropped when she noticed the faraway look in his eyes. His head was canted sideways, as if he was a rabid animal considering which threat to attack first. A shotgun slanted across his body like a hash mark.

"I'm so glad you're here, Griff. Finally," Grace said. "Where have you been?"

Grace watched Elaine out of her periphery. Elaine began to move Mahegan's rifle, triggering a reflexive response from Griffyn, who raised the butt of his shotgun and smashed it into Elaine's face.

Grace clenched her stomach but remained stoic. Her friend fell backward on top of Mahegan's rifle.

"Been trying to find your ass for two days," Griffyn said. "Where the hell *you* been?"

"It sure as hell took you long enough to get here," Grace said. "You told me to get in good with the lesbians, so I did. You told me to get close to the Indian, so I did. What haven't I done for you?"

Griffyn hitched his shoulder, as if he had a nervous twitch. "Well, go ahead and kill her," he said, handing her the shotgun. Before taking the weapon, Grace knelt and placed her hand against Elaine's neck.

"She's dead. No pulse. Check it out for yourself. Besides, we don't need anyone to hear the blast from the shotgun. You can call it in."

Griffyn said, "You're the technician. You say she's dead, she's dead."

Grace looked at Elaine, who was lying motionless in the dirt, and nodded. "She's dead. We done here?"

"Nope. Not until we get the Indian. Let me make this call." Griffyn pulled out a handheld radio and said, "Base, this is rover. Watchers neutralized."

Grace listened for the reply and heard a voice say, "Roger. Return to base."

"Let's go then," Grace said.

As they stepped along the narrow trail leading away from the boulder, she heard movement behind her.

"Not so fast, you two," Elaine said.

CHAPTER 38

MAHEGAN STOOD BEHIND THE DOOR AND LISTENED. HE HEARD Brand Throckmorton and his wife, Sharon, arguing.

"This thing's falling apart, you stupid moron!" Sharon shouted. "One person has single-handedly shut your ass down. If you weren't thinking with the head in your pants, maybe you could have pulled this off."

A muffled cough followed Sharon's outburst, and Mahegan knew it was a pistol report.

After a moment, Throckmorton screamed, "You bastard! You killed her!"

"Did you a favor," said a male voice. Mahegan's sense was that it was the elder Gunther's voice, but he couldn't be sure. "We can blame it on the Indian. Griff's got Grace Kagami and killed the dyke. Just cleaning up, Throck. That's all."

Mahegan heard a slight whimpering, the sound of Brand Throckmorton crying. He pictured him hovering over Sharon, imagining all he had lost, despite his infidelity.

If the watchers were out of play and Grace was a captive, Mahegan thought, the battlefield geometry had changed. What he had calculated as three different moving pieces now became two at best. He had no idea how reliable Diablo and Manuela would be in a combat scenario, but without the watchers pinning down the roughnecks at the wellhead, Mahegan would have no supporting fire. His freedom of maneuver would be restricted.

He left the door that separated the hallway from the main lodge. He turned around and looked to his left where the door to the tunnel was ajar. To his front was the door to the observation room. He took a few steps and turned right through the door to the control room, where Maeve was watching the chaos inside the nuclear rod pool. She looked catatonic.

"Look at me," Mahegan demanded.

Startled, Maeve turned and stuttered, "Y-yes?"

"Is there another control room anywhere around here? I need to find where they follow the cell phones."

"There was always a lot of activity down there in the infirmary, or what became the infirmary once you showed up."

Mahegan walked into the hallway and through the door to the tunnel. He checked several doors, all of which led to empty rooms, before he found one that was locked. Mahegan's knife made quick work of the flashing and the doorjamb, and soon he was in the cool air of the server room. From floor to ceiling he saw server racks and blades, as well as routers and high-tech gear he didn't recognize. He found a monitor that had twelve small insets with maps on them. Each showed the location, or the last known location, of a cell phone. It was a Stingray. Mahegan had used this technology in Afghanistan and Iraq to find the enemy. Now the enemy was using it to track employees, the watchers, and, ultimately, him.

Modern technology tracked the phones in the cloud, which required passwords he did not have time to hack. Knowing the phones could be tracked from another computer, Mahegan was banking on the idea that if he destroyed this setup, he might shut down the tracking of all communications for the operation. If he couldn't track anyone, then he didn't want anyone else having that capability, either. He did need to keep cell phone communications operational, however.

He carefully unplugged every wire and plug he could find that led into the monitor and the server feeding the monitor. Then he smashed the hardware on the dusty cement floor. Knowing that was the best he could do, he glanced at the other blinking and flashing servers. He didn't want to damage those, because that might impact Maeve's ability to maneuver the drill and see into the channel, which were other key elements of his plan.

Mahegan exited the server room and walked along the dark tunnel, listening to the cries of the wounded EB-5 workers he had locked in the room where he had found Maeve and Piper. He walked back to the door separating the lodge from the control room. He listened at the door, behind which Sharon had been shot.

"Jimmy, go back there and check on Ting and Chun. Blow the door with C-four if you have to," James Gunther directed. "I'm gonna take this knife and go cut up the Indian."

Mahegan walked back to the control room, where Maeve appeared more alert and was playing with the controls.

"I have an idea," she said.

"I'm open," he said. "Talk."

"This channel is very narrow from the base of the pool to this second kickoff point. It's three thousand feet below ground level but only about two feet wide, maybe eighteen inches in some places where I was more precise. The volume is pi times the radius squared times the height, which, like I said, is three thousand feet. One cubic foot is seven-point-four-eight gallons, so you've got to get word to the nuclear plant that they have to replace 281,990 gallons of water if I can block it at this kickoff point."

"You can collapse it at the kickoff point?" Mahegan asked, pointing at the display, which showed the vertical channel from the pool to where it made a horizontal turn, the kick off point.

"I can try. Had to do this once in Pak. It would be better if I had the perforating charges down there, but I can chew at it with the drill and try to block it. At least I can slow down the loss of water. I'll have to come about fifty yards back into the pipe to build a decent rock pile."

"And if we can't make that happen?"

"The pools drain, they're all connected, and we've got a nuclear explosion on the East Coast."

"If that's our best play, do that. I'll try to get word to Shearon Harris," Mahegan said.

He had no idea how he was going to contact the nuclear plant, but then a thought occurred to him. He heard Jim, he presumed, pounding on the door.

"Open up, Ting. Let's go. This is our operation, too."

Jim's hammering sounded like gunshots echoing down the long hallway. Mahegan looked at Maeve, who was staring at him with wide eyes. She needed him to buy her some time to collapse the channel, or they would have radioactive water spewing like a geyser into the wellhead in fifteen minutes or less.

Sam Blackmon stared at the image of the drill bit retracting into one of the many holes it had created in the bottom of the cooling pool. Red lights were flashing and sirens were wailing, as if a bombing raid were inbound.

"Stix, we've got to open the floodgates on the lake and fill the pools faster than they drain."

"I'm working it, boss. We haven't rehearsed that in a year, and there's some rust welding the door shut."

"Get down there with a crowbar and pry that puppy open if you have to," Blackmon said calmly in his commander's voice.

"Roger that," Stickman said. He punched a small button at the base of his ear that controlled the radio in his ear canal. "How we coming on opening the dam?" His voice was calm, like Blackmon's. They had operated together in Iraq, Afghanistan, and the Philippines, among other combat zones, and one thing they knew was that while the pressure was building, they had to react inversely, as they had trained themselves to do. The more pressure you had, the calmer you had to be.

"I'm heading down there," Stickman said.

"Boots on the ground. Can't beat it," Blackmon nodded as Stickman dashed through the command center doors.

The cooling pools were located in the basement of the nuclear reactor facility. A steady stream of water from the lake circulated through the facility, and some of it was diverted for the pools after extensive filtration and chemical testing. There would be no time for that, Blackmon thought. They would just need to bum-rush the lake water in like a flood. The idea would be to replace more than they were losing. But how the hell would they ever stop the loss with five holes in the bottom of the pool?

Blackmon could think of one way. He was a trained frogman, a certified military diver who could swim for miles underwater. There wasn't much Sam Blackmon couldn't do from a combat perspective, and if saving his country meant possibly sacrificing himself at the bottom of a highly radioactive pool, then that would be a risk worth taking.

He thought about his three daughters and his wife, who had endured their fair share of deployments and his absence from the home front. They lived in Holly Springs, North Carolina, just around the corner from the nuclear facility. Only in passing had they ever considered a nuclear catastrophe wiping out the Triangle region. It was the kind of jokey talk that he and Stickman and the rest of their buddies slung around during backyard barbecues.

"Let me just hold this burger up. All that radiation will cook it in a minute. . . ."

"Went fishing in the lake the other day. All the fish weighed ten pounds and had three eyes. . . ."

That kind of thing. Meanwhile, their children would be playing in the expansive backyard, on the swing set or in the tree fort. It was about as apple pie as you could get, Blackmon thought, and he wanted to keep it that way.

Stickman returned, breathing heavily. He knelt over in the doorway to the command center, with his hands on his knees.

"Boss, we got it open about a foot. Damn thing is rusted bad. But water's flowing into the holding pool."

"We need to make it a straight pass," Blackmon said. "No time for chemicals or cleansing. Just need the cold water on the racks and the rods that are now lying on the bottom of the pool."

"Roger that."

Blackmon grabbed his dive suit.

"That ain't what I think it is, is it?" asked Stickman.

"Depends on what you think it is."

"You will fry with those open racks and fuel rods down there. Ain't nothing you can do."

"I can plug the gaps," Blackmon said.

"With what? That damn thing punched five holes in the floor. It's all funneling out fast."

"I'll try to slide some of the casks over the holes. That'll slow it down."

"And then what?" asked Stickman.

"Have the pressure washer and the soap ready for me when I get back. It's the best we can do. Everyone needs to put hazmat suits on now."

Blackmon's friend and combat buddy stared at him for an eternity, eyes locked onto his. Stickman shook his head and said, "There's another way."

A security guard ran in, panting, as Stickman had before him.

"We've got the valve to the lake water open more. We've got a hundred gallons a second coming in from the lake. We're losing about that much, so it's going to be close."

"Your dive can wait, sir," Stickman said. "We've got this."

Blackmon suited up, walked to the air-lock chamber, and opened it with a swipe of his identification card.

"You know me. I've got to be where the action is," Blackmon said. He then stepped into the pressurized chamber, waited until the command center door closed, and pressed a button, opening the door to the stairwell that led down to the cooling pools.

Mahegan watched Maeve maneuver the joystick.

"I can buy you ten minutes, maybe," he said.

He quietly undid the locks that the Chinese had evidently put in place to keep Gunther and Throckmorton out of the control room as the mission moved into its final phase. Looking over his shoulder, he could see Maeve manipulating the drill bit as she reversed its course through the channel it had just scoured. She cursed a few times as her hand worked the joystick. Then he stepped out of the command center, into the hallway, and walked toward the door that led to the lodge. He leaned against the wall, steadied his breathing, and thought about his next move.

The rock wall pressed into his back as he listened to footsteps scrape along the dusty cement and dirt floor that led from the lodge to the door behind which he was hiding.

"Little bit of C-four never hurt anybody," Mahegan heard Jim say. "Not anybody that I cared about, anyway."

Mahegan tucked himself into the corner of the hallway where the doorjamb was located. The blast would be on the doorknob side of the door frame opposite his position. The door would blow outward, and the hinges next to his shoulder would either hold or be the last to give.

Mahegan looked at Maeve through the observation window of the control room. He could see on the display that the drill bit had reached the three-thousand-foot bottom kickoff point and that she was retracting it to her fifty-yard point. He saw her angle the drill upward to try to get enough rock to fall and block the water.

"Stand clear, Dad," Jim said on the other side of the door. Then, from a more distant vantage, he added, "Fire in the hole!"

The explosion was about the right size to knock a door down, Mahegan thought. The door flew open, mostly because Mahegan had removed the locks, and it still hung from the top hinge. He had braced for the blast, which landed directly on him, but his left shoulder took another hit that it didn't need to take. In a combat situation he didn't worry about it, but he made a note that he needed to do more swimming.

As the smoke settled, he heard Jim say, "I'll go in and find the Chinese. You go kick the Indian's ass."

Jim stepped into the hallway. The blast had knocked out the emergency lights, which the generator had been powering. The ambient glow of the monitors cast enough light for Jim to step past Mahegan without noticing him.

"Let me know what you got in there, son, before I drag my ass down there. Throck's up here, moaning about his old lady."

"You killed my wife!" Throckmorton was repeating from be-yond the hole in the wall where the door once was.

"Shut up, Throck," said Gunther. "I have to think of every damn thing. I'm going to go put this gun in the Indian's hands, let him shoot it a few times against the wall so he gets some gunpowder residue on him, and then stick it in his mouth. Problem solved. I'll even drop your wife down there with him. Make it look like a fight of some sort. Hell, she was boning everybody else. Why not the biggest guy around?"

"Shut up, you bastard," Throckmorton thundered.

Smoke still hung in the air like a dense fog. Mahegan could see that Jim was focused on the lights coming from the control room. He heard him whisper, "Dear Maeve," and was reminded that they had worked together in Afghanistan and that she had been abused in the worst possible way by him.

Now he really needed to take Jim quietly to avoid a rush from Gunther and Throckmorton. After slipping his knife from its calf sheath, he quietly opened the blade as he moved, stepping silently onto his heel, rolling against the side of his arch, and then pushing off the ball of his foot, as he had learned from his mother in Frisco in the happy days of his childhood. Each step was a de-liberate imitation of the way his forefathers had hunted for cen-turies. He and his mother would practice with a bow and arrow and a bale of hay as a makeshift circular target. First, the exercise was static, and he would just sit there. Next, she had him stalking "game," which was the target. She would reset the targets every day and have Jake walk from a different direction. The hay bale would be covered with tarps, to which she had tied ropes, and his mother would pull the tarps from the bale, which was Mahegan's signal to stop, aim, and shoot.

He thought of his mother as he watched Jim Gunther, the son, step three feet in front of him, within arm's reach. Mahegan could tell that Jim's radar was up, that he knew something was not right. But to Mahegan's advantage, Jim was moving slowly. In all of Mahegan's days of wrestling in high school and hand-to-hand combat training in the Army, he had learned that the best takedowns were always from the rear. Surprise and shock were at a premium.

Jim turned his head over his left shoulder, away from Mahegan, and said, "Something ain't right. It's just Cassidy down there in the control room."

Mahegan needed to act swiftly and with lethal force. Again, as always, his emotions were pushing against his rational thought. He needed logic, not passion. He was less than two feet from Jim's back, the knife firm in his right hand. In one rapid motion Mahegan looped his arm around Jim's neck and squeezed it like a vise, shutting down his vocal cords, and rammed the knife into Jim's right kidney. As he felt his hand touch Jim's back, he retracted the knife and brought it around to the front and into his gut, where he made a deep, long laceration that opened Jim's stomach, blood and intestines spilling over his hand. For good measure, after sliding the knife into the sheath on his calf, Mahegan reached up with both hands and snapped Jim's neck. Lowering him to the floor, Mahegan slid the body of his first true rival behind the unhinged door.

He looked up and saw Maeve staring at him through the glass observation window, her mouth wide open in a silent scream.

Then, in the wafting smoke, he turned and waited for James Gunther, fifteen years of anticipation surging through his veins like an electrical current.

CHAPTER 39

GRACE SNATCHED THE SHOTGUN FROM GRIFFYN'S HANDS, SLAMMED the stock into his stomach, and then chopped downward, striking him in the back of the head. She then performed an acrobatic twirl to sweep his legs out from underneath him with a forceful kick.

Remembering Elaine and her ready gun, Grace called over her shoulder, "Don't shoot him, Elaine. He needs to make a phone call."

"You were always a good faker, Grace," Elaine said. Grace could hear the smile in her voice. "I'm good, though. Love it when a plan comes together. Just squeeze him, okay? He broke my nose."

Griffyn was on the ground, with Grace on his back, tying his hands behind his back. Mahegan's ropes were coming in handy. The sounds were crisp and distinct in the cool night air: Griffyn's "Oomph" from Grace's back kick that had landed him on the ground; Grace's voice, clear and authoritative; Elaine's nasal wheeze as she adapted to breathing through her mouth alone. Locally, they were isolated out at the boulder that had been their hiding place for the past several weeks, as they monitored the fracking operation. In the bigger picture, their noises were drowned out by the industrial operation going on three hundred yards below them. Grace and Elaine had worked out a plan to implement if Griffyn ever compromised them. Grace would act as if she were with him, on his side, and Elaine would take the punishment, up to a point.

"Where's the phone?" Grace asked Griffyn.

"You'll never get away with this, Grace," he said. "You'll never live to tell about it."

"Means a lot coming from you, Griff, with you all tied up and everything."

"They'll kill you. You know that, right?"

"I know they'll try." Searching him, she found his iPhone tucked away in the inside of his North Face jacket. "Got it," Grace said. She took Griffyn's hand and pressed his thumb against the fingerprint sensor, activating the touch identification to open his phone.

"You ungrateful, insubordinate slut," Griffyn muttered when he realized what she was doing.

"That's one word for it," Grace said.

She began scrolling through the contacts and found the name Mahegan had given her, plus another that she thought might be useful. She called the first.

Sam Blackmon was staring at the backlit fuel rod cooling pools as the water level approached the tops of the racks fifty feet below the surface of the connected pools. The water looked a mint blue, he thought. They almost looked like those high-end swimming pools in the chic hotels that dotted sandy, white Caribbean beaches. His reality, though, was very different than the images running through his mind.

In a few minutes he would either burn to death or radiation would eat through his body. At his feet were five sheets of plywood, which he intended to drag into place over the holes in the damaged pool. He had had his crew drill holes in the center of each sheet of plywood using the tools from the reactor maintenance room. Then he had had them thread nylon cord through the holes in the plywood and tie it around the barbells they had scrounged from the weight room. The barbells would serve as sinkers, holding the plywood in place over the drilled holes.

He bent over and lifted a fifty-pound barbell and tossed it into the pool. The barbell pulled the four-by-eight-foot sheet of plywood to the bottom of the pool quickly. That was its purpose: to hold the plywood in place against the pool floor and keep the plywood from floating to the surface. The plywood had fluttered like a giant bass lure until the barbell reached the bottom of the pool. Now the sheet of plywood was suspended vertically, as if desperately trying to reach the surface.

He threw the remaining four barbells into the water, and they all landed in generally the same area, their respective sheets of plywood looking like arms raised, signaling for help. He adjusted the oxygen tank on his back and began to reach for his mask and regulator. In his reinforced Kevlar frogman dive suit, he carried a pistol in a watertight compartment and his cell phone in a vertical zipper pocket above his left breast. He felt the phone vibrate and considered not answering it, figuring it was probably just Stickman calling to tell him one last time not to go into the pool.

He fumbled the phone in his gloved hands, managed to press the green ANSWER button, and growled, "Hello."

"Colonel Blackmon, I was told to call you by someone who calls himself Manteo Six. He said you would know what that meant."

Blackmon listened to the female voice, fear hanging off her words like jagged icicles. The only Manteo Six he knew was a former Delta Force operator called Chayton Mahegan, whose unit had been known as the Warriors. General Savage had adopted him as a protégé until a mission went badly in Afghanistan. Blackmon had met Mahegan a few times and knew he was legit. If Mahegan was having someone call him, it most likely was important, but he had pressing matters directly in front of him as he watched the lake water swirl into the pool too slowly.

The brown tint indicated that Stickman had turned off the filtration system in an effort to accelerate the flow of water into the pool. They were fighting some laws of gravity, he knew, as the holes in the bottom of the pool followed a channel straight down, while the lake water flowed horizontally from the valve in the dam to the pool, like a stream. The math wasn't working in his favor. He examined the five sheets of plywood, knowing he had to get to work.

"I know Jake. What's he want? I've got a situation on my hands."

"So that's his real name? Jake?" Grace murmured.

"Jake Mahegan. What's he want?"

"A fracking drill has bored a hole in the bottom of your pool," Grace said.

"Actually, it has bored five holes," he said. "Tell me something I don't know, or I'm off the phone and going in to plug the gap."

"He's got someone in control of the drill, and he's having her block the hole at three thousand feet. That means you need to get two hundred eighty-two thousand gallons of water into the pool. The hole will consume that much, at least."

"Okay. That's useful. Who am I talking to?"

"Grace Kagami. I'm with the Raleigh Police Department. I borrowed Detective Griffyn's phone."

Blackmon did the math in his head. It would be an hour before he got three hundred thousand gallons into the pool. Way too long. Even their best-case estimate was ten thousand gallons a minute, which would cut it to thirty minutes. Still too long.

"Tell Mahegan we've got about five thousand gallons a minute coming in from the lake right now, but I'm trying to get it to ten thousand. We're losing it faster than we can add it."

"Okay. We need to notify emergency management for the state," Grace said. "That's not quick enough."

"We're working it. Is Mahegan taking care of whoever did this?"

"Yes, as we speak," Grace said.

"I wouldn't want to be them," Blackmon said.

"Roger that," Grace said.

Blackmon hung up and tossed the phone aside. It skittered away on the concrete. He pulled his mask over his face and flopped backward into the pool.

Grace looked at the phone and then at Elaine. "Where do we get these guys? He is about to jump in a pool of radioactive water to plug the gap."

"Damn."

"Okay, so what do we have? Mahegan with Cassidy at the drill.

Blackmon jumping in the pool. Maybe the Mexicans moving to the lodge. Us watching the Russian and other roughnecks and waiting on the call to kill them."

"About sums it up. Plus, your boss all tied up over there." Elaine turned her chin in the darkness toward the muted lump about twenty yards away on the dirt trail.

"When we first started watching these guys a few months ago, did you ever think it would come to this, Elaine?"

"I knew it wouldn't end well, but, no, nothing like this."

Grace and Elaine knelt behind the boulder, using night optics to look into the lighted pit below, where Petrov was screaming at five or six men. Through her optic, Grace saw one of the men shout at Petrov as he threw something over his shoulder toward the well. Immediately, Petrov scrambled toward the open hole. He wrestled the cap into place and then backed away, as if running from a crazed animal.

They stared in amazement as the metal cap covering the well pipe blew into the sky like a Frisbee, chased by fire leaping hundreds of feet into the air.

Mahegan let the smoke clear and walked into the large den of the lodge. He saw the Civil War–era knickknacks hanging from the fireplace mantel like trophies. He looked in every direction, only to see an open front door and headlights backing away. As the truck turned, the lights briefly highlighted the dead body of Sharon Throckmorton.

Gunther was heading either to the wellhead or to the rear entrance of the Underground Railroad tunnel that connected to the lodge. Now that he was out of it, Mahegan could picture the layout of the entire tunnel. The tunnel opened to the north and connected at this location about a mile to the south. Runaway slaves would follow the streambeds that today formed Harris and Jordan Lakes. They would huddle at the base of the high ground, where Throckmorton would later build his lodge. An old copper mine, most likely, provided safe passage beneath the ridge and west of Raleigh to the road that led farther west toward the Piedmont. There Levi Coffin's efforts had already paved the way for slaves to escape to the Northwest Territory, and away from Virginia, the cradle of the Confederacy.

Mahegan walked past Sharon Throckmorton's body and through the doorway, which was singed black from the explosives, and stepped over Jim Gunther's body. He saw Maeve Cassidy working diligently in the control room.

As he approached the door, she said, "I think I've got it." She pointed at the monitor that showed the three-thousand-foot drop from the nuclear plant, then the right-angled turn that was collapsed a few inches from the bend.

"Good. Can you pull the drill out and shoot more fracking fluid down the hole?" Mahegan asked. "If we push fluid down, it will help stop the flow of the radioactive waste."

"I don't control that from here. Those guys do," Maeve said. She pointed at the monitor that showed Petrov waving his arms wildly at the other men near the wellhead. "Someone would have to put the hose they have into the pipe and shoot the fracking fluid in. Then I can modulate the flow."

"Okay. I'll go down there and get it in. Which hose?"

Maeve moved the camera and showed Mahegan the fracking fluid hose system fifty feet from where Petrov was standing. "That one," she said, pointing at the screen again.

"Okay. Give me ten minutes."

As he turned to leave the tunnel, he heard Maeve say, "Oh, no."

Looking over his shoulder at the monitor, he saw Petrov arguing with a roughneck who was smoking a cigarette. The man was openly defiant toward Petrov and, gearing up to fight him, tossed the cigarette, perhaps without realizing that it might land in the well. The flaming ember flew into the open hole and down the pipe. Seeing the danger, Petrov quickly hefted the cap on the wellhead and backed away, shouting at his men, eyes wide with fear. The cap blew off the wellhead, and flame erupted into the night sky, beyond the top of the HD monitor.

"How did that happen? I thought you said the real vein was blocked," Mahegan said.

"It was. There's always leakage, though. You can never get it airtight. And you can't smell the gas like in your home. The power companies put that smell in there to avoid liability if there's a leak."

"I don't guess you've got any experience with or opinion on what this will do to the nuclear waste."

"Well, the fire will carry the radioactive isotopes up with it. You can't burn the neutrons, but you can spread them, so instead of destroying radiation, fire rearranges it, spreads it. That's why Chernobyl was so bad. Look at Hiroshima or Nagasaki. Same thing."

"You're pumping me full of confidence here, Maeve. How do you shut down the fire?"

"There's a shutdown valve at the wellhead, and the wheel to it is about fifty yards in the other direction from the fracking fluid hose. You've got to turn the big wheel, and it caps the well about a hundred yards below the ground."

"Either way, I've got to go down there."

"Yes."

Mahegan turned and ran through the burned-out door, avoiding the dead bodies, and scrambled through the den until he reached the lodge's front door. He wheeled around the side of the building and followed the trail to the wellhead. The fire illuminated his path, the shadows dancing like black ghosts. He remembered there was a fence, one he had helped build several days ago.

The gate was open, most likely because of the chaos of the evening. All Mahegan could think about was the fire collecting the invisible nuclear waste and spreading it like pollen through the crystalline night air, poisoning everything and everyone for possibly thousands of years.

Rounding the corner beyond the roughnecks' trailers, Mahegan could feel the heat licking at his skin. He saw five men backing away but staring at the fire, unaware of the lethal blend that was about to spew forth. He pulled out his cell phone and called Grace.

"I'm coming up on the wellhead. Shoot Petrov and the others. Just don't shoot me."

"We see you," Grace said. "Be careful."

Mahegan put the silenced phone in his pocket and paused, giving Elaine a moment to hit a few of them. Moving toward the fracking fluid system, he found the hose, which looked like a giant flexible tube. He secured the nozzle to the frame of the rig so that the spray would be generally in the direction of the wellhead. After studying the system, he texted Maeve and told her to shoot the fracking fluid when she saw him moving toward Petrov on the monitor.

She replied, **Roger.**

Grace spotted for Elaine.

"Okay, Petrov is the prime target. He's the one facing the other five guys. See if you can hit him."

A few seconds later the rifle coughed, and Petrov slapped at his arm, as if he'd been stung. He looked up in their direction. Grace heard another cough from Elaine's gun, and Petrov went down to one knee.

"This sight is good," Elaine said.

Grace heard the selector switch click and was momentarily confused, thinking Elaine was placing the weapon on safe. But then she heard three successive coughs in a row. Elaine had put the weapon on semiautomatic. She was firing into the group of men.

Grace's phone buzzed again. It was Mahegan.

"Tell her to stop. I've got it from here. If she sees someone coming after me, she can try to hit them, but she damn well better not shoot me."

"He said good job, but cease fire," Grace said to Elaine. "Shoot if someone gets near him."

Elaine looked up. "I heard him."

Grace looked through the goggles and saw Mahegan barreling toward the wounded Petrov. Then she saw a solid stream of fracking fluid disappear into the fire.

*   *   *

Mahegan took in Petrov's condition. The man appeared to have two wounds, one in the shoulder and one in the leg. *Not bad, Elaine*, Mahegan thought. Three of the other men were down, also, and two of them appeared dead. Another man, who was not wounded, had run toward him and past him without stopping.

He didn't waste any time on Petrov. Mahegan removed his pistol from his pocket and shot Petrov in the head. The Russian died, backlit by a fire that might kill them all, anyway.

Mahegan felt the spray from the fracking fluid slap into his back like pellets shot from an air rifle. He angled away from the fire and found the apparatus that controlled the shutdown valve that Maeve had described. There it was before him, a giant wheel, like a ship's helm. The temperature had to be at least 150 degrees where he was standing. His clothes were hot to the touch. He removed his shirt and wrapped it around the hot metal of the wheel, forming a barrier. Using his body to pivot into the device, he turned the wheel, felt it give, and pushed some more. He dug his heels into the dirt and pulled down on one of the spokes, trying to move the wheel in a clockwise direction. He felt it give, exerted more pressure, and felt it give again.

Sweat streamed from every pore of his body, only to evaporate in the intense heat. The hairs on his arms were singed. As he leaned forward, his metal belt buckle pushed into his abdomen, searing the skin beneath his navel. Again he pulled, and again the wheel responded, this time with less resistance. So he pulled with everything he had, his own lightning bolt scar screaming at him with pain, and he finally felt the wheel turn freely. The heat lessened as he pulled again. He felt something click into place and turned to see that the fire was gone.

Then he heard gunfire about a half a mile away, to the east of the lodge. It wasn't the watchers. They were to the west.

He walked toward the trailers, exhausted, and sat down against a blown-out tire on one of the big trucks. He watched the fracking fluid, which was mostly water, spray the entire gravel and dirt area that had been charred by the fire. The real issue now was at the nuclear plant. Could they get water into the pool quickly enough? His phone buzzed with a call from Grace.

"Yes?"

"Damn bravest thing I've ever seen."

"Did you get in touch with Blackmon?"

"Yes. He was going into the pool to cover the holes."

Mahegan thought a minute. Made sense. Then, remembering the shots just fired, he asked, "What's that shooting?"

"We saw some flashes at the lodge. My guess is the Mexicans are in a gunfight while everyone is trying to leave."

"Try calling them on that cell phone. Then call me back."

Within a minute Grace called him.

"Gunther answered."

CHAPTER 40

A T SIXTY FEET DEEP IN THE SPENT NUCLEAR FUEL ROD COOLING pool, Sam Blackmon's handheld gamma-ray spectrometer was pegging off the chart. The device looked like a flashlight with a handle, except it read the type and amount of radioactive material present. Through his diver's mask he could see the darkened lake water rushing past him, while his legs felt the tug of the water being sucked into the drilled holes in the bottom of the pool.

Figuring he was already fried, Blackmon went to work. He let the spectrometer hang from its tie-down on his wet suit and moved the fifty-pound barbells and plywood as close to the holes as possible. The idea was to have the weights dangle in the holes. That, coupled with the force of the water, would hold the plywood in place, staunching the flow of water out of the pool. At least that was the theory.

He lifted one barbell with each hand, tugging two sheets of plywood behind him. He found the holes and had to stand about fifteen feet away from the closest one to prevent himself from being sucked into the vortex. Even then, he was challenged to fight the pull of the rushing water into the five holes, which by now had collapsed into about three. He fought the undertow as if he were fighting a riptide at a North Carolina beach, feeling the water sweep between his legs and around his body. The plywood caught the current when he held his arms out, as if he were performing the iron cross on gymnastics rings. He let go of the barbells, and one sheet of plywood slapped onto one hole, covering it perfectly, the suction centering the rectangle. The other piece of plywood got caught sideways in one of the combined holes and was sucked into the channel, reminding Blackmon that something four feet wide could vanish into the abyss.

He fought his way back to grab two more of the barbells and had more success this time, covering the larger crevice with one sheet and then another smaller hole with another sheet, which left one more vacuuming hole to his left. Bernoulli's equation kicked in, though: the narrower the gap, the greater the acceleration of the fluid. He returned to the edge of the pool, where he had dropped the plywood and the barbells, and hoisted the remaining barbell and sheet of plywood. He trudged through the swirling water. He felt himself becoming weak and dizzy. His strength was ebbing as he felt the floor of the pool begin to tremble, as if the massive suction from beneath was going to cave in the entire structure.

Struggling over the spent fuel rods, which had been pulled toward the remaining hole, he felt his leg hit one as he tripped. His face smashed into the bottom of the pool, fracturing his mask. Water was running through the cracks. The rushing water pulled at the plywood, and he lost his grip on the barbell, which immediately wrapped around one of the fuel rods. He removed his knife from its ankle sheath and cut the nylon cord as he gripped the plywood in his other hand. Holding the sheet of plywood above his head, Sam Blackmon ran in slow motion through the swirling water toward the black hole. Upon finding it, he leapt directly into the abyss, assisted by the flowing current, and felt his fingers being crushed beneath the weight of the board as it was sucked onto the pool floor. He thought of his wife and children and the country he had served in combat as his hands eventually slipped free.

He was unconscious by the time he was pulled three thousand feet into the core of the earth.

CHAPTER 41

Mahegan found the keys in one of the black Ford F-150 pickup trucks that had been the standard vehicle for the EB-5 commandos. He turned the ignition and slammed the truck into gear, then bounced past the terrain scorched as black as midnight. He stopped the truck when he saw a figure about a hundred yards away walking through the smoke, like a fighter pilot emerging from a blazing crash.

Smoke still billowed from things burning: rubber tires, gasoline engines, and some of the trailers. To Mahegan, it looked exactly like a combat zone, which, of course, it was. He called Maeve on his cell phone as he stared at the figure walking toward him.

"Sitrep," he demanded. Mahegan knew that a soldier like Maeve would understand the acronym for "situation report."

"I've collapsed the parallel channel about sixty yards out. My drill bit is done, but I think we're okay so far. The fire actually helped underground. It melted some of the junk down there and helped firm up the stopgap I created."

"So we're okay?"

"I think so. Good job on the fire."

"Have you seen Gunther or Throckmorton?" Mahegan kept his eyes on the man walking steadily toward him from between the burning trailers.

"No. Place is like a ghost town. I don't hear anything except the wailing banshees down in the tunnel, where you stashed them. If they escape, I could be toast."

"I need you to stay with the drill in case the team inside the reactor needs you. And turn off the fracking hose."

"No problem. I said I'd make amends. Plus, I've got this pistol you left me."

"I can't make any promises, but I'll do what I can," Mahegan said.

"How's Piper?"

"She's with the watchers, so she's good."

Mahegan hung up the phone. He had a decision to make: stay here and fight whoever was coming at him or go to Throckmorton's house, to which he believed Gunther and Throckmorton would ultimately return. Watching the outline of the hulking figure wade through the smoke, he thought back to that first time he had stepped into Brand Throckmorton's house.

When he returned home after confronting the American Taliban in Dare County, Mahegan had visited Frisco, then ridden the ferry to Cedar Island and hitched a ride to Raleigh from a state worker heading that way.

He had said his name was Benny Cooper and that he was from the town of Kinston, North Carolina, which they passed on the way to Raleigh along Route 70. Predictably, the man had started talking about his job.

"I tell the state how much land is worth before they buy it from property owners to build roads or whatever we're going to build," the man had said. Mahegan had looked at him in his white blend shirt and polyester tie. He had a balding head and had somehow gotten dandruff on his headrest and neck.

"Everywhere I go," he said, "I hear about two guys during the Great Recession who bought up all the land in North Carolina that might have natural gas underneath it." Cooper said the term Great Recession *as if he were a preacher in a tent on a humid North Carolina Sunday and was talking about the devil.*

"Then they sell us—the people who have lived and worked here all our lives—back our own land for twice the price. I was just down here in Carteret County, closing the deal right next to the port and railhead. The state is building a big-ass natural gas pipeline that allows us to export nat-

ural gas. Now, doesn't that beat everything you've ever heard? We've got us energy independence if we're exporting natural gas, don't we, mister?"

For a good chunk of his life Mahegan had been fighting wars that revolved around the lack of energy independence, so he wasn't in total agreement with Benny Cooper.

"That's why I'm heading up to Raleigh. Gotta go brief the big guy. Throckmorton and Gunther seem to own everything we need for roads, fracking, construction. You name it, they have it. Word is that Throckmorton has all the senators and representatives in his pocket and that Gunther has first dibs on all the road projects in the state."

Mahegan adjusted himself in the marginally comfortable seat of the state car. "Interesting," he said as they passed Goldsboro.

"More than interesting," Cooper said. "I go appraise this land and give a damned good assessment of its value. Then Throckmorton and Gunther hire their own guy, and his estimate is at least one third higher than mine, sometimes a full half. That makes me look incompetent, don't it?"

Mahegan said, "No. Makes them look like thieves."

Cooper slapped his thigh, causing the car to list toward the shoulder before he could correct his mistake. "That's what I said! But nobody can touch these guys. Not even the attorney general. Everybody's on the damn take, is what I say. I mean, look at this document right here."

Cooper handed Mahegan a folder, which he opened. Thumbing through the documents inside it, he saw the names Brand Throckmorton and James Gunther mentioned multiple times. Throckmorton's address was listed as the address of record for both of the men.

Mahegan memorized it.

The man dropped him off by the state capitol, and Mahegan walked the short distance to Ridge Road on his first night in Raleigh. He scouted Throckmorton's house from the expansive backyard, noticing no signs of life. He entered through the basement beneath the deck. The house was empty, and his only goal was to find a lead on Gunther, as he had some newfound time on his hands. Mahegan spent precious little time inside, but he discovered one pearl of intelligence.

On the third story he found maps and graphs laid out across the floor and tables, mostly maps of land whose sale the state appraiser had bemoaned to Mahegan. There were two newspaper clippings that didn't be-

long. The first was from Maxton, and it was a story from fifteen years be-
fore about the murder of his mother and about how Gunther had tried to
save her. The article made Mahegan seethe, and it rekindled his determi-
nation to find Gunther sooner rather than later.

The second newspaper clipping involved his father, whom he had not
heard from since his mother's murder. Mahegan read the article, and pre-
pared to leave the clippings where he had found them when he came upon
a photograph paper-clipped to the back of the newspaper story. He had
stopped and lifted the photo from the paper clip. The image started the
process of Mahegan losing control, his emotions racing forward like un-
broken mustangs, but he heard the front door open two stories below. He
pocketed the picture and stole away through the back deck of the master.
On the way out he stopped to listen to the voices in the house, placing his
hand upon the sliding glass door that led to the deck.

He recognized Gunther's voice booming through the hallway.

Mahegan took a deep breath as he watched James Gunther trod through the detritus like a zombie in a dystopian world. Fire leapt around him, each flame like a trumpet signaling his arrival.

Mahegan watched Gunther stop about ten yards away, Petrov's dead body the only thing separating them. He momentarily wondered what had become of Papa Diablo and Manuela, and of Throckmorton, for that matter.

Mahegan stepped from the truck, intentionally leaving his pistol in the vehicle. This was personal for both of them, and it would be a man-to-man fight.

"Your mother was a good lay, Mahegan," Gunther started. "But killing your daddy was even better."

"Where is he?" Mahegan asked. "In some borrow pit? One of your road projects?"

"Something like that. Doesn't matter, does it? He's dead. She's dead. You're going to be dead in a few minutes. Can't you see? I win against your kind. Your daddy killed my friend and tried to make it look like a meth lab explosion. Police couldn't figure it out, but I sure did."

"I got two when I was fourteen, including your brother. My dad got one. And now here you are. Seems my kind is pretty good, don't you think?"

Mahegan scanned Gunther, who looked solid and strong. He remembered the man as being heavy, even though in a rage as a child Mahegan had once tossed him through a plate-glass window. Then he thought about his father's last visit to him in the juvenile detention center, where the authorities had placed him.

The picture he had found a few weeks ago in Throckmorton's third-story library—that first time in Throckmorton's Ridge Road home in Raleigh—was of his full-blooded Croatan Indian father tied naked to a tree, gutted and flayed. Gunther was in the picture, smiling and holding his father's lifeless head up, as if he had just killed a trophy buck.

"My mother put up more of a fight than your kid did when I killed him," Mahegan said. "Guy was just a weakling when it got right down to it. And there is only the one son. Gunther and Sons may have been wishful thinking, but your seed is gone from the earth."

With all the thoughts racing through his mind, he didn't need memories clogging his efficient fighter's mind-set. He needed to assess what he was seeing and what he wasn't seeing. What was present, and what wasn't present?

The state appraiser had mentioned Throckmorton and Gunther, as if the two were partners, like Bonnie and Clyde. Which left the question, where was Throckmorton? He hoped the watchers were still watching, as he got the sense that Gunther was stalling him, deceiving him into believing this was the ultimate showdown that he had been seeking.

As if to emphasize his point, Gunther said, "Then this is what you wanted, isn't it, boy? Come driving into our compound like you own the damn place. Dump Griffyn on the ground like he's a sack of garbage. That was you, wasn't it?"

"You know it was."

His mind raced as he pulled in the thick, smoky air. Mahegan was an athlete, and he needed oxygen for this face-off. Like in a western gunfight, the two men were squared off thirty feet apart, with a dead body between them. What was missing? Where was Throckmorton?

Then it came to him.

"You attacked my mother with three other men. You and Throckmorton killed my father when he found you at a construction site. You never operate alone, do you?"

Gunther was silent for a moment, and that was all it took for Mahegan to know that Throckmorton was somewhere on the ridge, most likely in finely stitched riding britches and top-of-the-line hunting apparel.

"Just you and me, boy."

"You know it isn't. But you're not the only one with backup," Mahegan said.

"Your Mexicans ain't going to be much help, son. Sorry about them two."

Mahegan saw the phone in Gunther's left breast shirt pocket. It was a rectangular bulge with a green light, indicating it was operational. He was talking to Throckmorton, or at least Throckmorton was listening to what he was saying. What was the cue to shoot? Mahegan wondered. How much time had Throckmorton needed to get into place? He guessed that Gunther had come along only after his partner had told him he was in position to shoot Mahegan. The watchers had most likely not seen Throckmorton.

Which meant he had to make Throckmorton miss once. He felt confident that the watchers could find the muzzle flash.

Gunther threw his hands up in the air, ostensibly as a gesture of exasperation, but Mahegan saw it as a signal.

"I guess there's nothing left to say," Gunther said.

Mahegan took that comment as the second half of the signal, like "Ready" and then "Aim."

The arms came down.

Mahegan stepped forward.

A rifle bellowed from the eastern ridge.

A bullet snapped past Mahegan's body at supersonic speed approximately three feet behind him. He felt the whoosh of the gun's round as it zipped through the air and heard the crack as it broke the sound barrier. The valley echoed with the sound of the first bullet.

"Missed," Mahegan said.

As he charged Gunther, he saw the man retrieve a knife from his belt. Mahegan still had his own knife on his shin. Two more thunderous booms rattled the valley. Two more bullets missed.

As he closed on Gunther's heavy frame, Mahegan heard the barely audible *cough, cough, cough* of his own silenced weapon. The watchers had his back.

Gunther was larger than he remembered. The man had hands the size of baseball mitts. His forearms, which showed beneath his rolled-up shirtsleeves, were bulging. He was barrel-chested, with arms equally as long as Mahegan's. The details of the memory of tossing him through the sliding glass door had evaporated like the fringes of a puddle in summer heat, leaving only the core behind. Now, those details came back to him with stunning clarity.

Mahegan had been a man possessed and had functioned beyond his fourteen-year-old capabilities, the same way a mother was moved to lift a three-ton car that was crushing her child. He had experienced a superhuman rush of adrenaline then, and now he felt a similar surge—though this time more controlled—coursing through him.

As he approached Gunther, Mahegan's first goal was to reverse positions with the man. He needed to move him away from the burning trailers and toward the gaping hole fitted with concrete pipes that went down three thousand feet into the earth. There was a steaming metal plate a hundred yards below the surface, and it had just smothered the gas fire. Mahegan thought this would be a good final resting place for a demon like Gunther. He visualized Gunther roasting there, as if atop a frying pan heated by the flames of hell.

But plans always changed, Mahegan knew, at first contact with the enemy. "Get inside your enemy's decision cycle and stay there," had been Mahegan's motto.

Gunther surprised him by pulling a pistol from his pocket as he closed the gap between them. Mahegan dove toward the arm lifting the gun and latched onto the massive forearm with two hands. The arm was as steady as a pull-up bar, unwavering beneath Mahegan's initial block.

The pistol fired two shots, which fractionally missed Mahegan's midsection. He planted his left foot inside Gunther's right foot, pushed Gunther's arm across his body, keeping the weapon aimed away from him, and drove into him with his shoulder. Two more shots were fired from Gunther's pistol, and they missed wildly.

Gunther was sturdy, like concrete, the business in which he had dwelled his entire life. Mahegan performed an inside trip wrestling move, using Gunther's weight against him. Gunther toppled over as Mahegan's shoulder rammed hard into Gunther's abdomen. Still, the man was in good physical condition and had perhaps gotten stronger over the past fifteen years. The two men landed on the ground, Mahegan on top of Gunther, who was now scrambling, having lost his preplanned advantages. Gunther's plan clearly had to change on contact with Mahegan, also.

Gunther's knife hand came arcing down, and the blade caught Mahegan in his right triceps. The cut burned, but he was focused on the more lethal pistol, which had at least two shots, if not more, remaining. He rolled off Gunther and wrapped his legs in scissors fashion around the man's neck as he flipped Gunther onto his stomach and ratcheted his pistol arm backward until two more shots were fired and the weapon dropped into the dirt.

With good leverage, Mahegan went for Gunther's knife-wielding hand, but Gunther managed a lucky stab into his thigh, which forced Mahegan to release the scissors lock on Gunther. Both men rolled away and stood, facing one another, but with their positions reversed.

Exactly as Mahegan wanted.

Mahegan took up a boxing stance and drove straight at Gunther, who raised his arms in brawler fashion. As Gunther tried to wheel to his left, Mahegan cut him off, forcing him back. He let Gunther get in a few jabs to his face, to make him think about hitting him instead of the fact that he was backing up toward the wellhead.

Mahegan unleashed a flurry of left jabs and right crosses, most connecting with Gunther's huge head. The target was certainly big enough, Mahegan thought. The issue was getting past those large hands and arms. Even with Mahegan's wingspan, Gunther was able to parry and thrust better than most men Mahegan had fought.

Two more jabs, though, and Mahegan was able to see the five-foot-wide wellhead hole. It needed to be that big initially for all the hoses, shape charges, drill lengths, and piping that the rough-necks had lowered into the well. Mahegan knew that it narrowed considerably beyond the one-hundred-yard shutdown valve, but he wasn't worried about that.

Gunther continued to back up, and it occurred to Mahegan that the man was not stupid. Gunther was a survivor. Perhaps he was planning to toss Mahegan into the pit of hell at the last second.

Mahegan steadied himself, thinking, *Slow is smooth. Smooth is fast. No mistakes.* This *was* the fight he had been seeking.

Less than a yard from the hole, Gunther telegraphed his move. Mahegan's years of wrestling and hand-to-hand combat had trained him to continuously monitor his opponent's entire body, from head to feet. On a quick downward glance, Mahegan noticed Gunther put his right foot forward, when he had been leading with his left. The only reason for such a move would be to duck a jab from Mahegan and then spin around behind him and let Mahegan's own weight carry him forward. Then he would need only a shove from Gunther to wind up in the abyss.

So Mahegan countered Gunther's step by treating him as a left-handed boxer and circling to his right, making Gunther punch awkwardly from his weak side. Mahegan fought through the big hands and the muscled forearms with his own might and began to pummel Gunther in the face, while avoiding getting inside his reach. It occurred to him that another strategy Gunther could employ would be to hug him and make Mahegan go down with him.

Gunther's heels were now at the concrete lip of the wellhead. Fire was raging all around them like an inferno. All the EB-5 trailers were burning. The heat was suffocating. The flames raged in a horseshoe around them as fracking equipment and vehicles burned and melted. The black smoke from rubber tires fouled the air with noxious fumes. Mahegan knew that Gunther had to be struggling to breathe, too.

The huge hands clasped him, though, and pulled Mahegan toward Gunther.

"Think you're so smart, Indian? Why don't we go into this hole together?"

Mahegan's weight leaned into Gunther, who had a smile frozen on his face. They were falling toward the hole, and Mahegan could see the hills where the watchers were hiding, the trees on the low ground, the graded lot, the gravel, and the hole. It all came rushing up toward him as Gunther then spun him around in a move worthy of an Olympic wrestler. He felt his head hit the ground on the far side of the hole and his feet catch on the concrete lip on the near side. Mahegan's arms were splayed on either side of the circular concrete prefab. There was nothing beneath two-thirds of his body except a frying pan, a sheet of metal, one hundred yards below.

Gunther hovered above him, spit coming off his demonic face, as if he was doing a push-up. His hands were on either side of the hole, and he was propping himself up two feet above Mahegan's precarious position.

"Got your mama. Got your daddy. Now I got you. That ought to do it, don't you think?"

Gunther lifted his foot to push Mahegan into the hole, like a man stepping into a trash can to make room for more garbage. Mahegan managed to brace himself with his arms as Gunther raised himself up for his final kick. Then Mahegan used his left foot to crash into Gunther's left knee, the joint that was bearing all of Gunther's massive weight. He heard the cracking of bone, the tearing of ligament, and the howling of an injured man, who, without thinking, used both hands to grab at his knee.

Mahegan spun to Gunther's right as Gunther fell to his left.

Gunther's head hit the concrete pipe with a thud. Mahegan delivered another well-placed kick to the destroyed knee joint, causing Gunther's body to buckle beneath its own weight. They had reversed positions.

For the first time Mahegan saw fear in Gunther's eyes. Throwing Gunther through the sliding glass door had been different. The man had been confused and perhaps a bit amused back then, even with the severe injuries he had suffered. But now Gunther's eyes showed that he knew his fate would be soon at hand, and that it wasn't going to be a happy ending. The man was hanging by the heels of his boots and the tips of his fingers as his inverted body hung like a V in the open pit.

Mahegan avoided Gunther's mistake of attempting to accelerate his fall into the abyss and instead let his adversary's body slowly sag into the hole. While he could have simply crushed the man's fingers as they clasped the lip of the wellhead, he chose to watch the man struggle.

He couldn't believe what he was hearing from Gunther's mouth. His voice, however faint, was whispering over and over, "Help me."

Mahegan took a few steps back and looked up the hill at the boulder, where he knew the watchers were, well, watching. He nodded.

He heard the coughs of his rifle, fired by Elaine, he presumed, and allowed her to get a measure of justice, as well.

The bullets found their mark on Gunther's body. His grip released, oddly causing his body to slap against the near side of the pipe as his boot heels mysteriously clung to the ledge upon which they had found purchase. Quickly, though, Gunther's sheer weight pulled him downward into the chasm.

Mahegan heard the thud on the metal plate one hundred yards below and what he figured was the sizzling of human skin.

He then walked over to the wheel he had used to close the shutdown valve. He turned the wheel in the opposite direction, until he felt Gunther's mass leave the plate. Reignited by a fresh dose of oxygen, the fire briefly licked at the sky again, like the tongue of a sneering reptile.

Mahegan quickly closed the valve, having served Gunther to the devouring beast below.

EPILOGUE

T WENTY-FOUR HOURS LATER, BACK AT HIS APARTMENT, MAHEGAN sat on his bed with his rucksack packed. He nodded at Grace. "You did good," he said.

She was dressed in tight-fitting jeans, an even tighter-fitting T-shirt, and wedges, which added to her height. Her hair was hanging loosely across her downturned face, some of it wet from tears. She hooked her hair behind her ears and looked at him.

"I don't understand why you have to go," Grace said. She sat on the bed next to him.

Mahegan was silent. He wasn't sure, either. Grace was someone he could spend time with in the future. He felt a twitch in his chest and fought it.

"It's what I do," Mahegan said.

"That doesn't make any frigging sense! What are you? A spy or something?"

Mahegan shook his head and changed the topic. "What are the environmentalists telling us?"

"Elaine is getting the update outside now. Word is that your friend Blackmon plugged the bottom of the pool enough to prevent oxygen from getting to the fuel rods."

"Old age is not an honorable death," Mahegan said. "Croatan saying. Rather die a hero than grow old. Sam may have saved all of us."

"I can't even fathom what he did. When you shot the water and the fracking fluid into the wellhead, that was a smart move, too. Beat back the flames, and the Geiger monitors are not showing substantial radiation in the air. The groundwater is a different matter, though. It'll take some time to test and see how much radiation actually leaked into the aquifer, if any."

A knock on the door indicated that Elaine was back from her phone call. Mahegan walked over and opened the door for her. With Elaine were Maeve Cassidy and Piper.

"Hey, sharpshooter," Mahegan said.

"Found these two out front with some badass dude with a crew cut."

"That dude is my boss," Mahegan said. "And my ride." He watched Grace and Elaine exchange glances.

"You're leaving? You can't leave," Elaine said. "Where are you going?"

"I am. I'm not sure where."

Grace stood. "Still have my number?"

Mahegan had gone through so many burner and cutout cell phones, he couldn't remember in which phone he had loaded the number. Once he arrived at Fort Bragg for his debriefing, he would have to process every phone and GPS he had acquired over the past week, so he was certain he would come across Grace's number.

"I know where to find you, Grace."

"This is some bullshit," Elaine said. Then, looking down at Piper and up at Maeve, she added, "Oh, sorry."

Maeve Cassidy walked up to Mahegan and hugged him. "Thank you. For everything," she said.

Mahegan nodded, thankful that there was one less child without a mother. Then he picked up his duffel bag, hugged the women, knelt in front of Piper, and said, "Love your mom."

The little girl nodded, as if she understood.

Walking out of the above-barn apartment and down the stairs, Mahegan saw Major General Savage leaning against a black Suburban.

"Let's go, Ranger, before you let them women convince you otherwise."

"You got something better?"

"You know I do, Jake. It's called Charlie Mike. Continue mission. Now, get in the car."

Mahegan glanced over his shoulder at the three women and Piper. They were staring at him through the window he had used to shoot the Russians. That was a fitting juxtaposition of his life, he figured: violence and love. At some point he would dispose of the violence, he hoped, and share his life with a woman who loved him.

As he rode back to Fort Bragg with General Savage, Mahegan thought of his mother and father and all that he had lost.

And the justice that he had finally delivered.

Acknowledgments

Thanks to my agent, Scott Miller of Trident Media Group. Scott continues to be a great mentor and friend. The team at Trident is so very talented, including Emily Ross, Nicole Robson, Brianna Weber, Sarah Bush, and Scott's assistant, Allisyn Shindle. Thank you for all you do in support of me and all of Trident's talented authors.

Thanks also to Gary Goldstein for his mentorship and friendship. Gary is an author's editor, supportive and engaged. The team at Kensington Publishing has been superb, including Karen Auerbach, Vida Engstrand, Alexandra Nicolajsen, Robin Cook, and Rosemary Silva. Thanks for making *Three Minutes to Midnight* the best book it can possibly be.

To friends and family in North Carolina and Virginia, thank you for your tremendous support. To my children, Brooke and Zachary, I love you and am so very proud of all that you have accomplished. And to my parents, Bob and Jerri Tata, and sister, Kendall, thank you for your unconditional love, commitment, and support. A son could not have asked for better parents or role models.

Finally, to all of the thousands of readers, thank you for your support, and comments. Please feel free to send me email from my website at www.ajtata.com.

For the record, I am making no political statement about fracking, and do believe that energy independence is a must for our country. Simply put, I looked at the map of the shale deposits in North Carolina as they ran beneath the nuclear power plant at Shearon Harris Lake and thought, "Interesting."